snapshot

A Jamieson Brothers Novel

D0099350

Also by
A n g i e   S t a n t o n

rock and a hard place:
A Jamieson Brothers Novel

n t o n

snapshot

A Jamieson Brothers Novel

HARPER TEEN
An Imprint of HarperCollinsPublishers

Angie Sta

HarperTeen is an imprint of HarperCollins Publishers.

Snapshot
Copyright © 2013 by Angie Stanton

HarperCollins Children's Books, a division of HarperCollins
Publishers, 10 East 53rd Street, New York, NY 10022.
www.epicreads.com

Library of Congress Cataloging-in-Publication Data
Stanton, Angie.
  Snapshot : a Jamieson brothers novel / Angie Stanton.
    pages cm
  Summary: "Marti, the reluctant rock princess, and Adam, the
undercover guitar wizard, fall for each other, but are in danger of
falling apart when tragedy strikes"— Provided by publisher.
  ISBN 978-0-06-227256-0 (pbk.)
  [1. Camps—Fiction. 2. Singers—Fiction. 3. Rock music—Fiction.
4. Celebrities—Fiction. 5. Love—Fiction. 6. Wisconsin—Fiction.] I. Title.
PZ7.S793247Sn 2013   2013012281
[Fic]—dc23   CIP
                                                              AC

Typography by Andrea Vandergrift
13 14 15 16 17 CG/RRDH 10 9 8 7 6 5 4 3 2 1
❖
First Edition

For Faith Black.

Thanks for pulling me out of the slush all those years ago.

snapshot

1

"*Shave* it all," Adam said, running his fingers through his loose, brown waves.

"You want me to shave off all your hair?" Peter, his older brother, held the electric shaver and looked at Adam's reflection in the mirror. "You know your fans are going to riot when they find out."

Adam grinned. "They'll learn to love the new look, when they eventually see it. The point is that I don't want anyone to recognize me at camp."

"It's bad enough Peter's chasing after Libby like a love-sick dog," Garrett, his oldest brother, said as he walked in. "Now you're acting like a twelve-year-old going to summer camp. Shoot me now."

Adam shrugged, unruffled by Garrett's words. "It's not just *any* summer camp, it's the Gallagher Institute Arts

Camp, and there won't be any twelve-year-olds there. Just high school kids."

Garrett leaned against the door frame. "I get it. You want to pretend you're a nobody and blend in. Good luck with that," he said in a condescending tone.

Peter tossed the shaver from one hand to the other. "Are you ready, or what?"

"You really think cutting off your trademark hair, the thing girls go crazy for, is going to keep them from recognizing you?" Garrett asked. "And what's so bad if they do? I thought you loved the attention."

Adam pushed his bangs back to check out how he'd look without his mop of hair. "It's photography camp, not a rock concert. I can't exactly spend two weeks with girls screaming and begging for my autograph every time they see me. I need to blend in."

"Plus"—Peter turned to Garrett—"no one would ever expect Adam to be at a camp in northern Wisconsin, especially without you, me, and a small entourage. People see what they expect to see: a nerdy guy with a bad haircut and no personality."

Adam shook his head. "Nice. Thanks for that. You gonna do this, or do I have to go ask Dad?"

"Relax. Sit still and let's do some damage here."

Adam perched on the stool in front of the bathroom mirror as Garrett looked on with a frown.

Peter examined Adam's hair. As he turned on the

shaver and placed it at Adam's hairline, Garrett said, "Give him a Mohawk."

Peter slid the buzzing razor through Adam's hair. Adam grinned as the locks dropped to the floor, revealing a two-inch strip of short hair. He reached up, felt the soft patch, and grinned. "Awesome."

Garrett shook his head. "I can't believe you're really doing this. Does Mom know?"

A few more swipes of the electric shaver, and Adam sported a buzz cut. He rubbed the bristles of his short hair and grinned. "No. Sometimes surprises are best."

Marti rolled down the window and inhaled the fresh scent of the north woods as Grandma slowed the car and drove the long, narrow road that led to camp.

"It even smells like fun," Grandma said.

"I can't believe I'm finally here." Marti leaned her head out the window and let the warm breeze blow her long hair. She breathed in the pine-, moss-, and wildflower-scented air. Two weeks away from her summer job at the Garden Centre, on a dream vacation. She couldn't wait to be surrounded by other kids who loved photography as much as she did.

They drove around a bend to discover a glimmering blue lake. A sandy beach dotted with kayaks, canoes, and small sailboats anchored the camp. A log cabin–style lodge was nestled on one side, and a sidewalk traced the edge of the lake on the other. Small cabins peppered the lakefront for as far as she could see.

"You'll have plenty to take pictures of, I can see that already," Grandma said, pulling to a stop in the parking lot. She nodded toward a young guy walking out of the main lodge; a couple of cameras crisscrossed his chest on long straps. He had an easygoing gait and his head bounced as if he were listening to music inside his head.

"Grandma! You are such a cougar."

"Oh, he's a few decades too young for me, but not for you."

Marti shook her head and rolled her eyes with a smile. She loved her grandmother, especially when she acted outrageous.

"I'm just saying." Grandma winked.

They exited the car and went around to the trunk. Marti collected her rolling bag packed with six months' worth of stuff. Grandma picked up the camera bag, handed it to Marti, and looked back at her new favorite target: the guy. He was talking to another kid on his way into the lodge. He said something and they both laughed.

"He's a cutie. You better make your move right away. You don't want some other girl to snatch him up."

"Grandma! It's a good thing there isn't an extra cabin or I could see you staying to check out all the guys!" But even from a distance, Marti noticed his handsome face. He wore a permanent smirk as if he'd just heard something really funny, and his eyes lit up when he laughed.

Marti and Grandma made their way toward the lodge. At the edge of the sidewalk, a pile of suitcases and bags was heaped next to a sign that said REGISTRATION with a painted arrow that pointed to the lodge.

"Looks like you can leave your bag here while we go in," Grandma said. Marti parked her bag at the edge of the pile.

The boy walked out of the lodge and headed over to a bag near Marti's feet.

"Hi! You here for photography camp, too?" he asked with an inviting smile. His hair, cut super short, showed off his strong jawline.

"No, actually, I'm here for orchestra camp," Marti responded with a straight face.

"Really? That's a mighty small violin." He smirked, eyeing the camera bag over her shoulder.

"It's a really small orchestra." Marti arched a flirty eyebrow.

"Is that so? Then I guess I won't have to worry that you'll keep me awake at night practicing." His eyes, a combination of amber with flecks of rich brown, connected with hers in a silent duel.

She fought back an excited smile. Marti didn't want him to know that he'd gotten under her skin. She didn't come to camp to meet a guy, but that would be a bonus.

"Marti, you shouldn't tease this young man. Now be

polite and introduce yourself. This is Marti, and it looks like you'll be getting to know each other, because you were right. She is here for photography camp."

"Nice to meet you, Marti. I'm Ada . . . uh, AJ." For an instant, she saw something flicker across his eyes, but then he smiled and it was gone.

AJ picked up a large duffel and slung the bag over his shoulder. "I guess I'll be seeing you around." He flashed Grandma an infectious grin and headed off for the path leading to the cabins.

"He's got spunk. I like him," Grandma said, watching him as he left. Marti eyed AJ as well.

Inside the lodge, a huge stone fireplace anchored the main wall. Wood carvings, bird feathers, and a few too many animal antlers for her taste covered the rest. Registration tables were set up in front of the fireplace with college-aged staffers checking people in.

"Hi! Welcome to the Gallagher Institute," a perky blond with a messy ponytail said.

"Hi, I'm Marti Hunter."

"I'm Melody. Did you bring your paperwork?"

"Right here." Grandma dug in her purse and pulled out an envelope with the camp forms and handed them to Melody.

"Perfect." She looked them over and checked her list. "Your cabin is Monet. Here's a camp map and a schedule of your photography classes and free time. At the next table, you can pick up a name tag. Dinner is at five thirty. If you want, you can take your guest to see your cabin before she has to leave."

"Thanks," Marti replied, gathering her map and name tag.

Once outside the rustic lodge, she hugged Grandma. "I still can't believe you let me come!"

"You deserve it, honey, but are you sure you didn't want to go to some rock band camp?" Grandma waited for her reaction, a concerned look on her face.

"Don't even say that! You know I don't want to be anything like my dad." Marti's dad, Steven Hunter, was the lead guitarist for the rock band Graphite Angels. Marti knew her grandma still worried that Marti would want to follow in his footsteps and become a rocker.

"Just checking. How do I know you won't change your mind and wish you were back in LA and not Wisconsin? There is so much more excitement out there, and our life is pretty ordinary in comparison."

"Grandma, LA was, like, six years ago, and you know I hated everything about it, especially my poor excuse of a father. There's nothing that could take me away from you . . . except for camp." Marti grinned.

When they arrived back at the car, Grandma rested against it.

"Are you okay?"

"I'm fine. Just a little winded. It's all this excitement

and fresh air. I'm not used to walking so far anymore."

Marti glanced at the sidewalk to the lodge, which wasn't really that far. "Maybe you better go to the doctor."

"I'm two steps ahead of you. I have a checkup on Monday."

"Good," she said, satisfied, but then thought again. "There isn't anything wrong, is there?"

"Of course not. You concentrate on making new friends and taking pictures. I can't wait to see them." She brushed a lock of Marti's hair off her face.

"I will. Do you want to come see my cabin?"

"No, I'd better be getting back. I've got a long ride ahead of me." She walked around to the driver's side. "For the next two weeks, I want you to relax."

Marti gave Grandma a squishy hug and breathed in her lilac-scented perfume. "I will. Love you."

"I love you, too." She climbed into the car and settled her purse on the passenger seat. Marti closed the car door for her.

"I know you're not allowed to use your phone, but be sure to write and tell me how things work out with that boy."

Marti shook her head. "I'll keep you posted, but don't get your hopes up. Boys aren't on my radar right now."

Grandma raised an eyebrow. "Now that's a big fib if ever I heard one." She reached out and gave Marti's hand a quick squeeze. "Have a wonderful time."

"I will." Marti stood out of the way as Grandma backed out of the spot and turned down the road that would lead her away from camp. Marti looked around at all the kids arriving and parents leaving. She hadn't been to a summer camp since fifth grade, and this was no average camp. This was the Gallagher Institute Art Camp for teens who wanted intense immersion in their subject of interest. Along with photography, the camp had drawing, painting, and orchestra, too.

She took the handle of her rolling suitcase and followed a trail of kids heading down the path to the lakefront cabins. Her adventure was about to begin, and she couldn't wait to see what it brought.

Adam followed the uneven sidewalk for what seemed like a half mile. But what was another few minutes' walk after two connecting flights and a three-hour ride from the airport? He was finally here!

Excitement buzzed through the air as he watched dozens of kids locate their cabins. He made his way down the path until he reached the last cabin. Two guys relaxed on a spacious, covered porch with their feet up on the railing. One, with loose, wavy, brown hair, wore a heavy-metal T-shirt and a devilish grin. The other sported expertly trimmed black hair and smart eyes that gleamed with adventure.

Adam rubbed his hand over his newly shortened hair.

Here goes nothing. He climbed the steps and stopped at the top. Cameras sat on the table between the two guys, along with a docking station playing some adequate indie tune. A quick peek in the cabin revealed what appeared to be a black light.

"What's up?" Adam nodded. Would they recognize him or would he blend into his new surroundings?

"Dude," the guy with black hair acknowledged. "Welcome to the Chateau!"

Adam looked to the other guy in confusion.

"We didn't like our cabin name, and since we're on a hill overlooking the lake, we renamed it the 'Chateau.'"

"Nice." Adam gazed out at the spectacular view. "I'm AJ."

"I'm Kyle." The guy with the wavy hair leaned forward to shake his hand.

"Justin," said the other, offering his hand. "Help yourself to a Dew. There's a cooler inside."

"You brought a cooler?" Adam lugged his gear into the cabin.

"I brought everything. And trust me. We are going to have the best time! You know what the Boy Scouts say: 'be prepared.'" Justin smiled in a way that said he'd probably never been a Boy Scout and if he had, he probably got kicked out.

"Dang, I wish I'd have thought of that," Adam said, looking down at his duffel bag.

"Technically, we're not supposed to, but as long as it's out of sight, the counselors won't bother us. We're the last camp of the summer, and I'm sure they're so sick of teenagers that they couldn't care less what we do."

"Check it out. Here comes another girl for the cabin next door." Kyle sat up, eager to get a better view.

Justin grabbed his camera. "Very nice. I can definitely work with that." He snapped a couple of pictures.

They watched the beautiful girl that Adam had met earlier, with the honey-blond hair and sassy spirit, pull her bag toward the cabin next door. "You might have to fight me for her," Adam challenged with a grin.

"We'll see about that," Kyle laughed.

"Guys, there are many fish in the proverbial sea of camp." Justin put his camera down, leaned back, and put his feet up.

Maybe, but Adam looked forward to trying to hook this particular little fish.

Marti's rolling bag bounced along the busy sidewalk. The forest of trees created a scent like nothing she'd ever experienced. Finally, she spied Monet, one of the last cabins.

Her stomach clenched as she shifted the many straps over her shoulder. She took a steadying breath, gripped the handle of her bag, and pulled it up to the cabin. As she mounted the three wooden steps to the front porch, the screen door flew open and a perky girl with a dusting of freckles, wavy, brown hair, and a button nose leaned out.

"Hi! Come on in." She held the door open.

"Hi!" Marti hauled her load through a screen porch and into a main room.

"I'm Kayla. Welcome to Monet!" she said, nearly bouncing out of her flip-flops.

"Thanks. I'm Marti." She lowered her bags to the floor and looked around at the knotty pine walls, worn wood floor, and four beds positioned around the room. "This is awesome."

"It's gotta be the best! We've got our own screened porch. The only other cabin with a porch is next door, but theirs isn't screened in."

Marti peeked out the window and saw a couple of guys hanging out on the porch.

Kayla followed her gaze. "Isn't it great? Two of the guys over there are really cute."

"You didn't waste any time checking things out." Marti immediately liked her.

"Heck, no! Gotta get the lay of the land right away. I'm a seasoned professional at summer camp. We're sitting on prime real estate here. We are the second-to-last cabin, we have a porch, we have an amazing view of the lake, and there's a hiking trail that starts on the other side of the guys' cabin."

Grumbling sounded from outside the cabin.

"Hang on!" Kayla hollered, ran to the porch, and

opened the door for the new girl.

Marti glanced around, noticing a small bedside table with a low lamp by each bed. Both sides of the room featured a dresser with a mirror. There was a sink with vanity and drawers beneath it, a large mirror over the top, and a bathroom located to the right.

"Brooke, this is Marti. Marti, meet Brooke." Kayla plopped down on a bed.

"Hi." Brooke wiped her brow, revealing large, almond-shaped eyes and long, silky hair. "That is one freakin' long walk."

"I know. I thought I'd never get here." Marti perched on the edge of the closest bed.

"Where can I dump this stuff?" Brooke surveyed the room.

"Anywhere you like, except this one." Kayla pointed to her coordinated bedding complete with neon-orange fur pillows and a purple makeup bag on the bedside stand.

Brooke heaved her leopard-print bags onto the bed next to Marti's and then sprawled on top, extending her long, tanned legs. "I can't tell you how glad I am to be here," she said with a megawatt smile.

The screen door creaked again, and their final cabin mate, a petite blond girl with large, green eyes and thin hair pulled into a ponytail walked in. She looked up as she struggled through the screen door. They all grabbed a bag off her shoulder or from her hand.

"Thanks," she said with a smile as innocent as her Hello Kitty T-shirt.

"I'm Kayla, and this is—"

"I'm Brooke," Brooke interrupted.

"Marti."

"Hi, I'm Haley," the new girl said.

There was a long pause, and then they all looked at each other and grinned.

This was going to be the best two weeks ever.

2

"*Welcome* to the Gallagher Institute's Summer Intensive. I'm Tony Johnson, camp manager," said a tall man who resembled a scarecrow with his long, pointy nose and spiky hair. "I see a few familiar faces out there—welcome back—and a lot of new faces, too. For the next couple of weeks you will be experiencing a highly intensive education from some of the best instructors in your field of interest. Now before I lose your attention, we need to go over a few housekeeping rules."

Marti huddled with her new friends at a long table with benches on each side. Huge windows revealed a clearing around the building, the lush forest provided the backdrop. It was almost like being outside.

"Did you see that guy with the black hair? He keeps looking over here," Brooke whispered, and peeked out the corner of her eye.

Marti glanced over to see not just one guy but also three of his friends eyeing their group. "They are totally checking us out," Marti said, her heart beating a little faster. The cute, dark-haired guy seemed to be tracking Brooke.

"The one with the wavy hair is kind of cute," Haley whispered as she chewed on her fingernail.

Marti looked at him. Bushy eyebrows framed his face.

"You can have him," Kayla declared. "I'm trying to decide between the other three."

"Do you think they're here for photography or one of the other programs?" Haley asked.

"With looks like his, I don't think he's here to dabble in the arts. I think he's here to dabble with the girls." Brooke met the dark, steamy guy's gaze.

Marti could tell that Brooke was in a class of her own where guys were involved.

"Intense," Kayla said with approval.

Tony droned on. "In a weather emergency, you'll hear the bell ringing. . . ."

"Check out the guy with the short hair. He is totally hot!" Kayla wiggled her little finger in his direction.

Marti peeked over at the guy she had talked to when Grandma dropped her off. He joked with his friends.

"His name is AJ. I met him when I first got here. He's nice." And he was easy on the eyes.

"I can definitely work with that," Brooke said, giving him the once-over.

AJ looked their way and smiled at Marti as the other girls giggled.

"That's it for tonight. I'll bore you with more details tomorrow." Tony clicked off the mic, and the kids broke into small groups.

As the girls walked through the lodge, Marti noticed a small room off the main area with overstuffed chairs, a bookcase packed with novels, an upright piano, and a couple of guitar cases.

"Hey, look." Haley pointed. "A piano. Anyone play?"

"Not a note," Kayla said. "My mom made me take piano lessons for an entire year, and I hated it. The music gene skipped over me and went to my brother."

"Is he older or younger?" Marti asked.

"Younger, but he acts like he knows everything. He's such a pain." Kayla rolled her eyes.

"My brother is older and he's impossible, but now he's at college, so it's a lot better." Brooke brushed a long, gleaming lock of hair from her face. "What about you, Marti? Any sibs?"

Marti considered telling them about her two half siblings: a brother and a sister who were total losers that she barely knew and never saw, but that seemed like too much information. "Nope. It's just me." Which was more or less true.

"Four sisters," Haley offered. "Two older and two younger. I'm lucky when my parents get my name right."

"On the positive side, there are lots of clothes you can borrow." Brooke grinned.

Outside, the warm day had turned into a balmy evening. The sun lay low in the western sky and sparkled across the calm lake.

"This is so gorgeous. Makes me want to start snapping pictures." Marti's fingers itched for her camera as they followed the path to the Nature Center, which was tucked in a clearing surrounded by tall trees. Tonight, they'd meet the other kids in the photography group. When they entered the cozy building, they discovered a large room where one side was the Nature Center with displays of driftwood, pressed leaves, butterflies mounted behind glass, and jars of mysterious bugs. The other half of the room boasted a large area rug along with two comfy couches and a dozen giant floor pillows in an array of colors. A piano was placed behind one couch and faced a stone fireplace.

"This place keeps getting better!" Marti wished she could live here forever.

"I know, isn't it great? I've been here the past two years." Kayla ran her finger along the fringe of a wall hanging.

"Really, you like it that much?" Marti asked.

"Yes and no. My parents want to keep me busy and pad my résumé for college apps. Plus, they hope it'll keep me out of trouble. The thing is, I've probably gotten into more trouble at camp than I would have if I stayed home. If they only knew." Her face broke into a sneaky grin.

"Let's grab the pillows." Brooke led the way, and they plopped down on large, comfy pillows in the corner as more kids arrived.

"Don't look now, but things just got better." Brooke tipped her head toward the guys from dinner.

Tall, dark, and steamy led the way. "Hey," he said to Brooke, and relaxed on a pillow next to hers.

Brooke arched a perfectly tweezed eyebrow and looked away, but then grinned at Marti and Kayla.

The girl from registration joined them. "Hi, everyone. I'm Melody and I'm your counselor." Melody wore frayed jeans and a Gallagher Institute T-shirt with an artist's paint palette embroidered in the corner.

Melody tucked an escaped strand of blond hair behind her ear and sank into the couch. "We're going to start off with one of those lame 'get to know you' games. Sorry." She smiled. "But first, let's start by going around the circle. Say your name and something about yourself, like where you're from."

Everyone looked around. No one wanted to start. Melody looked at AJ. "Why don't you start?"

His eyes widened, but he recovered quickly. "Okay. Sure. My name is AJ. And I'm from . . . Boise." He looked to the guy with dark hair the girls had been gawking at to go next.

"I'm Justin and I'm from Seattle."

"Hi, I'm Kyle and I'm from Naperville, Illinois," said

their roommate with the wavy hair.

"Hey. I'm Ryan and I'm from the Atlanta area."

Marti knew this was a prestigious camp and loved the idea that kids came from so far away. Haley was the first girl to answer, telling them she was from a small town in New Jersey. Marti told them she lived in Madison, Kayla drove up from Chicago, and Brooke was from Santa Fe.

"Great. Now, have any of you ever played Two Truths and a Lie?"

Marti nodded, along with most of the others.

"What's that?" whispered Haley.

"For those of you who don't know, each person takes a turn and tells two things about themselves that are the truth and one that's a lie. Then everyone guesses which one is the lie. I'll go first," Melody said. "I'm majoring in poli-sci, I'm allergic to horses, and I've been skydiving. Now you guys have to guess. Which one is the lie?"

"Skydiving," Marti called out. She couldn't imagine why anyone would ever want to leap from a plane.

"No, that's too obvious." AJ shook his head.

Marti didn't know if she should be irritated that he disagreed with her or if she should find a way to stop noticing the way his mouth curled into a smile every time he spoke.

"Is it the allergy to horses?" Haley asked.

"Yup, you got it," Melody answered. "Now let's split the group in half so it's a bit more manageable, and you guys can play. Let's have the people on the pillows be one group, and the rest on the couches be another."

Marti's group gathered up pillows and moved into a corner of the nature area where a taxidermied fox watched over them, and a fish tank containing tiny turtles bubbled.

"Okay, I'll go first." Kyle leaned back on his hands and blew his bangs out of his eyes. "I was born in Hawaii, I put ketchup on popcorn, and I can snort Jell-O from one nostril to the other."

"Oh, that's gross!" Haley groaned.

Everyone laughed, and Marti relaxed even more as she sensed these would be fun kids.

"So what's the lie?" Brooke asked.

"I bet it's the ketchup on popcorn," Marti said, "because no one would think of snorting Jell-O unless they'd done it." Marti tried to imagine how one went about snorting Jell-O.

"You got it." Kyle flashed a sexy grin her way, and Marti couldn't help but blush.

"I've got one," AJ offered, stretching out and crossing his long legs at the ankles. She was tempted to reach out and touch him. "My favorite musical group is that new boy band from England, I hate running, and when I was little I stuck peas up my nose."

"Boy band! No guy in their right mind would like a boy band," Kyle said.

"I think they're all kind of cute." Kayla ducked her head and nibbled on her lip. Marti bumped shoulders with her.

"Yeah, you're right," AJ laughed.

The game went around the circle, until Melody interrupted. "Okay, everyone. You have free time until lights-out at eleven."

"You've got to be kidding. It's not like we're six years old," Kyle complained.

"Sorry, bunk checks happen at eleven. Don't blame me. It's the rules. I don't make 'em."

"Well, I break 'em," Justin whispered under his breath.

"Wake-up bell is at seven thirty, and breakfast is at eight thirty. Tomorrow you'll be starting off with a project on perspective and also some black-and-white work. You guys have a full day, so off with you. I'll be by your cabins at eleven for lights-out." Melody slid the furniture back in place.

They all wandered out of the building into the balmy evening air.

"What do you want to do?" Kayla asked.

"I don't know. Let's explore," Marti suggested. "I've barely seen the camp yet."

As they walked toward the cabins, the guys followed.

"You girls want to party later?" Justin asked.

"What'd you have in mind?" Brooke flipped her hair. Marti was pretty sure Brooke wanted to do anything that involved Justin.

"Let's meet up at the ball field around eleven thirty. We'll bring the beverages." He grinned, which told Marti he wasn't bringing lemonade.

"Sounds good to me. What do you think?" Kayla looked to Marti and the other girls.

Marti nodded.

"Abso-freakin'-lutely," Brooke added.

"Awesome. We'll catch ya later, then. Come on, guys." He motioned up the path and AJ, Kyle, and Ryan followed.

A few minutes before eleven p.m. as the girls pretended to get ready for bed, Melody popped in. "Time for lights-out. I'll see you in the morning." The girls said good night as Melody flipped off the light and let the screen door softly creak closed as she went to the next cabin.

And then, the sounds of a cello came across the outdoor speakers. The strains of Brahms's lullaby floated through the air. Marti smiled as she lay in bed and listened to the haunting sound of the low strings' vibration. It was a beautiful piece when played in its entirety. She wondered who played it: one of the kids from camp or an instructor?

Finally, at eleven thirty, the four girls popped out of bed, changed clothes, and snuck down the dark, wooded path to the open ball field. They whispered and giggled as they followed Kayla's flashlight beam. In the middle of the field, they spotted the shadowed figures of the guys sitting in the grass around a small cooler.

"Oh my God, they totally brought booze!" Kayla whispered.

"How do you know it's booze? Maybe it's just soda." Haley sounded worried as if she'd never had a drink before.

"Don't worry. Stick with me, and I'll get you educated in the ways of the real world." Brooke slid her arm around Haley's shoulders and pulled her forward.

"Hey, guys," Marti said as they approached. "What's up?"

Justin swirled the contents of his red plastic cup. "We're debating whether vodka or brandy gets you drunk faster."

"Definitely brandy," Brooke stated with confidence.

Marti looked wide eyed at the others.

"I think we need to do a test to decide for ourselves." Kyle rubbed his hands together like a mad scientist.

At home, Marti didn't go out drinking. The last thing she wanted to do was worry her grandmother. But this was camp, and the odds of getting caught were pretty low. This was a perfect chance to finally cut loose.

"Okay, who's Team Brandy and who's Team Vodka?" AJ asked, turning to Marti as she knelt next to him and the cooler.

The low light of the moon illuminated his impish grin. Something about him seemed familiar, but she couldn't figure out what. He pulled more plastic cups from the cooler, along with a two-liter bottle of fruit punch.

"I'll try the vodka," Marti decided.

"Excellent choice. That puts two of us on Team Vodka."
His eyes flashed.

Marti's stomach tightened in a good way. So AJ already
put her on his team. "Want some help?" she asked.

"Absolutely." His eyes met hers, and Marti's stomach
did a little flip.

"Haley and I will go for the brandy." Brooke gave Haley
a look that said there would be no backing down.

"Awesome, come join us." Kyle scooted over to make
room. Brooke dragged a nervous Haley over to join him.

"I think that makes you a vodka girl tonight," Justin
said to Kayla.

"Twist my arm." She giggled and wiggled in between
Justin and Marti.

Marti put ice in the cups and held them as AJ poured
juice and a generous amount of booze. She admired how
the shadows from the moon defined the structure of his
face. He seemed to have a permanent glint in his eye as if
he were having more fun than anyone else. She couldn't
help but smile.

He took an empty cup and poured the drink between
the two cups to mix it up.

"You've done this before." She realized he was much
more experienced with booze than she was.

"Nah, this is how my brother used to make chocolate
milk." AJ finished, the corner of his mouth turned up in a
devilish grin.

Marti handed the cups down the line to the girls, and Justin made a toast. "Here's to an awesome two weeks."

They leaned in and tapped their plastic cups together. "Cheers."

Here's to uncharted territory. Marti took a drink, a little too big as the strong alcohol made her want to cough, but she choked it down.

"Here's to new friends." Haley raised her glass.

"Here's to what happens at camp stays at camp." Kyle looked straight at Kayla, and she raised an eyebrow before lifting her cup. They toasted again.

Marti toasted silently to Grandma. Grandma made up for Marti's absentee parents. She always found a way to make Marti's dreams come true. Not that Grandma had any idea Marti would be drinking her first night at camp. She felt a teeny bit guilty but brushed it away.

She leaned back on her hands and gazed at the night sky. The moon rose, illuminating the clearing. Stars twinkled as if telling her she was in for the time of her life.

"Nice view." Adam leaned back next to Marti and looked up. He liked how the treetops framed the edge of the playing field and the stars above.

"Sure is. At home, the stars don't look like this. Or if they do, I guess I just don't take the time to look." Marti sighed.

"I hear you. Plus, the lights of the city block out half of

the stars." Adam rarely thought about looking at the night sky. But here, away from big cities, bright lights, and a full schedule of appearances, he already found himself looking at the world with fresh eyes. He took a deep breath of the woodsy air.

"I wish I had my camera. I'd love to capture this."

"I know what you mean. I've been dying to break mine out, but I didn't want to look too eager." He glanced over to see her reaction, hoping he didn't sound like a total loser.

"I think you're in the right place to be a photography nerd," she laughed.

"Nerd! Where'd that come from?" He rubbed his head and wondered if the short hair had changed him so much he'd lost his cool factor.

"Come on, anyone who goes to an arts camp has got to be totally obsessed and kind of nerdy."

"I can honestly say I've never been called a nerd in my life. At least not to my face." *And not in any of the fan magazines, either.*

"My, my, a little sensitive, are we?" Marti teased.

"Hey, you're attacking my coolness. I've got a reputation to defend here. I can't let word get out that some hot girl thinks I'm a nerd." He hoped the compliment would impress her.

"Hot girl? You're trying awfully hard. Trouble getting dates back home?" She sipped her drink.

He shook his head. He noticed her smirk and wouldn't

mind shocking it off her with a kiss, but he didn't know if she even liked him.

She bumped his shoulder with hers. "What? Did I hit too close to home?"

"You have no idea." Her words made him want to laugh at the irony. Marti didn't know about all the thousands of girls who screamed his name at concerts. How many were dying to get close to him, and how he was the one who turned the girls down. Now here he was hanging out next to a beautiful girl with gorgeous eyes and a smile that made him never want to leave her. He finally had the perfect opportunity to get close to a girl and she seemed totally immune to him. He gulped his drink.

"That game tonight was totally lame," Justin said, bringing Adam out of his thoughts.

"No kidding. All that stuff about 'I don't like oranges, and I've never been to a baseball game.' Totally stupid." Kayla rolled her eyes.

"I know, let's go around and say something totally scandalous that's true."

"I don't have anything scandalous," Haley said, looking nervous again.

"Okay, something you'd never say online."

"I'm going first," Justin said. "But wait, I need a refill." He handed his glass to AJ, who poured him another brandy and fruit punch and passed it back.

More cups were passed for refills. Marti and AJ worked in tandem to complete the requests and then refilled their own. When everyone had their cup, they went around and told outrageous stories of things they'd done.

"Me first," Brooke said. "Once, when I was little, I knew I was going to be sick so I went right for my dad's open briefcase."

"Eww!" Marti scrunched up her face.

"My parents never forced me to eat tomatoes after that." She shrugged with satisfaction.

Adam thought about what outrageous thing he could share. He couldn't really tell them about trying to sneak into the Oval Office when he and his brothers sang at the White House for a special event. Or the time his brother Garrett hooked him up to the fly lines at Madison Square Garden and flew him around the stage. His dad had a fit because they were breaking union rules, and his mom had a fit because Garrett crashed him into the rigging and almost broke Adam's arm. It hurt so bad he could barely play guitar the next night, but the show had to go on. His dad blew a gasket on that one.

Adam wanted to enjoy the anonymity of being a regular guy while he was here. He took another sip of his drink, savoring the cool burn of the alcohol.

"My dad was so drunk one time he drove through the garage door." Justin raised his cup in the air.

"I can top that one," Marti spoke up. "When I was little, my dad made me drive him places when he had too much to drink."

"So? I used to drive before I had my license," Justin said.

Marti shook her head. "Well, I was ten years old." She slurred her words a little.

"No way." Adam looked at her, dumbfounded.

"That's when I went to live with my grandma."

"Where was your mom?" Haley asked with concern.

"In rehab." Marti looked around the circle, and Adam wondered if she wished she hadn't revealed her family dirt. "Who's next?"

He watched her tear the lip of her cup, creating little rips around the edge. He wanted to reach over and squeeze her hand or do something to let her know he cared. But his head felt a little fuzzy. He wasn't sure what to do with a pretty girl who talked tough but looked soft and smelled good, so he did nothing.

"AJ, what have you got?" Kayla asked.

"Um, well . . ." Adam didn't know what to say. Anything worth telling would reveal that his life was a whole lot bigger than anyone expected. He'd like to see if he could hit it off with a girl who wasn't fawning over the fact he was Adam Jamieson, lead guitarist for his band. If they learned his identity before getting to know him, he knew they'd treat him like a celebrity or a spoiled kid who got everything he wanted. Either way, he wasn't ready to spill it.

Plus, anything scandalous he said, whether it was true or a lie, could end up in the tabloids. If there was one thing his father hated, it was bad publicity.

"Can't really think of anything to top those stories." He hid behind another long drink of his beverage.

"Aw, come on, man," Kyle urged.

Marti watched him with narrowed eyes. "He's holding back. He's got secrets; he just doesn't want to share."

"Coward!" Brooke threw her empty cup at him.

"I don't." He laughed. "I'm an open book." He considered telling them that his brother Peter held up a sold-out concert by forty-five minutes because he was upset about a girl named Libby. Probably not a good idea.

Adam lifted his cup and drained the contents. "Okay, I've got one. My oldest brother called my other brother's girlfriend and told her he didn't want to go out with her anymore."

"Huh?" Ryan looked confused. "I'm confused."

"You're saying one brother called up the other brother's girlfriend and broke them up?" Brooke asked.

Adam nodded.

"Damn, that's seriously messed up," Justin said.

"That's terrible! What did your brother do when he found out? The one who lost his girlfriend?" Marti looked shocked.

"I've never seen him so pissed in all my life. Broken furniture and blood were involved."

"Did he get his girlfriend back?" Haley asked.

"Eventually, but it took a while." Adam wished he could share the long, sordid tale about Peter losing Libby and the national search Peter created to track her down, but knew he couldn't. Peter and Garrett wouldn't appreciate the details of their lives being told to total strangers. Enough of their lives were already in the tabloids.

"That reminds me, I've got one," Kyle said.

While Kyle confessed his next story, Marti scooted closer to Adam and whispered, "There's something about you that seems really familiar."

Adam leaned in, inhaling the floral scent of her hair. It blended perfectly with the woodsy setting. "Really?"

"Yes. It keeps nagging at me. I know you said you were from Boise, but have you ever lived in Madison?"

"No." But he'd cruised by the city on the interstate many times while touring the Midwest.

"You never lived there?"

He could see her trying to puzzle it out. "Nope. But I hear that all the time. I guess I have one of those common faces. I probably remind you of someone you go to school with."

"Maybe, but I don't think so." She tilted her head and scrutinized him in the moonlight.

Adam needed to get her mind off why she thought he looked familiar. Maybe she was a fan.

"What you said earlier about your dad. That's unbelievable."

"Yeah." Marti turned away and stared at the ground. "He's a piece of work."

"How were you able to drive? Did you crash? I mean, how did you get caught?"

"My dad would bring a couple of phone books for me to sit on and scootch the seat up really close to the steering wheel so I could reach the pedals. I never hit anything, probably because I was so terrified that I drove super slow. That's actually why we got pulled over."

Adam shook his head. "That is so messed up. Why would your dad put you behind the wheel at that age?"

"The short answer is that he's a pothead, alcoholic musician who thinks he's entitled to whatever he wants and laws aren't meant for him."

"Sorry. I shouldn't have asked." Dumbstruck by her words, Adam tipped his cup back only to find it empty. He fumbled with the cooler for a refill.

"No, it's fine. I don't usually talk about him. He's a washed-up rocker with absolutely no sense of responsibility. I guess the juice here made me talk too much."

Her dad was a musician? A rocker? Adam wondered if it was someone from the industry he'd heard of or just a small-time musician who'd never hit it big.

"I'm glad you live with your grandma and don't have

to see him." He moved closer and could see a light sprinkle of freckles on her nose. He liked Marti and how direct she was with her opinions. She didn't flutter around and try to be someone she wasn't.

"I don't plan on ever seeing him again. He's so screwed up." She peeked at Adam and smiled. "Sorry."

"No problem." He liked the cute way she grinned.

"You guys, everybody quiet!" Kayla whispered. "I see lights coming up the path."

"Shit!" Ryan said.

"Quick. Hide! Maybe they won't see us," Brooke said.

"The flashlight!" Justin dove for Brooke's flashlight and blocked the dim light with his body. He quickly turned it off.

They all scrambled out of the clearing in different directions, leaving the evidence of their party behind. Adam and Marti hid behind a large tree. Getting busted for drinking the first night at camp wasn't how he'd planned things to go, but it sure was a hell of a lot of fun.

Marti faced him with her back against the tree. He held her shoulders and peeked around to check on the intruders, enjoying their close proximity.

"Are they gone?" Her sweet breath warmed his neck.

"Shh," he whispered. She giggled, so he gently pressed his finger against her lips. "Shh. I can still see the flashlights." He took advantage of their nearness and gazed into her eyes. The dappled light from the moon beamed through

the tree branches onto her face. She watched him, so innocent and inviting. Did she know how pretty she was?

Her long lashes waved as they locked eyes. His thumbs
caressed her shoulders through her light sweatshirt. She felt
so delicate and real. Adam dipped his head and felt her soft
intake of breath, and then her beautiful lips met his. She
tasted citrusy sweet, and he kissed her slow and soft. The
tip of her tongue brushed his, and his body went on high
alert as the kiss deepened. He slipped one hand behind
her neck, the other around her waist, and pulled her close.
Marti didn't seem to mind as she trailed her fingers over
his back. Her other arm was pressed against his chest.

Adam didn't know if the alcohol made Marti so willing
or something else. Either way, he didn't care. She nestled
in his arms, all warm and soft, and he fought to control
himself. He wanted to mold her body to his and let his
hands linger over every inch of her. Instead, he lost himself
in her kisses, the softness of her hair, and how the touch
of her body tortured his senses. After too short a time,
their mouths parted. Marti's eyes reflected dark and glassy
in the low light. She sighed and a shy smile greeted him.
Suddenly, they heard rustling in the woods and discovered
the others emerging from their hiding spots.

"I would have liked to stay hidden out here a lot longer,"
Adam breathed in her ear.

Marti watched the others and looked disappointed.
"Me too."

"It's only the first night. Lots more nights ahead of us," he offered, tilting his head to catch her eye. Her smile brightened.

He leaned down and kissed her again, not quite ready to leave. He held her face and caressed her cheek with his thumb. Marti curved into him for a last kiss before they joined the others.

"I think we're clear. Whoever it was took some trail farther into the woods. I don't think they were looking for us." Kyle watched the trail.

"Oh my God! I've never been so scared in my life! I just about peed my pants." Haley swayed on her feet, and they all laughed.

"I guess we better get back," Kayla said, looking at Haley.

Adam snuck a peek at Marti and found her watching him, too.

"Make sure we grab all the bottles and cups. We don't want to leave any sign we were here." Justin flipped open the cooler and started tossing things in.

They packed up and headed back to the cabins. Clouds drifted in front of the moon, darkening their way. Brooke led with a single flashlight beam. Kyle and Ryan carried the cooler. The rest followed.

Marti stumbled on a root sticking out of the ground. "I can barely see. I'm going to break my neck out here."

Adam caught her arm and held her upright as they

fumbled their way along. "I've got you. I won't let you get hurt."

"Is that so?" she slurred in a sassy tone that made him smile.

Adam leaned close to her ear. "Promise." He wrapped his arm around her waist and tucked her in close.

Back at the cabins, Haley hightailed it to bed. Brooke and Justin flirted while the others went inside.

Adam and Marti stopped at a large oak tree between the two cabins. Small solar lights illuminated the walkway.

"That was fun tonight," she said, leaning against the tree.

"Sure was. I can't wait to see what happens tomorrow." Adam wanted to kiss her again but not in front of the others.

"So I guess I'll see you at breakfast."

"Sounds good." He smiled, looking forward to more time alone with her.

"Good night, AJ." Marti pushed away from the tree and brushed her hand against his before she disappeared into her cabin.

Adam took a quick look around at his new surroundings, his home for the next couple of weeks, and broke into an air-guitar riff.

3

The clang of the morning bell woke Marti way too early. She squirmed farther under the soft covers.

"This is supposed to be vacation. Why do we have to be awake so early?" Kayla groaned from across the room.

"My head is killing me," Haley complained from bed.

Marti gazed out the window at the placid lake, smiling as she remembered AJ's kisses. She touched her lips and bit back her grin. She couldn't wait to see him again.

"I've got ibuprofen." Brooke, already showered and dressed in cute shorts and a snug-fitting T-shirt, stood in front of the mirror and carefully applied mascara to her gorgeous eyes.

"Why are you up already?" Kayla's words were muffled by the pillow over her head.

"This"—Brooke waved her hand in front of her face and body—"doesn't happen all by itself."

"Ibuprofen would be great." Haley crawled out of bed, holding her head.

"I told you to drink two glasses of water before you went to bed last night. It works every time." Brooke inserted the wand back in her mascara and twisted it shut.

Marti stretched and took mental inventory. Her mouth felt dry, but she didn't have a headache despite drinking two of AJ's concoctions. *Ah, AJ.* She snuggled under the covers remembering the touch of his arms around her. Maybe Grandma was right and he was a good one.

Suddenly, a low eerie noise sounded.

"What's that?" Marti sat up in bed.

"That's a loon," Kayla mumbled, the pillow still muffling her words.

"A what?" Marti asked.

"A loon. It's a bird," Kayla answered.

"No way! A bird that sounds like that, I want to see." Marti tossed off the covers and went to the window. "There it is!"

"Where?" Haley joined her, toothbrush in mouth.

Marti scanned the surface of the water, but this time found nothing. "It's gone. Did it fly away?"

"No. They go underwater to fish. It'll pop up somewhere else in a minute," Kayla said.

Marti and Haley peered out the window and waited.

"That was so fun last night. And those guys! We struck gold on cabin location. They're all cute, but Justin . . . hello!"

Brooke said, still slaving away at the mirror. Marti didn't understand her need to try so hard. She had the perfect package even without all the added bells and whistles of makeup and styled hair.

"And how about the guy that Marti was talking to? AJ? He's pretty hot," Kayla said.

"I didn't really notice," Marti responded.

Kayla's pillow flew through the air and hit her square in the head. "Marti, don't make me come over there and hurt you. If you don't want AJ, I'll be glad to take him off your hands."

"I guess he's okay." Marti tossed it back. Kayla finally looked ready to roll out of bed.

Haley finished brushing her teeth. "What's up with all that stuff about your dad? Did you say he's a musician?"

Marti cringed. She usually didn't mention her dad, but now that the story was out, she knew they'd have questions about that dark part of her life.

"Making me drive him around is only one of many stupid things he's done, and yes, he's a musician." She grabbed a washcloth and ran it under warm water.

"What's his name? Anyone we would've heard of?" Haley asked.

"Steven Hunter," she said casually as she wiped the residual makeup from her face.

"Seriously?" Brooke perched on the edge of the vanity. "*The* Steven Hunter from the band Graphite Angels?"

"That's the one." Marti hung the washcloth on the towel bar and grabbed her toothbrush. People always had different reactions when they learned her dad's identity. Some were starstruck, and some didn't know or care who he was. Others were impressed and thought knowing Marti brought them closer to a celebrity. Except her dad wasn't really a celebrity anymore—unless he went on *Celebrity Rehab.*

"He is so hot!" Brooke's face lit up.

Marti raised her eyebrows in disgust.

"Brooke! That's gross! You're talking about Marti's dad," Haley said.

"Sorry, my bad." But Brooke didn't look apologetic. Marti brushed her teeth.

"That's wild. Whenever a Graphite Angels song comes on the air, my mom always cranks up the radio. They are really awesome! From a classic rock point of view," Kayla added for Marti's benefit.

Marti wiped her mouth with a towel. "Well, the group is nothing like they were. At least not the last time I saw them, and that was a long time ago."

"So what's he like? I mean, it must be cool to have a famous dad. It's, like, crazy, right?" Brooke asked. "Did you go to movie premieres and stuff like that?"

Marti moved to her dresser and pulled out a pair of shorts. "It's crazy all right," she said with a lack of enthusiasm. "Let's see. One year for my birthday there was this huge party with all my dad's friends and their kids. They brought in a big, castle-shaped bouncy tent, a cotton candy machine, and a fountain that spouted fruit punch." Marti remembered it like it was yesterday. She'd been so excited.

"That's so cool." Brooke's face was all dreamy.

"It was. Until my dad and his buddies got wasted and passed out in the bouncy tent." She pulled on her shorts then grabbed her hairbrush.

"Oh." Brooke's smile faded.

"Trust me, having a rock star for a dad sucks. I wouldn't wish it on my worst enemy." Marti tore the brush through her tangled hair and glanced out the window. Her grade-school friends had been horrified by his behavior. She'd run from the party, sobbing. The next day, when she stood up to her dad and told him what a terrible thing he'd done, she was ridiculed for crying like a baby at the party. That was the day Marti realized she could never trust him, and since then, she learned to hide her emotions. "I haven't seen him since I was ten years old and that's fine by me."

"Jeez, I'm sorry. I had no idea," Kayla apologized.

Marti shrugged and tossed the hairbrush on her bed. "That was a million years ago. And as bad as my parents are, my grandma is that many times as great. She's the one who found this camp for me. She is always doing awesome things." Marti didn't mention that she was here on a partial scholarship. No way could they afford the entire tuition.

"I'm glad she did, because now you're here, and we're

going to have a blast!" Haley bounced, and Marti smiled in return.

"Hey, there's the loon again!" Kayla pointed out the window.

Sure enough, halfway across the lake, Marti spied the pointy black head and long, low body floating serenely in the water. "I'm taking a picture of that!" She rushed to her cabinet, grabbed her camera, and flew out the door. Marti stepped into the cool morning air, glad to end the discussion about her dad. Thoughts of him always dredged up painful memories. When people found out about him, they became obsessed with talking about his greatness, as if he'd discovered a cure for cancer. No, he *was* the cancer.

She crossed the sidewalk and moved past a couple of large trees for a better view of the lake. Located up on a hill, their cabin offered a panoramic view.

Her sandals crunched on dry pine needles as she edged closer to the water, hoping to spy the elusive bird. She searched the lake as a *click-click* sound interrupted the quiet morning.

To her surprise, AJ sat farther down the hill. A warm flush ran through her as she remembered their kisses. He peered intensely through the camera lens and adjusted his focus. A few more clicks and he lowered his camera to check out what he'd taken. Appearing satisfied, he looked up and smiled at Marti as if he'd been waiting for her all morning.

Marti cursed herself for not finishing getting dressed. She joined AJ and crouched down in the pine needles. He smelled fresh from his morning shower. Along with the dewy scent of the morning woods, she couldn't imagine anything better.

"Morning." The sunlight sparkled off his eyes. "You see the loon?"

"Yes, but only for a second." She licked her lips. Did he remember their kiss? Or had he been too drunk to care?

"Quick, check it out before it goes back under. It's straight out there." AJ leaned his head close and pointed to where the large bird floated.

"That is so cool," Marti whispered, glad she'd taken time to brush her teeth. The loon let out a low, eerie call. She grinned at AJ and raised her camera, focused, and snapped a shot right as it dove under.

"Aw!" She lowered the camera and looked at AJ.

"Elusive, isn't it? I've been sitting here for fifteen minutes trying to get a good shot." AJ's friendly demeanor made her feel like she'd known him forever.

"Did you get one?"

"I think so. Here, check these out." He shared his camera with her and they peeked together at the dozen or so pictures he'd taken.

"Oh, I like that one!" Marti pointed to a shot where the loon's whole body could be seen in a close-up. "I think it was looking at you." She glanced at AJ and laughed.

"That's because I was calling to it."

"And how did you do that?" Marti listened to the low tones of his voice and watched his mouth move. Would he kiss her again?

"First off, you have to know how to speak fowl."

"You swore at the bird?" She raised an eyebrow.

"No!" He laughed. "I meant fowl, like the bird family, not foul as in language."

"I know. I was messing with you." Marti watched for his reaction.

AJ gave her a sly look and shook his head. "Nice one."

Together, they watched the loon as it swam through the placid water and sang out an occasional call. Sometimes it was a low wail and other times, a trill. Every so often, it dove under and they'd try to guess where it would pop up.

The sound of a creaking cabin door interrupted their moment. They turned and spotted the girls leaving their cabin, camera gear in tow. Despite Marti's disappointment that her time alone with AJ was over, she waved them over. "Hey, you guys, you should see this loon. It's amazing!"

"Hi," AJ greeted the girls and smiled so adorably that Marti actually felt a pang of jealousy. She wished he would save that smile only for her.

"That's great, but breakfast is in, like, five minutes," Brooke said, not even looking out at the lake.

"Oh, jeez." Marti stood up and realized she was still

wearing the T-shirt she'd slept in. She covered her chest with one arm as her face warmed. Had AJ noticed? She brushed the dirt and pine needles off her shorts with her other hand. "I'm not even ready."

"We'll save you a seat," Haley said.

"Thanks. I'll hurry." The girls started off for the lodge.

"Do you want me to wait?" AJ offered as the guys came out of his cabin.

"No, that's okay. But thanks for showing me the loon and everything."

"Anytime," he said in his sweet, easygoing way, and Marti hoped that meant soon.

By the time Marti arrived at the lodge with all her gear, breakfast was well underway.

"Thanks for saving me a seat." She hooked her camera strap over the back of the chair and squeezed in next to Kayla and Haley. Four girls she hadn't seen before occupied the other side of the table. Marti smiled a greeting.

"We saved you two pancakes and some bacon, but the eggs and sausage are gone." Kayla passed the near-empty platter to her.

"Thanks." Marti slid the food onto her plate. She glanced at the nearby tables but didn't see AJ or the guys.

"Good morning, campers." Tony's voice boomed out over the kids' chatter and clinking dishes. "This afternoon, swim tests will run from one o'clock until three, so be sure to get down to the lake. Lifeguard Brian will help you out. Also, there will be a volleyball tournament with games every afternoon, so be sure to support your team."

Marti scooted her chair back and shifted to the side for a better view of the tables in the back corner. She glanced around but still didn't see AJ. She craned her neck and finally spotted his group. A bunch of girls she hadn't noticed before sat with them. A cute, redheaded girl giggled and kept flipping her hair. AJ laughed and leaned closer, touching her arm.

Marti's heart sank. Great. He wasn't interested in just her. He was interested in any girl. AJ looked up and their eyes connected. Marti whipped back around. How could she have misjudged him? Last night he'd been drunk, yeah, but this morning she thought for sure that he liked her—at least a little.

Determined not to look desperate, she refused to look back again. She focused on a saltshaker and ate her cold pancakes. She needed to stop acting so obvious. If he was interested, he'd have to make a move.

After breakfast, their heavyset, balding photography instructor, Mike Sellers, reviewed the basics of depth of focus. He sent them on a hike to a railroad track on the other side of the lake for their first assignment.

After a thirty-minute hike, they reached the railroad tracks and found Mike and small clusters of kids setting up equipment and experimenting with different angles and light levels.

Marti's group walked on, because Brooke insisted they find Justin before picking a spot. She was hot on his trail. Marti was pretty sure Brooke would land the guy soon.

Another hundred yards around a bend, they found the guys. Ryan's equipment was set up and ready to go. Justin and Kyle relaxed on an outcropping of rock. Marti didn't see AJ at first but then saw him farther down, adjusting his tripod. As soon as he spotted her, he waved.

Her heart beat a little faster. She waved back and instantly wished she'd acted less eager. She was going to act friendly, not flirty. If he liked other girls, so what? In an effort to act nonchalant, she ignored him and chatted with the others. She could see Justin and Kyle weren't too invested in photography. Brooke was right; with Justin's good looks, he belonged in front of the camera, not behind it.

"I'm going to go check out what AJ's doing." Marti didn't care if the other kids weren't interested in the work. She turned and looked at AJ, who appeared to think the same. Plus, the assignment was a great excuse to go talk to him.

"Mind if I join you?" Haley asked.

Marti fought the urge to tell Haley no, since she knew

she'd sound like a jerk or desperate for a guy. "Not at all. Come on."

They caught up to AJ, who had picked an ideal location.

"Nice spot." Marti lowered her backpack carefully to the bed of gravel. A half mile down, the train tracks disappeared into a dark stone tunnel.

"Thanks. I thought it would work out pretty nice." His eyes followed her.

"Mind if we join you? Or is this a restricted area?" Haley asked.

"My train tunnel is your train tunnel." He winked, and Marti started thinking about his kisses again.

She admired the spot he'd picked for taking pictures and how the distance created an illusion of the tracks growing narrower and narrower until they faded into the mysterious passageway.

"Think any trains will come out of that tunnel while we're here?" In her mind, she screamed the real question she wanted to ask: *Did you kiss me because you wanted to or because you were drinking?* Maybe it was a good thing Haley was here.

"If one does, I hope I get a picture before it runs me over," AJ said.

"Now that would be a great live-action shot." Haley laughed.

Marti went to work unpacking her gear. She took her camera from its case and secured it safely to the tripod.

They took turns capturing shots of the tracks and the tunnel from various heights and shutter speeds. The warm sun promised a spectacular day ahead.

After thirty minutes, Marti perched on a large boulder with a bottle of water. "Did you hear that cello last night?"

"That was so great." Haley adjusted her camera settings.

"Whoever was playing sure knew their stuff," AJ said.

"I love classical music, and there's something about a cello. It's just so . . . mellow." Marti took a sip of her water.

"Do either of you play?" AJ sat on a nearby boulder.

"The cello? God, no. That would be a disaster," Marti said.

"I tried the guitar when I was younger, but I quit," Haley said, while hooking her camera to the tripod.

"Why'd you quit?" AJ tossed a small rock back and forth between his hands.

"You know the song 'Classical Gas'? Well, I really wanted to learn to play it, but it was too hard for me to hold down all the strings. Never could play a lick."

"That's too bad," he said.

"I love that song!" Marti said.

AJ raised an eyebrow. "Really?"

"I'm not kidding!" she laughed.

"How do you know 'Classical Gas'?" he asked.

"I heard it all the time when I was little." She almost said her dad played it to her at bedtime, when he happened to be around, but she didn't want to bring him up again.

"How about you, AJ? Do you play?" Haley asked.

He swiped a drink of his water and then stretched the fingers on his hand. "Me? Nah."

"How's everyone doing down here? Getting any good stuff?" Mike asked, joining them.

"Yeah, lots of great shots!" Marti said.

"Glad to hear it. Now, I need to have you gather your stuff and move about ten feet off the tracks."

"Why? What's up?" AJ asked.

Mike checked his watch. "In about three minutes, the eleven o'clock train will be coming through."

"Oh!" Haley lifted her tripod with the camera still attached and quickly moved it off the tracks.

Marti and AJ quickly tossed loose items in their packs, grabbed the rest of their gear, and joined Haley.

The distant sound of a train whistle startled her. She shared an excited look with AJ.

"Oh my God! The rest of my gear!" Haley looked at her gear scattered on the other side of the tracks.

Mike laughed. "Don't worry, plenty of time."

The three of them raced over, gathered everything up, and ran back.

The other kids in their group joined them, ready to catch pictures of the train. A couple more minutes with an occasional locomotive whistle, and the tracks begin to rumble.

Anticipation escalated as the noise grew. Marti expected the train to appear at any moment, but it didn't. The sound became louder and louder, bouncing off the tunnel walls. The distant light on the engine shone brighter. She grabbed AJ's arm with one hand, her camera poised with the other. He grinned at her.

Suddenly, the train engine burst through the tunnel. She fumbled with her camera and started snapping shots. The whistle blew loud, repetitive blasts, causing her to stop and cover her ears. AJ lowered his camera and put his arm around her and laughed. She ducked into his embrace to block out the earsplitting train whistle. He tipped her head up in time to see the engine pass. The engineer sat at the window and gave them a quick smile and a wave before letting loose on the whistle again.

Some in the group concentrated on getting train pictures, others plugged their ears, and Kyle took pictures of everyone's reactions.

As the sound faded, Marti stayed in AJ's secure arms a few seconds longer. He had strong arms and a solid chest, as if he could protect a girl from anything. She finally stepped away and smiled shyly, which was dumb, because they'd made out last night.

"That was awesome!" Ryan exclaimed.

"I can't believe we were so close." Haley's eyes followed the tracks.

"Everybody get something they liked?" Mike asked.

Marti looked at AJ, and he nodded.

4

After a late morning photography session on linear and vanishing-point perspective and then lunch, Marti and Haley walked down to the lakefront for their swim test.

"You and AJ sure seem to have something going," Haley said with a little grin.

"Oh, I don't know." Marti pretended it wasn't true. She still wasn't sure what was going on. She knew she liked him, and he was a super-nice guy, but . . .

"Come on, you two are so cute together, and I can tell he's totally into you!" Haley gushed.

"You think so?" Marti nibbled at her lip.

"Are you kidding me? He's always looking at you and haven't you noticed that he always manages to be right next to you?"

Marti grinned, a new bounce in her step. "He is pretty cute."

"That's an understatement. You know, he kind of reminds me of someone." Haley wrinkled her forehead.

"Me too!" Marti turned to Haley. "It's been bugging me ever since I met him. There's something that seems so familiar, but I can't figure it out." They stepped over a raised crack in the sidewalk.

"Okay, this is going to sound crazy, but he kind of reminds me of one of the brothers from the band Jamieson. You know, the youngest brother, Adam Jamieson?"

Marti tripped and stubbed her toe. "Ow!"

"Are you okay?"

"Yes," Marti groaned.

Marti tried to picture Adam Jamieson in her mind. She wasn't a fan of the band, or any rock band for that matter, but their music was everywhere, and she had to admit it was pretty good. Her best friend back home, Kristi, was a huge fan, owned all their music, and had their posters hanging in her room. The three brothers were all really great looking, but Kristi liked Peter best.

"I don't think so. Isn't Adam the one with all the curly hair?" Marti asked.

"Yeah, but there's something about when AJ smiles. I think he looks just like Adam Jamieson, minus all the hair, of course."

"Maybe." She tried to picture the posters on Kristi's wall, but she never paid close attention. Marti didn't understand the whole appeal of idolizing someone because they were in a movie or sang a song. It all seemed pretty shallow, which described her father to a tee.

Haley continued, "And AJ could stand for Adam Jamieson."

That captured Marti's attention. Her head whipped around to Haley and she was about to comment, but then Kayla ran down the path toward them.

"Hey, guys, wait up!"

Marti and Haley waited as Kayla skittered up, trying not to lose her flip-flops. Her ponytail bounced with each step. "I hate swim tests. Why can't they just take our word?" Kayla hugged her beach towel.

The girls chatted the rest of the way to the beach and joined the others who were in various stages of the test.

Marti shimmied out of her shorts and tank top, adjusted her coral-striped bikini bottom, and put her clothes in a pile covered by her towel. Together, the three waded into the cool lake.

"Oh my God, I hate cold water." Haley gripped her arms as they trudged to the lifeguard area.

"You three going as a group?" Brian, the camp life-guard, asked. He had that total laid-back lifeguard thing going on. The sun kissed his hair with blond highlights, and a bronze tan covered his body.

"Ready." Haley stood on her tiptoes.

"Hang on, we're ready, too," AJ called out as he and Kyle splashed through the shallow water toward them. AJ wore a pair of loud, floral swim trunks that on any other guy would be obnoxious, but looked perfect with AJ's fit body and handsome face.

Haley aimed a knowing look at Marti. "I told you, he likes you."

"Shut up," Marti whispered back, but inside her stomach flipped with joy.

"Okay, listen up. First, swim to the far buoy and back. Use whatever stroke you want. When you get back, go to that deep area over there." Brian gestured at a group bobbing up and down in the water. "Tread water for three minutes. Got it?"

They all nodded.

"Start whenever you're ready." Brian glanced out at the bobbers and checked his stopwatch.

"Race you!" Kyle called, and dove in, splashing Kayla, and started swimming. AJ dove in after him.

"Kyle is such an idiot." Kayla gave him a dirty look.

Marti, Haley, and Kayla stepped out farther until the depth forced them to swim.

As Marti did the sidestroke through the refreshing water, she wondered about Haley's comment. It would be so weird if AJ really were Adam Jamieson. Kristi, back home, would have a coronary if she found out Marti spent two whole weeks at camp with him. But she couldn't imagine in a million years what a guy like that, who spent his time touring and surrounded by groupies, would be doing in a remote location like the Gallagher Institute Arts Camp spending idle days taking nature pictures and hiking.

She reached the deep water at the same time as Haley. The other three were already treading water. Marti joined the circle right across from AJ.

"I hate this part," Kayla complained. "My body has absolutely no buoyancy. It's like I have concrete legs."

"This is nothing. At my school, the teacher made us tread water for five minutes with our clothes on." Haley bobbed as she spoke.

"They keep the pool at my school at, like, sixty degrees. Every day we thought we'd die of hypothermia." Marti spit water out after dipping too low.

"I can't imagine going to swimming class in the middle of the school day." AJ floated easily as he treaded water.

Marti tried to check him out to see if he resembled Adam Jamieson, but she couldn't tell because the sun reflected off the water, making it hard to see.

"Don't you have swimming at your school?" Haley asked. "Where do you go?"

AJ hesitated. "Well. Uh . . ."

Marti exchanged a questioning glance with Haley. They swooshed their hands through the water and cycled with their legs to keep their heads above the lake as they waited for him to answer.

"Actually, I don't go to school." He seemed a little embarrassed. Marti found it adorable, but wondered if he'd flunked out or something.

"Why not?" Haley asked. "Did you graduate early?"

"Or drop out?" Kyle looked hopeful.

AJ laughed. "No, I'm homeschooled."

"No way!" Kayla said. "Did you ever go to school or were you always homeschooled?"

"I went for a long time, just not the last few years. Hey, how long have we been treading water? Shouldn't we be done by now?"

Just then, the lifeguard blew the whistle.

"Time's up, come on in," he hollered.

"Thank God!" Haley swam for the stairs at the end of the dock.

Marti floated onto her back to rest her aching arms. She gazed up at the blue sky. Only a couple of small puffy clouds floated by. She'd never met someone who didn't go to school before. Now she wondered even more about him.

"You coming?" Kayla called out.

Marti flipped over and swam to the dock.

She shivered as Brian secured the swim band around her wrist. Goose bumps covered her arms, but the sun warmed her skin. "You guys all playing volleyball later?" he asked. "It's painters versus photographers. And I'm captain of the painters' team."

"Sure. I'll be there." Marti adjusted the blue wristband.

"You're going down!" Kayla taunted the lifeguard, and batted her lashes.

Brian laughed. "We'll see."

They wandered down the dock and gathered up their towels. Kayla spread hers out on the sand to get optimum sunshine. Haley placed her towel next to it. Marti wrapped hers around herself and looked at her fingers. "Look how wrinkled my fingers are."

AJ stepped closer. "Now that's attractive. They look like prunes."

"Let's see yours!" Marti reached for his hands and turned them over, loving the excuse to touch him.

"They're worse than yours," he laughed.

Marti noticed big, white bumps on the tips of each of his fingers. "What are those?"

AJ looked down. "Oh, they're just calluses from . . . It's nothing." He pulled his hands away.

Confused, Marti said nothing, but then realization dawned along with a heavy feeling in the pit of her gut. The only other time she'd seen calluses like that was when she lived with her dad. He had calluses on every finger, just like AJ, and used to say that was why he played guitar so well.

Marti looked straight at AJ. The carefree glint in his eyes dimmed. She examined his face. *He couldn't be. Could he?*

"What's wrong?" AJ asked with genuine concern. She didn't like where this was leading.

"I know what those calluses are from." She spoke quiet and serious and wrapped her towel tighter.

"I grip my camera too tight." He grinned that familiar smile that made her want to melt in his arms, but instead the ache in her stomach grew.

Marti shook her head and in a quiet voice said, "You are such a liar." She picked up her clothes, grabbed her sandals, and left the beach.

"Marti, what?" He followed behind.

When she reached the sidewalk away from the rest of the kids, she turned. "What's your name?"

AJ stepped back. "It's AJ."

"What's AJ stand for?" she demanded, knowing the answer before he spoke. A mixture of disappointment and dread surrounded her. She didn't want it to be true. She wanted him to be normal, good-looking, charming AJ.

He laughed nervously. "It stands for AJ. That's all."

"You've been playing us all along. I can't believe it!" She turned and stormed off.

"Wait up. Marti!" AJ caught up to her and blocked the way. His suit dripped water on the sidewalk.

She gave him the evil eye. He wouldn't even be honest with her, and she'd thought she was the one person he'd connected with. "You're lying. Again!"

"No, I'm not. What have I lied about?" He folded his arms across his chest.

"Everything! Probably. First off—your name! Your name is Adam, isn't it?"

He looked toward the lake and then up at the sky.

He pushed his hand through the short hair on his head and seemed startled. "My real name is Adam. So what? Sometimes I go by AJ."

Marti watched him battle some internal conflict. He clenched his jaw and kept looking one direction and then another.

Marti felt a sense of betrayal from him with every answer. "Right. And you told Haley you don't play guitar. But you do. The only way to get calluses like you have is to play guitar. A lot." She glared at him and could tell he was scrambling to figure out what to say that would have him in the least amount of hot water.

"I'm not playing guitar . . . while I'm at camp."

She huffed. *Why did he have to lie?*

"That's not a lie!"

"Well, guess what? You don't fool me. My dad is Steven Hunter. I've seen too much and known too many guys like you."

Adam's jaw dropped and she could tell he was shocked to hear her dad's identity. Marti hated to admit it, but Adam was just like her dad—easily telling lies if it made his life more convenient. Always looking out for himself before anyone else. She couldn't afford to fall for a guy like that. She had the emotional scars to prove it.

"Not only do you play guitar, but your name is Adam." She cocked her head to the side. "You are Adam Jamieson, aren't you?"

He glanced around to see if anyone heard. "Yes," he finally admitted.

A stab of betrayal shot through her heart. Why did he have to be a rocker? And why did he have to lie? She knew the answer. Because that's what rockers did—lie and hurt you until you cut them off. "And you've been playing us like a Les Paul ever since you got here. Well, guess what? Your secret's out!"

Marti stomped past. She didn't look back, and she didn't know if he followed her or not. She seriously couldn't care less.

Guys like Adam were always trouble. *Always.* Her dad, the king of messed-up, egotistical, selfish musicians, couldn't pull out of his driveway without doing something horrible like running over some little kid's bike. Given the chance, she knew Adam Jamieson would run over her emotions and break her heart just as easily.

She marched back to the cabin, gritting her teeth the whole way. She wanted to like AJ—no, Adam—but he lied from the word go, a sure sign of his true character. He might not be like her dad yet, but he was only sixteen. He had plenty of time to perfect the skill.

The last thing she needed was another loser in her life. Her mom was so screwed up on drugs that Grandma forbade her from coming around, and her dad was horrible. Marti spent the past six years wishing that man out of her life for good. And now Adam Jamieson showed up, tempting her back to that nightmare world. Well, she'd learned a thing or two and refused to let him do it.

Marti let the creaky screen door bang shut and took a long, hot shower to wash away her frustration.

Adam let Marti go. He had no idea why his real identity pissed her off so much. He figured that if the kids at camp found out, they'd be starstruck or at least a little impressed. So he hid his real name, big deal! He didn't want the whole camp to know that Adam, lead guitarist of the chart-topping band Jamieson, was on the property. Only Tony, the camp director, knew the truth.

And now Marti did, too.

He stood in the middle of the path, still wet from the swim test. He didn't feel like going back for his towel, so he followed the path to the cabin. No danger of running into Marti. She flew out of there so fast, she could be to town by now.

When he reached her cabin, he glanced over but didn't see her. He entered his cabin, unlocked his storage cabinet, and grabbed his cell phone. He knew cell phones weren't supposed to be used while on camp property, but this was an emergency.

He pulled on a T-shirt, slid on sandals, and took the hiking path that lead up to Eagle's Point. Once the cabins and beach were out of sight, he called his brother Peter. He had experienced plenty of his own girl problems the past year.

Peter picked up on the third ring. "How's Boy Scout camp?"

"Very funny." Adam relaxed at the sound of Peter's voice. They spent so much time together it felt odd to be apart these past couple days. "How's everything with Libby? Did she turn you down again?"

"Nice one. Nope, she's right here." Adam could hear the happiness in Peter's voice and was glad for him.

"Hi, Adam!" he heard Libby call through the phone.

"Tell her hi," Adam said. "So, where are you guys?"

"You're not gonna believe this. Wall Drug."

Adam burst into laughter. "What the heck are you doing there?" Wall Drug, famous for nothing more than serving free ice water, had grown into a tourist mecca.

"I know, but Libby saw the signs, so we had to stop."

"Bro, you are so whipped, it's pathetic." But deep down Adam wished he had someone special, too. He thought Marti might have been that person, but apparently not.

"So what's up? What has lured you away from making candles in the sand and singing 'Kumbaya'? Don't tell me. Since the girls don't know who you are, they'll have nothing to do with you."

"Not exactly." He hesitated. "See, there's this girl, and . . ."

"Hey, Libby, Adam's got a girl!" Peter yelled, ignoring Adam.

"Way to go, Adam!" Libby called back. "Don't break her heart."

Adam shook his head. Calling Peter was probably a mistake, as his brother couldn't see anything in the world other than his girlfriend. Heck, Peter probably didn't know if it was day or night.

"Sorry, so there's this girl. What's the problem? You finally get a girl alone, and you don't know what to do with her?"

Adam rolled his eyes. "No, she has this huge issue with musicians. Let's just say she hates us all."

"Harsh. Why, what did we ever do to her?"

"Her dad is Steven Hunter."

"No way! *The* Steven Hunter? Of Graphite Angels?"

"Yup, the one and only." Adam spied a log bench at the top of the hill and sat down.

"I've heard he's pretty messed up, so I guess I can understand why she doesn't like musicians. I mean he's a genius, but a dysfunctional genius. So you're afraid she'll figure out who you are?"

Adam ran his hand over his short hair realizing it had been a waste of time to shave it. "She just did."

"Oh. So now what?" Peter asked.

"That's just it. I don't know. Will she be so pissed off

that she tells everyone? Then everyone will be tweeting pics of me, and crazed fans will start showing up, or worse, paparazzi will start flooding into camp." He drew patterns in the dry dirt with the toe of his sandal. "No one else seems to recognize me. Should I ask her not to tell anybody?"

"Is she a reasonable girl? Can you talk to her?"

"Not right now. She's pissed off that I lied to her."

"Give her some time to cool down. If she doesn't spill it right away, you're probably okay."

"I guess. But how do I get her to stop hating me?" How could he get things back to how they were last night in the moonlight?

"That I can't help you with. Just be yourself and hopefully that won't make it worse." Peter laughed.

"Not real helpful." Adam gazed out across the expanse of crystal-blue lake. A warm breeze rustled the leaves on the trees.

"You know what they say," Peter said. "There's a fine line between love and hate."

"And right now I'm feeling the hate."

"Hey, I gotta go. We found one of those Mold-A-Rama machines that makes a plastic elephant."

"All right, well, thanks for the help," Adam said.

"Anytime. Oh, and could you build me a picture frame out of Popsicle sticks?"

"You know what you can do with those Popsicle sticks. Later."

Adam ended the call and leaned back against the bench. He sighed. He'd find a way to make Marti stop hating him. He just didn't know how . . . yet.

5

Marti tousled her long, damp hair. No need to use the hair dryer when outside the sun glowed bright and a light breeze blew on this eighty-degree day. She pulled on a pair of shorts, a coordinating tank, and with a flick of mascara, felt complete.

She slid the camera strap over her shoulder and headed back to the beach to join the others. The shower cooled her temper after the confrontation with AJ.

No, *Adam*. While she wanted nothing to do with Adam Jamieson, she wasn't about to let his presence ruin her time at camp. She couldn't wait to see if he fessed up his identity to the others or kept lying.

On the way to the beach, she stopped and captured several pictures as a butterfly fluttered from one black-eyed Susan to another. The vivid yellow-and-black flowers, together with the orange-and-black of the monarch, displayed a brilliant array of color against the forest-green backdrop. She reviewed the new pictures and knew she had some winners.

As she arrived at the beach, she spotted a group of kids gathered at the sand volleyball court.

"Hey, Marti, just in time. We need you on our team," Kyle called.

Kayla ran up. "Where did you disappear to? All of a sudden you were gone." Friendly concern lit her perky, freckled face.

"Sorry about that. I realized I promised to email my grandma and haven't yet. And then I figured I might as well shower while I was back at the cabin." Marti felt a little guilty that she was lying over someone as stupid as Adam, and that Grandma really would like an email, but she hadn't sent one.

"Oh. I kind of wondered if you and AJ snuck off to make out." Kayla grinned.

"No. He is totally not my type."

"Who's not your type?" Haley joined them.

"Oh, Kayla thought I was off with AJ, but that'll never happen. I promise you." She kicked at a pinecone on the ground.

"I thought you liked AJ." Haley looked confused, since only an hour earlier Marti kind of said exactly that.

"Yeah, well, after talking with him more, I realized I'm just not that into him," she said, shrugging.

"Really? Maybe I'll go after him," Kayla said.

Marti's head popped up. She certainly didn't want Adam, but she didn't want one of her friends with him, either. Wasn't that an unspoken girlfriend rule?

"Just kidding," Kayla said after catching the look on Marti's face.

"Okay," Marti said, happy to know Kayla really didn't have her eye on Adam. All of these conflicting feelings confused the heck out of her. If she didn't want to see him, why should she care if anyone else did? Why did she care? Her insides tangled into a jumbled mess.

"Girls! Hurry up. It's game time," Kyle called again.

Marti noticed that the whole gang—Brooke, Justin, and Ryan—assembled for the game, but not Adam. Had she hurt his feelings? If so, he sure needed to toughen up. What a wimpy rock star. A few others from the photography group filled out the team.

"Gather 'round." Justin waved them over, sporting only his swim trunks, sunglasses, and a bronzed body.

Marti kicked off her sandals and joined Team Photog.

"Okay, team, we're gonna go out there and crush 'em!" He put his hand in the middle of their circle, and they all placed theirs on top. After a team chant, they cheered and took their places on the court.

What Marti assumed would be a friendly game quickly turned intense. Adrenaline pumped through Marti as she relished the chance to blow off some steam.

"AJ! You're late! We need you," Kyle yelled.

Marti turned to find Adam jogging down the footpath barefoot, still wearing his swim trunks. Her shoulders tensed at the sight of him.

"Sorry, man." He ran up and joined them on the court, standing next to Marti.

She refused to look in his direction. She wouldn't give him the satisfaction of knowing how much he bothered her.

Justin served. This time they volleyed back and forth a few times. Then the ball soared right to Marti. She hustled to return it but smashed into Adam instead. The ball hit the sand.

"What the hell was that? I had it!" Marti yelled, and drilled him with her worst glare.

"You didn't call it. Someone had to get it." Adam ignored her biting tone.

"Well, *you* didn't." She rubbed her shoulder where they'd crashed.

"My bad." He shrugged and moved back into position. Marti fought the urge to smack him.

Within minutes, all the guys played shirtless and looked like a sweaty mess of tan, sand-covered bodies. The game went on with Adam continually moving into Marti's playing space. She muttered under her breath a lot. Finally, Team Photog won.

"Canteen is open. Anybody want something?" Haley asked.

"I'm in," Kayla said.

"Definitely." Marti joined them, along with a few others, as they wandered to the canteen over by the lodge. Most of the guys went back to the beach to cool off.

The girls ordered ice cream. Marti chose a toffee bar, and they all returned to a picnic table on the beach where they let the hot afternoon sun bake their skin.

"So, Marti, what's going on with you and AJ?" Brooke asked with a knowing look.

"Nothing. He bugs the heck out of me. He's so full of himself." Marti ripped the paper off her bar.

The silent look exchanged between the other girls did not go unnoticed.

"What?" Marti refused to share the whole story.

"If you ask me, it's like you two are performing a mating ritual." Brooke licked at her ice cream.

"Hardly! If anyone is doing a mating dance, it's you and Justin. I could feel the steam off of you two." Marti looked at the lake where the guys tossed a football back and forth in the water.

Brooke grinned. "I know. He is amazing." She waved at Justin.

"I say AJ is hot for Marti, and the more she pushes him away the more he's going to keep coming," Kayla said.

Marti clenched her teeth. That's what she didn't want, more attention from Adam. Let him chase after some other gullible girl. No, she didn't want that, either. It drove her nuts that he bothered her so much.

"And he looks pretty fine with his shirt off," Haley said, appreciating their view of the guys.

"Where's my camera when I need it?" Kayla slapped the table.

Marti picked up her own camera and snapped a couple of shots. "For you." She smiled at Kayla.

Marti watched the guys throw the ball. Adam wasn't overly buff. He was lean and fit, but obviously strong.

The guys charged out of the water and approached the picnic table. Kyle stood in front of Kayla and shook his mop of hair.

"God, Kyle, grow some manners, would you?" Kayla yelled.

Kyle grinned.

Adam's stare burned into Marti. She huffed and looked away.

"Want some?" Brooke held her ice cream up to Justin. He leaned in, took a lick, and smiled. Brooke grinned and took a lick of her own.

"Somebody needs to get a room," Haley said under her breath.

"Let's go. I'm hungry," Adam said to the guys.

The girls watched as the guys, dripping in their wet, tanned awesomeness, headed for the canteen.

"You know," Marti started, "if I didn't know better, I'd

say Kyle has a thing for Kayla."

"Oh, ick! You are so wrong. Seriously! You don't even know how wrong you are." Kayla scrunched her face in disgust.

"What? You just said the same thing to me about AJ." Marti laughed.

"That's different." Kayla squirmed.

"Sure it is." Marti looked out to the lake and hid a smile. She liked seeing someone else in the hot seat for once. Still, her mind kept drifting back to Adam, and she didn't know what the heck to do about it. Maybe she could drown him.

Later that night, during lights-out, instead of the low tones of the cello, the sound of an acoustic guitar came over the loudspeaker. The gentle plucking of strings played the Brahms lullaby.

"That's cool," Kayla whispered.

The sweet sounds of the lullaby played over the airwaves. Marti suspected immediately it might be Adam, but how the heck did he pull that off? He should be in his cabin, lights out. She pictured Adam in the lodge office, holed up with a guitar across his lap. Despite her anger with him, the blending chords soothed her.

Brooke fluffed her pillow. "I wonder who it is."

They knew now that the cello player was the camp director, Tony. Maybe he played guitar, too. Adam said he didn't want people to know who he was. Why would he risk anyone finding out he was the hotshot guitarist from Jamieson?

"I really like this," Haley purred.

The song came to a gentle end. Marti sighed. "Whoever it is, they sure know how to play."

And then another song began. This time it was upbeat and intricate.

Haley popped up in bed. "That's 'Classical Gas'!"

"I think someone snuck in the office and is going rogue. I've been coming here for years, and there is always only one song—the lullaby," Kayla informed them.

The girls sat up in their beds as moonlight shone through the windows. The music trailed and twined up and down the scales with chords and complex notes. Marti couldn't help herself. No average guitar player could perform at the expert level they heard. She imagined Adam's long fingers dancing over the strings, moving up and down the neck of the guitar.

"Sometimes my dad would play for me at bedtime when I was little," Marti recalled out loud. *When he wasn't on tour or too strung out from a hard day of partying.*

"That must have been so awesome," Brooke sighed.

"Yeah, it was." Her dad would sit on the side of the bed with his acoustic guitar. Usually, it was the Brahms lullaby, but as she grew older, he would play lots of different things.

Sometimes "Puff, the Magic Dragon," her all-time favorite, or Beatles music or Led Zeppelin. He'd take pretty much anything and play it in whatever style he was in the mood for. His long hair, the same shade of blond as hers, would fall forward like a curtain. His face softened and the distractions of his crazed world disappeared.

Those were their special moments, which happened less and less as she grew older. Strange. She hadn't thought anything positive about her dad in forever.

The guitar music suddenly changed key and tempo. A tiny part of Marti itched to see Adam play. She envisioned his easy smile and the way his body would move to the song as he went to that special place musicians go when they're really into it. Then she reminded herself who he was. Adam Jamieson. A rocker who would lie to get what he wanted. He'd grow more self-absorbed and spoiled as he grew up. He'd end up stomping all over everyone else.

The song ended and silence echoed in her heart. Despite herself, she wanted more.

Kayla whipped back her covers, still dressed in shorts and a tank top. "Do you think the coast is clear?"

"Oh yeah." Brooke smoothed down her clothes. "I heard Melody and Brian talking earlier. They're sneaking off to the bar tonight."

"I bet they're sneaking off to more than the bar," Kayla said.

"What are we going to do?" Haley sat cross-legged on her bed.

"I'll tell you what I think," Brooke announced. "We should go skinny-dipping!"

Marti's head swung around, her eyes wide.

"What? You aren't serious, are you?" Haley shot them a worried glance.

"Serious as a missed period," Brooke said.

"Why not? Let's live a little." Kayla bounced onto the edge of Haley's bed. "No guts, no glory!" She shook Haley playfully by the shoulders.

"But what if we get caught?" Haley's voice quivered.

"Then it will be the best story of your entire summer." Brooke pulled her long tresses back in a ponytail.

"Are we really gonna do this?" Marti asked, nervous but excited. She'd never done anything like it in her life. What would Grandma say if she found out? Marti smiled. Grandma would love it.

"Yes, we are! Now quick, get ready," Kayla said.

Marti loved how Kayla always seemed ready for a new adventure.

Haley looked at Marti across the moonlit room. "Oh boy."

Marti grinned. "We need something fun to remember when we get old and boring."

* * *

Ten minutes later, covered only by their beach towels, the girls of Monet tiptoed past the guys' dark cabin and to the forest path. Brooke boldly led the way with her flashlight down the trail leading to the water and a small sandy area. A perfect spot to wade in. Marti's stomach performed Olympic-level flip-flops as her body tingled with awareness.

"I feel so naked," Marti whispered.

"That's because you *are* naked," Kayla giggled.

The nearly full moon reflected off the water, and the lights from the distant lodge glowed like a string of holiday lights. Cricket chirps echoed in the air. The cooler night air chilled Marti's skin. She pulled the towel tighter, nearly dropping her flashlight.

"If I get caught, my mom is going to kill me," Haley groaned.

"Come on, there's far worse things we could get caught doing," Brooke reminded her.

Kayla laughed. "I think we should do a different outrageous thing every night."

They arrived at the sandy expanse and stood in a tight clump, staring at the water.

"Now what? Who's going first? 'Cause I can guarantee it won't be me," Marti said.

"And it won't be me," Haley added.

"We could all go at the same time," Kayla suggested.

Marti looked behind them to the darkened forest. Even though they were all alone and a towel covered her, she'd never felt so exposed.

"I'll go. I don't care." Brooke took a quick glance around before she tossed her towel aside and walked into the water.

As Adam reached his cabin door, he heard someone whisper, "AJ." He glanced around the darkened woods, straining to see.

"Psst. AJ! Over here."

The girls' cabin looked dark and unwelcoming, like Marti's feelings for him. He looked in the other direction toward the path and saw a shadowy figure step out. He squinted, recognizing Justin motioning for him.

Adam held up a finger, signaling that he'd need a minute to put his camera away. He used the excuse of leaving his camera at the lodge so that he could sneak back in to play the lights-out lullaby. Of course, he added a bit of his own flavor to the melody, but he didn't think Tony minded. Tony had been supportive of Adam attending camp and even changed his name on any paperwork that other employees would see.

"Bring it!" Justin whispered again, waving him over.

What the hell was up? Adam looked around to make sure no one saw him as he joined the guys in the shadows of the trees.

"Dude, what's going on?" he asked.

"Shh! They might hear you," Ryan said.

"Sorry." He lowered his voice. "Who might hear me?"

Justin nodded his chin toward the lake. "The girls."

Confused, Adam looked at each of the guys and their devilish grins.

"They're going skinny-dipping," Ryan whispered.

Adam's eyes widened, and he snapped his head to the direction of the beach.

"No, they're this way." Justin pointed and then silently led the way. The rest of the guys eagerly followed.

A couple of minutes later, they heard giggles and whispers. Adam peeked through the trees as the moon illuminated the four girls, each wrapped in only a towel.

Holy crap! Adam glanced at Justin, who grinned like he'd just produced the holy grail, which he sort of had.

With more stealth than a SWAT team, they crept closer to their prize. Adam recognized each girl by her silhouette and quickly spotted Marti. He wished he could figure out a way to make her stop hating him. He really hadn't done anything wrong.

Then Brooke looked around. The guys all crouched down in case she could see them. Suddenly, she tossed her towel aside and walked straight into the water. Her body, outlined by the moonlight, reflected off the water. Adam's jaw dropped. He'd never seen a naked girl before.

Before Adam could blink, Brooke moved out of sight, her form blocked by the other girls. Justin motioned to Adam's camera.

Adam fumbled to pull the case and lens cover off, but his fingers moved in slow motion. He glanced up to see if he missed anything. The guys motioned for him to hurry. He freed the camera and turned it on. The low mechanical sound seemed loud as thunder, but the girls didn't notice. He fumbled in the dark with the controls, trying to adjust the shutter speed for such low light. He didn't know if he had it right or not. At the last second, he remembered to turn the flash off.

He looked up. Brooke bobbed in the water, and the other three seemed ready to join her. He nodded to Justin and raised the camera, watching the action through the viewfinder.

The towels dropped and his finger pressed the shutter. He zoomed in, his eye drawn to Marti. She turned her head and he saw her naked body in silhouette. She laughed and he imagined her nervous excitement and guessed she'd be unwilling to back down from a dare. He smiled as she waded into the water. Her lithe body moved with grace.

For a moment, he felt like kind of a creep for stalking her, but he pushed the thought away as she turned, revealing her silhouette. She reached down and splashed the other girls, then sank under the water's dark cover.

He lowered the camera, dumbfounded, and glanced at the guys. Ryan wore the expression of a twelve-year-old boy with his first hard-on. Kyle turned his head away as if watching would burn off his corneas. Justin asked, "Should we join them?"

Adam looked from Justin to the girls playing in the water, and back again. "Hell, yeah!" He shoved the camera back in its case and stashed it behind the nearest tree.

Ryan bounced on his heels. "They are going to freak out!"

"I don't know if this is such a good idea," Kyle hedged.

"Come on, man. Don't wimp out on us now!" Justin led the charge as they broke out of the woods to the small clearing.

It only took a moment before Haley noticed them. "Oh my God! Look!" Her voice went so high, Adam thought she might cry. The others shrieked. Kayla and Marti moved into deeper water.

Brooke immediately took charge of the situation. "Hi, guys, want to join us?"

Adam figured Brooke probably planned the whole thing to work out this way.

"What are you doing?" Haley squeaked, sounding on the verge of tears.

"Oh, relax, they're harmless," Brooke said. "Aren't you?" she crooned.

"Totally." Justin pulled off his shirt.

Adam wanted to crack up as Haley began a new round of "oh my Gods!" Brooke looked encouraged. Marti and Kayla stayed far enough out that he couldn't see their reactions. Did he have the nerve to follow Justin? *Hell, yes!*

6

"*They* aren't really coming in, are they?" Marti asked.

"Sure looks like it," Kayla said with a grin that proved she liked the idea of sharing their private swimming beach with the guys.

Marti's jaw dropped as Justin boldly dropped his board shorts. Brooke glanced back at the girls with a proud smirk. Adam followed suit and for a moment Marti tried to think of a way to hide. Her panic quickly turned into excitement and her heart pounded. Only silky-smooth water covered her naked body.

She watched Adam kick his shorts away, and in that couple of seconds before he hit the water, Marti couldn't tear her eyes away. Her breath caught in her throat.

She'd never seen a naked guy before, except once at her friend Kristi's house. They'd looked at naked pictures of guys on the internet. The guys quickly headed to the deeper water.

"Jeez, it's cold." Ryan raised his hands above the water.

"Don't worry, it warms up fast." Kayla swished her hands through it.

Compared to the cool night air, the water felt warm, so Marti floated in about four feet deep with her shoulders below the water.

"Hey, Kyle, get your lily-white ass out here!" Brooke called to Kyle, fully dressed on the shore.

"Nah, I think I'll take a rain check." He looked away.

"Come on, man! Don't be a dick!" Justin hollered to him.

"Shh! Keep your voice down. Do you want us to get caught?" Haley chided.

"Maybe, could be fun," Justin said to Brooke, and she arched a seductive eyebrow. He swam closer and scooped her into his arms, cradle style. Brooke wrapped one arm around his neck and twirled the other in the water and laughed.

Marti couldn't stop thinking about their bodies touching. She knew she could never be so gutsy. She glanced at Adam and wished it was twenty-four hours ago. No one had ever kissed her the way he did. She pressed her lips together, recalling the sensation and the gentle touch of his hands, but that was the past.

"Oh my God." Haley moved a little farther away. "They

aren't gonna—you know—right here, are they?"

Kayla splashed the water. "Hard to say."

"Nice night for a swim." Adam swam up to Marti, his chin dipping into the water. The moonlight reflected off his dark eyes. His hands swished underwater, creating a tide that caressed her as it moved across her bare body. Her breathing hitched as she thought of Adam so close to her. She couldn't spot how near his hands might be.

"Hi, AJ," Kayla, the daring soul, cooed.

"Hey, Kayla," Adam answered her, clearly loving the situation. "Nice night for a swim."

He inched closer to Marti. Instinctively, she backed away.

"Oh my God! Oh my God!" Haley squealed in a high-pitched panic.

"What's wrong with her?" Ryan asked as if Haley was broken.

Marti glared at Ryan. "You okay, Haley?"

"Something rubbed against my leg!" she all but screeched.

"What!" Marti scanned the water for signs of something lurking. The guys were too far away to be pranking them.

"I'm serious!" she screamed again, and jumped up, covering her chest with her arms.

"What? What's going on?" Kayla asked in a panic.

"Something's in the water." Marti's voice quivered. She

hugged herself underwater and moved a few feet closer to shore, scanning the water the whole time. She hated that she couldn't see what was down there.

"Of course something's in the water," Adam chided, following her. "It's a lake. There are all kinds of fish and probably snapping turtles, too."

"Don't forget crawfish and snakes . . ." Ryan added.

Marti had had enough. No creepy fish were coming after her in the dark, but she didn't know how to get out without everyone, particularly Adam, seeing her naked.

"It just bit me!" Adam yelled, and splashed.

Marti, Haley, and Kayla screamed and the three girls made a beeline for the shore.

The guys laughed. "I'm kidding," Adam chuckled. "Come back."

But Marti wasn't taking any chances. She didn't care who saw her bare bottom, she didn't want any creepy water creatures biting her. She hit the shallow water and ran for the shore. She snatched her towel and covered herself, grabbed the flashlight, and took off up the trail like a shot, with Haley and Kayla right behind.

She heard the guys roar with laughter.

Jerks.

At breakfast the next morning, Marti froze Adam out. She didn't want him to think she'd forgiven his stunt with the biting fish last night or forgotten his lies. Not to mention the awkwardness of swimming naked together. She reminded herself that he was a rocker and possessed limited ability to be a normal, caring human being. She didn't need any more people like her dad in her life.

After breakfast, the photography group met in the Nature Center for their next assignment.

"Today, you're going to take water-related pictures utilizing the rule of thirds that we discussed last night. As you complete your assignment, I want you to really think about how you're framing your subjects, and be sure to incorporate the water's reflection to create unique perspective," Mike instructed, picking up a bowl containing slips of folded paper. "Go ahead and pick a partner. Each pair will select a topic from the bowl. Each slip has a different subject matter for you to photograph."

Relieved that this wasn't another large group where she'd be forced to hang with Adam, Marti turned to pair off with one of her friends, but Brooke wrapped her arm around Justin's, resting her head on his shoulder. No separating them in the foreseeable future.

Kayla glanced at Marti, then sidled up to Haley. "Haley, let's you and me go together."

"Okay." Haley looked at Marti and shrugged.

Ah, so this is how it's going to be. Marti saw through their sly maneuvers. They wanted her to be stuck with Adam.

Marti watched the other kids pair off, which left her

and Adam, who stood off to the side playing with his camera.

"Marti, this will give you a chance to make up with AJ," Kayla whispered, acting pleased with herself for pairing the two up.

"Come on, you guys. This is not funny," Marti muttered under her breath.

Haley tilted her head in Adam's direction. "He's a nice guy, and you know you like him."

Adam looked up, and Kayla nudged Marti in his direction. She shook her head and crossed her arms. Her friends needed to back off.

Adam glanced from her to his friends and back at her. The realization of the situation finally dawned on him. Clearly annoyed, he shook his head, seeming as unhappy about the pairing as she felt. At least she could be happy about that.

"Can I pick first?" Kayla asked.

"Sure." Mike handed the bowl to her. She scrambled the pieces around and pulled one out.

"Rowboats." She looked at Mike. "Seriously?"

"Seriously." He smiled in response.

Brooke took the bowl and pulled out a slip. She opened the paper and batted her eyes at Justin. "Waves, ripples, and reflections."

"Sexy," Justin growled. Brooke passed the bowl on and more slips were pulled until finally the bowl came to Marti.

She uncrossed her arms to accept it. One slip of paper remained. Uninterested and avoiding eye contact, she held the bowl out to Adam.

He grabbed the last paper and opened it. He muffled a laugh. Marti glanced up.

He rolled his eyes. "Loons."

Marti bit at the inside of her cheek and put the bowl back on the table. Of course, it would be loons.

"Very good," Mike said.

Kyle raised his hand. "Is it a race?"

"The picture that best features the water and lighting elements will receive a free camp T-shirt. Now, you will boat out to reach your subjects, so you've got all morning," Mike said. "You can take out any type of watercraft, but keep in mind the positioning you'll want. A sailboat might not be the best idea. Also, be sure to use a dry bag for anything you don't want to risk getting wet. It will keep your cameras safe and dry until you get to your destinations and again on your way back. We don't need any expensive cameras at the bottom of the lake. All right, off you go. Use your imaginations. I look forward to some amazing pictures."

The group dispersed out the lodge doors with cameras in hand and headed for the boats. A bunch of kids ran ahead and snagged the paddleboat and two rowboats. Marti didn't care what she ended up with. Hopefully, there wouldn't be enough boats and she could blow off this challenge.

At the waterfront shed, she picked out a life jacket and dry bag for her camera.

Haley joined her. "Marti, this is your chance, so be nice to him. You know the guy likes you."

Marti scowled. "Trust me. He doesn't like me. He hits on pretty much anything that shaves its legs."

Adam had a group of girls surrounding him, giggling like idiots. He probably wished he had a different partner, too. She imagined how the girls would act if they knew he wasn't AJ, the cute funny guy from camp, but Adam Jamieson, the lead guitarist for the band Jamieson. He could have any one of those girls in a heartbeat.

"And why shouldn't he hit on someone else, considering the way you've been ignoring the poor guy," Haley scolded.

Marti focused on swiping dried sand off a faded life jacket and slipped it on. "Well, he isn't my type."

"Okay, so if you don't like a tall, funny, hot guy who can't keep his eyes off you, what kind of guy do you like?"

"Someone short, fat, and ugly." Marti grabbed another life jacket and left Haley standing alone. She approached Adam and flung the life jacket at him. He caught it easily. "Come on, Romeo, let's get this over with."

"See you later," Adam called to the girls as he followed Marti to the remaining boats.

"Pick one." Marti crossed her arms with her hip hitched. The choice included two sailboats, a rusted-out, sunken rowboat, a single-person kayak, and a canoe.

Adam scanned their options. "Not much left."

"Yeah, well, if you weren't so busy hitting on the groupies back there, maybe we'd be in a solid rowboat." She opened up the dry bag and placed her camera inside.

"Lighten up. We're at camp, and this is supposed to be fun. Are you always this uptight?"

"I'm not uptight. I'm annoyed that I have to spend my entire morning with a shallow, self-centered rocker who thinks it's funny to deceive his new friends. Give me your camera." She held out her hand and waited as he stared at her.

"Ouch! Does that attitude work for you back home? You must have loads of boyfriends." Adam slapped his camera into her hand, then turned over the canoe and tossed in a paddle. A spider scurried around the edge. He used his life jacket to brush it out and then slipped the life jacket on.

Marti ignored his comment. She pushed the air out of the rubber bag and sealed it tight. "You know nothing about me. Don't pretend you do."

"I know you have a chip on your shoulder the size of a killer whale. And for whatever reason, I seem to represent your crappy childhood. Real mature." He slid the canoe halfway into the water.

"For your information, I've had a beautiful childhood living with my grandma. I haven't spent the past five years basking in some artificial environment of fan adoration."

She attached the dry bag to a crossbar toward the front of the boat. "About all you've done is build your ego by hiring a good special-effects producer so when you stand on a stage you appear like some demigod."

"Wow, you've been obsessing about this for a while," he said. "Gee, and I thought that all this time we were creating groundbreaking music that earned us five Grammy nods."

"Well, they also give Grammys to rappers, who make the worst music ever!" Marti knew she was being over-the-top harsh but she couldn't stop herself. She wanted to hurt him. When she thought of Adam, she remembered all the sadness and disappointment she'd suffered at the hands of her father.

Adam's face turned red and his eyes intense. "Do you even hear yourself? Just . . . just . . . oh, get in the damn boat!" he ordered, clenching his jaw.

"Fine." Marti stepped in the cool, shallow water, climbed into the front and sat with a thud on the metal seat. She turned.

Adam grabbed the back of the canoe and heaved it forward, causing Marti to lose her balance and almost fall backward. He grabbed the other paddle and threw it in, creating a loud clamor.

She spun around and glared. "What is your problem? You can't handle a couple of insults?"

Adam jumped into the back and settled in. "My problem is that I'm stuck with a girl who obviously has some serious daddy issues and can't see past her egocentric self."

"Oh!" *Daddy issues!* Marti wanted to take her paddle and smack him upside the head so hard he'd fall overboard. Daddy issues were the absolute last thing she had. As far as she was concerned, she didn't even have a dad!

"You're an asshole!" She shoved her paddle in the water.

"And I'm too polite to say what you are." The boat shifted forward across the water as Adam paddled away his anger.

Too upset to respond, Marti sat in silence and paddled. They continued to veer to the left. After some muttering from Adam, they found their rhythm and straightened it out.

The clear water ran deep as they floated farther from shore. Long strings of water dripped from her paddle with each pull. Below, she saw an occasional fish. A few minutes later, the sun and the gentle breeze soothed her nerves. Despite her rift with Adam, Marti relaxed. She sighed and rested her paddle across her lap. Adam's smooth strokes propelled them forward.

She didn't hate him, but lying was a deal breaker for her. Her mother lied to feed her addiction; her dad lied to get whatever he wanted. "Sure is pretty out here." She wondered if Adam would ever speak to her again.

Silence.

Just when she was about to try again, he spoke.

"If I could live anywhere, it would be on a nice lake like

this. Lots of trees and the sun sparkling across the water."

"We have lakes in Madison, but they're green and scummy. My grandma said she learned how to swim in those lakes. Now people don't even let their dogs go in."

"That sucks."

"Yeah." A warm wind created ripples on the water.

"So, I haven't spotted any loons yet. Where do you think we'll find them?"

"I heard the naturalist say they build their nests in the bog, over there." Marti pointed to the left side of the lake where a small inlet opened up.

"Okay, we have a plan. To the bog it is."

She resumed paddling, and Adam turned the canoe toward the far inlet. Together, they cruised along the top of the water. The other boaters were scattered across the lake. Occasional sounds of laughter and shouts could be heard.

"Can I ask a question? Without you getting mad?" Adam asked.

"Depends. Is it going to be a stupid question?" She smirked, knowing her words would annoy him.

"From your point of view, everything I say is stupid."

"True." She gloated.

"You didn't have to agree. That was your chance to say 'No, I think you're brilliant and witty.'"

"Nah, I wouldn't want to lie." She heard Adam chuckle.

"Okay, risking my fragile ego, and taking the chance that I'll be crushed by you once again, here goes: I know your dad was far from a stellar parent, but didn't you ever see the genius side of him?"

"Seriously?"

She lifted her paddle and turned in her seat. "After the things I told you, you're going to be like everyone else and go, 'Oh, but he's so talented. He's an icon. He's a frickin' master of his craft!'" Marti mimicked the words.

"I'll take that as a no. You are not ready to talk reasonably without flying into a rage."

Marti took a deep breath. "Fine. Here's my take on it: when a person is so irresponsible and self-centered that he can't look out for the basic needs of his own family and actually causes harm to his own children, that's totally unacceptable. And when he treats other people like they exist only to serve him, that's not only rude and offensive, it's wrong.

"No one should be allowed to step on other people just to build themselves up. That's the kind of guy my dad is, that's the way the guys in his band are, and that's the way all the other musicians who came around are. They couldn't care less about someone else unless there was something in it for them. So when you ask if I saw the genius side of him, my answer is no. I was busy trying to survive. I was busy trying to stay away when he was high on drugs. He would go into a hallucinated rage and think the furniture was going to eat him alive. Sometimes I would have to dodge the unexpected piles of vomit on the floor. And there were times when one of his groupies would wander in and pass out on my bed."

Marti was on a roll. Adam started this line of conversation, and now he'd have to hear it all.

"Then when the parties ended, he'd be hung over for the next day. If I so much as turned on the Disney Channel, he'd fly into a rage."

Adam finally spoke. "I'm sorry. I didn't realize. My family isn't like that at all."

"No one ever does see that side of the story. They just think about the genius. Well, there's a steep price paid by the people around him."

"It sucks he treated you that way, but stop confusing me with him. I'm not like that."

"Maybe not, but give it time." Behind her, she heard him swear.

A short while later, Marti spotted a wooden sign with *BOG* painted on in peeling letters.

"Look. There it is." She pointed.

They rounded the corner to a narrow inlet leading back to the bog. Around them grew tall weeds and water plants, creating a sort of secret entry. Thick clouds moved in and covered the sun and changed the bright day to overcast and dull. The buzz of a mosquito filled her ear. She fanned her hand in the air and regretted not bringing bug spray. The waterway became smaller until the overgrown plants brushed against their arms as they paddled carefully through the shallow, murky water. A low croaking sound came from up ahead.

"This is like out of a horror movie. Don't go into the bog! There's monsters in there!" Adam said in a spooky voice.

Marti tried to ignore him, but the eerie surroundings caused a chill to run up her spine. She shivered. "What do you think lives in here . . . I mean, other than loons?"

"And creatures from the deep? I don't know. Turtles, frogs, water snakes, I'd guess."

"Snakes?" She still hadn't recovered from last night's fish scare.

"I don't know. Probably. It's pretty swampy back here."

Marti tried to squish smaller in her seat so none of the overreaching plant growth touched her.

"Relax, I don't think a snake is going to jump into the boat and get you."

Suddenly, there was a loud clunk directly behind her. She screamed an earsplitting screech, leapt off her seat, and gripped the front of the canoe, tipping them dangerously to the side.

"What was that?" She cowered at the front, her breathing rapid.

Adam picked up one of his sandals and waved it. Its match lay on the bottom of the canoe behind Marti's seat. He burst into laughter.

"You are such a jerk!" She climbed back to her seat, wobbling the boat.

"You're such an easy mark." He continued to laugh.

"Don't ever try something like that again," she warned.

"Oh, relax. It's good to get your feathers ruffled once in a while. All that control makes you uptight."

Marti turned in her seat and glared.

"Speaking of which, any chance we had of finding the loons was ruined by your girly screams."

"That's your own fault." She grabbed the paddle she'd dropped into the water when she launched herself away from his sandal. Cool drops fell on her legs as she resumed paddling. She stopped to swat a mosquito biting her ankle.

They canoed another few minutes until the brush finally opened into an inlet of water—a secluded mini lake.

"This is amazing." Marti took in the private sanctuary, glad to be out of the narrows. Water bugs skated across the water, barely touching the surface. The chirps from unseen birds sang in the distance. Around the edge of the small inlet, brush arched over the water in lazy slumber. Disgusting, thick algae floated near the overgrowth donning an oily film from who knew what. Fish poo?

"Look. Over there." Adam pointed toward the far side of the water. A mound of sticks and plants created a low nest with a loon nestled inside.

"Quick, grab the cameras," Marti whispered.

"I can't reach them. They're closer to you."

Marti glanced back to see the dry bag she'd clipped to a crossbar about three feet behind her. She quietly set her paddle in the canoe and turned in her seat until she faced him. She crouched low and took a step, but the boat wobbled, and she let out a little squeal.

"Shh." Adam quieted her.

"Sorry," she whispered, then knelt on the square life-saving pad and crawled just far enough to reach the bag. She unhooked it, retrieved her camera, and slung the strap around her neck. She looked at the bag as Adam raised an eyebrow.

"Push it this way," he said.

"Hang on." Marti reached for her paddle and pushed the dry bag across the bottom of the canoe until Adam could reach it.

"Nice one." He grabbed the bag and his camera and glanced to see if they'd spooked the loon.

The next half hour, they drifted, capturing various snapshots of the loon. Marti remained facing Adam so they could talk quietly. Funny how they could get along when their focus was on something other than each other. Occasionally, Adam would slide his paddle in the water to adjust the position of the canoe.

After a while, the bird seemed agitated by their presence and raised its long neck. As it watched them, they noticed two babies peek out from underneath her.

"Do you see that?" Marti whispered. She raised her camera, feeling like a photographer for the Discovery Channel.

"That is so cool." Adam adjusted his focus as he looked through the lens and clicked away.

The curious chicks kept poking their heads out. The canoe drifted closer, allowing them better angles of the babies. Marti aimed and captured as many images as she could.

Suddenly, the mother let out a loud wail, stood up tall, stretched her long neck in the air, and flapped her wings.

"Uh-oh, Mama Loon is pissed." Adam lowered his camera and let it hang from his neck strap. He grabbed the paddle and maneuvered them farther away.

"That's incredible." As the canoe moved, Mama Loon hopped in the water with the chicks following right behind. She wailed a couple more times and then motored her way through the water to the narrow exit. The chicks swam after her in hot pursuit, which Marti found adorable.

Adam picked up his camera and scanned through his pictures. "These are so much better than the ones I got the other morning. She's so close in this one, I can count the spots on her back."

Marti scanned through her pictures, too. "I've got a perfect profile shot of her with the babies looking straight at the camera. This one could be an awesome birthday gift for my grandma."

Adam took a few more pictures of the bog, the tall reeds that blew in the wind, and some water lilies that floated on the surface.

Marti relaxed, watching Adam, so intent on his subjects. She felt the wind picking up. "We should probably head back soon."

"Yeah, I guess you're right." He turned off his camera and returned it to the dry bag. He slid the bag forward to Marti. She placed her camera next to his, sealed the bag tight, and clipped it to the crossbar.

As she was about to turn forward, she noticed Adam's sandal in the bottom of the canoe.

"You wanna toss me that?" Adam asked as he paddled them toward the channel.

"What, this?" Marti picked up his sandal and examined it. She offered up an innocent look.

Adam narrowed his eyes. "Just toss it to me, will you? Please."

"Nice touch with the please. Just for that, I will." Marti flung the sandal underhand high in the air. It sailed to the edge of the bog where it caught in the brush.

Marti laughed but then covered her mouth to hide her grin. "Oops."

Adam shook his head, but amusement sparkled in his eyes. "You had to do that, didn't you?"

"My bad." She shrugged and bit back her laughter. Paybacks were a bitch!

He shook his head and paddled toward the sandal. "You could give me a hand here." He eyed her paddle lying idle in the canoe.

Marti turned in her seat and helped paddle them to the edge of the bog. She pressed her lips tightly, biting back a fit of giggles. The water plants were especially dense near the edge, and the thick, green algae floated on top like a layer of sludge. Adam extended his arm, but couldn't quite reach the sandal suspended in the low brush. They drifted back out into deeper water.

They paddled in as close as they could get. This time, Adam used his paddle to try to knock the sandal loose, but the canoe floated out of reach before he could get to it.

Marti wondered why he was even bothering. "Just leave it. Let's go back."

"I'm not gonna just leave it. This is the only pair of sandals I brought, and I'm gonna get it back."

"You mean to say that a superrich rock star like yourself only has one pair of sandals?" She doubted it. He probably had closets full of designer guy duds.

"First off, I never said I was rich, and yes, I only have one pair of sandals."

"You're not rich?" She didn't believe it for a second.

"Look who's asking nosy questions now? I didn't say I wasn't rich, either. In fact, I have no idea." He struggled to reposition the canoe.

Marti spun around to face the back again. They were

going to be here a while since Mr. Tightwad wouldn't leave behind a stupid sandal. "How can you have no idea?"

"I don't. My parents have me on an allowance. My mom says too much financial freedom at an early age is unhealthy. That doesn't include band stuff, like guitars. Those are top-of-the-line. But my camera stuff, I have to save up for. I do get awesome stuff at Christmas, though." He pulled on the brush to hold the canoe in place. He still couldn't get to the sandal this way; he needed to let go to reach it.

She leaned back and watched the growing cloud cover roll in. "How do you know your parents aren't stealing all of your money?"

"I don't. Listen, if my parents end up blowing all the money or siphoning it off to some offshore account, they obviously want it more than I do. It's only money."

"How can you not care? You earned it." She watched him bat at the brush with the paddle while trying to hold them in place. The canoe rocked from side to side. She gripped the edges.

"I'm sixteen. What do I need with a bunch of money? When you think about it, it's not normal for a kid to be loaded. Aren't we supposed to earn our money when we're adults?" He jabbed at the brush again.

She admired how his T-shirt stretched across his shoulders and arms. "I've got to say, Rock Star, you surprise me."

"Maybe you shouldn't judge a book by its cover." He

poked at the brush, this time leaning way out and tilting the boat to a precarious angle.

"Adam! You're gonna flip us!"

"Just. About. Got it." With one more jab, he leaned farther and the canoe tipped too far.

Marti screamed and the canoe flipped before she had the forethought to close her mouth. Her body splashed into the cool, murky water.

7

Marti flailed underwater, and the long water-lily stems rubbed against her legs like the snakes she feared. She swished her legs to come up for air and discovered the water was only a few feet deep.

She popped up between the canoe and the edge of the bog. Adam held his arm high with the sandal. "I got it!"

"You jerk!" She tried to stand but her feet sank into thick muck on the bottom of the lake. She cringed. "Ew!" She tried to tread water to avoid the disgusting lake bed and swallowed some of the algae-laced water. She coughed and spit as she felt the slimy green beads of algae in her mouth.

Adam laughed. "My bad."

"How are we gonna get back in the canoe?" Marti tried not to whine or cry as the plants tangled around her limbs.

"First, we have to flip it over. I did this once with my

brothers." Adam moved to the edge of the canoe. As he pushed with his arms, he tried to stand, and Marti saw his surprise and disgust as his feet sank into the gunk.

She raised her eyebrows. "So now what, Sherlock?"

"This is gross."

She could tell he was trying to swish the lake sediment from his feet. He didn't seem to realize that oily-looking slime covered his head and streaked his face. Awareness hit. She touched her own face and cringed; slime covered her as well. She tried to scrape it away but knew it wasn't really working.

"Let's try to drag the canoe into deeper water, away from the plants," Adam suggested.

They towed the flipped boat away from the edge where their feet didn't touch bottom. The water became much better, but a thick layer of green algae still floated on the surface. Marti wiped her mouth and chin, praying she didn't swallow any more lake scum.

"Now what?" She held on to the edge.

"We need to get underneath and push it up and over."

"I'm not putting my head underwater again."

"Well, I don't know any other way to flip the canoe," he snapped.

"Can't we just try to lift this edge of it really fast?"

"It won't work. The boat will fill with water."

"Oh." She treaded water. Her life jacket rose up around her face as she bobbed.

"So feel underneath where the crossbars are. You're going to take a breath and pull yourself under the canoe. There will be plenty of air," he reassured her.

The idea of going into a small, claustrophobic space and trying to breathe set her heart thumping at a rapid pace. *Why couldn't we have gotten the assignment for something easy, like taking pictures of rocks?*

"When we're both in place, we're going to kick up with our legs and lift with our arms. As soon as we get the canoe far enough out of the water, we'll flip it to the side."

"And this is going to work?" She needed a guarantee.

"I hope so, because it's a long swim back to camp." He didn't appear as confident as she wished.

"You go first." No way would she go under there by herself.

"Okay. I'll see you on the other side." Adam grinned and his face turned all adorable, which made her want to splash green scum water at him. Why couldn't she stay mad at him? He was like some pesky fly that wouldn't leave her alone.

Adam's head dipped below the surface and didn't come up again. After a moment of panic, Marti saw the canoe move and heard a muffled call.

Crap. Her turn. She felt under the edge of the canoe for the crossbar. She faced the canoe, took a breath, and pulled herself under. Kicking forward, she pulled herself up on the other side.

Marti wiped the slime that coated her face and spit. She took a breath and opened her eyes to pitch blackness.

"Adam?" She hoped her voice didn't sound wobbly.

"I'm here." His voice echoed under the metal hull. His hand reached out and touched her arm. "How you doing?"

"Just great."

She heard his chuckle and pictured his impish grin. "Now that I've got you here alone, what would you like to do?"

"I want to get the hell out of here."

"Got it. Can you go to the crossbar right behind your seat? You should be able to reach out and grab it."

Marti reached forward until her hand bumped into the bar. "Got it."

"Good. I'll be at the bar on my end. On the count of three, we are going to lift up. As soon as the canoe is out of the water, push it to the right. You're going to have to kick up with your legs as hard as you can."

"Piece of cake," she said sarcastically, trying not to think about water snakes or snapping turtles.

"Good. So, on the count of three, lift. Ready? One. Two. Three!"

Marti pushed on the bar and immediately her head went underwater. She came up sputtering.

Adam spit water. "That didn't go so well."

"No kidding." Marti wondered if they could do this but didn't want to be the first to call it quits.

"Let's try it again. Ready?"

Marti positioned herself better and prepared to kick. "Ready."

"One. Two. Three!" Adam groaned out the three and she felt the boat shift on his end.

She pushed and kicked up in the water with all she had. The edge of the canoe lifted, but didn't even rise above the water. The weight brought it back down and she sputtered up again.

"I hate to say this," Adam said, spitting. "But I think we have to go where it's shallower so we have something to push against."

"You mean the muck? Won't we sink in?" The thought of it caused her to gag. *What lives under there?* She shuddered.

"Afraid so. I don't know how else we can get it over unless you want to swim through the muddy shallow channel."

"Oh God, I don't want to do this." But she knew she would. Complaining somehow helped.

"Come on. Push it this way. Something's on my leg and I'm afraid it's a leech."

"No!" Marti whined. "Please don't say leeches." She flutter kicked as fast as possible.

"A little farther," he said, not sounding too happy anymore.

When she had to scrunch up her legs to avoid the gooey

bottom, he called it enough.

"Okay, Here we go. One. Two. Three!"

Marti pushed with every ounce of muscle she had. Her bare feet pressed into the soft lake bed up to her ankles. She cringed, wondering what lived in the mud, but didn't want to complain and look like she couldn't handle a little mud.

The canoe rose out of the water. The instant it broke the surface, she felt Adam heave the boat to their right. She did the same and, miracle of miracles, it flipped.

She grabbed the edge of the canoe and pulled her feet out of the gunk, swishing them clean.

Adam floated next to the boat, out of breath. He rolled over in the water. Algae and who-knew-what-else covered his hair, face, and life jacket.

Marti couldn't help but laugh. "You look disgusting."

"You look like one of those creatures from the deep." His grin revealed white teeth behind his slimy face.

Marti reached up and discovered her hair was coated. She tried to wipe the slime off but it clung to her tangled hair.

"Give it up. Nothing less than a car wash is gonna get that out."

"How do we get in?" She switched her focus to the canoe floating high on the surface.

"I can hold it steady on one side and you can pull yourself in from the other."

"Okay." Marti swam to the other side and gripped the lip on the side of the canoe. This was going to be a lot harder than she thought. She kicked with her feet and pulled with her arms. The canoe rocked, despite Adam anchoring the other side. She rose out of the water, but not enough to even get an arm over the side. She let go and slid back into the water.

"Let me try that again," she said, hating to be defeated.

"Okay. You can do this," he encouraged.

This time she pulled again but made even less progress. She flopped back into the water; her arms burning from the effort. "What if you helped boost me in?"

Adam hesitated for a minute. "It's worth a try. I'll be right over."

With Adam behind her, she again reached for the lip of the canoe. He put his hands on her waist. Despite the craziness of the situation, the gentle touch of his hands brought her comfort.

"Okay, now!" She pulled with her arms and kicked with her legs. As Adam lifted her from the waist, she threw an arm over the edge of the canoe. She felt Adam's hands on her butt trying to push her into the boat.

She pulled with her arms, desperate to get in. She was close but couldn't pull herself in. The canoe tipped so far it started taking on water.

"Let go!" Adam hollered. She released her hold and fell back into the water. The canoe bounced upright.

They floated next to each other, both out of breath and exhausted.

Adam blew out a frustrated breath. "How about you hold the boat and I'll try to pull myself in?"

Marti nodded and reached for the edge of the canoe.

Adam swam to the opposite side. "Okay, hold tight and don't let go unless I tell you to."

She gripped firmly. Suddenly, the canoe jerked up out of the water, pulling Marti with it, but she held on as her face rubbed against the gritty aluminum. As fast as her side of the canoe came out of the water, it splashed back down. He made it.

Thank God.

But now she was alone in the water and didn't like it one bit. Adam's handsome face popped over the side, bringing her a sense of relief.

He locked eyes with her and held out his hand. "Ready?"

She nodded and gripped it like a lifeline.

He squared his jaw and tensed as he lifted her. He braced himself and leaned back in the boat so gravity would work to their advantage. Exhausted, Marti knew she was dead weight.

As she rose from the water, the canoe rocked and threatened to dump her back in, but Adam threw his weight backward and fell into his side of the boat, dragging her with him. She landed with her face on his chest, their life preservers a bulky cushion. Her legs hung over.

"I gotcha." He wrapped his arms around her and pulled her forward. Marti scrambled in. Her legs knocked the side as she fell on top of him, his knees on each side of her body. They slid sideways and lay in an algae-covered heap.

Marti didn't have the energy to get up off him yet. Plus, Adam still had his arms locked around her, which she kind of enjoyed, not that she'd ever admit it.

"Gee, that was easy," he joked, his mouth temptingly close.

She laughed. "I can't believe we actually did it. I thought we'd be trudging through sludge to get out of here."

He brushed a strand of hair from her face. "Nah, I'd never let that happen to you."

What a sweet thing to say. Not that it changed anything. A rocker was a rocker. "I guess we better get back. Do you think the cameras are okay?"

Adam glanced over her head toward the front. "I hope so. The bag looks like it's still sealed tight. I guess we won't know until we open it. I'd rather not do it here. Just in case."

"There will be no more flipped canoes!"

"No argument from me. I'll be glad to leave this spot behind." Adam slid toward the back of the canoe, then climbed over the bar and inched his way to his seat.

Marti followed his lead and crawled her way to the front. Thankfully, her paddle had been wedged under the bars and survived the flips. With her energy depleted, she couldn't have been more grateful.

"Now to find the other paddle." They looked in the water near the canoe. It couldn't have floated far. The wind picked up, causing them to drift. Her fingers felt cold to the bone.

"There it is." Marti pointed to the paddle floating in the lily pads a few feet away. She steered close enough that Adam was able to reach over and grab it.

"Hey, look what I found!" Adam reached down and pulled up his sandal.

"Unbelievable." Marti shook her head, reminded of the stupidity that started this fiasco.

"And there's the other one." He pointed to a spot not far from the front of the canoe.

"That is so not fair," Marti groaned.

"Why not?"

"Because I lost both of mine when you flipped the boat!" Her voice rang out an octave higher than normal.

"*I* flipped the boat? You're the one who threw my sandal overboard. I'd say it's your fault you lost your sandals. Bad karma, baby."

"Oh, shut up. Let's get out of here before you make some other lame-ass move." Marti shivered in her wet clothes. She didn't mean to be so bitchy, but Adam was so damn happy and she was cold and tired.

"So much for playing nice." Adam stuck his paddle in the water and pulled ahead with the force of a bulldozer. The canoe lurched forward.

Marti paddled on the other side, and it didn't take long for them to reach the narrow strait leading them out of the murky water and back to the main lake. The sky clouded over and the wind picked up even more. Marti shivered as each drip from her paddle tortured her goose bump–covered skin. Her stomach grumbled; it must be close to lunchtime.

She concentrated on paddling, silently blaming Adam for their crummy situation. Just because he got them back in the canoe didn't wash away his careless actions that caused this whole mess. The more she thought about it, the more steamed she became. It was easier to be mad at him and feel sorry for her cold, wet, miserable self than to remember how much she liked being wrapped in his arms.

After exiting the bog, they paddled past the point and spotted the distant beach. The strong wind made their task even harder. She put her head down and dragged the paddle through the water over and over again until her arms ached.

Adam tried to talk a couple of times but she shut him down. As they approached the dock, a bunch of kids came out to greet them. They wore dry sweatshirts instead of life jackets. Marti reached up and felt the clumps of algae drying in her hair.

Haley and Brooke waved. Marti brooded.

Kayla called out. "What happened? Where were you?"

"Adam flipped the canoe," she yelled back.

"Oh, now, that's real nice. Blame it all on me," Adam muttered.

A few more pulls and Marti stood up and yelled again. "This idiot, Adam, flipped the boat!"

Suddenly, the canoe rocked violently from side to side. Marti screamed and fell over the side, taking in a mouthful of water. She popped up with hair in her face. She flipped the soppy mess out of her eyes and turned on Adam. He sat in the back laughing and holding his gut. Her friends covered their mouths in shock while the guys cheered.

"You are the biggest jerk I've ever met. Oh. My. God. You are a dead man!" She fumed as she swam to the beach.

"Bring it on, baby! Bring it on!" he hollered after her.

She reached the shallow water of the swimming area and dragged her shivering, waterlogged body out of the lake. She looked up and Kyle snapped her picture. She glared. *Another asshole guy at camp.*

"Kyle! Put the camera down before I break your arm," Kayla snapped at him. He lowered the camera.

At least her girlfriends would stick up for her.

"You called him Adam!" Haley said, all excited. "I was right, wasn't I? He's Adam Jamieson!"

"What?" Kayla flipped around to see Adam land the canoe on the beach. "You think AJ is Adam Jamieson? As in the guitarist from Jamieson?" She looked from Haley to Marti to Adam and back. "Marti, is he really Adam Jamieson?"

"Yup," she snapped. Her numb fingers unhooked the life jacket and she shrugged it off.

"Are you serious? When did you figure it out?" The others gathered around when they heard of Adam's superstar identity. "Did he tell you himself? Did you know all along?"

"Listen. I'm wet and I'm cold and I'm pissed off. You want answers? Go ask him." She flung the life jacket toward the boat shed. "I'm going to take a shower. I'll see you at lunch."

Marti trudged barefoot past the group and down the long path to her cabin, stubbing her toe again along the way.

Adam climbed out of the canoe and slid the paddles neatly inside. He chuckled as he picked up his coveted sandals. He unhooked the dry bag. Marti stormed off so fast she forgot her camera. He'd hang on to it for a while, just to make her have to ask for it back.

Marti was ticked off again but he didn't mind. Before, she hated him for no good reason. This time it was on his terms. He couldn't resist dumping her and her high-and-mighty attitude into the lake. All in all, it had been a great day. The loons were spectacular and the whole fiasco with his sandals and flipping the canoe were the most fun he'd had in a long time . . . well, at least since skinny-dipping last night. He couldn't shake the two images of Marti. The one of her naked in the moonlight; the other with lake scum coating her hair. Both visuals were equally entertaining. He laughed out loud at the fact he'd been able to shut her up.

He pulled the canoe farther up the beach. A bunch of the kids talked in a huddle nearby.

"Hey, guys, what's up?" he asked.

"Nice job dumping Marti. Priceless, man." Ryan slapped him on the back.

Kyle whistled. "Boy is she pissed."

Adam shrugged. "What can I say? I have a gift."

The girls stared but didn't say a word.

"What?" He had ticked off one girl and now the whole gang turned on him. He never had this problem at concerts.

Brooke spoke first. "Are you really Adam Jamieson?"

Shit. He looked skyward. *She told them.*

"She couldn't keep it to herself," he said under his breath.

Kayla's eyes widened and she covered her mouth. "Oh my God. I never would have guessed it. You look so different with short hair."

Kyle snapped a picture.

"I don't think she meant to say it. She was so mad she just blurted out your name without realizing," Haley said apologetically. "But for the record, I thought you were Adam Jamieson a couple days ago."

Adam grimaced. *Great.* His days of being a regular

guy at camp were now over. He'd miss it. Being an equal with the others had been so nice. He slipped his life jacket off. "I've got to put this away." He trudged to the boat shed knowing from experience that they would treat him differently now. In an instant, they went from friends to enamored fans, following him. Kyle took another picture.

Adam glared. "Seriously?"

Kyle lowered the camera. "Sorry, dude."

And then the questions started.

"Why are you here?"

"Why'd you cut your hair? Was it so we wouldn't know who you were?"

"Are your brothers, Peter and Garrett, here, too? But we haven't recognized them?"

"Will you play for us?"

"Are you going to be in the talent show? 'Cause, man, you totally rock."

"Can I get my picture with you?"

"I can't wait to tweet this."

"My friends aren't gonna believe this."

"Would it be weird if I asked for your autograph?"

Adam sighed. These were his friends and he liked them all a lot. He didn't look forward to playing the celebrity with them.

"Okay, let me explain." He led them to a nearby picnic table where they all sat down. He looked at their faces and saw everything from idle curiosity to idol worship.

"Listen, I'll tell you everything but when we're done, I'd really like to go back to how things were before. If that's possible," he added.

"Dude, not possible," Justin said, shaking his head.

He sighed again. "Okay, here goes. Yes, I'm Adam Jamieson, and I'm in a band with my brothers, Peter and Garrett. We're on a two-week break, which never happens, so I had the chance to come here."

"Why would you want to come here of all places? Wouldn't you rather go to Fiji or Paris or someplace exotic?" Kayla asked.

Kyle reached over and flicked her in the arm. "Kayla, shut up and let him talk." She gave Kyle a murderous glare, which he ignored.

"The reason I came is because I love photography. More than just about anything. Plus, I've never been to camp and I knew this was my last chance." And it might end a lot sooner than he had hoped.

"Don't you love playing in the band?" Brooke tossed her hair and looked disappointed.

"Of course. I love the band and it's hard not playing guitar every day. But having a chance to attend the Gallagher Institute Arts Camp is like a dream come true."

"Wow, and I would have thought it was all the screaming girls," Justin said. Kyle and Ryan grinned in agreement.

Adam ignored them. "I don't get much opportunity to

be a regular guy. I didn't know if I could go incognito or if people would recognize me right away. At least I got three days out of it."

"You cut all your gorgeous hair off, just for three days of going undetected?" Haley sighed.

"Yup." He rubbed his hand over his short hair.

"Boy, are the girls gonna be mad when they see you," Kayla said.

"I think he looks better like this," Brooke said. "Older, sexier."

Adam smiled and shook his head. Their comments would be repeated soon enough in all the fan mags. "I know word will spread through camp now, and I get it. I'm a novelty, but I really want you guys to try to think of me as the guy you met three days ago. This is who I really am. I just happen to be in a band."

"Just a band?" Kyle said, his face showing offense.

"Okay, the best freakin' band that's ever hit the planet!" Adam grinned.

"Oh yeah. Now we're talking!" Kyle high-fived him.

"If it's okay with you guys, I'd like to try to keep this on the down low. I know stuff like this leaks to the press really fast, and as soon as it does I'll have to leave."

"No, I don't want you to leave!" Haley reached out and grabbed his arm. She looked down and realized what she'd done and pulled back.

"Neither do I. I love it here, and I love you guys. I never

get to do stuff like this. Ever. This is the most fun I've had in a long time."

Brooke pegged him with a look. "Even more fun than performing in Times Square on New Year's Eve?"

"Darn close."

Justin leaned in. "Here's what I think." Everyone huddled closer. "I say we keep this quiet. Don't tell anyone else. Not Mike, not Melody or Brian, and definitely not the other kids." Everyone nodded in agreement. "No tweeting it, no Facebook posts, nothing. At least not till camp is over."

His friends looked at one another. Could he dare hope they'd keep his secret?

"I'm in," Kyle said firmly.

Haley nodded. "Me too." And around the table it went, with each one agreeing to keep Adam's identity their private secret.

"You guys are awesome." Adam grinned. They'd just given him a new lease on life and he wouldn't forget it.

Marti's day went from bad to bizarro. She arrived late for lunch after a marathon shower that included washing her hair three times. She finally found her group at the farthest table from the entrance.

She squeezed in on the end next to Kayla. "What's up with the new table?"

"We decided we're going to help Adam, I mean AJ, keep his identity a secret. If we sit where people can't easily see him, they won't have a chance to recognize him and blow his cover." Adam sat in the middle with his back to most of the room.

"Unbelievable," Marti muttered, and rolled her eyes. Just what Adam needed, hero worship from their friends.

Later in the afternoon, while the guys downloaded the morning's photos onto computers in one corner of the library, which also served as a computer lab, and selected their top three shots to submit, the girls, who were already finished, hung out on the cozy couches with the Scrabble board.

"Why are you so hell-bent on not liking him?" Kayla asked. "I don't get it."

"He isn't who he seems," Marti replied, pulling at the fringe on the edge of a throw pillow.

Kayla formed the word *lover*. "What do you mean?"

"He comes off as all friendly and like he cares about us, but he doesn't. When he's not here, he has handlers who take care of everything for him. I bet he never even has to go get his own soda." Marti added her tiles to the board and created the word *asshole*.

Haley frowned. "That's harsh."

"Hey, AJ," Brooke hollered across the room. "Do you ever have to get your own soda?"

Adam glanced up from the computer screen, cocked his head, and sneered.

"I'll take that as a yes," Brooke said to Marti. "So what?

He has people who do stuff for him. He hasn't acted like he's 'all that' while he's been here. I'd say it's been the opposite."

Marti didn't want to argue but they didn't know the things she did. "He was lying to everyone all this time. That's wrong. You don't lie to people you care about." She hugged the pillow on her lap.

Kayla dropped her tiles and said, "That's not exactly true."

"Yes, it is. He lied about his name, where he lived, playing guitar. I can go on and on."

"No, it's not that. I'm saying that people lie all the time. That doesn't mean they don't care about people or that they're bad."

"What are you talking about?" Haley asked.

"I've been sort of keeping a secret from you guys, too." She cringed.

"Are you a famous rock star?" Brooke joked.

"I wish. No, remember the first night when we played Two Truths and a Lie? I said that I have a twin."

Marti tossed her a look. "Was that a lie?"

"No. That was true. The lie, or maybe I should say lack of truth, is that my twin is here at camp."

Marti sat forward. "Really? Why haven't we spotted her? I mean, a twin would be easy to see."

"My twin isn't a girl," Kayla admitted, and then waited for their reaction.

"Your twin is a brother?" Haley said, clearly surprised.

Brooke called across the room again. "Hey, guys, Kayla has a twin brother here at camp!"

The guys looked over, curious. She had their attention now.

"Seriously?" Kyle shook his head in annoyance. "I thought you were hell-bent against going there."

Kayla shrugged. "It kind of came up."

Marti looked at Kyle's wavy, brown hair and then at Kayla with her long, brown hair the exact same shade. "Kyle is your twin?"

"The one and only." Kyle laid his cards on the table in victory.

"But you don't even look alike, other than the shade of your hair," Brooke said.

The guys finished up on the computer and joined them. Kyle sauntered over and sank into the couch. The other three stretched out on the carpeted floor. Marti scrambled up the words she'd made.

"Now I get it. Before, I thought you guys really liked each other because you kept picking on him and he kept bugging you, but he was only being an annoying brother." Brooke laughed. "That is priceless."

"Why did you keep it a secret? I don't see what the big deal is about having a twin here," Marti said. Kyle was nice, friendly, and not a jerk or anything.

Kyle laid back and put his feet up on the couch. "Because

Kayla didn't want me to get in the way of her hooking up with some guy. Like I'd really care."

"You always scare the other guys away. They're afraid you're going to beat them up or something," Kayla said.

"Now it makes sense." Justin yawned. "Last night you didn't want to skinny-dip, not because you chickened out, but because you didn't want to swim naked with your sister."

Haley cringed. "Ew."

"Exactly. Swimming naked together ended when we were three. Not about to start that up again. Freud would go nuts with that," Kyle said.

"My point," Kayla stressed, glancing sideways to look at Marti, "is that sometimes we have our own reason for keeping a secret and it's not about hurting or deceiving anyone."

Adam tossed his hands in the air. "Thank you! I'm not the asshole she thinks I am."

Brooke patted his leg and batted her eyes. "We know."

Marti could imagine Brooke shifting her attention from Justin to Adam in a heartbeat, and her stomach grew queasy. Didn't the hot girl always end up with the rocker? She glanced at Justin. By the way he concentrated on a snag in the rug, Marti knew she wasn't the only one to suspect that Brooke might switch her affections.

8

Later that night, after surviving a snooze fest of a PowerPoint presentation on 35-mm-film processing, Marti found herself alone and miserable while the others were out raising hell. Somehow she felt that joining them would be saying she approved of Adam. And she didn't. He could do whatever he wanted and the others could all adore him, but she didn't have to participate.

Stir-crazy and trapped in her thoughts, she decided to take a late-night walk. The camp shut down by this hour and she doubted she'd run into anyone other than her friends sneaking around.

Her mind wandered back to Adam. She worked hard to keep problem people out of her life and while Adam hadn't actually done anything terrible—except lie—she knew the patterns of rockers and that eventually he'd turn the lives of everyone around him to garbage.

Marti ended up down near the lodge. She sat on a bench overlooking the lake for a while but her frustration and anger churned. Why couldn't she ignore Adam and stop letting everything he did annoy her?

Unable to relax, and finding her shoulders tense, she stood and wandered, ending up at the Nature Center. Soft lights from the turtle tank glowed through the window. She tried the door, and the handle turned easily, allowing her into the intimate comfort of the woodsy room. Orange and yellow embers smoldered in the stone fireplace. The bubbling fish tank was the only interruption in the quiet night.

Marti eyed the piano behind the couch. She approached, raised the cover, and slid her fingers across the smooth ivory. She sighed, pulled out the bench, and sat. She stared at the glistening coals in the fireplace. Her emotions matched them: fiery-hot and angry. What was wrong with her? She placed her hands on the piano keys, exhaled a deep breath, and played a chord.

Yes. The sound of the piano always made things better.

Slowly, she played one chord and then another. Each time, the sound resonated through her and released a bit more of the viselike strain that plagued her.

Marti closed her eyes and leaned into the next chord and the next, until they magically evolved into music. Tentatively, her fingers found the notes. The more she played, the better she felt. She didn't need to think about

Adam and how much his presence reminded her of so many unpleasant memories with her dad.

Her shoulders relaxed as she played her favorite classic. She started light and gentle, her fingers tinkling the keys, and then let the emotion of the piece sweep over her. As the crescendo built, she let out the anger and frustration she'd been battling. She lost herself as her hands moved over the keys.

Adam and the rest of their group, minus the stubborn-ass Marti, snuck away from the main lodge, where Kyle found a key and they raided the kitchen's walk-in freezer. Marti missed out on some amazing ice-cream concoctions. Her loss. Ryan took pictures of the whole thing for posterity.

With full bellies, they passed the beach, when Adam heard something. "Hold up for a second." He stopped and listened. "Hear that?"

"What? I don't hear anything." Brooke looked around.

He shushed her. "It sounds like a piano."

"Oh, I hear it, too. It's probably one of the counselors playing their iPod," Kayla said.

"Probably," Adam said, unconvinced. They started up the walk again, but that sound nagged at him. There was an emotional element that drew him in. "Hey, guys, I'm gonna go check it out. I'll catch up in a minute." For whatever reason, Adam felt the need to explore the source of the melody. He never realized what a strong presence music was in his life until he was away from it for a while.

"Do you want us to come with?" Haley offered.

"Nah, I'm good. Go on ahead. I'll be right behind."

"Okay." Kyle nodded and they took off.

Adam headed back toward the lodge, listening to the muffled piano music. He knew there was a piano in the main lodge but they'd just left there. He didn't see any buildings with lights on.

The music grew louder as he neared the Nature Center and he remembered the piano inside. Maybe Kayla was right that it was a recording, but the intense power of the performance drew him in.

Quietly, he entered the dim room. Because of the lack of moonlight from outside, his eyes needed a minute to adjust. Intense music filled the air. He stepped farther into the room and spotted a figure at the piano, swaying to the most amazing piece he'd ever heard. As his eyes adjusted to the low light, a quick toss of the piano player's long, golden hair caught his attention. Like a slap of cold water, he realized the musician was Marti. Momentarily stunned, his jaw dropped. This girl continued to surprise him.

He spied like a voyeur as she passionately pounded the keys, her hands moving at lightning speed up and down the keyboard. The music escalated with the increasing tempo. She swayed, oblivious to the rest of the world. Clearly, she was as lost in the music as he was lost in watching her.

The piece built in tension and energy until it transported

Adam to another place and world. He could tell it did the same for Marti as she took her aggression out in the form of a pulsing, pounding, musical masterpiece.

And then, with slow, gentle chords, she caressed the keys to a whisper and then, silence.

Adam didn't know if he wanted to applaud or cry at the beauty of her playing. Marti slumped in her seat, clearly spent. He wanted to embrace and kiss her and beg her to let him back in her world.

He approached the piano. "I thought you didn't like musicians and here you are rockin' it out."

Marti jumped and jerked around. "What are you doing in here?"

"Sorry, I didn't mean to startle you. I heard the music and had to check it out. I didn't realize I'd get a concert from a virtuoso."

"Not hardly." She pulled her hands away from the ivory keys.

"You never mentioned you play piano." He squeezed next to her on the piano bench. His leg brushed against hers.

"Like you never mentioned you play guitar for Jamieson." She scooted to the far edge of the bench.

"That's different." He really didn't want to start that whole argument again. "Who taught you to play?"

She cringed and looked away.

Instantly, he realized the answer. "Your dad."

She nodded and then seemed to sigh in defeat.

He waited, hoping she'd continue.

She trailed her fingers across the smooth ivories. "When I was a little girl, every once in a while he would sit me on his lap and teach me songs. They were never children's tunes, more like some super-simplified version of a classic."

"Like the Brahms lullaby?"

"Exactly."

"He taught you well. You're amazing."

"Not really. I swear the man is bipolar. He used to scream if he heard me practicing. Said it made him want to gouge his ears out." She mimicked her father's cruel, low voice.

Adam grimaced. "That's horrible. I can't believe he'd talk to you like that. You were a kid."

"He used to say a lot of things like that when he was drunk or high. He's a lot more than the rehearsed sound bites people hear in interviews. That was only one example of who he is. Anything less than perfection he considered a piece of . . . well, you know what I mean. But it drove me to practice harder." She lightly pressed one piano key and then another.

"I'm sorry he treated you like that. You deserve so much better." He couldn't get past the terrible story she told him. He knew of Steven Hunter's amazing accomplishments in the music industry. He was known as eccentric and unpredictable but Adam never realized how cruel he was to others, particularly his talented, beautiful daughter.

Marti reached for a music book laying on the piano and tapped her finger on it. "It's thanks to my grandma that I play well. She found me a great instructor and encouraged me to play."

"With talent like yours, you probably didn't need an instructor." Adam figured she inherited her genius musical gene from her dad, but knew she wouldn't want to hear it.

"Oh no, I do! I mean, playing does come easily, but I have to work hard on my technique."

Adam understood how playing came naturally. He felt the same way with the guitar. It just clicked. He could play as easily as he could breathe.

She slid her hand over the keys. "My instructor says I play like someone riding a motocross bike: wild and dangerous."

He leaned his elbow on the piano frame and angled toward her. "That's funny. I have to admit, I love wild and dangerous."

Marti smirked. Adam was happy to see her fighting back a smile. The light from the turtle tank cast a golden glow on her face. She looked vulnerable and open. "Can I ask you a question?"

"Sure," she said, sounding guarded.

"Why do you dislike me so much? I'm not whatever kind of awful guy you think I am. I'm not a drug addict, and I never will be. I'm not a loser. I'm like everyone else."

She shook her head and silky strands of hair fell forward. She pushed it back behind her ear and answered, "Not to hurt your feelings or anything, but you're not like everyone else. You are overpaid, coddled, and given every opportunity you could ever dream of. You live an entitled life."

"Wow, tell me how you really feel," he said, but didn't back away from her words. He wanted to get inside her head so he could show her who he really was.

"You asked." She laughed. "When's the last time you waited in line at the movies for popcorn?" She raised an eyebrow and drummed her fingers, waiting.

He grimaced. What could he say? The only movies he'd seen the past three years were when the theater manager snuck them in the side entrance after the previews started. Someone on staff always brought them whatever they wanted to eat, because, hell, he couldn't exactly walk into the lobby area. If someone recognized him and started making a big deal, it could ruin the movie for everyone.

She cocked her head. "See?"

"Okay, but it's pretty obvious why I can't do that. It's not like I have much choice in the matter."

"When's the last time you mowed your lawn? Do you even know how to wash a load of jeans?"

Adam opened his mouth to protest but stopped himself. He mowed the grass once when he was thirteen. After that, the band worked full-time to put their first album together. Then they promoted it at practically every school and mall across America. That's how they got their break. Fans put them on YouTube, and Jamieson went viral. After that, the record label picked them up and life had been insane ever since.

Marti cocked her pretty little head again. "You haven't done anything normal in years. Don't try to tell me otherwise. I know better."

"Fine, so sue me! I'm not like every other high school guy, but I didn't go looking for this, my brothers did. I got pulled into it because I played guitar." Better than both his brothers put together was more like it but he wasn't about to say that.

"While I may not know how to work a washing machine, I lost out on a lot of things, too." He gazed into her eyes, but she looked stubborn and unconvinced.

She pretended to ignore him.

"I used to love soccer. I played in a competitive league in middle school. We were really good but the first year the band started to take off, I had to quit. Our soccer team went undefeated. All my friends were on the team and I missed everything. I had to spend that summer squished into a van with my family and our equipment. We stayed at cheesy little roadside motels. We couldn't afford the kind that had a pool. My mom cooked our meals in the motel room in an electric frying pan. I ate enough

Hamburger Helper to last a lifetime."

Marti rolled her eyes and looked toward the cooling fireplace.

"And I haven't been to a friend's birthday party since that summer. Not one. The time my friends played laser tag, I was stuck on a six-hour drive to perform at a mall in a town no one ever even heard of."

"Poor baby," she cooed.

It sounded pretty trivial, but those things had hurt. "And the year they all went to my friend Scott's cabin, I was trapped in the recording studio for a whole month. It was July and I looked like an albino."

Marti picked up a music book and brushed her thumb across the edge, peeling through the pages. "Yeah, I guess that would suck, and it must have been hard to give up soccer."

He pressed his advantage. "Once the band started, I couldn't do any regular stuff. That's when I got my first real camera. I couldn't hang out with kids my age so I'd take pictures of them instead. It was like I became the boy in the plastic bubble. I couldn't exactly make lasting friendships, so I would take pictures. Plus, if you have a camera in front of your face, people don't recognize you."

She smiled, and his heart jumped. "Now will you let go of this crazy idea that I'm bad news?" He leaned over and gently bumped her shoulder with his. She didn't move away. *Progress!*

"Fine. You're not a horrible person. Yet." She grinned. "I just . . . I don't know. I would never want to be compared to all those other girls you've been with." She peeled the corner pages of the music book some more.

"What girls?"

Marti glared. "Duh! The girls you're always hugging and kissing. I'm not an idiot! I've seen the magazines; my friend buys them all the time."

Adam laughed. "You mean the fans." For a second, he thought she believed he had girlfriends.

"Yeah, the fans! There's a million of them! They're always hanging all over you."

"If I didn't know better, I'd say you're jealous." He leaned forward to catch her eye.

"Oh please." She rolled her eyes and crossed her arms. "Come on. You've been kissing all these girls, and I don't really want to become one on your long list."

A smirk curled the corner of Adam's mouth. "Marti, I've never really kissed a girl." He dipped his head in embarrassment. "Except, of course, you, that first night of camp." And right now, more than anything, he wanted to replay that night.

"Of course you have. Don't lie to me. I'm not stupid." She rolled her eyes.

He wanted to laugh. How could he explain it so she'd understand and he didn't look like a total dweeb? "Yes, I hug fans and kiss girls on the cheek all the time." Marti rolled her eyes again. "But! It's always at meet and greets and record signings. I've never actually talked to any of those girls for more than a minute and a half. I couldn't tell you any of their names or if they skinny-dip, hate loud train whistles, or swear when they get mad."

Her expression softened. "You know a lot of stuff about me."

"Yup." He was making progress.

"You've never even kissed a girl while playing Truth or Dare at a party? Or on the bus coming back from a football game?"

Adam cocked his head and raised an eyebrow. He watched the realization wash over Marti.

"Oh. You don't go to parties or football games." She nibbled her lower lip, which reminded him of its softness.

"Nope. You were my first real kiss," he said softly, and hoped he didn't sound too pitiful.

She peeked at him from behind her long, dark lashes. "You do realize that's kind of pathetic."

Adam chuckled. "That's an understatement! I'm supposed to be some sort of teen idol, and I never even had a decent kiss until three days ago."

Marti smiled in a satisfied way and he could tell she really liked that she'd been his first. He realized this was his moment, and he better not blow it. He drifted his fingers down her cheek, nudging her chin toward him. Softly, gently, he placed his lips on hers. An instant rush rocked him as he tasted the same soft mouth from the other night. He felt her tense but refused to stop.

He placed his hand on her neck and caressed her cheek with his thumb, feeling her body relax. She sighed in his mouth; her sweet breath warmed him. Marti was fast becoming his drug of choice. Everything about her made his body tingle. She was beautiful, sassy, strong, and her kisses transported him to a place he never wanted to leave.

Their kiss deepened and he knew she was putty in his hands, oblivious to the outside world. And then the worst thing happened.

The flash of a camera.

Marti jumped away; her hand covered her mouth. Stunned, they looked up to find Ryan and Kyle outside the window, laughing.

Marti looked at the guys and back at Adam. She rushed from his side and out of the room without another word, disappearing into the night.

Adam banged his head against the piano lid and swore.

The next day, Marti continued to avoid Adam. She couldn't believe how easily she'd let her guard down, but then the other guys showed up and she pictured Adam bragging about kissing her. On the other hand, she enjoyed hearing him talk about the sacrifices he made. He seemed more human. Still, it would be best to keep her distance.

Today, her friends still obsessed over protecting Adam's

identity. They didn't seem to notice that she hung back during their assignment on landscape composition. Plus, because they all wanted a little of Adam's celebrity gold to rub off on them, they stuck to his side, which annoyed her. Adam never got a chance to approach her—not that she wanted him to, but it would have been interesting to see if he did.

The afternoon turned cooler and a strong breeze kicked up. During free time, a bunch of kids went to play Ping-Pong in the rec hall. Marti zipped on a fleece jacket, slipped her camera strap over her head, and followed a trail that headed off behind the main lodge.

She desperately needed to escape all the Adam drama. The woods provided a huge canopy across the wide forest path. After a few minutes, the path led her into a low valley where a stone labyrinth wound in a peaceful circle. She thought about walking the maze but decided to leave it for another time. Instead, she climbed the hill on the other side and trekked down a narrow path.

As she hiked deeper into the forest, thoughts of Adam still pursued her. Whenever she thought about him, her emotions jumbled into a big, tangled mess. He wasn't a bad person. Not really. But his life would inevitably change him someday and she hated that thought.

The path curved and led her around the perimeter of the lake. The sky was a bright blue with big, white, puffy clouds sailing fast. The trees helped block the brisk breeze.

Still, she zipped her fleece higher. She discovered patches of wild trillium and paused to take a few pictures.

A while later, she came across some sort of lookout tower. She had walked so far, she wondered if she'd left camp property. She knew there was national forest land nearby; perhaps she was now on it. The tower's wooden ladder was aged with rusty nails. She shook it; it appeared secure. She carefully climbed the ten rungs and ended up in a six-by-six-foot lookout station. Or maybe it was a deer hunter's stand. The sides were constructed with wooden slats, like on a deck.

Looking out from all angles, she could see for miles. In one direction, she saw rolling hills of green forest. An occasional tree burst out in spurts of orange, as if it needed to remind everyone that autumn was near. In a couple weeks, she'd be back at school starting her junior year, and Grandma, newly retired, would have more time on her hands to work on her quilt projects.

This morning, she received a box in the mail: a tin of Grandma's homemade chocolate-chip cookies. Marti felt a twinge of guilt. She still hadn't sent her an email. She'd been having so much fun and then been so distracted by Adam that she forgot all about it. She would do it later today, or maybe tomorrow at the latest.

In another direction, storm clouds gathered and moved toward her. It would make for some awesome pictures.

Stepping carefully over the faded boards, she could see

across the lake to the beachfront of Gallagher Institute. The boats were pulled onshore in a neat row of bright colors. She removed her camera from its case and snapped a few pictures.

She didn't spot anyone on the beach as the wind created small waves on the water. One look at the canoes, and she thought of Adam and how he'd flipped their canoe to get his sandal. She smiled. In hindsight, it was pretty funny. The way he looked with beads of green algae clinging to his short hair, his determination to get the boat flipped right, and how he pulled her back in on top of him.

That reminded her of their kiss last night. She couldn't push it from her mind; it was so unexpected and perfect. For a guy who had never kissed before, he sure knew what he was doing. She shivered and touched her lips.

Marti needed to refocus, because thinking about Adam's kisses made her want him. She aimed her camera at the oncoming storm and clicked off a few more shots of rolling clouds. She sighed, wishing that Ryan and Kyle hadn't ruined last night's moment by taking pictures. It reminded her of her dad and the paparazzi. His image still popped up in gossip magazines every six months or so when he did some lame thing or another.

She cleared her head of those ugly thoughts of her dad and returned to the dreamy memory of Adam kissing her, behind the tree on the first night and then again last night. She sighed, lowering her gaze.

Out of the corner of her eye, she saw movement. Thirty feet away she spied Adam lowering his camera. He'd been watching her and taking pictures. She immediately blushed and felt infuriated by his spying but a part of her leapt with excitement, too.

She leaned over the edge. "You keep showing up, like mold in the basement."

He grinned his irresistible smile as if expecting her to say exactly that. "Room for one more in your tree fort?"

She pretended to think it over, but knew she couldn't stay away from him. "Sure, why not?"

Adam approached and climbed the ladder. "Awesome view. Whoa! Get a look at those clouds. We're gonna get nailed."

"I thought I'd get pictures of it coming in for the landscape assignment."

"Great idea. Mind if I join you?"

"No, it's fine."

Poor Adam, he acted so careful and polite around her, like he feared she'd get mad at him any second. Now she felt a little bad that he was so unsure of her reactions, but she kind of liked having the upper hand with Mr. Superconfident Rock Star. Bringing him down to size was something she could never do with her dad.

Adam held his camera on the railing of the stand, adjusted his settings, and took a couple of shots. Marti did the same.

The ominous clouds grew larger and darker as the front edge of the storm approached. They clicked off another shot about every fifteen seconds.

Marti eyed the rolling clouds. "Do you think we need to worry about lightning?"

"Doesn't look like a lightning storm. So far, it's just a front with high winds and rain. We had one like this before a big concert at Red Rocks Amphitheatre in Colorado earlier this summer. It was the coolest thing, but this is so much better—being right in it."

A huge blast of air gusted, blowing Marti's hair straight back. Her fleece became useless against the cold, gale-force winds.

"Hang on!" Adam yelled, leaning his body into it. Marti's heart pounded as the powerful storm loomed near. The black clouds rolled toward them with straight-line winds. She clicked off pictures faster.

The winds howled.

She gripped her camera and the railing. "This is wild!"

The tiny hairs on the back of her neck stood up. Electricity hummed through the air as a crack of thunder exploded like a cannon just as a bolt of lightning struck the tree Adam had stood near earlier. Marti dropped and flattened herself to the splintered boards of their precarious fort. With her face near the edge, she watched as the tree lit up in a fiery blaze and the dry ground around it started on fire as well. Had Adam still been there, he could have been killed.

"Holy crap!" Adam yelled.

Despite the fear running through her, Marti aimed her camera between the slats and took more pictures. The wind blew and spread the fire to adjoining trees.

She looked at Adam and saw her anxiety mirrored in his eyes.

"This could turn into a forest fire!" she yelled even though his face was inches from hers. He wrapped a protective arm around her; the other held his camera as he snapped pictures.

The pine needles sparked into flames and spread fast.

Adam started packing up his camera. "We better get out of here before this stand catches fire."

She couldn't agree more. As they started to move, huge raindrops plopped, and two seconds later, the heavens let loose a deluge of rain.

They pulled their cameras under their clothes to protect them from the onslaught. Thunder boomed and lightning crackled as the storm raged. Rain pounded down.

The wind howled, causing a tree near them to snap and crash into another. Marti ducked and flattened herself on the deck. Adam climbed over her body, using his to shield her from the violent attack of nature.

"Look at that! The rain is putting out the fire." Adam's

voice sounded in her ear as rain pelted. The drops that got past Adam's human barrier stung her bare legs. Despite the danger, she relaxed as his warm body lay tight to hers, protecting her from the elements.

Sure enough, the downpour doused the flames on the forest floor and quickly killed the tree fire. The winds passed, as did the lightning and thunder, but the cold, heavy rain continued on, soaking them to the skin.

The rain ran down Marti's face, plastering her hair to the side of her head. A waterfall poured off her nose. She looked at Adam and laughed. His infectious grin brought sunshine to the rain-drenched day.

She couldn't believe they kept finding themselves in trouble like this. Raindrops clung to his dark eyelashes and dribbled into his mouth. He spit water like a fountain. She had to admit she enjoyed getting stuck with him in these crazy situations.

If only he weren't a rocker.

9

Shivering, they broke out of the woods and arrived back at camp. Rain dripped off the trees as the wind blew through.

"I'm freezing." Marti's teeth chattered. She didn't look forward to the long trek back to their cabins at the far end of camp.

"Let's see if there's a fire going in the lodge." Goose bumps covered Adam's bare arms. He shivered but didn't complain.

"Good idea." She hugged herself tighter and they hurried their pace.

Once inside, Marti beelined to the crackling fire in the stone fireplace. Adam followed, his sandals squishing on the tile floor. They stood together on a large, braided rug holding their hands closer to the fire.

"Oh my God, where were you guys?" Kayla left a nearby

table where she was playing a board game with some guy and joined them.

"I thought it would be fun to get pictures of the incoming storm. I didn't think about the cold rain and wind." Marti turned to let her backside feel the fire. She sighed as the heat hit her bare legs.

"What a great idea. I wish I would have thought of it." Kayla sat on the stone hearth.

"Great idea until I got frostbite in August." Marti took off her rain-soaked fleece.

"You guys should go warm up in the sauna," Kayla said.

Adam dropped his hands. "There's a sauna here? Are you joking? Because if you are, I might hurt you."

"No, it's totally true. It's in the same building as the laundry room," she said.

He grinned at Marti. "Let's go."

"Kayla, will you hold on to my camera?" Marti held it out.

"Sure. AJ, I can take yours, too."

"Thanks." He handed it over and they headed for the sauna.

Adam opened the heavy wooden door, and a blast of hot, steamy air escaped. Marti sat on the slatted wooden bench and sighed, so happy to feel warmth again. The air smelled moist, like cedar. "This is heaven," she sighed.

Adam took a seat beside her and leaned back. His body

relaxed in the hot air. Marti leaned back and closed her eyes, letting the heat seep into her pores.

"Sure is," he agreed.

Marti opened one eye and found Adam watching her, a content smile on his face. She couldn't ignore the zing that shot through her. He kept pushing against her defenses, peeling back the layers to get to her. "You know, you are really annoying."

He grinned and his whole face lit up, making him even more difficult to resist. "I've heard that before." He scooted closer, his arm touching hers.

She looked at where their arms touched and arched her brow. "You're starting to push your luck."

"I'm just warming up. Drawing off your body heat."

"Is that so?" She bit back her smile. Adam never quit trying to get back in her good graces. She had to admit she really liked it.

"If I was pushing my luck, I'd do something like this." He leaned over, tangled his fingers in her wet hair, and captured her mouth with his.

Every time he kissed her, a jolt of some powerful drug flowed through her veins. She parted her lips and let his tongue mingle with hers. She lifted her hand to touch him, but then hesitated, unsure of what she wanted. Adam decided for her as he wrapped his arm around her shoulder and pulled her in closer.

When their lips parted to take a breath, Adam's eyes

turned dark with little flecks of gold passion sparkling in their brown depths. She could stay lost in his eyes forever. He brushed a lock of damp hair off her cheek.

"Or maybe I'd do something like this." Adam lifted her legs and slid them across his lap. Her breath caught as her skin pressed against his thighs. Adam leaned her back and seized her mouth again. Marti relaxed.

Adam's free hand caressed her neck and trickled down her arms. She reached up and touched his jawline, noticing the soft stubble that appeared since his morning shave. She let her fingers drift up to the hollow of his cheeks, to his cheekbones, and then to tickle his earlobes. He sighed in her mouth, letting Marti know she affected him, too.

She didn't know how long they made out, but the moist heat of the sauna, combined with the heat she and Adam created, rose to an intensity she couldn't control. Her previously cold-to-the-bone body now steamed like a firebrand. Her body pulsed with an awareness she'd never known.

Suddenly, the door to the sauna flew open, and Marti looked up to see Kayla. "Oops! Sorry." Kayla's mouth dropped open in surprise.

With her heart pounding, Marti smoothly lifted her legs off Adam's, pretending it was no big deal to be draped over a guy in the sauna.

"You need something, Kayla?" Adam asked with annoyance. He kept his arm around Marti.

"Uh, yeah. Now that the rain is done, I'm going out in

the paddleboat, and I didn't want to take your cameras." She didn't hold back her grin.

"Oh. Thanks. We should probably get back to the cabin and change anyway." Marti didn't want to leave Adam's side, but her inner censor knew she should. She heard a low groan from Adam.

"I'll leave the cameras out here so they don't get all steamy. I'll see you later." She placed the equipment on the floor outside the door. "And by the way, you can lock the sauna door from the inside." She grinned and winked.

Marti bit her lip and fought back her smile. She peeked at Adam out of the corner of her eye.

He flashed his eyebrows at her. "I'd love to be in a locked room alone with you, but I better get you out of here before we both die from heat exposure."

And what a way to die, Marti thought.

Back at her cabin, Marti climbed out of the shower and changed into her cutest pair of dark jeans and a T-shirt with a low V-neck. She applied her makeup a little more carefully than normal and was drying her hair when the other girls burst in.

"I knew it! So you and Adam Jamieson are a thing!" Haley squealed.

Marti glared at Kayla.

"What? Good news travels fast."

"Well? Tell us everything." Haley bounced onto her bed

and waited for Marti to spill the details, which was the last thing Marti intended to do.

"I don't know. It's not that big a deal." She put the hair dryer away.

"Not from what I hear," Brooke said suggestively. "I heard you were draped over his lap with his hands all over you. Not that I'm judging. I have an appreciation for sex."

"We were not having sex!" *Oh my God!* She couldn't believe they were going *there*. Marti sat on her bed and pulled a brush through her hair.

"Okay, great foreplay." Brooke smiled knowingly, and Marti now understood why any guy in her sights would be toast.

Haley sat up and faced Marti. "Are you going to have sex with him? I mean, oh my God! I know the girl who's having sex with Adam Jamieson! I can't believe it!" Haley flopped backward and hugged her pillow.

"And you *shouldn't* believe it, because it's *not* happening! You guys are totally out of control." She tossed her hairbrush on the table, picked up her lip gloss, and swiped some on. They made her sound like her mom, a groupie who chased famous musicians and hooked up with them. "All we did is kiss a couple times." *And grope each other like hormone-driven teenagers, which is pretty much what we are.*

Brooke and Kayla shared knowing looks, as if that confirmed that she and Adam were a hot-and-heavy deal.

"He's kissed you more than once? I knew it! I totally knew it!" Haley kicked her legs in the air.

Marti shook her head. "You guys are seriously messed up. We're just friends." Which was a big step up from a couple of days ago, when she couldn't stand looking at him.

"Of course you are," Kayla agreed, but her expression said otherwise.

A knock sounded at the door.

The girls stared straight at Marti.

"What?" But she knew what they were thinking and she hoped they were right.

"I bet it's Adam. He can't stay away from you!" Haley giggled.

"Come on in!" Brooke called out, showing off her professionally whitened smile.

Marti's heart pounded as Adam appeared in the doorway. He wore a vintage rock T-shirt and low-rise jeans that hugged his hips in the nicest way.

"Hi," he said, looking slightly nervous.

"Hi, yourself," Brooke returned.

Haley and Kayla watched like they were spectators at a zoo, not speaking a word.

Adam glanced around at their colorful bedspreads and girl stuff. "Nice cabin."

More awkward silence.

"So, you want to walk down to dinner?"

"Yes," she blurted quicker than she meant to. She slid

into her sandals and shot out the door. Anything to escape her nosy friends.

"Guess we'll see you at dinner," Adam said on the way out.

He had to know they'd been talking about him but he didn't seem to mind. They weren't two feet from the cabin when they heard peals of laughter coming from inside. Marti cringed. "Sorry."

Adam reached for her hand and linked his fingers with hers. "Don't be. I'm not."

On their way to the lodge, they took a detour behind the nurse's cabin and snuck in a few kisses. Adam could set her pulse racing in an instant. She couldn't put a finger on what changed her mind about him, but she was so glad she did.

The days passed like wildfire for Marti. Not in a million years would she have imagined she'd be with Adam Jamieson. She couldn't bear to spend time away from him and she was pretty sure he felt the same.

Much of their days were filled with lighting setups, darkroom work, and graphic imaging, but during their free time they swam and hung out on the raft with their friends, basking in the sun and soaking in the view of each other. At night, around the campfire, Adam roasted her marshmallows and let them burn a little bit, just the way she liked. Each morning before breakfast, they sat on the hill and watched for loons, and at night, met up to stargaze. Their make-out sessions heated up, too. Adam had lit a fire in her that couldn't be doused.

One balmy evening, on her way to meet Adam at the playing field, Marti munched on one of her grandmother's cookies. She arrived to discover Adam lying on a blanket with his hands behind his head. She stepped over him and boldly stood with one foot on each side of his hips. She wore a devious grin.

"Look what I found." She gazed down at him as she wiped the cookie crumbs off her hands.

He offered a sexy smile and reached over to caress the back of her calves.

"Whatcha doing out here all by your lonesome?" She threw him a flirty smile.

"Watching fireflies and waiting for a really hot girl to show up."

"Sorry, the hot girl couldn't make it, but she sent me in her place."

Adam propped himself up on his elbow. "Is that so?" His eyes traveled over her and stopped on her breasts.

"Hey, eyes up here," she scolded.

"The view's pretty good." He flashed her a naughty grin, and her stomach did a flip. "You'll have to come down here if you expect me to look anyplace else." He reached and curled his fingers under the waistband of her low-rise jeans and tugged her down.

Marti straddled him. A zing of sexual power hummed through her.

"How's that? Better?" He locked his dark, smoky eyes with hers.

"Yeah," she breathed, not trusting herself to say more.

Adam hooked his thumbs through her side belt loops and caressed her hips. "You're killing me." He pulled her forward and kissed her. They rolled over and Marti discovered the air filled with fireflies.

"Look at them. It's like magic." She snuggled up to him.

He trailed his fingers up and down her arm, creating little goose bumps on her skin. "When I was little, I used to catch fireflies. I was convinced that if I caught enough, I could put them all in a jar, and they could be a lantern, like in cartoons."

"That's so cute. When I was little, I thought they were fairies flying around to bring me magic. I was so obsessed; it was all I talked about. That's when my dad got me my tattoo."

"Your dad got you a tattoo?"

"Yup, but I must admit that I begged him. He and my mom both had all kinds of tattoos, so I thought I should have some, too."

"You were how old?"

"Seven."

"You weren't kidding when you said he's messed up. So where is it? I want to see it."

"I'm surprised you didn't notice it already. It's on my ankle."

Adam sat up and Marti immediately missed his warm, cozy body. He leaned over to check out her ankles. She crossed her legs at the knees so he could see it more easily.

"I'll be damned." He held her foot as if he were Prince Charming about to place a glass slipper on it.

"It doesn't actually look like a firefly. It's more of a cross between a fairy and a dragonfly."

"How'd he get someone to put a tattoo on a little kid?" He examined the tiny artwork, tracing it with his finger and sending tingles up her leg.

"When you're Steven Hunter, you always get your way. I wouldn't be surprised if drugs were involved, or an autographed picture. That tickles!" She giggled and moved her ankle out of his reach.

"Does it?" He grinned devilishly. "How about this?" His fingers lingered at her calf and then, light as a feather, danced up her leg. And even though she wore jeans, she felt every brush of his touch.

Marti nodded.

"And this?" He trailed his fingertips, soft as butterfly flutters, to her inner thigh.

"Um-hm," she sighed as he teased. Her body awoke with a powerful feeling she had never experienced before.

Adam crawled up next to her and trailed her neck with sweet, hot kisses while his nimble fingers danced lower.

Marti let out a small moan. The sensation of his hungry kisses and magic touch caused her to lose all sense of time and place.

"Marti, I want you so bad," he breathed in her ear.

Her heart pounded with a new intensity. "Oh God, I want you, too. . . ." She hesitated, knowing she should stop. They should wait. She always planned to save herself for a really good guy, the right guy. Adam might be that guy. Plus, they were under a blanket of stars in the most beautiful place she'd ever been. Every ounce of her wanted to be with Adam.

His eyes questioned her as he swallowed hard. "Have you ever?"

Marti shook her head once, slightly embarrassed. "No. Never."

Adam caressed her face. "Me neither. But I want to. With you."

Marti cupped his shoulder. "I want you, too," she declared.

Adam paused and leaned back. "Are you sure?"

She knew he'd be okay if she said no, but she didn't want to say no. She wanted to make love with him. More than anything.

"Positive."

He suddenly looked devastated. "I don't have a condom."

She wanted him so bad and couldn't let anything stop

them. Her period wasn't that long ago, so she was safe. "It's okay. This is the safe time of the month."

"Really?"

"Yeah," she said, blocking out responsible thoughts of protection.

Adam grinned in that way that made her insides turn somersaults. He showered her with kisses as their bodies tangled together under the light of the fireflies.

Later, when Adam kissed her good night outside of her darkened cabin, a glow lit her from within. She didn't want to leave him. She didn't want to go to bed unless he could be with her. He wrapped his strong arms around her. She leaned her face against his chest and noticed his scent mingled with hers. They were one with each other. Could she die of happiness? Even if she did, it would be worth it.

"Go! Go! Go!" Adam's friends chanted the next day during free time as they took turns on a rope swing.

"You can do it, baby!" Adam encouraged Marti, who looked terrified but sexy as hell in her bikini. They were both flying high since they made love last night. He'd never experienced such euphoria in his life.

She gripped the rope, jumped in the air, and screamed as she sailed past the rocky drop-off and out over the lake. She let go and splashed into the water.

She popped up. "That was awesome!"

Adam grinned, proud of his beautiful, gutsy girlfriend.

"Come on, Rock Star, show us what you've got. Or can't you perform without a sold-out stadium?" she taunted.

"Harsh," Kyle said with a laugh.

"Wish I would have thought of that one," Justin said from his spot with the others near the cliff's edge, which dropped about ten feet. Kyle and Kayla knew about this place—which was on private property—from a previous year's camp.

The rest of his friends watched. They had all taken their turns to swing over the edge and past the rocky shoreline below. The bottom dropped off to deep water another couple of feet from there.

"You better be able to swim fast, 'cause you're going down." Adam hauled the rope up the hill.

"Ooh, I'm so scared," she teased, treading water.

"Kyle, would you hold this for a sec?"

Kyle took the thick rope while Adam disappeared around the side of the old shed. He found a woodpile to climb and then hoisted himself onto the roof.

"Nice." Kyle swung the rope up to him.

The added height churned the nerves in his gut, but he knew the water was deep with no protruding rocks. They explored it before trespassing onto this absent cabin owner's property.

"Adam, you're crazy. That's too high. You could break your neck," Haley warned, biting at her thumbnail.

"Piece of cake."

"Look at who's the big man now," Marti taunted.

Adam gripped the rope and jumped. He sailed out over the lake more free and alive than he'd ever felt. Instead of letting go and dropping into the water like everyone expected, he hung on for a second swing out.

"Let go!" Brooke yelled.

He shot them a smug look as the pendulum he rode swung back toward shore.

"Show off!" Marti called from the water.

He reveled in the warm air as he flew like Tarzan. As he approached the cliff, a huge crack sounded. The rope lurched lower. Just as he swung toward the land, the tree branch broke.

He dropped like a shot. Panic struck.

He was falling.

Everything moved in slow motion.

Shrieks filled the air. He hoped his voice wasn't one of them.

The safety of the water was too far away. The cliff wall came at him fast. He tried to brace himself.

His body smashed into the jagged rock, knocking the air from his lungs. His shoulder scraped against the coarse stone while the force of the impact jarred his hip. Searing pain like he'd never felt before shot through his body.

He tumbled like a rag doll down the cliff face, feeling each contusion to his body. In an attempt to break his fall, he held out his arm, trying to brace for further impact. The boulders below would not be kind. Pain lanced into his wrist as he heard his bone snap; his body crumbling like a useless heap between the rocks.

And then, everything went black.

10

"Adam!" He heard his name screamed over and over.

Stunned, he couldn't quite answer. His face was pressed against a gritty boulder. He attempted to move, but a jolt of pain shot through his pinned left arm, so he decided against it. He took a breath, feeling it scorch his throat. His shoulder throbbed and was jammed between the rocks.

"Adam, please talk to me!" Marti yelled for him, her voice growing near.

"I'm okay," he said with a shaky breath, convincing himself more than anything.

His adrenaline pumped and he began to panic. *Was* he okay? He needed to calm down. He managed another deep breath. *Better.* He'd hit so hard he felt useless to even try to move. He rested a second, afraid to find out how badly he'd been hurt.

He lay on his left side, his arm under him. The angle

prevented him from getting up. His right arm was free and appeared uninjured. He moved his leg and flexed his feet. They seemed fine, too. He sighed in relief.

The others were shouting, but it sounded distant in his freaked-out brain. He took another breath. He tried to shift to a sitting position using his left hand to push him up among the rocks. Pain lanced through his arm and into his shoulder. He doubled over.

Shit.

Something was seriously wrong with his left arm, which was beginning to swell. *Damn.* He used his right hand and carefully lifted his wrist and cradled it. Throbbing pain pounded from the area of injury. His hip ached like a son of a bitch. He knew he'd need a lot more than a Band-Aid and an ice pack.

One glance at his arm and he knew it would be a while before he could hold a guitar. He leaned his head back and glanced skyward. Life had been so perfect, and now he royally screwed it up.

He was a dead man. His dad would kill him and if he didn't, his oldest brother, Garrett, would. *Can we still tour if I can't play? Will we have to postpone?* All the hard realities struck him like a bucket of cold water. He hung his head. *What the hell was I thinking to jump off that roof?*

Marti climbed out of the water, over the rocks and boulders, scraping her legs raw to reach Adam. She could see him moving around, so at least he wasn't dead, thank God. As she got closer, she noticed huge scrapes on his side, shoulder, and legs.

"Are you okay?" She crouched down, trying not to drip all over him. *Please let him be okay.* She didn't know what she'd do if he wasn't.

"Looks like I'll live." He offered her a strained smile. It was nothing like his normal, adorable grin. Scratches and dirt and a tinge of blood covered his handsome face. He tried to get up but winced in pain.

"Don't move! What if you broke your back?" She reached toward him but wasn't sure where to touch him without causing more pain. She pulled her hands away.

"I didn't break my back. I jammed my arm against the rock pretty hard, but I think that's it." He sounded more annoyed than anything else, which was a good sign.

She sighed in relief. "What can I do? Tell me what to do." She needed to help and not sit by helplessly.

"If you could help pull me up, that would be great. I can't get off these damn rocks without letting go of my arm."

Marti spotted the other guys frantically climbing over the rocks to reach them. She gave them a thumbs-up.

"Hang on a second. The guys are almost here. They'll be more help than I am."

"Please tell me that Ryan doesn't have his camera."

She laughed. "No, he doesn't. You're safe for the moment."

Justin arrived first. "Dude, you missed the whole point. You were supposed to fall *into* the water. I thought I explained that."

Adam glared at him. "Screw you. Now get me the hell up."

"Yup. He's fine." Kyle grinned.

Justin reached down and held Adam's upper arm firmly. "You tell me when you're ready."

"Hang on a sec." He positioned his feet against a boulder. "Ready."

Justin pulled him up off the rocks, holding Adam's shoulder with his other hand.

Adam grimaced but found his balance while cradling his injured arm. His face screwed up in pain. "Damn, that hurts."

Marti and Justin exchanged worried glances. He was really hurt and not in a way that could stay hidden. Would he be able to take pictures with his injury, or play guitar? She knew they'd have to tell Tony and get him to a doctor. What if he had to leave camp? They had broken the rules and were all in deep trouble.

"Let's get off these rocks before some other idiot comes sailing over the side of the cliff," Kyle joked.

With the guys supporting him, Adam climbed over the rocks to the path leading back up the hill. Marti followed close behind and noticed that Adam never released his injured arm.

The girls met them on the path and they all trekked back to camp. She could see Adam grit his teeth when his arm got jostled, but he didn't complain again. She prayed his injury wasn't too severe.

"Mom! No! Do not come! I'm fine." Adam held the phone with his good arm.

"You're in the hospital! I'm not going to sit here while you need medical attention," his mother insisted.

"I'll be out of here in an hour and back at camp. It's a simple broken arm. No big deal. There's no reason for you to make the trip from San Antonio. I've got only five days left of camp and then I'm coming home anyway." There was no way they could make him leave camp, or Marti, and they better not try. He didn't care how badly he'd been battered and bruised, he was staying put.

"Don't use that tone with your mother," his dad warned. *Great, Mom put the call on speaker.* "You brought this on yourself. You know better than to act so irresponsibly. You need to start thinking about more than just yourself. What in God's name made you act like that?"

"Dad. I wasn't trying to break my arm. The tree branch broke."

"Adam, I'm no fool. We both know you were trespassing on private property. That's another issue I've got to deal with. Not to mention the media problem this will create."

Adam cringed. His dad was right. He couldn't hide his

identity on medical records and someone at the hospital would likely blab. He'd already received interested looks from the X-ray technician. A lot of curious medical staff kept popping in to see if he needed another blanket, apple juice, a magazine, or whatever excuse they could come up with.

"The doctor said you'll be in a cast four to six weeks! Do you realize how many appearances and concerts that affects? This is a logistical nightmare. If I didn't already have heart issues, this would definitely give me some."

The old man played dirty, throwing down the heart-attack card. "Dad, I'm sorry."

His mother interrupted. "Jett, calm down. We'll get it all sorted out."

"Nonsense. Adam made all these commitments and now what do we do? Jamieson's lead guitarist can't play."

Adam wanted to remind his dad that *he* hadn't made any commitments! His dad made them, along with his brother Garrett. Adam's guilt weighed heavy. He knew he screwed up the tour and basically the whole damn schedule. How could he possibly play with a broken arm? Would they keep their performance schedule or cancel? He hoped like hell they didn't cancel, but then again, it would piss him off if someone else played lead guitar.

"Adam, I'm calling the airline the second I hang up. I'll be there tomorrow and we'll get this smoothed out," his mother said.

"Mom, please. I *never* get a break! I'm always wherever you tell me to be. Have I ever complained once about giving up my freedom for the band?"

He didn't want to whine, but she had to see it his way. "This is important to me. I'll never get another chance to go to a camp like this. There are only a few days left and if I go home now, what will I do other than sit around and be miserable? Please, I'm begging you. Don't make me come home. Let me stay."

Silence.

The seconds passed like minutes.

"I never knew you felt that way." She sounded emotional. "But you're my youngest, my baby. I know you hate it when I say that, but you're so far away, and you're hurt, and I love you. I worry."

"I love you, too, Mom. But I'm not a child anymore. I've been living the life of an adult for a long time. I'll be okay for another few days. I promise."

He sensed her indecision and knew he had her. While his mom was fiercely protective, she also fought to keep as much normalcy in her kids' lives as possible. When they traveled, it was the whole family in their tour bus; no one else joined them. No managers or entourage. Just family. They stopped and had picnic lunches and played Frisbee. His mom found out-of-the-way places where they could sneak in and go-cart or watch a demolition derby at a small county fair.

"Promise me, no more crazy stuff. I can't take another

phone call from an emergency room."

"I promise." He smiled and wished he could reach through the phone lines and hug her. He had the coolest mom.

"In the meantime," his dad said. "I'm having your X-rays forwarded to a specialist here. I want to make absolutely sure there will be no permanent damage."

"I understand."

"So, you're having a good time?" his mom asked, her voice soft. "You've made nice friends?"

"I'm having the best time of my life, and I've made great friends." He thought of Marti and knew he didn't dare bring up a girl. His dad would have a coronary right then and there.

"That's good. We'll let you go, but be sure to have your camp director call when everything is settled."

"I will. Don't worry about anything. I'll give you a call in a couple of days."

They said their good-byes and Adam hung up, glad to end the long, stressful call.

Now he needed the doctor to release him so he could get back to Marti. Tony wouldn't let her or anyone else come with him to the hospital. He knew she must be worried sick.

The curtain of his room opened, and a hospital orderly peeked in. "Hi. Would it be okay if I got your picture? My daughter is a huge fan and is going to be so excited when she finds out you were here." She looked both ways to make sure no one saw her breaking the rules.

Despite his true feelings, Adam smiled and gave his stock answer. "Sure. I'd love to."

Finally back from the emergency room, Adam lay on his bed with Marti curled at his side. The others were down at the campfire. With his good arm around her, he ran his fingers through her sun-streaked hair.

"You know you scared me to death today," she whispered.

"Scared you? For a second, I thought I was a goner." He shuddered and held her closer.

His phone started playing the Jamieson song "Angel Kisses."

"That's my brother Peter." He tried to reach the phone but couldn't.

Marti handed it to him. "Here you go. Is he going to be mad?"

"Who knows?" He answered the phone, making sure Marti was still snuggled against him. "Hey, Pete."

"If you were so hell-bent on quitting the band, you could have just said so. You didn't have to go and break your arm," his brother said, amusement lacing his words.

Adam grinned. "So you're not disowning me?"

"Hell, yes! I disowned you the day you peed in my dresser drawer."

"I was four! And I was sleepwalking." He laughed and Marti watched, looking confused. He traced circles on her arm with his finger.

"That's still debatable," Peter argued.

Marti nuzzled his neck, which made it very hard to think straight. He tickled her side to get her to stop.

"What are we gonna do?" Adam asked. "Is there a way to make this work out?"

"Hell, no. You screwed up big-time! Garrett's having a field day with this one, so be glad you're not within swinging distance."

"I should have figured." Garrett took the bossy-older-brother role to new heights.

"So now what?" Adam couldn't escape the pit in his stomach.

"I figure we'll find someone new. Someone who can actually play the guitar and not just imitate *Guitar Hero*!" Peter taunted.

"Good luck with that!" Adam laughed. "And while you're at it, see if you can find someone who can actually sing lead."

Adam loved to banter with Peter. He'd never realized it before, but Peter was his best friend, the person he trusted more than anyone else.

"Hey, whatever happened with that girl? The one who hated you because you're a musician?"

"That would be Marti." She popped up at the sound of

her name. "She ended up yelling my real name in front of a bunch of kids. I had to drown her."

Marti shot him a dirty look and started pulling on his leg hairs.

"Ow!"

"She's there with you?" Peter asked.

"Yeah, I convinced her of my manly charms and now she's lovesick like some adoring fan." Adam started laughing.

"You are such a jerk!" She grabbed a pillow and whacked him.

"Where are you and Libby now?" Adam held the phone with his shoulder and ear and held out his uninjured hand to Marti. She took it, and he pulled her close.

"We're actually headed your direction."

"Why?" His heart stopped cold. Did his mom tell Peter to come get him? To haul his ass out of camp after all the chaos he created?

"Calm down. We're going to northern Minnesota. Did you know that the Mississippi River starts out up there?"

"And you're going there why? Don't answer that. It's because you're in love. Dude, you are so whipped."

"Pretty much." Peter laughed.

Adam hung up, tossed his phone away, and held Marti with his good arm. He kissed her forehead and rubbed his nose against hers. "You know, no one's going to be back for at least an hour."

She nipped a quick kiss. "Is that so?" She trailed her toes over his calf, sending fireworks straight to his core. "What about your arm? It must hurt a lot."

"Not at all. You are my drug of choice and I plan to overdose."

Within minutes, Marti found herself naked as Adam covered her body with hot kisses. Every tender spot he touched hummed with joy. She caressed his strong shoulders and chest, being mindful of his injuries. Nasty scrapes and bruises from the fall marred his beautiful body. She wanted to kiss each one better.

They lay on their sides so he wouldn't cause pain to his arm and bruised side. His fingers trailed from her cheek and down her neck. He dipped his head and kissed her. She felt naughty but more alive than ever.

Adam's fingers skimmed over her hip. She looked at him; deep, heady passion filled his eyes. He wanted her as much as she wanted him. He trailed tiny kisses on her neck. She turned her head to offer access. He took full advantage, kissing and nuzzling behind her ear.

Marti sighed. She never knew she could feel this way.

"We should stop," Adam groaned unconvincingly. "We can't do this again without protection."

"I know. We should stop, but not yet." Together, they had flipped on some sort of switch inside each other, turning on arousal and passion, and she didn't want to turn it off. She curled her legs over his to hold him in place.

"Marti, I want you so bad. You're killing me."

She squirmed, reluctant to let go. He felt so damn good. She wanted more of him but didn't know how to ask. "Please," she whispered in his ear.

He looked at her, his face inches from hers. The touch of his breath on her cheek. "Oh God, Marti. Don't tempt me." His voice filled with agony.

Suddenly, hurried footsteps sounded on the front porch and Kyle sprang through the door.

"Oh shit!" He turned his back on their intimate moment.

"Kyle, get the hell out!" Adam yelled, and pulled up the sheet to cover Marti.

Her face burned with embarrassment. *Why did he have to come in now?* How would she ever look him in the eye again?

"Sorry, Tony's on his way here!" Kyle huffed, out of breath. He obviously ran the whole way.

"What?" Adam sat up.

"Get dressed! He's looking for Marti and he doesn't look happy." Kyle turned and spoke to the wall.

Marti sat up, clinging to the thin sheet. "Why? What did I do?"

Adam glanced at their obvious disarray.

"Oh my God!" She leapt out of bed and fished around for her clothes.

While Adam fumbled for his shorts, Kyle exited to the porch, watching for Tony.

She pulled up her shorts. "Where's my bra? Oh crap." She looked under the bed but couldn't find it.

"Forget it. Put on your shirt." Adam turned it right side out and tossed it to her.

Marti pulled it over her head. She smoothed down her hair while Adam straightened up the bed.

"Hurry up, he's coming!" Kyle warned through the screen door.

She slipped into her sandals and stepped onto the open porch. Maybe Tony wouldn't realize what they had been doing. *Oh God, what am I supposed to say? What if he calls Grandma?* She couldn't believe this. How humiliating!

Adam and Kyle joined her. She shared a freaked-out look with Adam as the camp director approached.

"Hi, Tony. Kyle said you were looking for me? I was just checking on Adam," she said brightly, trying to sound as normal as possible.

Tony looked at the three of them and then settled his gaze on her. *Oh crap. He knows!* Her face heated.

"Marti, I need to talk to you."

Adam stepped to her side, which was the sweetest thing. He chose to face the firing squad with her.

"This is a private matter. Guys, would you excuse us please?" Tony stepped aside to allow Marti to join him.

She sobered, wondering if she was in trouble. Anything

she'd done wrong this week, she'd done with Adam or with their entire group. Why would he single her out?

"What's going on?" she asked tentatively, walking away from the guys.

Tony remained silent until they reached her cabin. "I have some very difficult news to give you."

She looked at him, his face serious and sad. Her heart stopped cold. Dread filled her gut. "What?" She faced him, not wanting to imagine his news. "Please just tell me."

"Let's go inside." He motioned to her cabin.

She swallowed; each second he didn't speak felt like hours. "No. Tell me here. Tell me now."

He hesitated. She looked across to Adam and Kyle watching from their porch. They could see something serious was going down.

Tony sighed. "I'm so very sorry to tell you this. Your grandmother passed away this morning."

11

She felt the blood drain from her face. "What?" She covered her mouth to stifle her cry. "No," she whispered and shook her head. "Grandma just sent me cookies." Tony was wrong. Someone else's grandma had died, not hers. He had the wrong camper.

"I just received a call from a woman named Ruth Jensen. She said she's a good friend of your grandmother's and that you know her well."

Marti nodded at the mention of Grandma's friend and neighbor, but she no longer wanted to hear his words. This couldn't be happening. She wanted him to stop.

"Your grandmother was in the hospital for a heart procedure and died from a heart attack during it."

Her eyes welled. "Please tell me this isn't true and that you're making this up." She'd accept any horrible excuse for a tragic joke if he'd take back his words and say it wasn't true.

"I wish it wasn't." Tony seemed about to cry, too. "Ruth said that your mother is coming to get you in the morning. It's too long a drive to start tonight, and she is understandably upset."

Marti felt an eerie chaos surround her. It seemed like she stood alone inside a giant vacuum while everything else sped by in a foggy haze. Tony spoke, but the words didn't really register. *Something about my mother?*

"If you'd like to sleep in the nurse's cabin tonight, that would be fine. It might be best."

Grandma is gone. She died from a heart attack. Marti didn't know Grandma had a heart problem. She'd been out of breath lately and tired easily, but Grandma never mentioned it or complained.

"I have Ruth's number for you. She said to call her as soon as you are able. I guess your mother is unavailable."

Grandma mentioned a doctor's appointment while I was at camp. Why didn't I see the signs?

Tony looked away. Marti followed his gaze to find her friends gathered on the sidewalk. Concern and curiosity showed on their faces. She looked back at Tony and then to her cabin door.

"Thank you. I think I'll go inside now," she uttered in a strained voice.

Marti opened the creaky screen door and entered the

cabin. She looked at her bed. The colorful bedspread that Grandma bought her. Her camera—a Christmas gift from Grandma. She saw the cookie tin on her bedside, the lid ajar, its contents nearly gone.

Numb and dazed, she walked to the sink and glanced in the mirror. She didn't recognize the reflection. She turned and glanced out the window to find Adam and all her friends gathered around Tony. The curiosity on their faces shifted to shock. She looked away and wandered the small cabin. She should do something, but what? What should she do? She knew her mother would be useless. She couldn't believe the woman actually offered to come get her. Marti sank onto her bed.

Grandma died.

She couldn't call her. She couldn't talk to her ever again. A fresh wave of grief arose, breaking through the numbness. Her throat tightened as she fought back the sobs. She stood.

She wanted to rush to Grandma's side, to give her comfort, but it was too late. Any comfort she could offer should have been given the last few days. Grandma was gone. She died on a sterile, cold table with no one she loved nearby. It wasn't fair. Marti should have been there. Instead, she was here, goofing off, having unprotected sex. Shame consumed her.

The door creaked open but she didn't look up. Adam's hand appeared on her arm.

"Marti, I'm so sorry."

She nodded. What could she say?

"What can I do?"

She turned and faced him. "There's nothing anyone can do anymore." Tears rolled down her face. She choked back her sobs.

Adam embraced her, his body warm and comforting. His good arm wrapped around her like a strong safety net. His cast pressed against her back, reminding her of how fragile life could be. She rested her head against his chest. The beat of his heart sounded in her ear. He stroked her hair and kissed the top of her head.

She didn't want to move because that meant facing reality. In Adam's arms, nothing else mattered. She didn't want to face reality, she didn't want to think of what happened next. She didn't want to have to figure anything out. She wanted to stay in his cocoon of protection.

The door squeaked again and the girls appeared, their faces stricken. Adam released her, and Marti let each of her friends hug her and tell her how bad they felt. It was nice they said the words, but none of it really made any difference. Nothing changed the situation or made it more tolerable.

The guys stood awkwardly on the porch. She knew they cared but they didn't know what to do or say. Neither did she. She grimaced and shrugged. They returned the helpless gesture.

"Do you want anything?" Haley asked gently. "I can go get you something."

"No." She shook her head. The silence in the cabin made it hard to breathe.

Adam rested his hand on the small of her back. "Do you want to be alone?"

She glanced around, suddenly feeling claustrophobic. "I want to get out of here."

"Sure, whatever you want."

Marti went to her dresser, dug to the bottom of the drawer, and located her phone. She hadn't used it once and now it was too late. Her breath hitched back a sob. She slipped her phone into her shorts pocket.

They all waited expectantly, as if she was supposed to lead them through this tragedy. She offered a tight smile, squeezed past her friends, and hurried toward the door. Adam joined her outside.

"I think I'd like to be by myself for a while. I might make a couple of calls." She looked away quickly, because if she lost herself in his eyes she might lose control and she didn't want to do that.

"Okay, whatever you want." He hugged her close, but suddenly all she wanted was to escape.

Adam waited on the front porch of his cabin for Marti to return. Lights-out came and went and still she didn't. Too worried to sit any longer, he took off looking for her.

He remembered the terror he experienced last year when his dad suffered a heart attack. He could imagine Marti's agony.

Normally, the group went off on some rule-breaking mission at night, but tonight none of them could muster any interest. For the first time, they stayed in their cabins, conducting a silent vigil for Marti and her grandma.

When he didn't find her on the dock or at the beach, he realized where she must be. He heard the music before he saw her shadowy form at the piano, in the comfort of the Nature Center.

Inside, the pulsing strains of Bach filled the room. Marti bent over the piano keys and played like a mad scientist. He noticed a bottle of vodka and a half-empty glass sat on the piano. He wondered when she'd gotten her hands on Justin's liquor stash. Probably when they were down at the campfire.

He sighed in relief that she was okay, sort of. She played the mournful tune with passion and heartache. When it ended, he quietly approached and sat on the edge of the bench.

She reached for the glass and took a long, slow drink.

"You doing okay?"

"Um-hum." She put the glass down. "Wanna join me for a drink?" She gazed at him through sad, red eyes.

"Sure." He reached in the bag containing her contraband and found a small stack of plastic cups and the fruit punch. He poured a drink and took a sip. It reminded him of the night they met, when he kissed her for the first time.

"Is there anything I can do for you?"

"I just want to play." She focused on the piano as if it was some sort of lifeline. And maybe it was.

"All right. But if you don't mind, I'm going to stay."

She nodded and began her next somber, classical piece.

Adam noticed someone walking outside. He rose to check it out, and discovered Tony, also checking up on Marti.

"She's kind of obsessed in there with playing." The melancholy tune drifted out to them.

Tony nodded. "That's probably a good thing. It's a healthy way for her to let her emotions out."

Adam hoped Tony wouldn't go inside and discover the not-so-healthy vodka. "If it's okay with you, I thought I'd sit up with her."

"That's fine. I understand her parents are out of the picture and that she lived with her grandmother. Poor kid. She's got a rough road ahead of her." Tony scratched his chin. "How's your arm feeling?"

"It aches, but I'm fine."

"That's good. There's never a dull moment around here. Well, if either of you needs anything, come get me."

Adam nodded and went back inside. Marti didn't even pause when he picked up his drink. He tossed a couple of pieces of wood on the dying embers in the fireplace. Sparks flew, reminding him of the fireflies they watched a couple of nights ago.

He took a comfortable spot on the couch with his drink. He leaned back against the side arm with his legs stretched out so he could watch Marti and still give her space.

She played song after song. He couldn't believe her repertoire. She played each piece like a master. Her dad definitely passed his musical genius on to her. He wondered how Marti felt about that or if she even realized.

She paused after each number and drank. He probably should tell her to stop, but this seemed pretty innocent, and he was here if she needed him.

Marti played another classical piece. Her mastery of the piano blew his mind. Under different circumstances, he would love to play together. Her on the piano, him on the guitar. He tried to move his hand and realized the restraints of the cast. *Shit.* More crappy reality. But nothing compared to what she faced.

She'd be leaving tomorrow, and he hadn't let himself think about it until now. It sounded crazy, but he was pretty sure he loved her. Everyone would say they were too young, but he couldn't deny what he felt.

The music stopped and Marti sat quietly. She glanced up, offered him a crooked smile, then joined him on the couch and lay with her head on his chest, molding her body against his.

He rubbed her back with his good arm and pushed a

lock of hair from her face. She sighed and kissed him on the mouth. Adam didn't mean to get turned on, but Marti's sexy mouth was hungry and aggressive. She tasted of vodka and fruit punch and passion.

They kissed and whispered and moved their bodies together until he could barely stand it.

Adam brought his hand down and stilled her. "I don't think that's a good idea."

"Sure it is. It's a great idea." She pushed his hands away.

"Marti, you just lost your grandma. You're upset. I don't think this is a good time."

"Are you kidding? It's the best time." She paused. "You could have died hitting those rocks yesterday. I could die on my ride home tomorrow. Plus, I have no idea if I'll ever see you again."

And honestly, neither did he. He wanted to; he planned to. "Of course, you'll see me again. Now that you're in my life, I'm not gonna let you disappear."

A spark of happiness glinted in her eye. She smiled and pulled off her shirt, tossing it away.

"What are you doing? Someone could walk in at any moment!"

"No, they won't. It's the middle of the night. Plus, if they did, who cares?" She got up and slid out of her shorts.

She gazed at him, all sexy and vulnerable. "Will you make love to me? Because I need you more right now than I need to breathe," she whispered.

He saw the hunger and desperation in her eyes. He swallowed. "Of course I want you. I'll always want you. Come here." Adam needed to get this situation under control and fast, but he didn't want to hurt her, and he sure didn't want her to hate him in the morning.

Marti slid in next to him, her beautiful body against his. He pulled a blanket over the top of them and kissed her on the forehead. She looked confused. "Marti, I am here for you and I'm not going to leave, but we're not going to make love tonight."

She looked at him with the saddest eyes.

"Shh. It's going to be okay."

He held her gently and she began to cry. He felt certain they were tears of grief and not rejection. Her tiny body shook as the tears fell. He comforted her as best he could until she finally quieted and fell asleep in his arms.

Adam awoke, rubbed the sleep from his eyes, and realized they'd been asleep for the past couple of hours. Marti's face looked so peaceful in the low light. He wished he could let her sleep, instead of waking her to the reality of her grandmother's death, but he knew he must.

"Marti." He brushed a lock of hair from her cheek. "Wake up," he said softly.

"Hmm." She moaned and snuggled closer.

He tipped up her chin. "I need you to put your clothes on. I'm not gonna let you get caught like this." He gazed at her naked body, illuminated by the warm glow of the dying fire. He felt the familiar pang of desire stir within and forced himself to ignore it.

Marti nodded and peeled herself away from him and dressed.

Adam felt an immediate void and wanted to pull her back. "Do you want to go back to the cabin and take a shower or crawl into your bed?" he offered.

"No. I don't want to face anyone else. Can we stay here?"

She looked so small and fragile, such a shift from her usually strong, stubborn persona. "You bet." Adam threw a couple more pieces of wood on the fire. He grabbed a soft fleece blanket and positioned the throw pillows on the couch. He lay down with his back against it. "Come here."

She snuggled up against him as he arranged the blanket. With his cast-covered arm under the pillow, he wrapped his other arm protectively around her.

The fire began to crackle and flames licked at the wood. "You must be exhausted. Do you think you can sleep?" His low voice rumbled in her ear.

"Probably not. I keep trying to pretend Grandma isn't gone, but it won't stop popping into my head, and I can't stop thinking about what a horrible way it was to die. I wonder if she was scared going into the hospital. Did she know she might die? Why didn't she call and tell me this was happening? I would have come home."

"I don't know." He caressed her hair.

A log crackled and sparks flew. He rubbed his bare foot against her tattooed ankle. They watched the flames in comfortable silence.

"After tomorrow, will I ever see you again?" she asked in the most unemotional way, as if she asked if it might rain tomorrow. Apparently, his earlier reassurances didn't sink in.

"You will if I have anything to do with it. And trust me, I will do whatever it takes." He squeezed her gently. He didn't know how he would say good-bye. Now that Marti was in his life, the rest of it didn't seem to matter. He thought about all the girls he flirted with at record signings and meet and greets. He felt so shallow. They meant nothing.

"Do you think you'll ever be able to come to Madison?" She turned and their faces nearly touched.

"Is that where you'll be?" he asked, and wished he hadn't.

"Where else would I be?" Confusion marred her perfect face.

"I don't know. I thought you might have to move or something." He didn't see how she could stay by herself, but maybe her mom would step up.

"No way. Grandma might be gone but I know she would want me to stay in the apartment. Plus, I still have school and my friends. Oh, I have a cat. Did I ever mention that?"

"No, you didn't." He laughed. "What's its name?"

"Her name is Kahlúa."

"That's a funny name." He inhaled the scent of her hair, a mixture of strawberry and pine. "And why did you name it Kahlúa? Does your cat drink?"

"Two reasons. First, because she's the color of Kahlúa and cream, Grandma's favorite cocktail. And second . . ." Marti became quiet and hesitant.

"What's second?" he urged.

She wiggled onto her back and looked at Adam. "I can't believe I'm telling you this." She rolled her eyes. "Grandma didn't want me to feel bad about my strange name, so she thought we should name the cat Kahlúa."

"I don't get it. What's so strange about Marti? What's it short for?" He tried to think of name origins for Marti. "Is it Martina? Or Martha? I don't know if I want to be dating a girl named Martha," he teased.

"Close, but not quite. It's . . . Martini." She grabbed the blanket and covered her head.

Adam laughed and tugged the blanket down. "Your real name is Martini? As in 'shaken, not stirred'?"

"Yes." She pouted in the most adorable way.

"And why did your parents name you Martini?" He tried to stifle his laugh but couldn't.

"Because my dad is a moron and thought it would be fun to name his kids after booze."

"You have siblings?"

"Halves. And we have absolutely nothing in common,

other than a little DNA. The oldest is my half sister, Brandy. And the other is my half brother, Jack. They are total losers, too."

"What's so bad about the name Jack?"

"Jack Daniel's, as in whiskey," she said with meaning.

"Oh. I see." But he didn't see how her dad could be so off the wall or how her mom would allow it.

"Now you see why Grandma didn't want me to feel bad? Teachers would say it on the first day of school, and the kids would have a field day. I'm going to change it when I turn eighteen."

"What to?"

"I don't know. I haven't decided yet." Marti yawned.

"How about you close your eyes and see if you can sleep a little?"

"I don't want to miss a minute of being with you."

"You won't. I'll be right here the whole time." He caressed her arm with his thumb.

"Would you sing to me? The only time I've heard you sing was that morning with the loons."

"If you close your eyes, I'll sing to you."

She gazed up at him. "Deal. But nothing hard rock, I hate . . ."

"Shh." He placed a finger on her lips and grinned. "I know, you hate rock music."

She laughed and closed her eyes. He looked at her beautiful face and wanted to kiss her cute little mouth.

"I'm waiting," she said, but kept her eyes closed.

"All right, let's see. Nothing rock. How about something classic?"

He started to hum, and after a few bars, Marti giggled. "I can't believe you're humming 'Classical Gas.'"

"Shh. You're interrupting my concert. You know people pay a lot of money to hear me perform."

"Oh, here we go again. Big rock-star ego." Her face smiled a big, sleepy grin. He thanked God he'd given her something to smile about.

"Shh. Try to go to sleep." He resumed humming the song and caressed her cheek. She relaxed her body and after a few minutes drifted off to sleep. Adam watched her for a long time until a single tear rolled down his face. He quickly wiped it away.

12

The next morning, Marti felt like crap after all the alcohol she consumed the night before. She stood under the weak spray of the shower, gladly accepting her throbbing headache. She deserved it, and so much more, for how thoughtless she'd been with Grandma. She couldn't get the water hot enough to clean away her sins.

While Grandma lay dead, Marti got drunk and tried to have sex. *What an idiot!* Grandma worked so hard to provide Marti with a better life than her parents had and what did she do? She literally screwed it all away.

Marti squirted more bodywash onto the washcloth and scrubbed her skin. Was she turning into her mother? God, she hoped not. What if she was pregnant? *Oh shit, no!*

And the drinking. Marti had always avoided it before, but this week, it came easily. Like it did with her dad. Neither of her parents had any self-control and, apparently, Marti didn't, either.

Was God punishing her for such bad behavior? She was absolutely turning out like her parents, and that soured her stomach.

She leaned against the shower wall, resting her head against the cool metal. She needed to calm down. She was nearly positive it was the wrong time of the month for her to get pregnant. Fate wouldn't punish her like that. Would it?

Please, oh please, God. Don't let me be pregnant. Anything but that.

"All set?" Tony asked later that morning as Marti and Adam reached the main lodge. They left her bags outside.

"Yeah," she answered. Her mother would be here in the next hour, and somehow she needed to brace herself for the meeting. Her mother had never been a big part of her life. She was too busy being an addict. But in times of trouble, family pulled together. Marti hoped.

"We left out some pastries and fresh fruit for you in the dining room. I know you didn't eat this morning."

"Thanks." Food didn't interest her. Nothing did, other than getting home where she could be in the apartment and hold Grandma's stuff and try to remember everything they ever did together. She tried to remember her voice, but it was fading. Maybe if she was home, it would bring them closer together again.

"Adam, I have some not-so-good news for you." Tony unfurled a local newspaper and showed him the headline.

ROCK GUITARIST ADAM JAMIESON INJURED AT THE GALLAGHER INSTITUTE ARTS CAMP.

A concert picture of Adam appeared below the headline along with a story about his ER visit and more.

"Great. Just what I don't need to deal with right now," Adam mumbled.

"I know. There are only a few more days left of camp, so hopefully we can get through without too much disruption."

Adam shook his head. "We'll see."

Marti knew she would be long gone before any paparazzi fallout began. She wished they'd leave him alone.

"I'll be in my office if you need anything."

Tony left, and Marti and Adam sat outside on a carved, wooden love seat that overlooked the driveway and beach area.

"You don't need to wait with me," she said.

"I want to. I want to spend every last second together. Plus, how many kinds of jerk would I be if I left you now?"

Marti wanted him there and wanted to push him away at the same time. He was part of the reason she strayed down the wrong path. If it weren't for Adam, she definitely wouldn't have had sex. Not that she wasn't an equal, willing participant, but still. He was like a magnet that pulled her closer.

And as if Adam were reading her mind, he said, "So you know how we, um, didn't use anything?"

"Yeah."

"Will you let me know once you know for sure that everything's okay?" He stared off into the distance, probably as uncomfortable talking about it as she was. "I know you said it was okay, but still. I'll feel a lot better when we know for sure."

Marti nodded. "Of course. I'll tell you right away."

Two hours later, they were still waiting as the other kids came in for lunch. Word about her grandmother's death had spread, and she received many sad looks.

"Marti! You're still here!" Haley rushed over. "I thought you'd be long gone by now."

"My mom was never good about being on time." Her mom wasn't very good at much of anything, except maybe creating chaos and doing drugs. She'd been in and out of rehab too many times to remember.

"Come join us for lunch," Brooke said.

Marti shook her head, not up for the attention or pity. "Thanks, but I'm just not hungry." She watched the endless stream of campers as they went in for lunch. She could smell the food and hear the clinking of dishes.

"I'm gonna go get you some lunch. You need to eat." Adam left her alone to fetch some food. That's when the reality of how alone she really was finally set in.

Her mother was never someone she could count on, even now, during a family crisis. Marti had learned at an early age to never ask her mother for anything, but come on, a ride home for her grandmother's funeral would be nice.

A car pulled into camp. Her heart leapt. Her mom finally arrived. She didn't recognize the car, but then who knew what her mother drove these days. But her joy disappeared when she saw the car loaded with teenage girls. They spilled out, giggling and checking out the camp.

Adam, holding two plates with his uninjured hand and a water bottle in his other, pushed the door open with his shoulder. "Grilled ham and cheese, chips, and I got you two pickles." He smiled with affectionate concern and handed her a plate.

"Thanks." She smiled weakly.

Adam sat and took a huge bite of his sandwich. Marti pointed toward the girls. "I wonder who they are?"

He looked up as the girls headed toward the lodge. "Oh no!" he said with a mouthful of food.

"What?" Marti asked, and then the shrieks began.

"Oh my God! That's him! Right there!" one of the girls squealed.

"He looks just like the picture in the paper, only with his hair cut off. Look there's his cast," said another.

"Hi!" Another waved, and they came at him like a torpedo.

These girls had seen the newspaper.

Adam turned to Marti. "I am so sorry. This is the last thing you need right now."

Marti wasn't sure what to say. She was both fascinated and dumbstruck. If nothing else, the invasion distracted her from her own problems.

"Hi, my name's Chelsea, and I heard that you were here, and even though I've only got my temps, I just had to drive here!" The girl bubbled over with glee.

"You cut your hair! It looks so awesome! I totally love you!" gushed a petite little thing with dark skin and braces.

"Can I have your autograph and get a picture?" a short, chunky girl asked.

Adam finished chewing his food and swallowed. He looked at Marti again, frustration brewing in his eyes. "Would you go find Tony for me, please?"

"And miss this? No way." She smirked.

He shook his head, then set his plate down and stood. "Hi. Who wants a picture first?"

Adam posed with each girl and then all the girls, and then signed his autograph on their fan magazines and CDs.

"I want to sign your cast!" the chunky girl said.

"Well, I'd rather not. . . ."

The girl didn't even pause before scribbling her name and putting a big heart around it.

Marti's jaw dropped. She looked at him, stunned. Adam frowned, clearly not enjoying one second of this invasion.

The other girls took out pens and left their hideous marks on his cast as well.

Two more cars pulled into the lot with even more girls piling out.

The girl with braces waved and yelled. "He's right here! Adam's right here!"

Adam groaned, pleading with his eyes for Marti to help. "Please, will you go get Tony for me?"

"My God, I had no idea how persistent teenage girls could be, and I'm a camp director!"

Adam and Marti were tucked safely in Tony's office, out of sight of any more camp-crashing groupies.

"I've set up a checkpoint at the entrance. No one else can get in unless they have official business. Marti, security knows we're expecting your mom anytime now, so don't worry, they won't turn her away."

"The checkpoint will help, but I'll tell you right now, if they want into camp, they'll find a way," Adam said.

Marti wasn't saying much and he worried about her. They'd been sitting there so long, Adam wondered if her mother was really coming. He didn't want to voice his concern and make her feel more upset than she really was.

"If you'll excuse me a minute, I'm going to step outside and make a call," Adam said.

He exited through the sliding doors of Tony's office out onto a small patio and driveway that allowed service vehicles an area to unload. He placed his call, hoping he wouldn't get voice mail.

"Hey, little brother, what's up?" Peter answered.

"Time for Plan B," Adam said.

The afternoon dragged, dinner came and went, along with three girls who got into camp via boat, and four more by hiking through the woods. Marti's mom hadn't shown. Marti called Ruth Jenkins again, Grandma's friend. They both agreed that something had happened, and her mother had let her down yet again. Ruth said she couldn't drive that far anymore, and could Marti ask the camp director to find a way to get her back in time for Grandma's memorial service the next day?

Marti slumped in a chair inside the lodge like a forgotten orphan. Her luggage mocked her. Despite the fact she wanted Adam with her, she needed out of camp so bad she couldn't stand it. She no longer fit here.

Her friends wanted to wait with her, but she wouldn't allow it. Even though they had exchanged phone numbers and Facebook info, every time they went off to another activity, they hugged her good-bye again. Exhausted from the emotional toll, Marti finally told them no more good-byes. She couldn't handle their parting words one more time. All she wanted was to be home and see Grandma's room, use her hand lotion, and sit in her favorite chair. Anything that would bring Marti closer to her, if only for a second.

Adam stayed by her side. They ran out of words hours ago. What more could be said? He slid his arm around her and she leaned her head on his shoulder. "I just want to go home," she whispered.

"I know. Soon." He played with the ends of her hair.

"She's not coming." Marti willed herself not to cry.

"I know." He kissed the top of her head.

She closed her eyes, and they sat in silence. Suddenly, she heard what sounded like a large truck. Then she heard the kids at the volleyball court talking with excitement.

Marti opened her eyes to see a huge bus wind around the bend into camp. Her eyes went large.

"Your ride is here," Adam murmured in her ear.

"Is that . . ."

He smiled, and his face looked so adorable she wanted to hug him. "That's the Jamieson tour bus, or one of them, I should say. Shall we?" He stood and held out a hand.

Her eyes welled up at his thoughtfulness. *How did he get a tour bus here so fast?* She didn't even realize herself until a couple of hours ago that her mom had abandoned her again.

"Thank you." She took his hand, and together they gathered her bags and headed to the parking lot. A crowd of curious campers had already formed.

The bus rolled to a stop, a loud whoosh of air sounded, and the door opened. Adam hopped aboard. Marti waited, unsure of what to do. A few seconds later, Adam reappeared with someone who, Marti surmised, could only be his brother Peter.

She couldn't hide her smile. They looked like brothers. Very similar, but very different, too. Peter's hair was a lot longer and lighter colored, with more subtle waves than the ones that Adam had cut off. His smile was friendly and kind, but not infectious and playful like Adam's. The brothers spoke quietly. Adam said something, and Peter laughed and bumped his shoulder.

They clearly cared a lot about each other. Marti wondered if his whole family was on the bus. Was his oldest brother, Garrett, there? From the little she heard about him, she feared he wouldn't be very nice. She didn't really want to face his whole family even though they were giving her the most important ride of her life.

Adam brought Peter over. "Marti, this is my brother Peter."

"Hi," she said, shaking his outstretched hand.

"I'm really sorry to hear about your grandmother." His eyes were warm and sincere.

"Thank you." She nodded.

A girl with long, blond hair and a friendly smile appeared at Peter's side.

"And this is my girlfriend, Libby."

"Nice to meet you," Libby said. "I'm so sorry about your grandmother, and I'm glad we can help out."

Marti relaxed a little. "Hi. Nice to meet you, too."

Adam put his arm around her. "If you don't mind, Peter and I should talk to the other campers for a little bit. Everyone's been so supportive in keeping my secret, and they deserve a few minutes before I leave camp with you."

"Of course, no problem." She really wanted to leave that instant but didn't want to be selfish, so she hugged Adam and whispered in his ear, "Thank you."

"You're welcome."

"Want to come on board? I'll show you around," Libby offered.

"I'd like that." She followed Libby into the spacious tour bus and received the grand tour while the guys took their time and talked with each camper and allowed lots of pictures. Her heart warmed at Adam's generous spirit. All during camp he wanted to pretend he was nobody, but now that he was leaving, he wanted to give back to their friends, and even the people who never suspected who he was.

Haley looked like she was in seventh heaven standing between the two rockers and having her picture taken. All of Marti's friends had turned into little groupies. She wished she had the strength to go say good-bye one more time, but she didn't. She hoped they'd understand.

After a few minutes, one of the counselors arrived with Adam's packed bags. The guys waved their final farewells and came aboard.

"Ready to hit the road?" Peter asked.

Marti smiled. "You bet, but where's the driver?"

"You're looking at him." Peter grinned and looked more like Adam for a second.

Marti gaped at Adam. "Is that legal?"

"Yes, he's licensed, and he's a good driver. I can drive the bus, too, but I'm too young to try for my motor coach license yet."

"Okay," she said with doubt as Peter sat in the driver's seat and buckled up.

Adam slid the giant coach window open so they could wave good-bye.

Peter put the bus into gear and slowly pulled away. Marti waved at her amazing friends. Brooke's model-perfect face looked as if she was ready to cry. Then came Kayla with a tear rolling down her cheek and finally Haley—who openly cried.

Adam wrapped his arm around Marti as they slowly passed by everyone.

Marti had shared the special secret of Adam with these friends. They knew her troubled background with her parents and a lot about her family. They knew her so well, and while she'd talk to them online, she'd probably never see them again. She swallowed down a sob and leaned out the window to wave a final good-bye. The tour bus turned around the bend, and her friends disappeared from sight.

13

Adam waited as Marti inserted her key into her grandma's front door. He knew this must be difficult for her, not having Grandma there to greet her, or even her cat, Kahlúa. Marti had told him that the neighbor was watching the cat. This time, only silence would greet her. Marti let out a breath and a wave of dread washed over him. He couldn't imagine coming back to an empty home after a family member died.

He gently squeezed her shoulder in support. She tried to convince him to say good-bye outside, but he refused. He understood she might want privacy, but he couldn't bear for her to enter alone.

Marti turned the key and nudged the door open. Inside, the kitchen light burned bright, illuminating cream-colored walls and a dining room table covered with a floral table-cloth. He wondered if her grandma forgot to turn off the light before her trip to the hospital. Maybe her friend Ruth left a light on for Marti.

She stepped into the apartment first. He followed, carrying in her luggage. He didn't know what to expect, but this sure wasn't it. An acrid smell of stale cigarette smoke assaulted his senses. The place looked a mess. Drawers to the desk were partially open, with papers scattered on the floor. A pile of ripped-open mail littered the kitchen. An open closet revealed boxes and empty tubs lying on their sides, their contents dumped in heaps.

Marti glanced at him, her face showing confusion. So, apparently, this wasn't normal. Had they been robbed?

A glance into the kitchen revealed dirty dishes and empty take-out containers. Empty diet soda cans cluttered the counter.

Adam wanted to grab Marti's hand and stop her when she moved to the entry of the small living room. Her body tensed and she stopped. Adam followed and discovered a sleeping woman draped limply across the sofa.

He glanced at the coffee table and saw more empty soda cans, a lighter, a hypodermic needle, a teaspoon, and a small square of paper containing a dusty, white substance. *What the hell is going on here?*

Marti closed her eyes and, with a clenched jaw, approached the rail-thin woman.

"Mom! Wake up," she said in a biting tone to the slack-jawed woman with dark circles under her eyes.

Adam tried to hide his shock. This nearly comatose woman was Marti's mother?

"Mom! Tami!" She hollered this time, but her mother didn't budge.

Adam inched a little closer and touched her arm. "Marti, she doesn't look so good. Maybe we should call 911." He wanted to help, but this was far beyond anything he'd ever dealt with.

"She's fine. I've seen her like this too many times to keep count. This is her preferred state." This was a new side to Marti that he'd never seen. She stood rigid, her eyes piercing and her mouth in a pinched line. She returned to the passed-out woman. "Mom!" This time Marti reached down and slapped her mother's cheek, quick and firm. "Wake up!"

The skeletal frame stirred and moaned. Adam fought the urge to stand between the two and protect Marti.

As her mother blinked and tried to focus, Marti went through the contents on the coffee table, nudging the drug paraphernalia with her finger. Her mother's purse spilled open with cigarettes, a couple of pill bottles, scratched sunglasses, and a checkbook. Marti picked it up and opened it.

"You stole Grandma's checkbook?"

"Hey, baby." The woman smiled and her head lolled to the side.

Marti snatched the checkbook and paged through. Her jaw dropped. "You emptied it! What is wrong with you?"

Marti threw the checkbook on the table. She rifled through the purse and found a bank envelope. She splayed three twenty-dollar bills in her hand.

"This is it? This is all that's left?" Marti glanced Adam's way, and he hoped he didn't look as stunned as he felt.

"I'm so sorry you had to see this. You should go," Marti said softly.

He looked deep into her eyes. "No way, Marti. I can't leave you here." He gestured toward her mother and hoped Marti could see how dangerous this woman might be.

"Yes, you can. You don't want to be a part of this. Trust me." She wore the stubborn expression he'd come to know and love.

"Let me call my mom. She'll help figure this out. No way should you have to deal with this on your own."

"No, Adam. Your mom has better things to do than try to fix my problems. I can handle this. I've done it before when I was a whole lot younger. When the drugs and money are gone, Mom will disappear. I just need to get her through the funeral. Grandma's friend Ruth will help me."

Her stoic expression broke his heart. No doubt she could get through it, but he wanted to protect her from these evils and heartaches.

Marti took Adam's arm, led him to the hallway, and pulled the door closed to block out the horror that lay on the couch.

"Everything about this is wrong," he said. He couldn't

leave without her. "Come get on the bus with me. You can't stay here tonight."

She reached over and caressed his face, comforting him.

"This is my home. Granted, it's royally screwed up, but it'll be fine. This is just a blip. Tomorrow is Grandma's funeral. I need to see her one more time . . . and say good-bye." Her voice cracked.

He couldn't believe how grown-up she'd become in one short day. Instead of the playful, feisty girl he'd grown to love, she'd evolved into a calm, take-charge person.

He sighed. "You shouldn't have to do this by yourself. Your mom should be handling this."

"My mom never acted like a mother. That's why I lived with my dad all those years. She's incapable."

He placed a hand on the wall just over her shoulder. He leaned in to capture her attention. "I know you won't like this idea, but maybe you should call him, for help."

Marti offered a weak smile. "That would be a nightmare. His world is barely any better."

"How about—"

"Adam, no. Peter and Libby are waiting, and I don't really want them to come in and see the screwed-up mess in there."

"You're killing me," he whispered, and pulled her into an embrace. Her body was so small compared to the troubles she faced. "I feel so damn useless." He kissed the top of her head and fought back tears.

"Trust me. I can handle anything." She stepped back and held his face in her hands, as if not expecting to see him again for a long time. If ever. "I need you to say good-bye and go."

"I can't leave you. It wasn't supposed to happen like this." He toyed with her silky hair, missing how perfect their lives had been two short days ago.

"We still would have had to say good-bye in a couple days. It's just a little sooner than we thought."

"Marti!" her mother mumbled from somewhere in the apartment.

Dread shadowed Marti's face. She pleaded with her eyes.

"I know. I'll go, but come here a second." He wrapped his arms around her and inhaled her intoxicating scent. He tilted her head up and captured her mouth in a final desperate kiss. He tried to forge a snapshot of this moment in his mind.

"Marti?" The apartment door opened and her mother appeared, eyes half-open. She stumbled against the door frame. A loopy smile appeared on her parched lips. "Oops, looks like I'm interrupting."

"Please go," Marti begged him. The pain in her voice convinced him.

"Okay, but I'll be back. I don't know when, but I will."

He pecked her quickly on the mouth and stepped away. He took one final look and left her alone to fend for herself.

The next day, Marti reflected over how uncomfortable the funeral had been as her best friend, Kristi, drove her home. She balanced a foil-covered Tater-Tot casserole on her lap—a gift from a lady in Grandma's book club. Cookies would have been nicer.

Somehow, she had managed to get her mother to the funeral this morning, but despite Marti's best efforts, she couldn't keep the strung-out woman from delivering an embarrassing eulogy.

Tami sobbed and blithered as she confessed her pain and regret for being such a disappointment. Thankfully, her mother disappeared immediately after the funeral, but that left Marti on her own to face the throngs of Grandma's friends and coworkers who attended the luncheon afterward in the church basement.

"Such a tragedy, such a loss, you poor dear," they all said. All eyes looked upon her with pity and everyone had questions about what Marti would do next. Even Kristi wasn't immune. At least Kristi had the guts to come right out and ask.

"What are you going to do?" She glanced at Marti as she drove, tapping her fingers on the steering wheel to the beat of the radio.

"Nothing has to change. I'll keep living at Grandma's."

Kristi's forehead creased in concern. "But how will you pay for things? You know you could always call your dad."

"No! I am not calling my dad or involving him in any way. I'll figure out a way to do this myself. I know Grandma had life insurance, so that should cover the rent for a while. I'll get a job to cover the other stuff."

Marti thought about how her mother emptied out Grandma's checking account. A wave of anger washed over her. She fought the urge to call the police, but knew it wouldn't do much other than to get her mom arrested. Marti would never see that money again; it had been injected into her mother's veins.

"Will they let you do that?" Kristi's expression resembled the women's faces at the church luncheon.

"They're going to have to because I'm not living with either of my parents. I don't even know if my mom has a place. Last I heard, she lived in some crappy motel." The tinfoil-covered hot dish crinkled as Marti shifted in her seat.

"But you're underage. There's probably some law against you living by yourself. I mean, if there wasn't, more kids would move away from home."

Marti didn't want to think about it right now. It had been a long day.

"I wish you could move in with me." Kristi chewed at her lip. "I could ask again."

"No. Your dad's been out of work for almost a year. I understand. Don't worry. I'll work it out." And despite the nagging voice of doubt in the back of her mind, she'd keep believing it.

Kristi pulled into the apartment parking lot. Marti spotted Grandma's car with the trunk popped open.

"Oh no!" Marti slid the casserole onto the seat and jumped out before Kristi could fully stop the car. She rushed over and found Grandma's flat-screen TV, along with her DVD player and old stereo receiver in the trunk. Looking at the stolen items made Marti furious. Her shoulders tensed. What more had her mother taken?

Marti looked in the car window and spotted her laptop and two cameras on the backseat. Hot rage boiled through her. She clenched her jaw.

"What's going on?" Kristi joined her. "Isn't that your stuff?"

"I'm going to kill my mother." Marti yanked open the door and grabbed her cameras, pulling the straps safely around her neck. This time her mother had gone too far. Her hands shook as she lifted out her laptop. She had spent nearly a year saving up for it, and it held practically every picture she'd ever taken.

Their toaster oven lay next to a clock radio. Then she spotted her grandmother's jewelry box spilling onto the floor. Marti felt a stab to her heart. She used to open it as a kid and listen to the beautiful melody while playing with

Grandma's jewelry. Her mother was going further than just stealing valuables; she was trying to steal Marti's memories.

"Here, take this quick and lock it in your car." She scooped the jewelry back in the box and handed it off to Kristi. Kristi's eyes grew wide.

"Now. Hurry!"

Kristi rushed off to hide the keepsakes. Marti knew the box mainly consisted of cheap costume jewelry, but some pieces were gifts to her grandmother from her grandfather. Plus, Grandma kept her wedding brooch in that box and had told Marti she could wear it at her wedding someday, too.

Marti carried her belongings back into the apartment, each step a painful reminder of the grandmother she lost and the mother she despised. She opened the door. Her mom knelt in the hall closet, rifling through its contents. A strange man with bloodshot eyes exited Marti's bedroom carrying her small TV. Her pink tote bag hung from his shoulder—her special camera lens and iPod inside.

"What the hell are you doing?" she exploded.

The tall man with dark, scraggly hair stopped in his tracks. Her mother jumped like a thief caught in the act, which she was.

"That's my stuff! Put it back or I'm calling the police!" Marti confronted them, crossing her arms in front of her.

Inside, she was shaken to her core, but if she didn't stop them, no one would.

"Oh, hi. I was looking for my dad's old coin collection." Her mother's wild eyes turned back to the box and dumped it on the floor. Clearly, she was high on something.

"Stop it! Don't you have a shred of decency? Show some respect! Grandma's only been gone a few days." Marti dropped her laptop on the couch.

Her mother stood and brushed frizzy, neglected hair off her hollow face. "Oh, Marti, relax. She's gone and couldn't care less what happens to her stuff. And it's all mine now anyway."

Marti narrowed her eyes. "What do you mean it's all yours?"

"Mom had a will, and as her only child, I'm her sole beneficiary." She curled her lip in spiteful disdain.

Marti fought the shock from her mother's words. She always thought Grandma would take care of her. Why didn't Grandma leave her belongings to Marti? It didn't make sense. "That can't be true. You're lying."

"Afraid not. It's all in black and white. I found the will in Mom's bottom dresser drawer. Signed and notarized. This place has to be cleaned out anyway, so I don't know why you've got your undies in such a twist."

The dirtbag in the hall tried to inch past with Marti's stuff. She turned on him. "Put it down! Now!" She glared at the unwashed man. He lowered the pile to the ground and stepped away, focusing on the floor.

Kristi appeared at the door and gasped. Marti kept her eyes glued on her mother. "Kristi, go get the apartment manager. He lives in four B. And if he's not home, call 911 and report a robbery."

"And what the hell do you think the apartment manager or police are going to do? I'm not breaking the law," her mother spat back.

"For one, I'll have them search you for drugs." Marti glared, but her bravado faded fast. If her mother's words about the will rang true, well, she didn't know what she'd do.

"Fine. I'll give you two days. You can take the will to whoever the hell you want. It's legal. And then I'm coming back for the rest." She glared. "Come on, Mike. Let's go cash in this load."

The tension between them was so thick Marti could barely breathe. Marti wished she had the nerve to reach out and slap her. Her mother strolled by with a snide confidence that turned Marti's stomach. The grotesque man followed, eyeing her laptop.

After they left, she watched out the window until her mother drove Grandma's car away. Grandma taught Marti how to drive in that car. She was scheduled to take her driver's test in a couple of weeks. She sighed in defeat.

Glancing around the disheveled apartment, she

discovered every storage area turned upside down. She spotted Grandma's expensive Lladro figurine broken on the floor. The emotions Marti worked so hard to control bubbled up. Why were all these horrible things happening? A sob broke free. Grandma was a sweet, wonderful woman. She didn't deserve to die, and she didn't deserve to have her beautiful things treated this way.

As Marti picked up the shattered pieces of Grandma's life, Kristi returned with Gary, the apartment manager. Kristi searched the room with fear in her eyes.

"It's okay, they're gone. But she's coming back in two days for the rest."

Gary, a middle-aged man whose stomach hung over his belt, took one look and shook his head. "I was afraid something like this would happen."

"What am I going to do?" she asked him, a trusted friend of Grandma's.

"Actually, we need to talk about that," he said, closing the desk drawers. Apparently, he, too, needed to create some sense of order in all this disarray.

"Hello?" Grandma's friend Ruth appeared at the door. She lived at the end of the first-floor hallway. She'd been so kind and helpful with organizing Grandma's funeral arrangements.

"Hi, Ruth. I'm glad you're here." Gary welcomed her in.

"Dear Lord, what has Tami done this time?" Ruth pinched her lips and blinked away her tears.

"She's taking everything of value and selling it. She said it all belongs to her. She doesn't want to keep anything," Marti whined. "That can't be true, can it? Grandma would never do that; she knew Mom could never be trusted." She failed to keep the emotion out of her voice.

"Come sit down, dear. We need to talk." Ruth sat on the couch and patted the cushion.

Marti wiped her nose with the back of her hand and sat at the other end. Gary leaned against the desk, facing them. Kristi watched from the edge of the room.

Ruth sighed. The pain of Grandma's death hit her hard, too. "Marti, your mother spoke the truth about your grandma's will. The reason I know is because I'm the executor." Ruth fished in her purse and pulled out a thick, white envelope that read LAST WILL AND TESTAMENT.

"The last time Judy updated her will was after your mother came out of rehab. You were eleven. She always wanted to believe the best in her daughter, and thought Tami had finally beat her drug addiction. Unfortunately, she was wrong." Ruth slid the papers out of the envelope and handed them to Marti.

"You were a minor then and still are today. Your grandmother never expected to die so young." Ruth paused, took off her glasses, and wiped her eyes. "It's so unfair. Your grandmother was an eternal optimist. She always thought Tami would turn her life around and always thought she'd be here for you. If she had any inkling of her impending death, I know she would have handled her legal matters differently."

Marti's mind swam in confusion.

"Even if she did leave her estate to you, there is very little left. Over the years, Judy spent all her savings and most of her retirement money on your mother's treatments and legal troubles. Tami was her daughter, and she would have done anything if she thought it would fix her addiction problem. And she didn't want you to go without, so she dipped in some more."

Marti never knew she'd used up all her money. Grandma always took care of everyone else, so this shouldn't have been a surprise. Now she understood how Grandma came up with the money for her expensive camp.

The weight of the situation threatened to bring Marti to her knees. "What am I going to do? I have to figure out how to pay the rent."

Ruth shared a glance with Gary. He grimaced.

"That leads us to another matter. Marti, you're only sixteen. You can't live here," Gary said.

"Why not? I will work full-time if I need to pay the rent. I can do it." She'd find a way to balance it with school.

Gary sank his hands in his pockets. "It's not even about the money, which you are too young to handle anyway. You're a minor. It's illegal for me to rent to anyone under eighteen years of age."

Marti watched her world grow smaller. Darker. She

picked at the edge of her skirt. "But you know me! I'd come up with it. You know I would." Her eyes darted between Gary and Ruth.

"I don't own this place, I only manage it. It's the law, Marti. I'm sorry." He looked at her with sad eyes, unable to budge on the topic.

This couldn't be happening. Why was he saying all these things?

"Marti, you can't live by yourself," Ruth said, and delivered a long, knowing look.

Confused, Marti wondered what Ruth was getting at. She couldn't live by herself, so who was she supposed to live with? Ruth? And then realization hit.

"No way! I am not living with my mother!" She crossed her arms and stared at the uncomfortable pair of heels she still wore.

"No. Your mother is not an option."

Marti sighed in relief.

"However . . ." Ruth paused and Marti's head snapped up. "You have a father. He is far more stable than your mother has ever been."

"No!" Her heart sank. She turned to Kristi, who appeared just as shocked. There was no way she would live with her dad. Ever.

"I hate him! And trust me, he would never want me anyway."

"Actually," Ruth said in a calm, slow voice, "he does."

Marti's eyes widened as the remains of her normal life shattered. She shook her head and begged, "Please, no. You can't make me go there."

"He is your father and is legally responsible for your well-being."

Well-being? The man couldn't see past his nicotine-stained fingers. "Maybe I could live with you," Marti suggested out of desperation. "I'd be really helpful and would get a job. I'd be really good. I promise."

Ruth ignored her pleas. "Your father has the resources to take care of you. In fact, he sounded very happy about seeing you again. I think he regrets how poorly things went when you were younger. I think he wants to redeem him-self."

"You talked to him?" she asked in a defeated whisper.

"Yesterday." Ruth let the news hang there. She knew all this time that Marti would be shipped away from every-thing she knew and hadn't bothered to tell her.

Things were moving too fast. Her throat tightened. "But he lives in California. That's half a world away! I can't leave my friends and my school." Marti felt the urge to run to her room, slam the door, and bury her sobs in her pillow.

"I know a lot is happening, but we need to make sure you're safe and well cared for. Your grandmother would have wanted that."

Marti blinked back her tears. Grandma would never want her to live with her dad. Maybe she could run away, but with what? Her mother had just stolen anything of monetary value. Then she thought of Adam. Was it only yesterday she was at camp with him? It seemed like a lifetime since he held her in his arms and made her feel safe and special.

"Marti?" Gary interrupted her thoughts.

She looked at him. "Yes?"

"You can stay here for another week to pack up and say good-bye to your friends, but after that, either your mother takes over the rent, which I don't see happening, or I have to list it for a new tenant."

Ruth added, a cheery tone in her voice, "You'll be able to move to California before school begins. It will be a wonderful new start. You'll make lots of new friends."

Marti glanced at Kristi, who had remained quiet and now looked devastated. They both knew it would *not* be wonderful.

It would be a disaster.

14

Ruth wouldn't leave. She forced Marti to eat some dinner and then washed the dishes, placing them in the dish rack and covering them with a white dish towel, just like Grandma did. After Ruth helped put the apartment back together, Marti insisted the woman leave. But then she popped back over to bring Kahlúa home. The cat padded off to her bed, as if nothing was amiss.

Kristi offered to sleep over, but Marti wanted to be alone so she could call Adam. She hadn't told Kristi about him yet. Too much had happened in the last twenty-four hours, and Marti wanted privacy.

At long last, everyone went home. Marti wandered through the quiet apartment trying to soak up any remaining essence of Grandma. Thoughts of dread over her move to LA tried to consume her. She pushed them away.

Grandma's bedroom remained a mess from her

mother's maniacal search. Marti tucked the clothing items back in the drawers and closed them.

She sat on the edge of the bed and smoothed the faded yellow spread. Her finger caught on a hole in the fabric, the material frayed from too many washings. Marti felt the same. The fabric of her life always had flaws, but now it was ripped beyond repair. She sighed. How was she going to survive this?

Marti slid one of Grandma's pillows across the bed and hugged it. The familiar scent of Grandma's perfume wafted to her. Marti buried her face in the soft pillowcase and wished she could hug her grandmother one last time.

She thought of Adam and how he'd been such a rock, staying by her side and convincing Peter to bring the tour bus to camp so she could get home. She longed to feel Adam's arms around her. She missed the way he tucked her into his body, as if they were created for each other.

She gathered up both pillows, took them to her room, snuggled up at the head of the bed, and called him on his cell. As the phone rang, giddiness tingled through her, and she smiled for the first time since learning of Grandma's death. Thank God for Adam. Somehow, he would help her through this.

The phone rang again. And again. Her smile faded. She assumed that Adam would be waiting for her call, anxious to talk. She hadn't spoken to him since he left late last night. She didn't even know if he was home yet or still on the tour bus with Peter and Libby.

The phone rang again and then went to his voice mail. Her heart sank that she couldn't reach out to him, but the sound of his voice soothed her.

"It's Adam. Leave me a message." *Beep.*

Short and sweet. What did she expect? A recorded message just for her? "Oh, hi, Adam. It's Marti. I, um, didn't expect your voice mail. This is sort of weird." She laughed nervously. "I just wanted to talk. You know. Today was Grandma's funeral." She paused, not sure what to say next. "Call me . . . if you want to."

She ended the call and tossed the phone on the bed. *What an idiot!* Now that they weren't at camp, she didn't even know how to talk to him. Marti stared up at the glow-in-the-dark stars stuck to her ceiling. Grandma put them there years ago. They didn't glow anymore. Nothing did.

Maybe summer camp was just that. A summer fling with a guy, and now it was over, like everything else. But he wasn't just any guy. He was a rocker! She fell back on her bed and covered her face. Like that would ever work. She shook her head.

Why would he want anything to do with her now? She was totally a fool. Not only had she slept with him, she'd thrown herself at him. Marti cringed, remembering her bold behavior that night in the Nature Center after Grandma died. Is that what her mother was like at her age? Sleeping with guys any chance she got? Marti hugged herself and rocked. No. She was not like her mother and never would be.

Her phone rang.

She scrambled to answer it. "Hello."

"Hi!" Adam's sweet, beautiful voice rang across the phone waves. "Sorry I missed your call. It's pretty crazy here."

"That's okay. Are you still on the bus?" She gripped the phone like a lifeline.

"No, I'm back in San Antonio. Peter had strict instructions to get me on a direct flight from O'Hare. He's taking Libby to Boston, where she's starting school soon. He bought a condo there, so he's gonna get things set up and then we're all meeting in New York in a few days to work."

"Wow, that was fast. I figured you'd be on the bus for a couple days."

"Not when my dad has other plans. He has me seeing a specialist for my arm. He doesn't trust the doctors in Wisconsin. But enough about me. How are you? How was the funeral?" His voice turned soft and kind like the Adam she remembered, and she wanted to transport herself to him through the phone.

"It was fine. It didn't really seem real." She recalled her mother's blathering in front of everyone and how much she had wanted to tell her to shut up.

"Are you doing okay?"

"Yeah, I'll be fine. It's just hard." She sighed.

"I wish I could be there," he said, and she heard the longing in his voice.

"Me too." She sank back into her pillows, imagining him curled beside her. "Things are happening so fast. I don't really know what to do."

"What's going on?"

"To start off, my mom has been horrible."

"Hang on a sec," he interrupted.

Marti heard mumbling in the background.

"Sorry about that. It's a little hectic here."

"What's going on?"

"In a nutshell, my life. I forgot how insane things always are. I wish I could morph us back to camp and never leave."

"Me too. Can you imagine how great that would be? I'd stay forever." She picked up a stuffed bear and petted its soft fur.

"Hang on," Adam said again, and then started talking to someone in the background. She overhead him say, "I know. I said I'm getting off."

He sounded irritated as he continued talking to someone else. "Give me a second, will you?" After more mumbling, he came back on the line.

"Marti, I've gotta go. I'm sorry. I'll try to call you later."

"Okay. Sure." She heard more mumbling and the phone clicked off.

She looked at the dark phone, empty and void. She

didn't get a chance to tell him about her mom stealing everything in the apartment or how she missed her grandma so much she couldn't bear it or, more important, that they were forcing her to live with her dad. She glanced around her room. The colorful pictures and keepsakes of her life would soon be packed away. She'd be alone in that strange mansion with no one to count on.

She hugged Grandma's pillows and buried her face in them, willing herself not to cry.

"God, Mom! I was trying to talk," Adam complained in a low voice so the other people in the medical imaging waiting area wouldn't hear.

"Don't use that tone with me," she scolded. "You can call your friends anytime. These people are trying to do their jobs." She tilted her head toward the technician who waited with his arms crossed. "Now give me your phone. I'll hold on to it while you're having your MRI."

He ignored her request. "Marti's grandmother just died, and today was the funeral. It was a pretty important phone call." He shot her the stubborn look he generally reserved for his brothers.

"I'm sorry your friend lost his grandmother, but you know better than to call when you're in the middle of something." She held open her hand.

Adam didn't bother to correct her. He stood and handed over the phone.

"Thank you. I'll return it when we leave. Do you want me to come in with you?"

"What do you think?" he snapped and walked away.

Hours later, he walked out of the San Antonio Medical Center with a new cast. The specialist determined that the location of his break would allow for a different type of cast that would provide him enough mobility in his hand and fingers to play guitar. He sighed in relief that he wouldn't have to deal with the nightmare of not being able to play.

"May I please have my phone back now?" he asked his mother with as much patience as he could muster.

She dug through her bag and pulled it out. "Here you go."

He snatched it from her hand and looked at it. "Great! The battery's dead."

"And that's my fault how?" she asked.

"You didn't give me a chance to turn it off."

"You know, I'm getting tired of that tone. What's gotten into you? I thought camp would be good for you, but it seems to have been the opposite. You got into trouble, you broke your arm, and you've turned surly."

"What happened is that I finally got the chance to *be* a teenager. Teenagers are supposed to be surly." He tried to look tough, but a smile curled at the corner of his mouth.

His mom grinned. Adam could never stay mad at her.

* * *

The next morning, Marti packed while Kristi looked on. "Let me get this straight. You expect me to believe that you're going out with Adam Jamieson?" Kristi asked.

Marti was glad to see her best friend after spending a depressing night alone. She grinned and nodded. She, too, found it hard to believe she was with Adam.

"Shut up! That isn't possible!" Kristi said from where she leaned against a pile of pillows.

"I know!" Marti hugged her yearbooks before putting them in a box with her photo albums. Her room had become a mess with all her stuff being sorted for packing, pitching, or donating.

"Prove it." Kristi raised a skeptical eyebrow.

"Hang on." Marti grabbed her laptop and brought up her photo gallery. Kristi hovered over her shoulder. First, Marti brought up a picture of Adam with the guys in the lake throwing a football. She zoomed in on Adam.

"Oh. My. God. That's him! But he cut his hair!"

"Here's more." Marti clicked through picture after picture of her new friends. Kayla had sent her a huge folder of photos she collected from everyone. They'd become a lifeline for Marti. She showed pictures of them hanging in the Nature Center, sneaking drinks around the campfire, and Marti's favorites—her and Adam at the beach.

Then she stopped on a close-up of the two of them. Adam took the picture by holding his camera in front of them. They looked so happy, their heads tilted together.

Kristi reached out and touched Adam's face on the screen. "You really are going out with Adam Jamieson! I can't believe it." Kristi plopped on the bed and kept scanning the pictures. "Is he a good kisser?"

"Oh yeah." Marti recalled the magical touch of his lips, soft and yet firm, and he tasted like . . . like Adam.

"Are you blushing?" Kristi put the laptop down and focused her attention on Marti. "So what else did you do?"

Marti tried to bite back her smile but couldn't. She pressed her lips together so she wouldn't spill the news.

"Okay, that's it. You're telling me everything!"

Marti fell back on the bed, hugging a pillow over her face, and squealed.

Kristi pulled it back. "Did you? You know," Kristi asked suggestively.

At first, Marti hesitated, but then nodded. "Yes!" She covered her face with the pillow again.

"I can't believe it. My best friend did it with Adam Jamieson!" Kristi shook her head, struggling to come to grips with Marti's reality.

Marti rolled over. "But you can't tell anyone. Swear it!"

"Who am I going to tell?"

Marti grabbed her arm. "No, seriously. You can't tell anyone! Okay? No Facebook, or Twitter, or anything!"

"Why not? Aren't you, I don't know, proud?"

"Kristi, shut up! It's not like that."

Marti's mind transported her back to that night in the

woods and the way Adam trailed his fingers over her hip and down her legs, how his breath warmed her skin from the cool night air. He made her crazy.

"Hello! Earth to Marti!" Kristi shook her.

Marti smiled and bit her lip. "Just . . . swear to me you'll never breathe a word."

"I swear," Kristi said, her eyes glued on Marti.

"It was really nice," Marti began quietly.

"We were going to do it again but got interrupted." She buried her head in her hands. "Does that make me a slut?" She didn't feel like a slut, but when she spent time alone with Adam, her body took over and she lost all control.

"Of course you're not a slut! I can tell you really like him. But what about him? I hate to be the wet blanket, but he probably sleeps with a ton of girls. Please tell me you used protection."

She did not want to admit her stupidity, but her face told the story.

Kristi's face fell. "Oh, Marti, what if you're pregnant?"

Marti refused to consider that possibility. "No. It's not like we planned it. It just . . . happened." She fought a sudden urge to vomit. What would she do if she was pregnant?

"It's going to be okay. I know it is," Kristi decided.

"What if it's not?"

"Don't think like that. You will be fine. Fate wouldn't be that cruel."

"Come on. My grandmother died and left me homeless.

I have to go live with my freakazoid dad. Don't bad things usually happen in threes?"

"I've never heard that. Nope. You've got something great coming your way."

At that moment, her phone rang. Marti grabbed it off her dresser.

"Is it him?" Kristi craned her neck to see.

Marti peeked at the display and grinned in relief. "Yup!" Secretly, she'd worried he'd never call again.

"I can't believe it! Adam Jamieson is calling your phone! Can I say hi? No, no. That would be weird."

"Calm down." She laughed and answered the phone. "Hi."

"Hey, how are you? I'm sorry I had to cut you off last night." Adam's voice sounded relaxed and unhurried.

Kristi crowded next to Marti with her ear up against hers. "I'm good. Listen, my friend is here, and she's a huge fan."

Kristi started waving and miming not to mention her and then rolled her eyes as Marti did.

"If you don't mind, I'd like to put you on speaker."

Adam chuckled. "Sure, go ahead."

"Okay, Kristi, this is Adam. Adam, this is Kristi."

Kristi perched next to the phone and twisted the edge of her shirt. "Hi," she said, acting shy.

"Hi, Kristi. How ya doing?" Adam's superstar voice answered, and Marti wanted to kiss him for being so nice.

"I can't believe it's really you!"

"Yup, it's me."

The three talked for a couple of minutes and then Kristi, flying high from rubbing elbows with a rock star, said she had to go pick up her little sister from a friend's house. Marti stayed on the phone as she closed the apartment door after her.

"Okay, she's gone."

"She seems really nice," he said, sounding more laid-back now that it was the two of them.

"She's the best. I don't know what I'm gonna do without her." The reality of her new life kept creeping up. It was becoming nearly impossible to ignore.

"What do you mean?"

"Oh, Adam, so much has happened. My life is a nightmare." The thought of teen pregnancy flashed in her mind, and she shook her head to erase it. No reason to freak him out when she was probably fine. "I'm being forced to go live with my dad."

"No way! But he's terrible."

"I know," she breathed, finally able to let her guard down with the one person she trusted more than anyone.

"Oh, Marti, that sucks so bad. I can't even get my head around it."

"Yeah, if someone were to ask me what the worst punishment they could ever give me would be, I'd answer, 'Living with my mom or dad.' So I guess I must have done something really bad."

"Stop talking like that. None of this is your fault, and you know it. I wish I could fly in there and steal you away." He quieted. She wished he could, too, but they both knew it would never happen. "When do you have to leave?"

"Tomorrow." Her heart ached.

"That's fast," he said, his voice somber.

"No one's asked me what I want." She sighed and wiped her hand over her face. The toll of losing Grandma and now her home was catching up with her. "My mom has been ransacking Grandma's apartment, so I guess it's probably better that I won't have to watch that anymore." Marti had moved all the old pictures and a handful of keepsakes for safekeeping with Ruth. Marti's mother would never notice they were missing.

"What's new with you?" She lay on the couch and stared at the ceiling, pretending they were on his bed at camp.

"I've got a new cast! So now I can play guitar again."

"That's great! I'm so happy for you."

"Thanks. We leave for New York in two days. We're having a bunch of meetings, shooting a video. And . . . get a load of this: we're playing on *SNL*!"

She sat up. "Congratulations! Are you nervous?"

"Are you kidding? I'm totally psyched." He laughed.

Marti thought about how amazing it would be to spend a week in New York and appear on one of the biggest shows ever. She realized how busy his life would keep him. She couldn't help but ask, "I'm never going to see you again, am I?"

She stood up and paced the apartment. The future looked bleaker by the minute. It made total sense in the karma of her life that he'd be next to leave. Plus, he lived the life of a musician. Even if he wanted to stay in her life, she knew his career would keep him away from her.

"Yes, of course you'll see me again. I just don't know when. Now that you'll be on the West Coast, maybe it will be easier than a trip to Madison. I'll figure something out. I promise."

She wanted to believe him and fought to keep her spirits up but was losing the battle. Marti spied a framed picture of her and Grandma and removed it from its shelf. She stared at it.

"Adam, I do *not* want to move in with my dad. This is a really bad idea." A huge, dreadful fog hung over her ever since Ruth delivered the bad news. She couldn't shake the eerie feeling.

"He wouldn't hurt you, would he?"

She didn't want him to worry. "No, I've never seen him hurt a fly, at least not physically." She wandered back to her bedroom with the picture.

"Good."

But good was the last thing this was. She tried to put on a happy face as her life tumbled upside down and inside out, but she ached for all that was lost: Grandma, Kristi and her friends in Madison, and Adam, who said he'd planned to stay a part of her life. What were the odds of that? Long-distance relationships were impossible, especially if one of the people involved was a pinup boy for one of the biggest bands on the planet.

She put the framed picture in her suitcase and zipped it shut. "Enough about me. Tell me something happy."

15

The next night, Marti stepped off the plane at LAX, worried she might not recognize her dad. Six years had passed since she left LA, and other than an occasional paparazzi shot in a magazine, she hadn't seen or spoken to him.

After waiting an hour for him to arrive and taking a few cursory loops around baggage claim, Marti knew he wasn't coming. Why did this surprise her? Her parents always left her high and dry when she needed them most.

When her dad didn't answer the phone number Ruth provided, Marti had no other choice than to blow a huge chunk of her limited cash on a cab.

Now she stood before her dad's Hollywood mansion with a pile of luggage and a cat carrier imprisoning a very unhappy Kahlúa. A dozen cars, ranging from shiny sports cars to beat-up compacts, crowded the large circular drive.

Marti felt transported back to her ten-year-old self as she looked at the chrome-and-glass front door. What if her dad didn't want her? What if Ruth made up the whole story just to get rid of her? Ruth wouldn't be that cruel, would she? And what a turn of events to want her dad's attention now when she had wanted nothing to do with him for so long.

Loud music carried to the front of the house. Marti didn't know what to do. She didn't want to go in, but she couldn't stand outside all day, either. Should she ring the doorbell? This wasn't her house, but it was now her home. If she did ring, would anyone even hear? Probably not.

Kahlúa meowed in annoyance, and Marti knew the cat needed out. She wrung her hands wishing for an escape, but this was her new reality.

She blinked back her worry and readjusted her purse strap. She stepped up to the massive glass door and gazed through the cut glass. A kaleidoscope of color appeared on the other side. She took a deep breath and opened the door.

The music blared louder. She stepped inside the air-conditioned entryway and scanned the area for occupants. No one. She all but tiptoed into the enormous great room. The cream-colored furniture and glass-topped chrome coffee tables were all new since she'd last been here. They were arranged in cozy clusters for maximum socializing. A giant, flat-screen TV anchored one wall, and a fireplace, another. One side of the room featured floor-to-ceiling windows that overlooked a massive pool area, complete with a waterfall and a small army of guests. The mansion perched at the top of a steep hill and overlooked the city and the less financially endowed residents below.

Marti tried to spot her dad in the crowd, but only saw strangers in various modes of dress: from bathing suits, shorts and shirts, to dresses and business suits. She dreaded the idea of going out there to find him, but she didn't want to move in unannounced, either.

Marti crossed the great room to the open veranda doors. The California sun blasted warmth. In addition to the partygoers outside, she saw a long bar with a bartender and plenty of seating areas filled by the throng of guests. Off to the side, in the shade, a marble table held a buffet of silver chafing dishes. As Marti gawked at the crowd and tried to locate her father, a woman with silky, black hair approached, wearing a red bikini top and tiny scrap of material serving as a sarong wrapped around her narrow hips.

"You're late! The caterer is already set up in the kitchen. It's off through those doors." The petite woman, with breasts so huge they threatened to bust out of her top, pointed a long, fake fingernail in the direction of the kitchen.

Marti stared. Was she in the wrong house? Had her dad moved?

"Hello!" The woman snapped her fingers in Marti's

face, any shred of patience gone. "Are you deaf? It's that way!"

"I'm not with the caterer," Marti mumbled, looking down at her unfashionable jeans and T-shirt.

"Then why the hell are you here?"

"I'm here to see my dad. He lives here." Marti tried to spot him before this lunatic went postal.

"Your dad lives here?" She looked unconvinced. "Honey, I think you've got the wrong house."

Marti looked at the room inside and saw one of her dad's Grammys on the same pillar it had rested on since she left. "No, this is his house. That's his Grammy over there." She pointed her chipped fingernail at the award.

The dark-haired woman narrowed her eyes. "Is that so? Honey, I don't know who you think you are, but you can pack up your gold-digging ass and find the door."

"No! He's expecting me. Where is he?" Marti craned her neck to see if her dad was poolside.

"If he was expecting you, I'd be the first to know." She looked Marti up and down, her lip curled in a snarl. "Fine, I'll play your game." She spun on her stilettos and sauntered away, swinging her hips.

Marti raised her eyebrows as the woman strutted over to a group seated near the pool. She placed her hands on each arm of a low, padded chair and spoke to someone, her behind thrust deliberately in the air. Marti looked away.

When Marti glanced back, she saw a man stand and nudge the half-naked woman out of the way. With a bong in one hand and a lighter in the other, he spied Marti and called out.

"Martini! You're here!"

Not much had changed with Dad.

The woman frowned, creasing her perfectly made-up face.

Steven Hunter pushed the bong into the hands of the guy next to him and ambled over, his smile bright and genuine. A mix of panic, dread, and even a little hope passed through Marti, as her father crossed the terrace. Maybe she wasn't all alone in this world after all.

He still wore his rocker hair long and straggled. Gray blended in with his blond, showing his fifty-four years. He wore swim trunks low on his hips, and his tattooed chest and arms were bronzed from the Southern California sun. His aging skin sagged on his thin frame. He still looked every bit the rocker, with diamond studs in his ears and numerous gold chains and leather necklaces around his neck. Despite his dilated eyes, he seemed happy to see her.

Marti's heart leapt, and for a moment she forgot about all his wrongdoings. She became the little girl whose daddy sang her back to sleep after a bad dream.

"Look at my baby! She's all grown up."

Marti smiled as her dad engulfed her in a hug. His long hair brushed her shoulder. She didn't quite know what to do. She hugged back a little. He smelled the same—like aftershave, Scotch, and pot.

"Steven, you never mentioned you had another daughter." The woman in the red bikini droned with annoyance. "Or that she was stopping by today."

He released Marti. "Didn't I, Courtney? I thought I did." He looked at Marti and smiled, and then confusion clouded his eyes. "How'd you get here?"

"I took a cab," she said, wondering how he'd respond.

"Shit. I was supposed to send someone, wasn't I? Damn, I'm sorry." He rubbed his weary eyes.

At least he had the decency to act remorseful.

"Well, you're here now!" He put his arm around her. "Hey, everyone, this is my daughter, Martini, and she's come home to stay." He sounded every bit the proud father. Marti blushed at the sound of her given name and nodded to the nearby guests who acted all happy but probably couldn't care less.

Courtney stepped closer. "What! You never told me she existed, let alone that she was moving in!" The woman lowered her voice to a whisper and spoke between clenched teeth. She was a force to be reckoned with, despite her waiflike frame planted in five-inch heels. The other guests watched as if hoping for a show.

"Of course she's moving in. My kids are always welcome here." He looked back at Marti. "I can't believe how much you've grown up. Isn't she beautiful?" he said to some nearby friends, including a guy with chin-length stringy hair and eyes that looked her up and down. They all nodded in agreement. Marti guessed they were part of her dad's current entourage of people who hung around to build him up and tell him how great he was in exchange for free booze, drugs, and a good time.

Courtney pinched her collagen-filled lips together, and her eyes aimed daggers at Marti.

"Let's celebrate! I think there's some champagne around here somewhere. Courtney, where's the champagne?" he asked.

Courtney stomped off in a huff. The partygoers cheered in approval and her dad joined them to accept his false accolades. They went back to their clusters and conversations as if she'd never arrived.

Marti glanced around. No one even seemed to notice her anymore. How quickly she'd been forgotten. She slowly backed away and reentered the house. She had no interest in the champagne or celebrating. She'd been up since six a.m., and all she wanted was to change into more comfortable clothes and be alone.

She lugged her bags and the annoyed Kahlúa into the entryway. She didn't know how her dad would feel about having a cat in the place, so she hustled her upstairs and out of sight before it became an issue for him or the bitchy Courtney.

Marti wondered exactly who Courtney was. The woman seemed to think she was in charge of the place, but that wasn't true, based on the fact that Courtney knew nothing about Marti. No doubt the woman was sleeping with her dad. She looked like a wannabe actress who hoped her dad's tarnished celebrity status would launch her career. *Good luck with that!*

After climbing the long staircase that wound the perimeter of the great room, Marti took the hallway to the north wing bedrooms. The south wing featured a music room, a library, a den, a couple of offices, and an enormous meeting room. More rooms existed on the third level, but were rarely used, because, heck, how many rooms did one past-his-prime rocker need?

Memories washed over her as she carried Kahlúa down the wide, marble-floored hall. The same strange picture of a dog with three heads hung on the wall.

She passed the bedroom door of her half sister, Brandy. She'd be in her mid-twenties now. Did she still live here? Marti remembered Brandy's numerous nose piercings and pitch-black dyed hair.

Next came her half brother Jack's room. He had been a mighty terror. If her dad's past drug use had affected any of his kids, Jack was the one. All her memories of Jack involved him getting into trouble, like climbing on the roof or taking their dad's car out when he was thirteen.

Then she came to the door of her old room. Farther down were guest bedrooms and at the very end, her dad's master suite.

Was any of her stuff still there? Was her Barbie bedspread still on the bed, or her rock collection? She'd been pulled out of there so fast, she took very few of her childhood items.

Marti turned the knob, pushed the door open, and took a step back.

Her little-girl bedroom had been turned into some sort of ancient voodoo room. Wooden masks lined the walls along with spears and shields. All her furniture had been replaced with heavy, dark pieces. The light pink walls were now the color of dried blood. One shelf held necklaces made from some sort of animal teeth. Another featured skulls. She hoped to God they weren't human.

No way could she stay in this room! She backed away and pulled the door shut. She shuddered at the violation of her childhood space.

She crossed the hall and checked a couple of other rooms, settling on a tidy, spacious room with a queen-sized bed, light beige walls, and a balcony overlooking the pool.

Marti set Kahlúa's crate on the floor and fetched the rest of her bags. After hauling her four suitcases up the steps, she let Kahlúa out of the carrier and brought her a glass of water from the attached bathroom. Kahlúa ignored the water, obviously not happy about their cross-country trek, either.

"Hey, it's not my fault," she said. Marti searched the room and found a washtub stashed in the cupboard under the bathroom sink. She opened her bags and searched until she found the small bag of kitty litter. She knew she might not get to a store for a while, so she came as prepared as possible. She poured the gritty litter into the tub and placed it in the bathroom in the far corner near the shower with showerheads on three sides.

Marti rifled around a little more in her luggage and found the framed picture of her and Grandma at their favorite restaurant after Marti's eighth-grade graduation. She placed it on the bed stand, then sat on the floor and leaned against the bed as Kahlúa nosed around the room, checking out her new digs.

The party outside grew louder. She hugged her legs and listened to the strangers having a good time in her new home.

Oh, Adam, what am I going to do? She wished desperately she could call him but knew he was en route to New York.

She was on her own.

The two-hour time difference caused Marti to wake early to a sunny California day. Kahlúa slept inside one of Marti's open suitcases. After throwing on a T-shirt and shorts, Marti wandered downstairs to get the lay of the land.

The vast great room was littered with empty bottles, glassware, a multitude of ashtrays, lighters, and the familiar bong.

The open patio doors revealed a man in a white polo shirt and shorts cleaning the pool. The scene reminded her of staying at a hotel once where the help cleaned up while the guests slept. Warm air wafted in and tickled her skin, making her think maybe life would be okay.

She wandered down the hall to the kitchen for something to eat. Inside the restaurant-sized kitchen, designed for catering companies instead of families, she found the granite counters covered with dirty glassware, serving dishes crusted over with dried hummus, and a platter containing the remains of a congealed smoked salmon.

If Marti hadn't heard the clink of silverware, she might have missed the tiny figure working at the sink. Marti moved around the edge of the giant island to get a closer peek.

"Rosa?" she asked.

The middle-aged woman looked up from her work. Her round cheeks and bobbed haircut hadn't changed a bit. "Yes." She took one look at Marti and squinted her dark brown eyes as if trying to puzzle something out. Then her eyebrows rose. She pulled her hands from the soapy dishwater and grabbed a towel. "Marti? Is that you?"

Marti nodded and smiled.

Rosa dried her hands in haste and came at her like a mama bear to a lost cub. "Oh my goodness, look at you! All grown up and such a pretty girl." Rosa held Marti's face between her damp hands.

Marti smiled again. She had forgotten all about Rosa. She had worked for her dad all those years ago and had been one of the only constants in Marti's chaotic life.

"What are you doing here? Mr. Hunter never said you were coming!"

Apparently, he didn't tell his girlfriend, either. "My grandma died." Marti's voice cracked before the words were out.

"Oh, you poor girl. That is terrible." She wrapped her aging arms around Marti and patted her back. "I only met your grandmother once, but I could tell she was a fine lady. Things will be okay, you will see."

Marti swallowed back her tears. Crying wouldn't accomplish anything.

Rosa sighed and released her. "You must be very hungry. Let me get you something to eat. Sit up at the counter."

Marti sat while Rosa went to work pulling items from the industrial-sized refrigerator. "He didn't even remember to pick me up at the airport."

"That is no surprise to me. Your father, he is loony. He fried his brain a long time ago. Too many bad drugs."

Before she knew it, Rosa set a dish of fresh strawberries,

blueberries, and bananas along with two slices of crusty toast, spread with blackberry jelly, in front of Marti.

Marti sank her teeth into the warm bread. Satisfied, Rosa went back to her work, this time humming a happy tune.

After thanking Rosa for breakfast, Marti decided to check out what had changed in the mansion since she'd been gone. She passed the library with books she knew no one ever read and the smoking room with dark wood, dark walls, and the heavy scent of cigars. The game room was made complete with an antique pool table with inlaid wood and carved legs. Her dad's favorite arcade games from when he was a kid—*Galaga*, *Asteroids*, and *Ms. Pac-Man*—lined the wall. Every room featured framed photographs of her dad with famous people, including rock legends and even a couple of past presidents.

When she arrived at the music room, she lingered in the doorway. Inside, a grand piano anchored the room. Drawn by some invisible pull, she entered and rested her hands on the polished wood. She considered raising the lid to touch the ivory keys, but her stomach clenched and she decided not to. Instead, she examined the numerous guitars propped in their stands around the room. A different guitar for each kind of music. Her dad kept a saxophone, an oboe, and a trumpet on display. In this room, unlike the others, there were no pictures of famous people or even of her dad, which was a rarity since the man always surrounded himself with his own image.

The decorations in this room were things that inspired him. His first guitar hung on the wall over the fireplace. The flyer from his first gig with his high school buddies was pinned up next to his Eagle pin from Boy Scouts. Hard to picture her dad as a Scout, let alone an Eagle.

She walked the perimeter of the room, taking in the tokens of his life that meant so much to him. As a little girl, she never noticed these things. Maybe he added them more recently.

When she reached the far wall, she found more pictures, but not like the ones adorning the rest of the mansion. Surprised to see herself, Marti walked closer to check out the picture of her, about four years old, at the beach. She wore the brightest, sweetest smile. Her light blond hair blew in the wind around her sun-kissed, chubby cheeks. The little girl in the picture didn't have a care in the world.

Next, she found pictures of Jack and Brandy. They varied from pictures of them as little kids through their teen years. One picture featured all three of them the Christmas before she left. Marti looked young and innocent, while Jack was about fourteen, his hair long, and he wore a sullen expression. Brandy, the oldest, must have been about nineteen. Her hair was cropped short, dyed black, and spiked out in rebellion. Her face featured a nose and lip piercing, along with several on her ears. Dark makeup outlined the eyes of the troubled girl. Marti wondered what this messed-up girl ended up doing with her life. When Marti moved to Wisconsin at age ten, they never tried to stay in touch. Not that they were ever close.

As she scanned the pictures, she came across one of a beautiful blond girl wearing a wedding dress. The girl looked radiant but Marti didn't recognize her.

Marti wandered through the remaining rooms on that floor and then back to the great room. During the time Marti explored, Rosa had cleaned the disaster of a room, leaving no hint of the previous mess.

The sound of splashing water attracted Marti's attention. She walked onto the terrace and discovered her father swimming smooth clean strokes across the pool. This was new.

She stood in the doorway. She didn't really belong here, and she barely knew the man in the pool. He was her father, but he was mostly a stranger. He spent all of thirty seconds talking to her yesterday. He hadn't given her enough thought to pick her up from the airport or even send someone in his place. She was no more to him than something to brag about. He'd created a kid. Big deal.

Her dad reached the far end of the pool and hopped out, revealing his naked butt. *Eww!* Marti whipped around and stepped into the great room to find Courtney perched on a pristine beige couch eating Cheetos. She wore tiny shorts and a tight-fitting tank top. Her mussed hair and lack of makeup gave her an air of youth and innocence, which Courtney ruined by speaking.

"You're still here." She crunched down another Cheeto.

What did she expect? For Marti to disappear overnight? "Still here," Marti stated, her voice solid even if her future wasn't.

"So, how long is this little visit of yours?" Courtney licked cheese residue from her fingers.

Marti sank her hands into her pockets. What could she say? This was her new home, because otherwise she was homeless? That her dad was the only one left on the planet who could take her in? Before she could come up with a lame answer, Courtney continued.

"Because I've got a lot of plans, and they don't include some doe-eyed, long-lost daughter." Courtney's laser-sharp eyes pierced Marti.

Her dad entered with a towel the color of the ocean wrapped around his hips. "Hey, everybody's up. Did you have fun last night?" he asked Marti, and plopped down in the middle of the couch.

He hadn't realized Marti left the party after a minute and a half. "It was great." She tried not to roll her eyes.

Courtney slid next to her dad. "I was just telling Martini that we have some big stuff coming up."

Her dad reached into the drawer on the coffee table and pulled out a joint and a lighter.

"We're in the final negotiations to star in a new show. We're about to start filming a reality show: *Lifestyles of the Rich and Rockin'*."

Her dad lit the joint and took a long drag. He held it in for a while and then blew the stinky smoke into the air.

"This show is going to be huge," Courtney said. "The producer said I'm going to be the next reality star 'It Girl'! I'm going to be bigger than . . . than anyone!"

"You're planning a comeback?" Marti asked her dad as he slowly got stoned.

"Yup," he said, holding his breath, then exhaled. "The band's meeting here tomorrow night. I've been working on new material to put with our greatest hits. It's going to be our best tour yet."

Courtney nuzzled up to Marti's dad and drew little circles on his neck with her finger.

"So, sweetie, how long is Martini going to visit?"

Despite his dilated eyes, he responded right away. "As long as she wants. I imagine at least until she finishes high school."

Courtney's eyes flashed rage. Marti knew Courtney would do everything in her power to make sure Marti didn't *want* to stay very long.

"School? Are you sure that's a good idea with all the film crews moving in here?"

"She can be part of the show."

What? No way did Marti plan on being part of a reality

show or any other show, for that matter. She needed to get them off the subject of her being part of their train-wreck lives. "Speaking of school, I probably need to get registered. It must start soon."

"Courtney will help you. Won't you, honey? She's good at organizing things." He picked up the TV remote and aimed it at the mammoth flat screen. He tuned it to some show about buying junk from forgotten storage units.

Courtney smiled sweetly at Marti's dad and then turned an evil sneer on Marti. "I'd like nothing better."

Message received. Marti took the signal and retreated to her room.

16

Adam hated red-eye flights, because even though they had the comfort and privacy of first class, he could never sleep. So while his parents and brother Garrett snoozed like babies, he watched three action flicks and tried not to miss Marti. The wheels touched down at JFK, and Adam practically jumped off the plane.

To make it less likely he'd be recognized, he pulled on a cap and dipped his head as they deplaned. It helped that they looked like a family on vacation, and that Peter wasn't along to create the more recognizable trio of Jamieson.

Adam's dad called ahead to Roger, their head of security. By the time they reached the airport exit, an SUV with tinted windows waited at the curb. Adam hopped in the far back and stretched out while the others climbed in. Within seconds, they were on their way to the hotel, no one the wiser of the band members passing by. Someone on Roger's team would wait for their mountain of luggage and bring it to the hotel.

The ride downtown took an hour. Adam sent Marti a text. With the time change, she'd still be asleep, which is what he wanted to be. He loved New York City. Something about the energy there felt different than anywhere else. But as they drove farther into the heart of the city, the towering skyscrapers crowded closer than he recalled. This claustrophobic feeling must have been due to all that time spent in the woods in Wisconsin—where open space was plentiful and the air smelled . . . clean.

They pulled up in front of the Waldorf. Doormen welcomed them into the upscale hotel known for excellent security. Adam brought up the rear of their jet-lagged group. Roger directed them to the elevator, and they arrived without incident. They would occupy two large suites; he and his parents in one and Peter and Garrett in another. They still treated him like a child, which annoyed Adam to no end.

He dumped his bag on the floor, fell onto the couch, and put his feet up.

"Adam, shoes off the sofa," his mother ordered.

He toed them off and covered his eyes with his arm, wanting nothing more than to sleep. He listened as his mother created the family nest as she did whenever they were at a hotel for more than a day or two. He heard Roger set his heavy travel cases on the floor and fish out schedules that would be the master plan for this week, this month, and probably the entire year.

As Adam drifted off, he heard a knock. The door opened and Peter and their manager, Wally, walked in. Great, he couldn't even catch five minutes.

"Hi, Mom," Peter said. He pushed Adam's legs off the couch so he could sit.

"Can't a guy sleep?" Adam groaned, and opened one eye. Peter looked too damn happy.

"You can sleep when you're dead," Garrett said. He texted on his phone from one of the comfortable side chairs.

"If I don't get any sleep, I will be dead," Adam answered.

"It's always hard the first day after a red-eye," his mother said. "You'll be fine. Do you want something caffeinated to drink?" She offered up a couple of pre-ordered sodas.

"A Dew. Please," he added to keep her happy.

"Okay, boys, here we go." Wally, middle-aged and balding, pulled up a chair from the dining table to their seating area. Dad took the chair next to Garrett's, and Mom sat on the arm of the sofa near Peter.

"We have a lot of catching up to do because of our two weeks off. The schedule is packed."

"Thanks for that, Pete," Garrett shot across the room.

"You're welcome!" He smiled.

Adam could see Peter was still riding high from his two weeks with Libby and setting up his new digs in Boston. Peter had the promise of seeing Libby often. Whereas, Adam had no idea when he'd get to see Marti again. Longing tugged at his heart. Damn, he missed her.

Wally continued. "This afternoon we've got a production meeting on the video shoot from one to three p.m. At three thirty, we've squeezed in fittings for all of your appearances this week. Dinner will be with a publisher and his team. They will be pitching ideas for the book. Then, at ten p.m., you've got a photo shoot."

"Starting at ten? Are you serious?" Adam saw his possibilities for sleep disappearing. He wished he could sneak back to camp and crawl in his bunk.

"We're showcasing the band in the exciting New York nightlife. We'll start in Times Square, so it will be a bit of a press when the theaters let out. Then tomorrow is another hectic day, starting off with a magazine interview at eight."

He and Peter groaned. Adam knew he'd be lucky if he got four hours of sleep, and considering he didn't get any last night, he'd be dragging big-time. He covered his head with a throw pillow and slunk down on the couch.

The schedule only got worse as Wally outlined the video shoot, rehearsals, and more interviews.

Why was he doing this again? Oh yeah, love of his art.

And the fact that his family wouldn't let him out of it even if he wanted. Heck, his dad had his broken arm recast so he could still play guitar.

Nope. No choices. This was his life for the foreseeable future. Marti and camp seemed like a million years ago.

Later that afternoon, when Marti could avoid her hunger pangs no longer, she ventured down to the kitchen. She was paranoid that she might run into Courtney, but instead was startled to find her dad in the kitchen, leaning over a bowl of Froot Loops.

"Oh, hi," she said awkwardly. What would it take to feel comfortable around him again?

"Want some?" He offered the box.

"No thanks." She opened the fridge in hopes of finding leftovers from last night's buffet or something more edible than processed food. On the top shelf, with a note that read *Welcome home* taped to it was a covered plate of sandwiches and a container of pasta salad. She pulled the items out and placed them on the counter. "Look what Rosa left."

"She always liked you." Her dad smiled and a drop of milk rolled down his unshaven chin. He swiped it away. "She wouldn't speak to me for a month after you left."

The sparkle of his blue eyes gave Marti hope that deep down he really did care. She watched his calloused hands as he took another mouthful of cereal, remembering him playing guitar when she was small. Marti put a sandwich and some salad on a plate.

"Want some?" she offered.

"You bet," he said, and watched Marti fix him a plate. "You know, I'd do just about anything rather than go to a funeral or talk about death, but I want you to know that I'm sorry about your grandma. She was a nice lady and always treated me well. Even when I didn't deserve it." He looked uncomfortable and then lifted his bowl and drank the remaining milk.

Marti took a bite of her sandwich and chewed on his words. "Thanks," she said, unsure what else to say.

They sat in awkward silence.

"You want to hear my new music?"

Marti's head popped up. "Sure."

"Come on, bring your plate. Just don't tell Rosa." He winked and the feeling of acceptance cheered her up.

"Where's Courtney?" She looked around, fearful of being caught by the pint-sized witch.

"She's off shopping with her brother, Nigel. She wants new clothes for the show."

They carried their plates to the music room where Marti curled up in a comfortable chair while her dad selected a guitar and pulled a straight-back chair closer.

He tuned the guitar using his perfect pitch, plucking each string and adjusting the tuning pegs. Satisfied, he began to play. Marti watched his gifted hands strum and dance over the strings, creating a masterpiece. He tossed his hair back.

"What do you think?" he asked when he finished. His expression open, he seemed to really want her opinion.

"I like it." She smiled. "I really do. What's it called?"

"Evolution," he answered, and began the next tune.

Marti placed her empty plate on the side table and tucked her feet beneath her as intricate rifts and melodies sounded from the guitar. He played song after song for her. The sound of his trademark raspy vocals rang out in the room. She enjoyed this rare, private concert from her dad, the famous Steven Hunter. She could see why he was considered such an icon. When he looked up and smiled, it accentuated the crow's feet on his weathered face.

"Is the band really going to tour?" she asked.

"That's the plan. We're having a party here tomorrow night and starting rehearsals next week. Then we'll hit the studio to record the new tracks. The tour starts in late October. I think this might be the perfect time to put the band back up on top." His eyes lit up as he talked about all of the plans.

Marti liked hearing the excitement in his voice. It had been years since the band had done anything, and she wanted to see her dad happy versus destructive. His happiness reminded her of Adam, and a pang of emptiness thumped in her stomach.

"There you are! I've been looking all over." Courtney strutted in, wearing skinny jeans so tight she could barely bend her legs. "Nigel and I just got back from shopping. I wanted to show you everything I bought. What are you doing in here?" Nigel appeared behind her. Marti recognized his stringy, dark hair from the night before. His eyes appeared stoned and his shoulders sagged as he lingered in the doorway.

"Playing Marti some of the new material. Did you have fun shopping?"

"Of course. But why are you playing it for her? You never play for me." Courtney pouted and sidled up to him, wrapping one arm around his shoulder and slipping her other hand down the neck of his T-shirt.

"Because you can never sit through more than one song. Martini is a wonderful listener." Marti let her dad's compliment soak in. It had been so long since either of her parents said nice things to her.

"I'll listen anytime you want, baby." She leaned closer and rubbed her ample breasts against his shoulder.

Marti took the cue to leave. "Thanks for letting me hear your songs, Dad." She liked being able to say his name without feeling angry. She picked up her plate and left, but as she passed Nigel, she felt his eyes follow her down the hall. She made a mental note to keep her distance.

Back in her room, Marti texted Adam about hearing her dad's new material. He was in some meeting, but texted back how jealous he was that she got a private concert of new Steven Hunter music. She knew Adam meant it.

She spent the afternoon unpacking her four large suitcases. The rest of her stuff was left behind for her mother to paw through and get rid of. She did leave a box of keepsakes with Kristi until she could have them shipped, and she left a box of important papers and old family photos that Ruth promised to keep safe until Marti was older. Marti didn't trust that her stuff was safe here, either. Too many people came and went and did what they wanted. Having her cameras and laptop here was risky enough.

Kahlúa seemed to like one of the suitcases so much that Marti decided to let her use it as a permanent bed.

The afternoon sun warmed her room, and the cool breeze reminded her of camp. Unfortunately, as the afternoon turned into early evening, voices traveled up to her room. She glanced out the window to find people milling around the pool. The alcohol flowed and, as the voices intensified, so did the music.

Marti spotted Courtney laughing with her brother and saw her dad holding court with his bong. She rolled her eyes. She didn't want to go downstairs, but the scent of something grilling caught her attention, and it had been a while since lunch.

She snuck down and was able to successfully snag a plate of kebabs along with grilled mango from one of the caterers. As she balanced her plate and soda while opening her door, Kahlúa snuck out.

"Aw crap. Kahlúa!" She set the food on her dresser and went off to catch Kahlúa before she got too far.

The cat trotted down the steps and into the great room. Marti found her pawing at the corner of the sofa. She snuck up from behind and scooped her up. Kahlúa meowed loudly.

"Naughty cat," Marti scolded, and kissed her on the head. She turned to find Courtney and Nigel watching.

Nigel took a slurp of his half-finished beer. "Well, lookie here. Someone's keeping secrets."

Courtney glared, her collagen-filled lips forming an ugly sneer.

Nigel approached, swaying on his feet. Marti wished he'd fall on his face.

He leered at Marti. "I want to pet your kitty."

Marti hugged Kahlúa tighter and recoiled a step back.

"What's the matter? I play nice," Nigel slurred and dragged his finger down her arm.

Marti jerked away. She desperately prayed someone would come interrupt, but no one did.

Nigel moved closer, his odious hot breath turning her stomach sour. "Here, kitty, kitty, kitty." He scratched roughly behind Kahlúa's ears and fixated on Marti. "See, she wants to play a little game of cat and mouse. Don't you, girl?"

Courtney laughed with wicked satisfaction. "Nigel, you are so bad!"

"What?" he said.

Kahlúa meowed loudly from Marti squeezing her too tight. Without another word, Marti ran up the steps and back to her room.

She tossed the cat onto the bed and slammed the door shut and locked it. Her pulse raced. She braced herself against the door and looked around the room; her eyes settled on the dresser. She pushed it over until it blocked the door.

Out of breath, Marti sank onto the bed. She grabbed Kahlúa and held her close. Marti pressed her face against the cat's soft fur and tried to calm down, although she doubted she could. She couldn't believe Nigel. His words kept repeating in her head, causing her to want to run farther away. Maybe a good TV show would distract her. She snapped it on and flipped through channels until she found a movie about earthquakes and tidal waves. Yep, the end of the world would certainly be a nice solution to her problems.

Later, she heard the sound of yelling and swearing from below. She peeked out the window and saw a brawl taking place on the terrace. She couldn't tell who was fighting. Most of the partyers ignored it; others laughed and cheered the drunken idiots on.

Marti pulled back in shock as one guy punched another in the gut. She couldn't watch the violence. She texted Adam to see if, by any chance, he was still awake. It would be two in the morning in New York. She didn't want to bother him, and apparently she hadn't, since he called her right back.

"Hi! I thought you'd be sleeping. I hope I didn't wake you."

"No. We just got in. What's up? Is everything okay?"

"Oh, not much. I couldn't sleep." She looked at her dresser blocking the door and the curtains blocking out the violence by the pool. She didn't mention either to Adam. Instead, they talked about his crazy day and her dad's impromptu concert. They talked for nearly an hour when Adam yawned for the umpteenth time.

"Adam, you have to get some sleep. We have to hang up."

"I know, but I love hearing your voice. It makes me think you're nearby and not three thousand miles away."

Marti snuggled under her covers, wishing he was beside her. "What's your schedule like tomorrow?"

"Horrible. We have interviews and start the video shoot, so I won't have my phone for most of the day." He sounded exhausted and she felt bad for keeping him up.

"That's okay. I'll talk to you when you can."

"Sounds good. Good night," he whispered softly.

His words sounded like a love caress, and she felt so much better. "Night."

When Marti came downstairs the next morning, she discovered a couple of passed-out drunks in the great room. It didn't stop Rosa from running her noisy vacuum cleaner, which gave Marti a bit of satisfaction.

Determined to avoid Courtney and Nigel, Marti stuffed her camera into her shoulder bag and went for a long walk.

She inhaled the fresh air and enjoyed the quiet morning after such an insane night. She meandered by one mansion after another. It appeared that no one actually lived in their multimillion-dollar homes. The homes were so enormous that barely ten feet separated one monstrosity from the next.

She spotted workers everywhere, pruning this or mulching that. Sprinklers kept the lawns lush and green as a golf course. She snuck a few pictures of flowering trees and manicured gardens. Some houses featured marble pillars that stood three stories high. Others were nearly all glass, like her dad's place.

She reminisced about camp, which seemed like a lifetime ago. Marti missed her friends, but knew from a few emails that they were all busy with their jobs, sports, and starting school. She ached for Adam. Marti couldn't believe they'd been together every day, and now he was back to his life as a rocker. His days were packed with meetings, interviews, and appearances. She understood why camp meant so much to him. He never got the chance to relax and be a teenager.

Marti walked down Sunset Plaza Drive to a strip of small stores and coffee shops. The day was warming up fast, and she decided to go in and order iced coffee with a shot of white chocolate. She sat at a bistro table toward the back and watched people come and go.

A couple of girls her age bought a coffee and left. She wondered if she'd be going to the same school as they did. And when did school start? She needed to figure that out. It was doubtful her dad gave it any thought. And Marti didn't want Courtney helping her out. Maybe Rosa would.

A young woman with a baby strapped to her front ordered next. The checkout girl oohed over the little one.

Marti squirmed. Babies were cute, but she didn't want one. Not now, maybe not ever, considering her poor excuse for parents. She thought of Adam. She still hadn't gotten her period, but she couldn't be pregnant, could she? She swirled her beverage with the straw as the woman sat down and the baby gurgled and cooed.

Marti couldn't watch. She grabbed her drink and made for the door. She did not need to be thinking about babies.

Outside, she drew a deep breath of smoggy LA air. Reality. But the reality of living in the uncertainty of LA was no better than not knowing if she was pregnant.

A few doors down, she spied a drugstore. Before she could overthink it, she went in and found the section with pregnancy tests. Should she buy one and end her misery, or maybe make it worse?

She reached for a box and at the last second changed her mind. She snatched her hand back and instead bought a few magazines and a soda.

Marti headed back to her dad's. Thoughts of her illicit behavior with Adam weighed heavy on her mind. How many times had her mom bought a pregnancy test after irresponsible sex? Then Marti remembered hearing her parents fight one time about who should take care of Marti. Her mother screamed that she'd wanted to abort the pregnancy, but her dad had convinced her not to. He loved kids, not that he ever proved it by the way he treated them.

Marti had been born to a mother who never wanted her. How many other unwanted pregnancies had her mom ended? Marti shuddered. She did not want to be her mother, but was she already following in her footsteps? She rubbed her lower belly. Still flat. She would wait a few more days before buying a test.

Normally, Marti didn't pray, but in this instance she thought a few prayers couldn't hurt. "Please, God, don't let me be pregnant. If you let me not be pregnant, I promise I'll never have sex again." She thought for a moment. "At least not without birth control," she added, as she didn't want to lie to God.

As she approached the mansion, a Mercedes convertible sped by with Courtney driving and Nigel in the passenger seat. Courtney pulled in and parked in the circular drive.

Marti stopped in her tracks. *Crap.* She didn't want to deal with them—at all. Avoidance would be better, so she sat on a stone ledge outside the property next door and waited for the pair to go inside.

It wasn't even a minute later when a tow truck pulled into her dad's driveway. It turned around in the drive and backed up to the bumper of the little convertible.

Marti watched as the driver jumped out of the cab, pulled out some sort of cable, and hooked it to the back of the convertible. Marti fished in her bag for her camera. This guy was stealing her dad's car! She knew Courtney could never afford a Mercedes. She couldn't stop him, but she could at least get a picture of his license plate. By the time she had the lens cover off and the camera turned on, the tow truck pulled the car away. She'd only caught a couple shots.

She rushed into the house and found her dad lounging on the couch with a cigarette between his fingers and watching some pawnshop program on the big screen. Courtney sat on the other end of the couch and pulled items out of her shopping bags. Nigel drank a beer.

"Dad! A truck just towed away your convertible!"

"What!" Courtney shrieked, dropping her latest acquisitions, and bolted for the front door.

Her dad frowned and continued watching his show.

"Shit!" Courtney yelled from the entryway. "My car!" She stormed back into the living room.

"Technically, it was my car, not yours," Marti's dad said, his voice devoid of concern. Marti saw him roll his eyes when Courtney wasn't looking.

Courtney huffed and turned to Marti. "Why didn't you stop them?"

Marti shrank back. "I . . . I didn't realize what they were doing until it was too late."

"Steven! Aren't you going to do something?" Courtney loomed before him with her lacquered fingernails pressing into her hips.

"What do you want me to do? You insisted that if I paid the down payment, you'd make the monthly payments." He leveled his bloodshot eyes on Courtney. "Looks like you missed a payment . . . or four." He turned his attention back to the TV.

Courtney knelt on the floor next to him and caressed his thigh. "Oh, baby. I missed a couple payments. I didn't mean to, but they're so expensive, and my allowance doesn't cover everything I need."

Allowance? Seriously?

"Help me out this one time and pay off my back payments," she cooed into his ear. "I'll make it worth your while, I promise, baby."

Marti cringed and turned away. Nigel leered.

"No." Her dad pushed Courtney away, aimed his remote at the TV, and cranked the volume. "The bank's closed."

Courtney turned on Marti again. "This is all your fault!"

"What did I do?"

"For one, you little snot, you could have stopped the

tow truck from taking my car!" she yelled.

Marti didn't know what to say. Her dad didn't flinch, zoned in on the TV. No reaction. *Great.* The guy with the tow truck had moved so fast he wasn't parked for more than twenty seconds. By the time she figured out what was happening, he was on his way.

"Secondly, you're here! What the hell are you doing here anyway? Steven and I are perfect together, and now you're ruining everything!" For a small woman she had a lot of volume. "We never get to be alone anymore!" Courtney's face turned an angry hue of red.

"But Nigel is always here," Marti pointed out.

"Of course he's here. He's my brother. I told you that! Are you stupid?" she bellowed.

"Sorry." Marti backed away.

"Courtney?" Her dad reached out and patted her butt. "The band is coming over in a couple hours. Did you get everything ordered?"

"Yes!" she snapped. "But I don't know why I do everything for you. What have you done for me lately?"

Marti's dad raised an eyebrow and eyed Courtney in a way that made Marti even more ill at ease.

Courtney's personality flipped like a dime. "Oh, baby, you know I'm teasing. I love you so much. You know I'd do anything for you." She took his hand and kissed it. "In fact, I better go check on some things."

As Courtney turned away, Marti saw her shoot a look

at Nigel. Courtney left the room and a moment later, Nigel followed. He stepped close to Marti as he passed. So close that he would have brushed against her if she hadn't stepped back.

Marti stood in the room with the TV blaring and her dad totally ignoring the scene that just took place.

"Well...I guess I'll go upstairs and email some friends." She waited, but her dad didn't seem to hear, so she backed away until she neared the stairs. When she arrived at her room, the door stood ajar.

Dang it. She knew she closed it before leaving. "Kahlúa!" She discovered the cat curled up in the sun on top of a T-shirt Marti had left on the floor. Marti scanned her room for anything missing or out of place. Her dad couldn't care less what she had in her room, but Courtney or Nigel might be nosy.

Her blood boiled at the thought of either of them nosing around her stuff. And if it was Nigel, well, that gave her the creeps even more.

Everything felt so messed up. Why couldn't anything be simple anymore? Her mind wandered to Adam again.

She picked up her phone and checked it. No messages, no texts. What did he say he had going today? Was it the meeting with the planning committee about performing in Times Square on New Year's?

how's nyc? she texted. That seemed generic enough. No pressure, not pushy. If he wanted to answer, it couldn't be that hard to sneak a text back. She waited and watched.

The phone screen remained blank. She sighed. The empty screen mirrored the feeling in her heart. Empty. Silent. Dark. Why did she always feel so alone?

The answer was simple: because she was.

17

$\mathcal{A}$ couple of hours later, Marti paged through the last of her magazines. Losing herself in the latest fashions and Hollywood gossip helped distract her from her own world. Nothing like useless news items to soothe the mind.

Through her open patio door, Marti heard loud talking and laughing from people downstairs. Sounded like another troop of caterers bringing in food for tonight's big bash. She sighed.

A click sounded, and Marti looked up to see Courtney barge in. Her hot-pink spandex top and leather lace-up pants left little to the imagination.

"Knock much?" Marti said.

Courtney sauntered in.

"I see you've made yourself at home," she said, looking around the room with haughty disdain.

"Not nearly as much as you have." Marti wondered

how the woman walked in her sky-high platform heels. Courtney wandered around the room and stopped at the desk. She glanced at the jewelry and lotion bottles strewn about, then poked at Marti's handbag so it fell open.

Marti leapt off the bed and snatched the bag from Courtney's reach. "Keep your hands off my stuff! Is there a reason you barged in here?"

"Your dad wants you to come down and meet the band. He wants to show you off like a new toy." Courtney flicked a speck of lint off her top.

"I've already met the band. I've known them since I was a baby." Marti set her bag on the bedside table. "I was around here long before you, and I'll be around long after you're gone."

"Ooh, kitty has claws," Courtney taunted as she went out the door, leaving it open.

"You let my cat out!"

Courtney's shrill laugh could be heard all the way down the hall.

Great. Now she had no choice but to go say hi to the Graphite Angels, who, as far as Marti was concerned, were anything but angels.

Marti walked into the middle-aged fray of a band who'd seen their better days. She would have preferred to look for Kahlúa and retreat to her room, but Grandma raised her with better manners than that.

"Martini! Come on over—you remember the guys!" Her dad couldn't hide his joy. It was nice to see him happy over something as simple as a band reunion. He wore outrageous reptile-patterned pants with a bright pink leopard-print shirt; numerous pendants hung from his neck on leather cords. Her rocker dad was in fine form.

At first, she didn't recognize the men. She pasted a smile on her face and joined the motley crew. A heavyset black man with a large bald spot took one look at Marti and broke into a grin.

"This can't possibly be the little cupcake who used to play inside my drum cases." He held his arms wide.

"Teddy!" Marti stepped into his bear hug. He hadn't changed a bit, if you didn't count the extra forty pounds and the hair loss.

"This is Martini? Not possible," Frank, the lead singer, said, inhaling his cigarette. He wore skinny jeans, a black T-shirt, and a fedora.

"Hi, Frank," she said, remembering the screaming matches he and her dad used to have.

"Steven, there's no way a guy as ugly as you could have a daughter as beautiful as this," said Jon. Jon played bass, and his long rocker hair had turned a lovely shade of gray.

Marti blushed, and her dad puffed up with pride. As she greeted and hugged each band member, she remembered the good times from long ago. Most of those good times unfortunately ended ugly. She noticed Courtney outside the reunion circle, ignored, at least for the moment. She wore a sneer of displeasure. Marti bet Courtney wasn't used to *not* being the center of attention.

While Marti only meant to say hi and leave, she got caught up in visiting with these men from her childhood. She enjoyed feeling like she belonged, for a change. In a way, her dad's band was part of her family, and she didn't have much family left.

The band members talked about the upcoming tour and tossed around ideas. Frank expressed a definite opinion as to how it should go. Marti could tell her dad didn't agree by the way he ignored every comment. Even so, the atmosphere stayed upbeat. Within an hour, more people arrived, none of whom she recognized.

"Hey, Martini, come on over and say hi to Jack," her dad called.

Jack? As in my half brother, Jack Daniels Hunter? Last time she saw him, he was fourteen and a holy terror, spraying graffiti on the side of buildings, shoplifting, and smoking dope.

She joined her dad but didn't spot Jack. Then she saw a guy talking to Courtney. He was the height of her dad, but with scruffy blond hair, wearing a baggy T-shirt. His jeans hung from his skinny hips.

"Jack, remember your sister Martini?" her dad said.

Jack glanced up, his eyes droopy. He looked Marti up

and down as if she were a pair of shoes he'd forgotten. "No shit?"

Yup, that was Jack. Not much had changed in six years. "No shit," Marti mirrored his answer.

"Cool," he said to his long-lost sister, and turned to their dad. "Hey, Steven." Jack never called him "Dad." "You talk to your agent about my band yet?"

"We'll talk about it another time," he answered.

"Why haven't you called him? All we need is someone to give us a damn break! Jesus, man, you won't even help out your own son."

Their dad got up close in Jack's face. "I said we'll talk about this tomorrow." And he walked away. "I need a drink. Anybody need a drink?" he called to the room in general.

Several cheers of agreement rose, and the bunch headed out to the pool bar.

"Asswipe," Jack growled under his breath, and stormed off the other way.

Courtney smiled like a satisfied cat, which reminded Marti that she'd forgotten to look for Kahlúa.

A moment of panic struck. If Kahlúa ran off, Marti didn't know if she could find her way back. The mansion was built on the side of a steep hill, home to plenty of wild animals. Kahlúa could be a quick dinner to a coyote. Ignoring Courtney, Marti turned and began her search.

It took her a while to search all the rooms with open doors. She peeked under beds and large furniture. She searched the yoga room, the breakfast room, and the sitting room filled with platinum records and trophies. Nothing.

Back in the great room, she tried to be more discreet. Most of the guests were outside and well on their way to a raging hangover. Above the din of voices, she heard a couple of people arguing. Now that felt familiar! A nice evening escalating into a full-out brawl. She better find the darn cat and fast.

A new ruckus sounded outside and then laughter. She looked out the patio doors to see Nigel, decked out in a silky shirt and dress pants, gripping Kahlúa by the scruff of the neck.

"Look what I found," he bragged. "Sweet little cat. She wanted to join the party."

Oh no! Marti rushed outside. Her heart pounded as he swung her cat around by the fur of her neck. Marti fought the urge to barrel out there and demand he set her cat down, because instinct told her he'd do the opposite.

Kahlúa meowed her frustration. Nigel glanced in Marti's direction and saw her fury. He turned the cat's face toward him. "What's that you say? Kitty wants to go for a swim?"

The group around him laughed. He watched Marti's anger turn to fear.

"If you insist," he said to the cat, and walked to the edge of the deep end.

"Nigel! Put her down!" Marti yelled, running toward him.

His eyes narrowed. He smirked and flung Kahlúa into the pool. The onlookers roared with laughter.

"No!" Marti screamed, but no one heard. She rushed to the side as Kahlúa floated to the top and started swimming, which, she had to admit, did look funny.

Nigel stared at Marti in challenge. Kahlúa swam to the edge of the pool a few feet past him. Marti rushed to fetch her.

Nigel stepped in her path.

Rage boiled in Marti. She wanted to smash his face in. Instead, she shoved him hard. In his inebriated state, he couldn't catch himself. He splashed into the pool, fancy clothes and all.

Marti rushed to the side of the pool in time to scoop Kahlúa out. The sopping-wet, angry cat meowed loudly. If Kahlúa still had claws, Marti would have been toast.

A pissed-off Nigel came up sputtering. "You little bitch!"

The guests continued to laugh.

"Next time, I'll break the little sucker's neck!" he yelled.

A deafening roar suddenly sounded from the house. She looked up as someone on a motorcycle rode through the great room into the pool area, revving the engine.

This party was getting way out of hand. Marti rushed

back into the house, holding Kahlúa tighter. The stinker mewed and bit Marti's neck.

Marti rubbed her sore neck where the little teeth had pricked her. "Thanks a lot!" she said to the cat. "I try to be nice and save you and you bite me."

Adam tried to shake away his desperate need for sleep. Morning shows were the worst. The band had to be there at the butt crack of dawn for sound check. Last night they were only supposed to work until midnight on the video shoot but, as always, technical screwups kept them there till after two a.m. Three and a half hours of sleep was not cutting it.

So here he was, on a stage in Times Square with his brothers. Normal people were still in bed, not shivering in the early morning hours. Temporary fencing held back the growing crowd of die-hard fans who kept yelling his name.

He'd waved and smiled a few times, but really just wanted to be left alone. He kept searching the crowd of faces, but the one face he wanted to see—Marti's—wasn't there. He turned his back to the fans, effectively blocking out their neediness. The band was only rehearsing. The show wasn't for another two hours. He'd let Garrett and Peter handle the fans for a change.

The guitar in his hands became his only solace. While the guys waited for the sound engineers to do their thing, Adam absentmindedly played one riff after another. He didn't even think about playing; he'd lived and breathed it for so long, playing was like chewing food. He just did it.

Peter tossed the cordless mic in the air and caught it with ease. "Have you talked to Marti lately?"

Adam winced, feeling the separation from her in more ways than one. "Not since the day before yesterday. We've texted, but that's about it. With this crappy schedule and the time difference, we can't seem to connect."

"How's she doing at her dad's in LA? I know she didn't want to go."

"She says she's fine, but I can tell something's not right. She always sounds so lost." The fact that he couldn't do anything to help tore at his heart. Plus, he'd had new worries when it came to Marti, which he'd been ignoring.

"That's gotta suck. I wish she could get to know Libby more. I think Libby could really help her through this. She was left to fend for herself, so she knows what Marti's going through."

"I don't know how that would happen when even I can't spend time with her. This distance is killing me."

Peter raised an eyebrow. "Wow, I'd say you're whipped."

Adam pushed a hand through his hair. It had grown back in fast, and the ends were beginning to curl. "All I know is I can't get her out of my mind. I've never met anyone like Marti, and I need to be with her. It's like I'm dying a slow death. Suffocating or something."

"Jeez, you do have it bad." Peter laughed, and Adam

wanted to wipe the grin off his face.

"You know, I thought if anyone would understand how I feel, it would be you." Adam couldn't hide the pain in his eyes.

"Sorry, man, you're right. It's just everything is finally working in my life, and I've never been happier." Peter waved at a group of girls showing off a *We love you, Peter!* sign.

"Yeah, I can see that every minute of every day." Adam strummed a few bars of "Classical Gas." "I need to get to LA. I'm worried about her. There's a lot she isn't telling me."

"Like what?"

Adam looked at Peter's mic. "Is that thing on?"

Peter checked it. "No. It's off." He set it at the front of the stage and turned back to Adam. "What's on your mind?"

Adam didn't know how to say it. Hell, he didn't *want* to say it. He glanced at Peter, who waited expectantly. Then he blurted it out. "I'm worried that Marti might be pregnant."

Peter's eyes widened.

Garrett appeared at Adam's side. "Did you just say what I think you did?"

Adam swore at the heavens. The last person who needed to know his business was Garrett. "This doesn't concern you. Walk away."

"Hell, it doesn't! If it leaks out that you knocked up some girl, we're going to have a hailstorm of bad press."

Adam resisted the urge to slug him. Press was the least of his worries.

"What's wrong with you? Are you out of your mind? Getting a girl pregnant! You're a bigger idiot than I thought!" Garrett pushed Adam.

"Listen, jerk-off! You don't know anything about this." Adam shoved Garrett. Garrett barely caught himself. Girls in the crowd pointed and started snapping pictures.

Peter stepped between them. "Whoa! Cool off! On stage isn't the place to be talking about this. Garrett, if you want bad press, go ahead and start a fight for the fans to photograph."

Garrett huffed.

"Adam, put it out of your head until after the concert."

Like he could ever do that! Now that he'd voiced his concern, the problem seemed bigger than ever. Combined with how heartsick he felt for Marti, he couldn't stand being here.

"You know this is going to break Mom's heart," Garrett said.

Adam got back in Garrett's face before Peter could intercede. "You are NOT going to tell her!"

"Of course not, douche bag, but it will! I knew taking that break was a bad idea."

"Garrett, back off!" Peter barked.

Adam appreciated the buffer.

"And you," Peter added, "stop being such an easy mark.

Let's get this show over with, and then you and I are going to talk."

Adam stepped to one side of the stage, and Garrett sidled to the other. Adam didn't say another word.

Peter shot him a supportive nod.

Adam frowned. He sighed, and they moved on with the sound check.

The four-song mini concert went well. Adam's saving grace was that he could lose himself in the performance. For that half hour, he let the energy of the music and the fans carry him. Times Square wasn't such a bad place to perform.

As soon as they finished, said their on-air thanks to the morning show hosts, and were out of sight of the crowd, Garrett tried to corner him.

Peter intervened. "Not so fast. Garrett, why don't you stay and help Wally and Dad with the postshow wrap-up. Adam and I are going for a run."

"I don't run," Adam grumbled.

"You do today." Peter pushed Adam into the car parked next to the backstage area for an easy exit. Peter closed the door, leaving Garrett alone with a bewildered manager, Wally, and their confused dad. "Let's go," he told the driver.

Back at the hotel, Peter tossed a pair of shorts and a fresh T-shirt at Adam. They avoided the other suite and their mother.

"Peter, I don't need to go for a run," Adam said.

"Yes, you do! Now shut up and change your clothes."
Peter walked away, leaving Adam no choice.

A few minutes later, they stepped out of the hotel. Peter wore a baseball cap, and Adam, aviator shades. Peter started a slow jog. Adam had no choice but to follow. In a few minutes, they hit the edge of Central Park. Seeing the trees and green grass caused Adam to sigh with relief. It reminded him of camp, and his memories with Marti brought him peace.

They jogged a slow, easy pace for several minutes until Peter finally spoke.

"You want to talk about it?" he asked.

"Not really." But then Adam did anyway. He talked about how he and Marti met and how much she hated him at first. He told Peter how much fun they had together and how everything about her just fit. Peter stayed quiet as Adam let it all out.

"She's smart and funny and stubborn. She's so damn beautiful, and I think I love her." There, he said it. It had been on his mind for a while now.

Peter looked at him. "Did you tell her?"

"Hell, no!"

Peter laughed. "Why not?"

"Beats me. How do I even know if it's really love? I've never felt like this before. Maybe it's just . . . I don't know. . . ."

Peter shook his head. "Dude, you're the only one who

can figure that one out. My guess is that you already have."

Adam chewed on the thought as they passed a shimmering blue lake with people rowing boats. Marti would like it here. He thought about their misadventure with the canoe and smiled.

"But I can't figure out how I'm ever going to see her. Why open that door when I can't promise her anything?" Adam dragged in each breath.

"What do you have to promise her?"

"A relationship, I guess. How are you and Libby going to handle the distance thing?"

"First off, living in Boston will make a huge difference. My place is only ten minutes from her campus housing. I've been working with Wally about better scheduling. I don't want to be zigzagging the country all the time when we could concentrate on the West Coast for a week or two and then be back out East again. We'll add more East Coast concerts, and I convinced Dad and Garrett that we should record our next album out here, too."

Anything Peter did to be close to Libby kept Adam farther from Marti. Adam's breath labored. He thought he was in shape, but he couldn't keep up with Peter, who hadn't even broken a sweat.

"Why should we hop around the country all the time? It doesn't make sense," Peter said.

"And they're doing it? How the heck did you make that happen?" If Peter's hopes came true, his wouldn't. Adam spied a water fountain. "Hold up a sec, I need a drink."

They stopped, and Adam took a long sip of water.

"A lot of carefully worded conversations and logic. When Dad and Garrett saw the advantages for the band, they were on board."

Adam nodded and wiped his mouth. How could he work Marti into the insanity of his life? Short of bringing her on tour, which he didn't see happening, he just didn't know.

Peter took a drink and then eyed Adam. "You gonna tell me about this pregnancy scare?"

Adam sighed. "There's not much to tell. She might be or she might not be. I don't know." He avoided eye contact with Peter.

"What happened? Did the condom break?"

Adam started jogging again. "There was no condom."

Peter stopped dead in his tracks.

"I know!" Adam bent over with his hands on his knees. "I'm an idiot, and now I'm paying the price."

"I think that's yet to be determined. What are you going to do? Have you two talked about it?"

"Not since camp, and that's been almost two weeks. I think we're both too afraid to bring it up." He straightened, and they walked side by side.

"Well, that would be an excellent place to start. Find out what's going on and take it from there."

Adam shook his head in defeat. "What if she *is*

pregnant? I'm not ready to be a dad. Hell, I'm not even smart enough to buy condoms. How would I ever be able to take care of a kid?"

"Let's take this one day at a time. We'll deal with whatever happens."

Adam felt better being able to talk it through with Peter, even if they hadn't solved anything. "Thanks for not going postal."

"No problem. Plus, I kind of like the ring of *Uncle Peter!*" His brother punched him in the shoulder, grinned, and took off running, leaving Adam in the dust.

18

Marti slept in the next morning. The noise had kept on late into the night. She looked out the window. Broken furniture littered the terrace area, and more surprising, a motorcycle rested at the bottom of the pool. She shook her head. The Graphite Angels loved and fought like brothers. What a bunch of idiots. She couldn't imagine Adam and his brothers acting so stupid.

After feeding Kahlúa and pulling the bedroom door shut, she wasted no time in searching for a different bedroom. She wanted one far from the pool and this part of the house where she kept running into Courtney.

When she reached the main wing, she checked out the bedrooms there. One room had a black leather bedspread and red walls. *Definitely not.* Another stored furniture covered in drop cloths. A third revealed two people passed out in bed. As she backed away, she realized she knew them.

Courtney and Jack! Holy crap! As silently as possible, she closed the door, but not before Courtney's eyes popped open.

Crap, crap, double crap!

She did not want Courtney to come out and confront her. She rushed up the steps to the third floor. Panting against the wall at the top, she braced herself for sounds of a cursing Courtney.

After a minute, she didn't hear anything, so she hoped she imagined the whole thing. Courtney sleeping with Jack? How messed up was that? She didn't know if she should blame Courtney or Jack. Probably both! Marti wasn't about to go downstairs, so she decided to check out the south wing of the third floor. This part of the house was farthest from the pool. Maybe that would help with the late-night noise.

The first rooms on each side were unused offices, linen closets, or storage. About halfway down on the side facing the street was the theater. She'd forgotten how she and her half sister, Brandy, used to watch movies in there. It was one of the few things they did together. One end of the room held a full bar and concessions area. On the opposite end, a movie screen covered the entire wall, and rows of leather recliners, each with side tables for drinks and snacks, sat across from it. There were no windows, so the room felt like a real movie theater.

As she wandered back into the hall, she couldn't shake

the vile picture of Courtney and Jack together. What was wrong with them? What would her dad say if he knew? Would he even care? Hard to say. She didn't plan on getting involved. They could live their dysfunctional lives however they wanted.

Across the hall, she passed bathrooms and a room with half a dozen file cabinets and storage shelves. Beyond that, she found the bonus prize! Marti opened the door to a corner suite that she never even knew existed.

The room was large and airy, with windows overlooking the city, and she fell in love with it. Tarps covered the furniture. She pulled them away to reveal a king-sized bed, dressers, desk, and sitting area.

Not bad! Behind one door, she discovered a walk-in closet the size of her bedroom back in Wisconsin. Except that she didn't have a bedroom there anymore. She frowned and pulled the door shut. Another door revealed an enormous master bath, complete with marble floors and state-of-the-art shower. Positioned under a large window was a huge, whirlpool tub. How weird would it be to take a bath in front of a giant window? But the house sat at the top of a steep hill and the room was on the third floor. Not much chance anyone would see her.

She grinned at the decadence. On her way out, she spotted a dial on the wall for turning on the heated floor. How many ways could she say awesome! This was perfect! And so much quieter. This should prevent any chance meetings with Courtney.

Marti checked with Rosa to make sure that her family and the partyers had gone. Jack had left, Courtney was out shopping, and her dad was attending some tour meetings. She spent the morning making up the new bed and moving her stuff to her secret suite. Kahlúa seemed happy with all the sunny spots to sleep in.

After grabbing lunch, she wandered down to the music room. The grand piano beckoned. She trailed her fingers over the polished wood, itching to play. She checked over her shoulder to make sure she hadn't been followed. Marti sat and lifted the lid to reveal the smooth ivory keys.

She missed her small upright piano back home. By now, the piano would be long gone, along with whatever else remained in the apartment. Her shoulders drooped as she let herself reminisce about Grandma, and how she would work on piecing her quilts while Marti practiced. What a perfect life they shared. Marti tried not to think about it very often because it hurt so bad whenever she opened that door. She sighed, placed her hands on the piano keys, and began to play.

Hearing the rich tones soothed her in a way nothing else could. The music lifted some of the weight she carried. She attacked the keys with fervor, pounding out Mozart.

"Hot damn, girl! When did you learn to play like that?" Marti's dad entered the room in his meeting attire, which consisted of purple pants, snakeskin boots, a jacket with a bright-colored scarf draped around his neck, and a black fedora.

"I'm sorry, I didn't mean to bother you. I should have closed the door." She tried to read his mood, hoping he wouldn't fly off the handle or criticize her.

"Hell, no, you didn't bother me. That was some insane playing. Who taught you?"

"You did," Marti answered.

"Not like that, I didn't! I don't know who your grandmother found to teach you, but that was awesome!"

"Thank you," she said, smiling.

"Don't thank me, you're the one with the talent." He rested his hands on the piano and looked at her.

Marti squirmed a little, not used to such attention. He slapped the piano lid again. "I've got something to show you, want to see it?" He smiled with such kindness that she saw the father who used to play her to sleep with the magic of his guitar.

"Sure." She closed the piano and followed him outside.

There in the circular drive she saw the cutest little Mustang convertible.

"What do you think?" He leaned against the lemon-yellow exterior.

"It's great! Is it for Courtney?" After the fit the woman

had thrown yesterday, she could picture her dad replacing her repossessed car with this one.

"Hell, no! It's for you!"

"What?" Had he lost all grip on reality?

"Happy birthday!" He grinned.

"But . . . but . . . my birthday isn't until . . ."

"Next week. I know. The fifth. It's an early gift." He chuckled, pleased with her reaction. "Do you like it?"

"Are you serious? I love it!" Marti touched the yellow hood. She couldn't believe he even knew when her birthday was, let alone remembered it. "It's beautiful. But are you sure? This . . . this is too much."

"Nah, it's exactly what you should drive. Wanna take it for a spin?" He acted like an eager teenage boy.

"I don't have my license yet."

"When has that ever stopped us?" He winked. So he *did* remember those idiotic times, and he thought they were funny. Unbelievable.

"I should go get my temps. They're from Wisconsin, but they should count here."

"Nonsense. You're with me. Let's go." He tossed the keys to Marti, which she barely caught, and before she could protest, he stretched his long limbs into the car.

"Okay!" Marti slid behind the wheel on the butter-soft, leather seats and turned the key. The engine purred smoothly. With jitters dancing in her stomach, she pulled out onto the canyon road.

Her dad cranked up the stereo and relaxed with his arm resting on the car door. Marti couldn't wipe the grin off her face as she navigated the curvy roads. *He bought me a car! An amazing car!* After a few minutes, he directed her to the highway, and she sped up. The wind whipped through her hair. Her dad laughed, removed his hat, and put it on the floor.

Marti wanted to squeal with the joy of being out of the house, of spending semi-normal time with her dad.

After several miles, he directed her toward an exit, and she ended up on a road that hugged the coast. With a lower speed limit, they were able to talk while watching the ocean crash upon the shore.

Most of the conversation centered around him, his upcoming reunion tour, and all the plans. She could see how much making a successful comeback meant to him. She hoped it worked. He deserved it. He wasn't a bad person, just kind of irresponsible and self-absorbed. But how could she complain when he just handed her a new car! She couldn't wait to tell Adam about her dad's amazing gift.

Eventually, the conversation turned to other things. "Last night I saw Jack, but I haven't heard about Brandy. What's she up to?" Marti tried to sound casual about the question, because she expected him to say Brandy was in jail, hooked on drugs, or something. His answer caught her totally off guard.

"She's a nurse," he said.

"Really?" Marti tried to hide her shock.

"Yup, she got married last year to a guy in film editing and production. They live on the East Coast."

"Wow." Marti had to digest that one. How did her sister turn her life around?

"Yeah, she turned out real well, and I can see that you will, too. You've got your head on straight. Now Jack, he's another story. That boy has been a problem since the word go."

Marti thought back to this morning when she found Jack and Courtney in bed together. Her dad didn't appear to know, and she wasn't about to mention it. Finally, they were spending quality time together and she didn't want to ruin it.

On the way back, they swung by a drive-thru for drinks. She considered telling him about Adam but wasn't sure it was a good idea. She had no idea how he'd react and it might complicate her life more. Windblown and relaxed, they returned home with her car properly broken in. As Marti climbed out, Courtney pulled up in a dented, gray Mazda. Marti's nerves zoomed to high alert.

Courtney's face pinched into a haughty glare. She stalked over to Marti's dad as he untangled himself from the small vehicle. "What's this?" she snapped.

Unfazed by Courtney's temper, he replied, "It's Marti's new car."

Courtney's eyes widened. She crossed her arms and hitched her hip. "What do you mean, Marti's car? She doesn't need a car. She's a kid! I, on the other hand, need a car."

Marti wanted to slink away and avoid the scene, but she was stuck. Plus, she couldn't deny she wanted to see how this played out.

"You're barely twenty-one. *You're* practically a child! And lately, you've been acting like one, too." He took a gulp of his soda, paying no attention to Courtney's rising rage.

Twenty-one! Holy crap. Marti assumed Courtney was in her late twenties based on the way she dressed. And honestly, who, at twenty-one, would want to be hanging out with an old man like her dad?

"Don't you see she's trying to break us up?" Courtney whined, and waved her arms in an overdramatic display of poor acting skills. "She's always interfering and pulling you away from me. You never spend time with me anymore."

"Maybe that has something to do with you being joined at the hip with Nigel." Her dad raised a skeptical eyebrow in Courtney's direction.

"He's my brother! What can I do? He's bored and has no one else to spend time with."

"Is that it? I thought he just hung around to freeload off my good nature. Rethink your position, Courtney. It's getting old." Her dad put his hat back on and sauntered into the house as if he didn't have a care in the world.

Marti bit back her smile. She was so proud he didn't take Courtney's crap and give in.

"Wipe that smirk off your face or I'll wipe it off for you. And listen up, you little bitch. You better watch what you say or you might find gouges on the doors of your pretty little car."

Marti sobered. She knew it wasn't an idle threat.

"That's more like it. And in the future, don't stick your nose where it doesn't belong." Courtney spun on her heel and left Marti alone in the driveway to contemplate this new threat.

Just when things between Marti and her dad were looking up, Courtney had to remind her of all the other issues she still faced in this screwed-up household.

Jamieson was filming their latest video with the Brooklyn Bridge as a backdrop. It was going to look awesome, but unfortunately, it meant another night shoot. The minute the director called a break to adjust the lighting, Adam snuck in a quick call to Marti.

"Adam?" Marti answered.

"Hi! I didn't wake you up, did I?" He grabbed a cookie and stepped away from the production tent.

"No. I was messing around with photos on my laptop. I'm avoiding Courtney. The pictures of that storm and the fire from the lightning strike are so cool. Hey, I thought you were supposed to be at a night shoot."

"I am. I've got a couple minutes and wanted to hear your voice." A brisk wind blew off the East River, causing him to shiver. He turned his back against the breeze.

"I needed to hear a friendly voice, so I'm glad you called." Marti's voice sounded sweet and lyrical to his ears, but the touch of sadness was unmistakable.

"What's going on?" He took a bite of his oatmeal-raisin cookie.

Marti sighed. "Oh, Courtney is making life difficult, that's all. Don't worry."

Adam didn't like how Marti kept her troubles to herself. He knew she didn't like being in LA, but she wouldn't open up about it. "Are you sure?" He felt helpless.

"It'll take someone a lot bigger than Courtney to take me down." She laughed, but it sounded hollow.

She always blamed her troubles on her dad's girlfriend, but was it really an unwanted pregnancy on her mind? Now probably wasn't the best time to bring it up, but he couldn't keep quiet anymore. He needed to know. He paced away from the production area and gazed at the historic bridge. "We haven't talked about what happened at camp."

"What do you mean?"

"You know, you and me . . . aw, hell, did you get it yet? Your . . . uh . . ." Why was this so damn hard to talk about?

Marti didn't answer right away, and each second seemed like an eternity. Then finally, in a quiet, defeated voice, she said, "No."

His heart sank. "Shit." He wanted this problem to go away. He didn't want to face the reality that she might be pregnant.

"No kidding."

"Do you think you are?" He had hoped so badly this was a false alarm and she'd have good news.

"I don't know. I really don't." She sighed, and he wished he was with her right now. "I almost bought a test," she added.

"Oh!" She must be really worried. He chomped off another bite of tasteless cookie.

Wally stepped out of the production tent. "Adam, we're ready to go."

Adam nodded to Wally but stayed focused on Marti.

"So are you gonna buy one?"

"I'm afraid to. There's been so much crappy stuff happening, and I don't want any more bad news. I'm afraid that if I take the test and I am, it'll erase all the good stuff with us, and I don't want to lose that. You're about the only really good thing I have left."

"You're not going to lose me. No matter what." God, he wanted to see her now more than ever. When they were together, they could handle anything. "What are you going to do?"

"I thought I'd give it a few more days."

"And your grandma died, and that was really stressful. Can that make you not get it?" He didn't know how these things worked, but maybe stress was the problem. She'd sure had enough of that. In fact, that was probably the reason she was late. He sighed over this tiny window of hope.

"Maybe. I'm not really sure."

Wally waved to Adam and pointed at his watch. Adam nodded and held up a finger for one more minute. Wally nodded and ducked back into the tent.

"I'm getting the evil eye here, so I better go."

"Okay. Well, good luck with the shoot."

"I'll call you tomorrow."

"Okay. Bye."

"Bye." The words *I love you* were on the tip of his tongue, but he didn't say them. Aw, hell. He felt like a jerk. She might be pregnant with his baby, and he was too chicken to say "I love you." He tossed the rest of the cookie into the river.

Adam pocketed his phone and followed Wally into the tent. If he wanted to see Marti, he needed to make it happen. "Hey, Wally, got a sec?"

"Sure, Adam. How are you holding up?"

"I'm exhausted, but what's new? Actually, I wanted to ask you about something that might help me."

"What's that?"

"Do we have any free days coming up? I know the New York commitments are winding down. Is there a day and a half or two that I could take a quick break?"

Wally eyed him. Adam had never asked for anything

before, and he hoped his manager would sense his desperation.

"Let's see." Wally opened his binder and paged through. "We should wrap up the video tonight. *SNL* is tomorrow night. After that, we have a couple of interviews, approval of new cover art, and some other business stuff." He turned the page. "The two days after that, you're all in Boston. I hear your parents are going to get a place there. They're moving home base from San Antonio to Boston."

"What? Where'd you hear that?" That was news to Adam. His parents never mentioned a word about moving, and their secrets were beginning to piss him off.

His dad walked in. He had suffered a heart attack last year but was back to his stubborn, domineering self.

"You're moving us to Boston, and no one bothered to tell me," Adam said.

"Didn't I mention it?" His dad shuffled through some papers without bothering to look at him.

"No, you didn't mention it. Don't I ever get a say in anything?"

His father paused and focused his gray eyes on Adam. "What would you say? Why do you care all of a sudden?"

Garrett walked in with their mom trailing right behind.

"I happen to care a lot! And I'm tired of being treated like a third-rate citizen in this family."

"You're only sixteen. What'd you expect?" Garrett interrupted. "Are we gonna finish this scene or not?"

Adam held up his hand. "I expect to be treated equally. I'm one-third of this band. I think I've earned the right to be in on major decisions. You force me to sit in on stupid meetings for book pitches and choosing cover photos and then you exclude me from something as important as where I live?"

"I'm sorry, Adam. You never seemed to care either way about most things," Mom said.

"I care now! And so it's clear, I'm not going to Boston with you. I'm going to see a friend in LA!"

He stormed out, not caring that he left his family standing there in shock. It was about time they started taking him seriously.

Marti decided to stay out of Courtney's way for the next couple of days. She would rather hide out in her room than deal with her, so Marti settled in for marathon TV. She texted with Adam whenever he had a quick break, which wasn't often. Last time they'd talked, he sounded frustrated. Neither of them were doing what they wanted anymore, and the fear of her being pregnant weighed heavier each day.

Annoyed by the latest episode about a five-year-old screaming for more Gummi Bears instead of a spray tan, Marti turned off the TV and grabbed her camera. She had told Adam about her car, but she hadn't sent him a picture.

Downstairs she found her dad parked in his regular

spot in front of the TV. The room reeked. He lounged, eyes glazed over at some show about hoarders, while munching on sour cream and onion potato chips.

Marti didn't bother to say hi as he seemed too zoned out to notice her anyway. She passed through the mudroom to the garage, opened the door, and, with a spring in her step, headed for her new car. She loved her cute, yellow convertible, but when she came around the side of her dad's silver Hummer, she found her new car and a sight so disturbing she wanted to gag: Courtney and Nigel going at it against her car!

19

"Oh my God!" She couldn't keep the disgust from her voice.

Courtney sat on the hood of the car with her legs wrapped around Nigel.

They stopped and looked up in surprise. Courtney pushed Nigel away.

"What the hell are you doing nosing around?" she snapped.

It took a moment for Marti to find her words. There was just too much to say.

"You guys are seriously messed up!"

"You are such an idiot. He's not my brother. Obviously." Courtney adjusted her top.

"He's not?" Marti looked from one to the other.

"Of course not."

Nigel didn't seem to care that Marti discovered him with Courtney.

"But why would you say he is?" How warped could a person be?

Courtney shook her head and rolled her eyes. "Are you really that stupid?"

Marti then realized that Courtney had told everyone Nigel was her brother so she could spend time with him here, at her dad's place. "You are a horrible person! Wait until my dad hears this!" Courtney had crossed the line big-time. It was bad enough she cheated on Marti's dad with Jack, but now Nigel, too?

Courtney stepped in front of her. "Don't even think about running to Daddy. You're going to turn around, go back in the house, and crawl into a hole somewhere. You aren't going to breathe a word of this to anyone."

"Hell, yes, I am!"

"No. You're not!" Courtney said with renewed fury, as if she'd read Marti's thoughts. "Because if you do tell, some unfortunate little incidents will start coming your way. Wouldn't it be terrible if you woke up some morning with your hair cut off?"

Marti recoiled.

"That's right. You're going to go back in the house and not breathe a word. And you're going to leave your car keys on the counter for me so I can *borrow* your car for a few days."

Marti shot Courtney a mutinous look. No way in hell was she going to let Courtney take her new car.

"Now, now. It would be a real tragedy if you found your precious cat floating dead in the pool. Wouldn't it?" Courtney said with a hideous purr.

"You bitch!"

"Think carefully before you say anything you'll regret. So many nasty things could happen." She snapped her fingers in the air and then looked at Marti's camera. "All your treasures could just disappear."

Marti gripped her camera tighter.

"Off you go. Go back to your little cave." Courtney waved her away.

Dumbstruck as to what to do, Marti obeyed. Courtney was more malicious than Marti could have ever imagined. And she wouldn't put it past Courtney to follow through with her threats.

Marti robotically returned to the house and the great room. She stood, frozen, still unsure of what to do. There was a madwoman in the garage, and her dad should know, but she didn't want to take a chance that Courtney would flip out and hurt her or Kahlúa.

"What's up?" her dad said, all mellowed out.

"Hey," she said, trying to keep her voice even and her hands from shaking.

As Marti contemplated what to do, Courtney sauntered in. She passed Marti and delivered an evil stare, then bent over Marti's dad and gave him a big, sloppy kiss. Marti turned her head in disgust.

Nigel slithered in, lit up a cigarette, and watched Marti from the patio door. She could tell by the look in his eye that he loved Courtney's manipulation.

"Hi, honey," Courtney cooed to Marti's dad. "Listen, we've got the movie premiere tonight, and I really need a new pair of earrings. Do you want to come shopping with Nigel and me?"

"No, you go ahead. Unless Martini wants to go." He glanced up at Marti.

"No!" *God, no!* She couldn't believe he'd even suggest it!

"Are you sure? It'd be fun! We could get manis and pedis, too." Courtney batted her eyelashes, feigning innocence. Marti wanted to out her right then and there but didn't have the guts.

"Nope, I've got stuff to do," Marti said as nicely as she could manage, which wasn't very.

"Aw, too bad. Well, then do you mind if I borrow your car?"

Marti held her breath. She looked to her dad to see if he'd defend her and her car, but instead he nodded off. "Um . . . yeah, I guess so."

"Oh, goody! You are such a doll!" Courtney grinned.

Marti spent the next few hours trying to calm down. No matter what Marti did, she knew Courtney would find a way to crush her. The woman was pure manipulating evil.

Then Adam called and said he was coming to see her in two days! Finally, something to be happy about. Hungry and bored with hiding out, she ventured downstairs and opened the refrigerator while humming one of Adam's tunes. She peeked inside the numerous food containers. One advantage to all the catered food was the nice variety of leftovers.

She selected Thai shrimp kebabs, broccoli salad, potato skins, and three mini cheesecakes. While the kebabs and skins heated in the microwave, she danced around the kitchen.

Her excitement couldn't be contained. Two days! She couldn't wait to lay eyes on him. She popped a cheesecake in her mouth.

After all the threats and drama from Courtney, Marti was relieved to have an empty house for a change. Tonight, her dad and Courtney were at a movie premiere. Courtney insisted that if Graphite Angels planned on reigniting their previous success, then Steven Hunter, the rock icon, needed to start making red carpet appearances.

The microwave dinged. Marti did a quick spin before removing her plate. She loaded on the salad and set the desserts on top. With the plate in one hand and a glass of lemonade in the other, she pushed the fridge door closed with her hip.

Dancing to the music in her head, she passed through the great room carrying her dinner back to her luxury digs and the movie she had queued up, ready to watch.

She turned the corner, and Nigel stepped into her path.

20

Marti stopped dead in her tracks and nearly dropped her dishes.

"What's put you in such a good mood?" Nigel's lip curled. The smell of booze and cigarettes permeated from him.

"Courtney's not here. She's out for the night," Marti blurted before he could strike up any more small talk.

"I know. She's at the movie premiere with your dad." He took a step closer.

Marti swallowed, wishing her hands were free.

"I thought I'd swing by and pay you a little visit. I wouldn't want you to get lonely."

The hair on the back of her neck stood up. She didn't want to talk to him. She wanted him to go away but didn't know how to make him leave.

"What? Playing coy?" He took another step forward.

Marti edged back. He helped himself to a mini cheesecake from her plate and popped it in his mouth, chewing with his mouth open. Lust loomed in his eyes, alerting her fight-or-flight instinct.

The plate in her hand grew heavy. She wanted to smash it in his face. How could she get him out of here?

She stood tall and in a matter-of-fact tone said, "Well, I'll tell Courtney you stopped by. I'm sure she'll call as soon as she's back." Marti tried to appear confident as she waited for him to turn around and go, but feared he saw right through her.

Nigel leered until she squirmed. He laughed and reached to brush a lock of hair off her face. Marti flinched and stepped back.

"Don't touch me," she warned, and took another step back. Her pulse raced.

"I'll show you a good time. You'll love it," he whispered in her ear. His stinking breath burned her neck.

Marti threw the contents of her lemonade in his face and turned to flee, praying he would take the warning and leave her alone. Before she moved two feet, he grabbed her by the shoulders. The dishes crashed to the tile floor and shattered. He shoved her against the wall and pinned her arms.

"You little bitch!" he spat. "You think you're better than me?"

Marti's eyes opened wide with fear. "No." She shook

her head. Her heart pounded.

Nigel tried to kiss her. She turned her head to the side. He struggled to reach her lips, but Marti fought him. "No!" Her hands were sweating, and her breath came quick and short.

Releasing her upper arms, he grabbed her chin and held it in place. He came at her with his big, sloppy mouth. She shoved his face away, but then he used his body to press her against the wall. He groped her breasts.

Marti clawed to no avail. He was an immovable wall. She kicked out with her legs and caught him in the groin, but not nearly hard enough. Still, he jerked away, and she ran for it.

"Not so fast." He yanked her back by the hair.

She struggled and screamed, but Nigel was too strong. He spun her around and slapped her hard across the face, but she still fought. He shoved her back against the wall. Her head hit the drywall so hard her teeth knocked together, stunning her.

Nigel took the advantage and pressed up against her, securing her wrists. Tears streamed down her face. She knew he was winning this battle. She lashed out with kicks, but he blocked her every time. Terror and helplessness overwhelmed her.

Marti turned her head away as he came at her again. He slurped at her neck. She couldn't stop his disgusting attack. He overpowered her.

Suddenly, Nigel's body was ripped away.

"What the hell are you doing?" her dad roared, and threw Nigel into the marble-topped coffee table.

Hugging her violated body, Marti slid down the wall. Tears poured from her eyes, and she gasped for breath.

Courtney shrieked. "Steven, what are you doing?"

Her dad ignored Courtney and went after Nigel, who'd risen to his feet.

"How dare you touch my daughter!" He slammed his fist into Nigel's face.

"Have you lost your mind? You're hurting him!" Courtney rushed over and grabbed his punching arm.

"Get the hell out of my way." Her dad shoved Courtney back and punched Nigel twice more in the gut. Nigel tried to escape the blows, but her dad grabbed him and, with alarming strength, hurled him against the wall. Courtney screamed as Nigel's body crumpled onto the glass-covered floor.

Marti watched in horror as her father attacked the now-bloody Nigel. Her teeth chattered, and she couldn't control the shudders that racked her as she huddled nearby.

He slammed Nigel's head against the floor. "Don't you ever touch my daughter again!" Marti barely recognized her father as rage transformed him into a dangerous maniac.

Courtney screamed. "You're going to kill him! Steven! Stop it!" She tried to pull him off, with no success.

Marti feared Courtney was right but remained frozen in terror. She gasped.

Her dad looked up, and Marti knew he saw the shock in her eyes as she witnessed his attack. He stopped and climbed off Nigel.

Courtney rushed to Nigel, crying.

"Get him out of here," her dad yelled. His hair hung in his face. "I don't ever want to see him in my house again!"

He stepped across the glass and food and knelt before Marti. Her teeth still chattered uncontrollably.

"Are you okay?" he asked gently. His blue eyes searched hers. His lip bled.

Marti nodded and wiped at her runny nose with her arm.

"I'm so sorry." He placed his hands on each side of her head and softly kissed her forehead.

She nodded again, her adrenaline trying to shift out of high gear. She watched Nigel scramble to his feet and stagger out, Courtney right behind. The door slammed. Marti released an anguished breath.

"Did he hurt you?" The concern in her dad's eyes revealed the love he couldn't say in words.

"No," she blubbered.

He leaned forward and held her in his arms. Her body shook as she tried not to sob. "It's okay, let it out." Her dad patted her back, and she cried like a baby. "I won't ever let him hurt you again. I promise."

After a minute, he released her, and she wiped her face. They looked at the mess on the floor.

"I take it you haven't had dinner yet."

Marti offered a tiny smile. "No."

"How about you go take a nice shower and I'll order pizza?"

"That sounds really good." Marti accepted his help to stand. "How come you're home so early?" If he hadn't come back when he did . . . She shuddered at the image of what might have happened.

"The premiere was a joke. Ten minutes on the red carpet posing for pictures and then they expected me to sit through a two-hour movie set in outer space. Not interested."

"Thank you," Marti said.

"I would do anything for you," he said. "Now go get cleaned up. I'll figure out what to do with this mess."

Marti rubbed the bump on her head and went upstairs. Her arms hurt from where Nigel grabbed her. She'd probably have bruises tomorrow. She still quivered from her terrible ordeal with Nigel, but her dad had saved her, and she could never be more grateful.

At the top of the steps, she turned around to see her dad staring at the evidence of Nigel's attack—the shattered dinner plate and food strewn across the floor. His body stiffened. He grabbed a ceramic lamp off a coffee table and, with an anguished roar, flung it to the floor.

After a long shower in which she tried to scrub away Nigel's touch, Marti went downstairs with her damp hair neatly combed, and wearing a pair of sweats and a baggy T-shirt. After the horrible incident, she needed some quiet time with her dad; pizza together sounded great. For the first time in her life, she felt thankful to have him.

The doorbell rang and as Marti turned to answer it, the door burst open with a couple of young women in short skirts and high heels. One carried a pizza box, the other, two bottles of wine. Marti's heart sank. She hung back as they rushed past to greet her dad, who reclined on the sofa, already half baked. He offered up the bong to his new guests.

Marti waited a minute to see if he remembered her or their plans. One girl uncorked the wine while the other turned up the stereo. Her dad tapped more pot into his pipe. He forgot about Marti just as easily as he forgot about the pizza. Marti crept back upstairs to her room, her appetite gone.

She should have known his words were too good to be true. Why did she let her guard down and believe he might actually be a decent guy for more than a few minutes at a time?

Marti climbed on her bed and hugged her legs tight. She looked out at the city lights below. So many people out there, but she was totally alone. A tear rolled down her face.

She swiped it away. She needed to be tougher. Right then, she decided to never cry because of any of these people ever again.

Still shaken from the night before, Marti lingered in the kitchen and watched while Rosa gave it a thorough cleaning. The shattered glass in the great room had disappeared. Rosa didn't ask any questions. She never did.

To pass the time, Marti snapped pictures of various kitchen items: the reflection in a spoon, the pattern in the granite countertop, the spots on a banana. The only good thing about last night was that Nigel would never be allowed in the mansion again. *Thank God.*

All she wanted now was to see Adam. One more day. An eternity.

As she focused her lens on a fern, she heard yelling. Marti glanced at Rosa. "What do you think that's about?"

"I don't want to know. It's best that way." Rosa sprayed disinfectant on the refrigerator handle and wiped.

Marti left the kitchen to investigate the latest drama. She peeked into the great room. Courtney stalked after her dad. He wore faded jeans, frayed on the bottom, and no shirt. His long hair hid most of his face. Marti stepped back, out of sight.

"How could you? I'm gone one night, and you cheat on me! You bastard!"

Her dad ignored Courtney's verbal attack. He rubbed

his stubble-covered face, yawned, then picked up his pipe.

"Steven! Look at me!" she shrieked. "I am your girl-friend. Don't think you can bring those sluts into my bed!"

"It's my bed," he said, searching for a lighter.

"Well, I picked out the bedding! And don't change the damn subject! First, you turn into a lunatic and attack Nigel for absolutely no reason."

Marti stifled a gasp and ducked out of sight.

The two women from the night before appeared from upstairs with mussed hair and shoes in hand. They looked used up and old, a lot like Marti's mom.

"You whores! Get the hell out!"

"Back off, bitch. What's your problem?" asked one.

Courtney approached the woman, waving a finger in her face. "You're my problem! Get your bad hair extensions out of here before I rip them from your head!"

Marti cowered in fear even though Courtney's anger was directed at the two women.

"We were invited!" the other one said.

"Well, I'm uninviting you!" Courtney picked up the decorative poker and swung it in their direction.

The women rushed for the door. "Bye, Steven. Call me!" called one. The other scurried out, not willing to take a chance with psycho Courtney.

"Bye, girls." Marti's dad waved. "Catch you next time."

Courtney spun around. "Catch them next time? You cheating piece of crap!" she snarled. "You even look at another woman again and I'll end you."

"Don't you think that's a bit melodramatic?" he asked, his voice disinterested. "You know what? I'm tired of your self-centered lies and manipulation. It's time for you to go." He located a lighter under some magazines, and his face brightened. He raised the lighter to the pipe.

"Excuse me! You're dismissing me? Are you out of your mind?"

Her dad lowered his pipe and fixed his eyes on Courtney. "You can play your games with me all you want. You can lie and cheat all you please. I couldn't give a shit. But your *boyfriend* assaulted my daughter. That's unforgivable. We're done." His steely, sharp eyes stared Courtney down.

Marti couldn't believe it. She still wasn't used to feeling like she really mattered to her dad, so every time he stuck up for her, it surprised her all over again.

"What? Nigel isn't my boyfriend!" Courtney had the gall to act outraged. "And Marti's lying. She's been trying to split you and me up since she got here!" Courtney's face turned red. She rushed to Steven's side and knelt, grabbing his arms. "Oh, baby, don't you see what's going on?" She pouted, and Marti hoped her dad wouldn't fall for her lies yet again.

He tossed the pipe and lighter on the table. "Listen, you can pretend that Nigel's your brother till the end of time, but I've known for months who he is and what you've been doing. Courtney, I didn't bother to deal with you before, but now I am. Get your freeloading ass off my property."

"No one treats me like that!" She stepped away and glowered down at him. "You can't throw me out. I live here. All my things are here."

"Sweetheart, I just did. And I paid for all your things, so that makes them mine." He leaned back with his hands behind his head and waited for her to leave.

"You won't get away with this."

"Watch me."

"If you think you can screw me over, think again!" She swung the fireplace poker and brought it down on a glass-top table.

He flinched at the flying glass but didn't move from his spot on the sofa. Marti ducked back behind the corner.

"Courtney, put the poker down," he said, his tone suggesting annoyance more than anything else.

"Not on your life. Two can play this game. You try to destroy my life, I'll destroy yours, too!" She swung again and took out a ceramic lamp.

Marti watched as her dad got up and approached Courtney. He appeared calm and unconcerned. He smoothly evaded her swing and hugged her from behind, pinning her arms. He swung her struggling body from side to side until she lost her grip on the weapon.

"You are no longer welcome here," he spoke evenly, carrying her to the front door as she kicked and screamed.

He set her down long enough to open the door.

"I wouldn't stay with you if you paid me!"

"Honey, I've been paying you for months. The free ride is over. Now go! And don't come back!" He pushed her out and slammed the door in her startled face, locking it.

Pounding started. "Let me in! No one treats me like this and gets away with it! You better watch your back, because I'm coming for you!" she screamed hysterically.

Her dad ambled back to the couch. "That felt good." He smiled.

Marti came around the corner. She couldn't believe he actually came to his senses and threw her out. "Aren't you worried she's gonna do something bad?"

"Nah, she'll be on to her next victim in a couple of days. Girls like her always are."

The pounding and screaming finally stopped.

"Hey, Rosa?" he hollered.

Rosa appeared. "Yes, Mr. Hunter?"

"I think we should celebrate Courtney's departure. Would you call the caterer? Make it something special. We're marking a new era!"

"Yes, right away. And then I'll clean up the glass." Rosa bustled off with a satisfied smile.

He glanced at the mess. "Oh yeah, good idea." He picked up the pipe again, and this time lit it.

And that was it? The woman tried to destroy his home with a fireplace poker and now he was planning a party?

She didn't understand him and probably never would, but she was happy to have Courtney and Nigel out of her life. She felt emotionally exhausted, but at least things were finally looking up.

Adam leaned back in the limo with his arm over his eyes. Press interviews were a pain. The same questions asked over and over. Do the brothers get along? How'd you break your arm? Can you still play? What's a typical day for a teen idol? "I can't wait to get this day over with and get out of New York."

Everyone became extra quiet. Adam moved his arm and glanced at his parents, brothers, and Wally, all crammed in the stretch limo.

His mother avoided his eyes as did Peter and his dad. Garrett stared and said nothing.

"What?" Adam asked, already annoyed, but received no answers. He knew he wouldn't like whatever it was they weren't telling him.

"You've got to tell him. You can't keep him in the dark all the time," Peter said to their parents.

His mom and dad looked at each other, both with an expression of guilt. "Well? What?" Adam demanded.

His father cleared his throat. "Adam, things don't always work out the way we plan."

"I knew it! You're not gonna let me go to LA!" When they said nothing, yet looked guilty as charged, he threw his hands in the air. "Unbelievable! You were never gonna let me go, were you? You just said yes to shut me up. That's bullshit!" He slammed his fist against the leather seat.

"Adam, enough!" his father barked. "You have no reason to talk like that!"

"You're saying that I can't go?" He wanted to hear them speak the words that would ruin his plans again.

His dad didn't answer. Instead, he said, "There's a high-profile fund-raiser tomorrow night, and it's an opportunity for some great press."

"And when were you going to tell me this?" he said through clenched teeth, fighting the urge to blow up at them.

"The reason we didn't tell you is because we knew you'd act like a big baby, and we didn't want to deal with it," Garrett said, looking down his nose at Adam.

Adam shot Garrett a death stare. "You are the biggest horse's ass. How does this awesome opportunity drop out of the air the day before? You wanna tell me that?"

"The other band had to cancel, so we got the gig. It's math, Adam; with the new album dropping, we need every bit of press we can get."

"I don't give a shit about the album. I need a life! You can't keep controlling my every minute."

"Adam!" his mom reprimanded again. He ignored her.

"Ah, actually, yeah, we can. You're underage." Garrett pulled at the cuffs of his shirt.

"Garrett, stop badgering your brother. Adam, you can't expect to take off whenever you please to see some new friend. You have obligations," his mother intervened.

"That you guys made without asking me! Again!" *Damn them!* When would he ever get a choice in his life?

"Honey, your friend will understand. These things happen," his mother said calmly, trying to soothe him. "What's his name again? Marty?"

Garrett interrupted. "Mom, he's not going to see a guy. He's going to chase after some girl he met at camp." Garrett shot Adam a childish "I got one up on you" look.

Adam drilled Garrett with a venomous glare.

"Oh, for crying out loud, you've got to be kidding me. All this over a girl?" his dad huffed.

His mother looked appalled. "Adam! Is that true?"

"It doesn't matter who I want to see. It's no one's business but mine!"

"If it's that important to you, we can probably find time in the next couple of weeks. If I can't make it, we'll have Roger fly out with you," his mother offered.

"I don't need a chaperone, and I'm not waiting a couple weeks just to have you book me into some other bullshit commitment!"

"What is so urgent that you need to go tomorrow?" she asked.

He knew his mom wanted him to be happy, but nothing would help at the rate they were going.

"He wants to go see if his new girlfriend is knocked up," Garrett blurted.

"What!" his mother exclaimed, and her face turned pale.

"You asshole!" Adam flew across the limo and tackled Garrett. He tried to get a punch in, but between the leather seats and the movement of the vehicle, Garrett evaded him.

Adam wrestled him to the floor and put a choke hold on him, ignoring the yelling of everyone else.

His father yanked him off Garrett, which was no easy task in the crowded limo.

"Let me go!" He fought his way out of his father's grip and slid back into a seat, ready to punch out a window. He avoided his mother's devastated expression.

"Adam, explain yourself," his dad demanded.

"You really think I'm going to talk about this right now, in front of everyone?" He wanted to kill Garrett.

"Damn right, you're going to discuss it right now! What is wrong with you?"

Adam crossed his arms and shook his head. *Absolutely not. We are not talking about this!*

"She's the daughter of Steven Hunter," Garrett provided, earning another glare from Adam.

"Garrett, shut up!" Peter warned.

His parents shared a confused glance. "As in the Graphite Angels?" his dad asked.

"That's the one," Garrett boasted.

"Oh, dear Lord," his mother breathed out.

"At least he lost his virginity to a rock princess!" Garrett grinned, so proud of himself. Adam fought the urge to knock out his front teeth. If he weren't trapped inside a moving limo with his parents watching, he'd do it!

"Garrett! That's enough!" their father bellowed.

Garrett smiled smugly, satisfied with himself.

"This is just great! Not only do you control my life, you think it's fine to discuss my personal issues like it's national news. When the rest of you want to plan my life, you go right ahead and do it. But as soon as I have something private, you think you can all butt right in. It's going to stop!"

His mother covered her mouth with her hand. His father looked fit to be tied, while Garrett relaxed.

"You may not want to discuss it, but I assure you, young man, you will," his father blustered.

The limo stopped at a red light.

"Well, guess what?" Adam said. "I'm not going to talk about it now or ever. And you know what else? I'm not in the mood to do interviews today." He shot them a calm, silent look.

His mother's forehead creased and his dad looked more pissed off, but that wasn't Adam's problem. Peter shook his head in frustration.

"You know what? Garrett likes to speak for me, so he can handle it. I am so sick and tired of all this bullshit! This family. This life. All of it!" He glanced around at everyone, and all he saw was their inability to understand him.

"I'm sick of doing what everyone else wants. I quit!"

The stoplight turned green. Adam opened the door and as the limo began to move, he hopped out into the slow-moving traffic.

"Adam!" his mother screamed.

"Let him shake it off. Give him some space," Peter said as Adam slammed the door.

The limo kept going, the driver unaware he'd lost a passenger. Adam dodged the traffic and crossed the street.

Shake it off? You bet. He planned to shake off New York and his overbearing family. He was so sick and tired of them running his life and making decisions without including him. Let them figure out how to handle this one! He needed to see Marti, and he refused to delay it any longer.

After a quick cab ride back to the Waldorf, he grabbed a duffel bag and stuffed in a couple of changes of clothes. Then he did something he knew he shouldn't. He went to the safe in the master bedroom and entered his parents' wedding anniversary date—the code they always used for hotel safes.

The safe clicked open, and he pulled out a small bag containing cash and credit cards in his dad's name. Adam took five hundred dollars and one of the charge cards. He closed the safe, hoping he'd make it out of the city before anyone noticed he was gone.

Once outside, he hailed a cab and hopped in. "How long to the airport?"

"Which one?" the cabbie asked, with a foreign accent.

"Which is closer?"

"This time of day, it shouldn't take much more than forty minutes to LaGuardia."

"Perfect. If you can make that thirty minutes, I've got another fifty bucks for you."

The cabbie grinned. "Hang on!" He swerved the car around a delivery truck and floored it through a yellow light.

Adam braced himself as the cabbie cruised through the maze of traffic. Adam called the airline for the next flight out. *Bingo!* If traffic didn't hold them up, he could be airborne and on his way to see Marti in a little over an hour.

He sat back, a huge grin across his face. There would be hell to pay later, but he didn't care. By tonight, he'd be with Marti. When they were together, life was so much better. They needed to find out once and for all if she was pregnant. Neither he nor Marti wanted that, but if she was, they'd deal with it together.

While he stood in the security line at the airport, his phone rang. The caller ID displayed his dad's number. He silenced the ringer. After removing his shoes and belt and walking through the X-ray machine, he saw two more missed calls from his mother and Garrett. He didn't plan on talking to any of them until he was safely on his way.

A text popped up from Peter: *where are you?*

Adam contemplated what to tell him. Certainly not the truth. His dad would stop him from boarding the plane in an instant.

Adam texted back: *central park. i needed to blow off some steam.*

don't be too mad at them. they can't help it. Peter texted.

of course they can. Adam texted back.

Peter knew only too well how overbearing their family could be. They had once sabotaged his relationship with his girlfriend, Libby. It took many months before Peter tracked her down and they were reunited. Adam refused to let it happen to him and Marti.

He pocketed the phone and hurried to the gate. Only a few people remained in line to board. *I just made it!* Onboard, he took his window seat in the middle section of the plane. He couldn't remember the last time he flew coach.

The flight attendant instructed him to turn off his phone, which he gladly did. A few minutes later, he was airborne. He'd never felt so free in his entire life. And Marti didn't know he was coming a day early. He couldn't wait to surprise her.

Without Courtney around, there was a wild, celebratory mood in the air. Marti had seen enough bad behavior since she arrived and decided to hole up in her room and avoid any drama.

A strong wind blew through her open bedroom patio door, along with raucous sounds from below. Marti glanced out as she slid the door closed. Even though her room was far from the pool area, she still heard the massive crowd. She pulled the curtains closed to shut out the crazies. "What do you think, Kahlúa?" The cat lounged on a pile of clothes Marti hadn't put away.

Tonight, Adam would perform on *SNL* with his brothers, and tomorrow he'd fly out to see her. Her heart fluttered with joy. She could hardly stand the wait. Life was turning a corner. Everything was going to be fine. She and Adam could talk about it and maybe she'd take the test when he was here.

She cranked up the Jamieson tunes and imagined she was singing along, live in concert. She picked out a bottle of purple nail polish and settled in to paint her toenails.

Once all her toes received two coats, she considered painting her fingernails as well. As the brush touched her first nail, she heard a loud beeping that sounded like a smoke alarm. She turned down the music and sure enough, a smoke alarm bleated loudly in the hall. Lord only knew what insanity was happening at the party. Someone probably lit the couch on fire with a cigarette.

As she rose from the bed to check the hall, her nose wrinkled at a strong, smoky odor. She opened the door.

A wall of black smoke poured down the hall toward her. Her jaw dropped and she watched, stupefied. Billowing clouds rolled and bounced to the ceiling.

The house was on fire!

21

Marti slammed the door and leaned against it.

Oh shit, oh shit, oh shit!

Her adrenaline kicked into panic mode.

The mansion was on fire! Really big, swallow-you-whole kind of fire!

Acrid smells began to fill the air. She pictured the growing wall of black death behind the door.

Her mind raced. She had to get out fast! If she went down the hall, she'd probably die of smoke inhalation, or she'd run straight into the fire.

She rushed to the patio door and yanked it open. She stepped onto the balcony, the wind whipped the hot air around. Flames licked from below.

"Oh God, it's really on fire! But where are all the people?" she said out loud. Not even a half hour ago, the place had been jammed with guests. Now, she saw no one below.

The howl of sirens filled the air, clashing with the constant bleat of the smoke alarm. *Thank God.* Fire trucks were on their way.

She rushed back inside, closing the patio door. Marti grabbed her laptop and shoved it in her backpack, then her picture of Grandma and her cameras. Her heart pounded as the crackling and roar of the fire grew louder.

Tendrils of smoke curled under her bedroom door. The fire was spreading fast, or at least the smoke was. Didn't most people die of smoke inhalation and not the actual fire? She needed to keep the smoke out if she wanted to survive until help arrived. She grabbed pillows off her bed and jammed them against the bottom of the door.

Then she realized the firefighters might come from the balcony. She stepped back out into the inferno and swallowed her panic. What if they didn't get to her in time? She'd have to jump. It was the only way down. She quickly did the calculations in her head. The first-floor ceiling was probably sixteen feet high, the second floor was the same. That put her at over thirty feet up. Way too high. Could she survive the fall?

The cement slab below was cluttered with wrought-iron furniture, trash bins, and lawn equipment. None of it looked like a safe landing.

If she jumped, she'd break a leg, maybe her neck. A small, ornamental tree grew to the side of the patio, but was too far for her to reach and way too small for Marti to land in without killing herself. She returned to her room, closing the door tightly behind her, and checked for other escape options.

Kahlúa mewed, unhappy with the smoky stench. The sight of her cat crying for help set Marti into action. She would not let Kahlúa die in this fire! This was one thing she could control.

She hoped.

Marti approached her beloved cat. Kahlúa tried to dart away but Marti scooped her up. "Gotcha!"

She pulled Kahlúa close. "This is going to be scary, but you're smart and stubborn and I know you can do it!"

Marti opened the balcony door and scorching air blasted her. The fire was spreading fast! New terror hit as she edged her way into the volcano-like winds.

"You'd better have nine lives, 'cause I think you're going to need them." She kissed Kahlúa on the head, then gently gripped her by the nape of the neck. With every ounce of nerve and strength Marti possessed, she tossed the cat as far as she could toward the distant tree.

Kahlúa screamed and disappeared into the thick, bushy foliage. Marti prayed she hadn't just killed her. Tears welled in her eyes. She would never be able to erase the mental snapshot of her cat flailing through the smoke-filled air.

A spray of sparks flew at her. She jumped back into the bedroom, yanked the door closed, and dropped to the floor.

A couple of sparks had made it inside and burned holes in the carpet. She grabbed a shoe and furiously rubbed them out, frightened by how quickly the carpet burned.

Marti's throat tightened. She swallowed back her panic. No one even knew she was up here. Rosa did, but Rosa wasn't here. Her dad would have no idea. For all he knew, she was at the party.

Smoke seeped into the room from air ducts like the hands of death. Oh God. She would die alone, and they might never find her. Adam would hear about her death on the news.

She wanted to call and hear his voice one last time. She picked up her phone, about to dial, but realized her only hope might be to call 911.

She entered the number and the first ring took forever. Outside, sparks flew by like the fireflies at summer camp.

"Hello, 911, Emergency Call Center. What is your emergency?"

"My house is on fire, and I'm trapped!" She tried to stay calm.

"What is your name, please?"

"Marti Hunter, and I'm at my dad's house." She recited the address. "I'm trapped, and I can't get out!"

"Marti, try to calm down. We have units on-site. Where in the house are you?" the woman said in a slow, patient voice.

"I'm on the third floor at the far end of the south wing. Please have someone help me." Marti spit the words out as fast as she could.

"I'm alerting them now. Exactly what room are you in?"

Marti gave her all the details of her location and the entrances. The smell of the burning mansion began to overpower her. Outside, flames reached the balcony.

"The fire's at the balcony door!" she cried.

"Marti, I need you to stay low to the ground and try to calm down. Help is on the way. They will find you, but you need to keep your wits," the dispatcher continued in a soothing voice.

Marti wanted to scream. "I am. I will." She fixated on the flames outside her patio door dancing higher and higher. She gripped the phone with sweaty hands, not sure if it was nerves or the intense heat. She coughed as the air thickened and dropped the phone. As she fumbled to pick it up, she accidentally ended the call. Marti rested her head on her hands and thought of Adam and how badly she wanted to see him again. If the firefighters couldn't get to her in time, she might not. Ever.

The air in the room darkened. Marti looked up. Smoke now poured through the air vents like a waterfall.

"Oh no!" She quickly pressed Adam's number and waited for what felt like an eternity as his phone rang and rang. Her heart sank. He wasn't going to pick up. His voice mail answered and she thought about hanging up, but then decided not to.

At the sound of the beep, she cleared her throat and tried to sound normal.

The wheels touched down at LAX. Adam wanted to whoop with excitement. Instead, he drummed his fingers on the armrest until he could finally deplane. He turned on his phone and saw he had twelve messages.

No big surprise. By now his family would be livid. He had missed the *SNL* performance. Funny thing, he didn't even care. He meant it when he said he quit the band. He didn't need their overbearing manipulation anymore. He could do whatever he wanted.

Walking through the terminal with a cap pulled low on his brow, he fought to hide his grin. Soon, he'd be with Marti. He couldn't wait to see the look on her face when he showed up at her door.

He passed a sports bar and noticed people crowded around the TVs. He paused for a second to see the news network reporting on a major fire in the Hollywood Hills. He began to walk away when he noticed the message feed at the bottom of the screen. *Live Footage: Steven Hunter's Hollywood Hills Mansion in Flames.*

Adam nearly dropped his bag. He pushed closer. A newscaster reported: "Steven Hunter, lead guitarist for the legendary rock band Graphite Angels, was hosting a party when flames broke out. We still don't know if all attendees made it out safely, but will bring you an update as soon as we have it. The cause of the fire is yet unknown, but high winds have caused the fire to spread quickly, making it more difficult to contain."

Marti!

He pushed out of the crowd and called her as he rushed for the airport exit.

"Pick up, pick up, pick up," he muttered.

The phone rang and rang until finally he heard her voice, raw and tense!

"Hello?"

"Marti! Oh my God, I'm so glad to hear your voice. I just saw the news. Is that your house? Are you okay?"

"Oh, Adam, I'm so sorry."

He heard her sniff back tears. Dread washed over him. "Why are you sorry, what's wrong?"

"I wanted to see you so badly."

He heard her sniffle and cough. He stopped dead in his tracks. "Marti, where are you? Are you safe?"

"I'm trapped in my room. I can't get out! And the smoke is getting really bad." She coughed again.

His blood ran cold. "Marti, I'm here! I'm in LA. I'm coming right now." He started to run.

"Really? You came early."

He pictured the smile on her tear-streaked face and

wanted to cry. "Tell me, where in your room are you?" He ran through the baggage claim area and out the doors, looking frantically for a cab. He spotted the taxi stand and rushed to a random cab.

"I'm on the floor, near my bed."

"Are you okay? Are you hurt?" His pulse raced. He needed to reach her and she was still so far away.

"I'm okay. It's getting hard to breathe, and it's really hot. It makes the heat in the sauna at camp seem like air-conditioning."

He detected the panic just under the surface of her voice, as if she was fighting to stay calm.

"Marti, can you get to a bathroom?" He focused on how to keep her safe.

"Yeah," Marti said.

"Do it!"

The cabbie turned to him, annoyed. "Sorry, kid, you've got to wait in line like everyone else. I can't take you till I get to the head of the line."

Adam pulled the phone away from his mouth. "This is a huge emergency. I can't wait in line. Please take me!" He pulled a bunch of bills out of his wallet and tossed them on the seat.

The surly man nodded. "Let's go."

He told the driver the address. "Marti?"

"I'm here. I'm in the bathroom."

"Close the door! Now fill the bathtub with water."

Adam ignored the cabbie's curious look in the rearview mirror. He racked his brain trying to think of things she could do that would help her.

"Get a towel wet and block the bottom of the door." The image of the burning mansion he'd seen on TV kept filling his mind. Flames engulfed half the building.

Marti coughed some more. "Okay. Done."

"Now get in the bathtub. You'll be safer. And cover your mouth with something so it's easier to breathe."

"You want me to take my clothes off, too?" She laughed and then started to hack.

He smiled. "You're such a smart-ass." For a moment, he forgot the danger surrounding Marti. Her coughing brought reality crashing back. He could tell it was getting harder for her to speak.

"Adam, I'm gonna hang up now," she wheezed.

"No! Don't. I'm on my way, and I want you to stay on the phone with me until I get there." He feared that if he let her hang up, he'd lose her forever.

"Adam." She coughed harder. "I'm scared."

She sounded small and distant. "I know. I'm scared, too, but it's going to be all right. I know it is." He prayed it would be. The cabbie glanced in the rearview mirror and then averted his eyes when Adam caught him.

"I'm having trouble getting air." She coughed uncontrollably. He pictured her struggling to find clean air. "After I hang up, call 911. Tell them I'm in the bathroom. They know where the bedroom is, but not that I'm in the tub."

Her voice sounded resigned, and he knew she was trying to say good-bye. He wouldn't let her.

"I will." His voice broke. She tried to say something, but was racked with more coughing. He gripped the phone like a lifeline, like if he only held on tight enough, she'd be okay. He waited for her to catch her breath, but all he heard was uncontrollable coughing.

The phone went dead.

"Marti! Marti!" He yelled into the phone, but she was gone. He dialed her back, but she didn't pick up. His hand dropped to his side. He stared out the window, his world falling to pieces.

Marti's phone dropped over the edge of the tub as she choked out cough after cough. The air, so hot, burned her lungs. She wrung out a washcloth and held it over her face. That helped. She concentrated all her energy on trying to breathe.

The house crackled and roared as fire ate through it. Outside the bathroom window, flames grew higher and higher, threatening to close in. Marti clung to the sides of the tub, trying to blink through the thickening air. The fumes made her nauseous, and her throat burned.

She didn't want to die. She was too young. The water pressure slowed, but still ran. Maybe the water in the tub would save her. Each breath scorched her throat raw. She hacked, trying to get air, but each breath provided less oxygen. She clawed at the washcloth, desperate to breathe through it. Too much soot coated her throat. She dipped underwater where the cool liquid soothed her body but still starved her of air. She burst up from the water gasping, the cloth still over her mouth.

She couldn't breathe.

Trapped in the cab, Adam was going insane. He kept bouncing his leg up and down and telling himself Marti would be okay. She had to be. He wouldn't accept anything less.

"Please hurry," he said again to the driver.

"Doing the best I can," he replied, and Adam had to agree; the man drove like a maniac.

He scanned his phone, hoping Marti would call back and say this was all a big misunderstanding and that she was fine and relaxing by a pool somewhere. He glanced through all the missed calls from his family and zeroed in on Marti's. She'd left him a message! From what he could tell, she had called right before he landed. He played the message.

"Hi, Adam, I just was calling to say hi, but I guess you're busy."

He heard the strain in her voice. Damn it! Why had he missed her call?

"You know, in case I don't see you tomorrow, I wanted

to let you know how much I love you. I never said it to you, but I always wanted to. You are the best thing that's ever happened to me. I wish we could spend more time together."

He could hear the fear in her voice as she struggled to get the words out. She coughed. "I better get going, but know that I love you, and thank you for . . . for everything." She muffled a cry. "Bye."

The call ended. She had called to say good-bye. Adam tried to force down his emotions. He ran a hand through his hair. He knew her so well. Of course she wouldn't mention the fire or the danger.

He clicked off his phone and wanted to scream. But instead, he silently sent her strength. *Marti, I'm trying to get there. Be brave. Hang on.*

The highway curved, and the cab took an exit onto a side road. In the distance, flames lit the night sky.

"Holy shit, get a look at that fire!" the cabbie said.

For the first time in his life, Adam felt a cold, stark fear. His throat went dry. "My girlfriend's trapped in that fire," he said in a whisper.

The cabbie glanced in the rearview mirror. His eyes said what Adam refused to believe.

She'd never make it out alive.

22

A noise sounded over the roaring fire. Marti muffled her chokes to listen, sharpening her senses. She heard it again and sat up. She tried to call out, "I'm here!" but choked on the words.

"This is the Fire Department. Is anyone here?" They sounded loud and close. She called out again and her throat felt like the Sahara Desert.

A bright light appeared, moving low on the floor from the direction of the doorway. "This is the Fire Department. Is anyone here?"

"Yes!" She waved her arm while climbing over the side of the tub. The light caught her movement and zeroed in. She flopped onto the floor like a dead fish. The light came closer until she could see the looming figure of a fireman leaning over her.

Thank God!

He looked like some sort of alien with his huge oxygen mask. "Is there anyone else here?" he asked, the sound somehow amplified through his mask.

Marti shook her head. "No."

"Are you able to walk?"

"Yes," she choked out with a nod.

"Take my hand." He held out a large, gloved hand. She placed her hand in his and he pulled her to her feet, helping her keep her balance. "We're going to move as fast as we can. Are you ready?"

Marti nodded to the masked hero as she struggled for air. They took a few steps, with him leading her by the hand. She doubled over, coughing from the thicker smoke.

Before she realized what was happening, he scooped her into his arms and moved quickly through her room and into the hall. She clung to him with her head tucked into his chest. She closed her eyes to block out the gritty soot and toxic fumes. The strong arms held her firm as he rushed down the hallway to the stairs. She prayed he could get her out before she suffocated. She opened her eyes long enough to see they were coming down the stairs into the great room. The other side of the room was lit by vicious flames. The heat was so intense she feared being baked alive, but she was able to suck in a scorching breath.

Marti held on with all her might, holding back her coughs as best she could. Suddenly, cool air hit her skin. She opened her eyes and found herself outside. The pristine circular drive looked like a war zone of fire trucks and rescue equipment. An army of firefighters roamed the grounds. The mansion burned like the fires of Hell.

When they were a safe distance away, her rescuer gently set her feet on the grass and held her steady. Marti couldn't suck in the fresh air fast enough, but each breath still caused her to choke and gag. She hacked and fell to her knees and vomited until her stomach had nothing left.

A moment later, soothing voices offered assistance. Her fireman helped her to her feet. "I'm going to turn you over to the EMTs. They'll take good care of you."

He'd taken his mask off and looked like a normal man, with a sooty, sweat-streaked face.

"Thank you," she croaked, barely able to make a sound.

"You're welcome," he said with a smile, and Marti wanted to weep with gratitude.

The EMTs led her to an ambulance. Before she even sat on the back fender, they placed an oxygen mask over her mouth and nose. She felt immediate relief through the burned rawness of her nose and throat.

A blood pressure cuff appeared on her arm and a brown-haired, kind-eyed EMT shone a penlight in each of her eyes.

I am alive. I made it! She saw everything but felt slow to react. The EMT asked her questions and she didn't know if she answered or not. In the distance, crowds of people watched the spectacle of the fire. Some of them were probably from the party.

She thought of her dad and experienced a new nightmare. "My dad!" She pulled off the oxygen mask.

"He's fine. He's safe. You can see him later." They placed the oxygen mask back on.

Marti sighed in relief and concentrated on dragging clean air into her lungs.

"This is as close as I can get," the cabbie said over his shoulder. His expression said that only bad news lay ahead.

"Thanks." Adam handed over the fare.

"Good luck, kid. I hope your friend is okay."

Adam nodded stiffly. He only had thoughts for Marti. Was she alive? Did they find her yet? Did they get her out in time?

He ran through the throngs of onlookers, panic growing with each step. His heart pounded out of his chest. The fire lit up the night sky like a fireworks finale. Noisy news helicopters flew overhead. He passed numerous reporters and camera crews filming live, and photographers snapping pictures.

A few street barricades held the public back. He pushed through the crowd only to have a police officer stop him. "You need to stay back."

Adam halted, out of his mind, ready to run into the burning building if he had to. "You don't understand. My girlfriend is in there. . . ."

"Okay, calm down. Who's your girlfriend?"

"Marti Hunter. She's trapped in a third-floor bathroom."

"I'll relay that information to the Fire Department. Just hang on."

The cop was wasting Adam's time. So he desperately looked for a way around the barricade. The officer turned to hear a radio message. Adam took advantage of the distraction. He ran as fast as he could and disappeared into the melee.

As he got closer, blasting heat radiated from the firestorm. He didn't know where to look or who to ask, so he ran up to the first fireman he saw. "Did they get the girl out?"

"I'm not sure, but hang on and I'll see if I can find out."

Adam felt like he was about to lose his mind while the fireman radioed in the question. A lot of static came back, but no answer. Adam couldn't wait around another second. Frantic and determined for answers, he took off in search of Marti.

He spotted two ambulances, one with a couple of middle-aged guys near it. Two EMTs stood next to the second ambulance, helping a person covered in soot. The person's face was smudged and dirty, with bright white eyes staring out. It must have been pure hell in that house. Adam's heart tightened as he thought of Marti fighting for her life.

The person he'd been looking at tore off the oxygen

mask and yelled something, but Adam couldn't hear it. He moved on, but the person by the ambulance waved, pushed off the medical personnel, and ran toward him. He couldn't imagine a fan recognizing him at a time like this, especially someone who'd just been in a fire.

He froze for a second.

Marti?

As the person came closer, he realized it was a girl. She called out again.

"Adam!" Her voice sounded rough, like sandpaper.

"Marti!" He couldn't believe it. He sprinted across the lawn to reach her. The world stopped turning as he took in her smoke-ravaged body. Every inch of her was black and sooty. Her hair and clothes were wet. The moment he reached her, he pulled her into his arms and held her tightly. He vowed to never let her go.

"Adam!" she cried with a cough.

He touched her hair and her back, assuring himself she'd really made it. He held her trembling body, silently cursing his cast for getting in the way. "I was afraid I'd lost you." She molded herself to him and cried.

He held her face and looked into her beautiful eyes. How had he not recognized her? "You scared me so bad!"

"I can't believe you're here." She smiled, revealing soot-covered teeth. She coughed again.

He held her as she doubled over. She continued to hack. "Are you okay?"

"I'm fine," she wheezed.

"Come on. Let's get you back to the ambulance and let them take care of you." He knew she'd never go on her own; she was that stubborn.

Adam rode along when they transferred Marti to the hospital. As the ambulance drove away, the mansion crashed in on itself, the firefighters losing the battle. Adam had been scared when he had fallen onto the rocks at camp. He had worried about his injury and that he'd let people down. But now, as they left the destruction, he realized how close he'd come to experiencing true despair, losing Marti.

He still couldn't believe he had arrived when he did. What if he would have waited until tomorrow? Was there some mystical force that had made him ditch his family in New York and hop a plane? He didn't know. But he thanked the heavens he had.

They delivered Marti to the ER at Cedars-Sinai Medical Center. She looked like a refugee from a war-torn country. The staff buzzed with efficiency, asking her questions and setting up the room.

A nurse entered data in a computer. "What are your parents' names and numbers? We need to contact them right away."

Marti glanced at Adam with uncertainty and removed the oxygen mask. "My mom lives in Wisconsin, but no one knows where she is. My dad is Steven Hunter. He was in the house, but I don't know where he is now."

She coughed, but not as bad as before.

The nurse glanced at Marti with sympathetic eyes. "I'll see what I can do to find out where he is. And who is this?" She referred to Adam.

"This is my boyfriend."

Adam could swear Marti blushed behind her soot-smeared face. "Adam Jamieson."

The nurse smiled. "You sure are connected to some famous musicians."

Marti grinned.

"We're going to take you for some X-rays. Perhaps Adam should leave the room while I ask you some personal questions."

"No, it's okay."

"We're going to do a chest X-ray. Is there any chance you're pregnant?" The nurse spoke softly as if she didn't want to embarrass her.

Marti swallowed and locked eyes with him. He waited to see how she'd respond. She looked down and twisted the blanket. "I don't know. Maybe."

The nurse glanced up, surprised. "I see. All right, why don't you sit tight, and I'll be back in a minute."

The second the nurse left, Adam joined Marti and took her hand. "I guess we're gonna find out once and for all." His chest tightened. He prayed she wouldn't be pregnant. His life would be changed forever if she was, and he knew he wasn't ready for a baby.

"I'm afraid," she murmured, and he wished he could protect her from more devastating news. She didn't need anything else in her life to go wrong.

"I know. Me too."

The nurse returned along with a woman who carried a caddy full of tubes and bottles. "I'm going to draw some blood panels," the lab technician said.

Adam squeezed Marti's hand and stepped away while the woman drew several tubes of blood.

"There you go. All done." She labeled the last tube and removed her latex gloves.

"Marti, let's get you cleaned up and into something more comfortable while we're waiting for your lab results. Adam, we have waiting areas around the corner. Actually, you should go to room 206. It's a private waiting area, where you won't be disturbed."

He understood. Cedars-Sinai was known as the celebrity hospital, and the staff knew how to handle high-profile patients better than anyone. Adam wasn't a patient, but he didn't need to deal with strangers knowing he was there.

"Okay, I'll be nearby. Come get me when you're ready." He gave Marti's hand another squeeze as she pulled the oxygen mask back over her face and leaned her head against the pillow, defeat in her eyes.

The nurse ushered him to the private waiting room, which looked like someone's living room with lots of comfortable couches, a flat-screen TV, DVDs, and a counter with coffee as well as a fridge packed with snacks. He thought about all that had happened, how he quit the band and left his family high and dry, and how close he came to losing Marti. He didn't know what happened to her dad yet, but it sounded like he was accounted for.

The mansion was destroyed, so neither Marti nor her dad had a home anymore. Where would Marti go? How would she live? Her dad was supposed to go on tour in a couple of months. Where would that leave Marti?

He pulled out his phone and turned it on. He'd been avoiding his family. He could only deal with one crisis at a time. He brought up his contacts and pressed CALL. Even though it was the middle of the night in New York, the phone only rang twice before it was answered.

"Adam, where are you?"

"Mom, I'm at Cedars-Sinai. I really need your help."

23

Marti adjusted the blanket across her lap. She felt half human again after washing off the stinky filth. The nurse had to help her put on a hospital gown before she fell into bed.

The curtain opened, and Adam peeked in. "Hi!" He rewarded her with his adorable smile that always made her feel giddy.

"You look great." He took her dewy hand and kissed it.

"I washed my hair three times to get it clean." She didn't mention that she also needed to sit on a shower chair because she had coughed so much she felt dizzy.

He lifted a lock of her hair and inhaled. "I think it still has a hint of eau de campfire."

A doctor pulled back the curtain and entered. "The smell is going to last for a while. You inhaled enough smoke that it'll take some time to work out of your system."

Adam released her hand.

The doctor focused on Marti. "Would you like your friend to step out while we discuss your test results?"

Marti glanced quickly at Adam. "No, he should hear them, too." She felt her face heat in shame.

"Very well. Your pregnancy test came back negative. You are not pregnant."

"Thank God! That is so great." She fought the urge to leap out of bed and cheer. Adam let out a sigh.

"Yes, it is," the doctor agreed. "With that said, I recommend you see your regular physician about birth control. Now, let's get you in for a chest X-ray to make sure your lungs are clear. You appear to be doing well, all things considered. I'm going to keep you on an IV drip overnight, and we'll be monitoring your oxygen levels. I'll check on you again in the morning, and we'll take it from there."

"Thank you so much." Marti couldn't have heard better news. She felt lighter than air with this huge weight off her shoulders. The doctor left and she grinned at Adam. Everything would be okay. They would be okay.

"You're not pregnant," he whispered. His face lit up like a Christmas tree. He pulled her into his arms. "I love you so much."

"I love you, too," she whispered in his ear. They were getting a fresh start. Her stupid decisions hadn't ruined her life. She reached for his face. Everything about him was perfect. He leaned back, and she touched his hair. "It's growing. It's starting to curl."

"You're funny." He shook his head. The amber-colored flecks in his eyes seemed to glow as he smiled at her.

"Your hair is so cute. I can't wait until it's longer and I can curl my fingers around it." She ran her hands over the soft, brown strands.

They heard a commotion outside her room.

"I know she's here, so either you tell me where, or I'll barge into every room!"

"I think that's my dad!" She looked at Adam in surprise. "Dad?" She sat up and called out, even though it hurt her throat.

"Martini! Where are you, baby?" he hollered back.

Marti grinned at Adam. "I'm in here!" She started to get out of bed.

"Whoa! Slow down there. You're hooked up to an IV." Adam stopped her before she took off, but she perched with her legs dangling over the side.

The curtain swooshed open and there stood her dad in a hospital gown, bandages on his legs and a cast on his left arm. He took one look at Marti and started to cry.

"Mr. Hunter, you need to get in the wheelchair. You shouldn't be walking," a flustered nurse, with a wheelchair beside her, chided.

Adam retreated to a corner of the room to allow space for her dad.

"Dad, don't cry." Marti had never seen him so emotional.

His tears proved he truly cared.

He hobbled forward. "Are you okay? Are you hurt?" He cupped her face between his hands. She noticed areas of his trademark hair were singed off.

"I inhaled a lot of smoke, but I'm fine."

"Thank God." He pulled her into a hug. "I was so scared. I couldn't find you. I thought something terrible had happened. I'm so sorry. This is all my fault."

She hugged him with all her might. He was far from perfect, but he wasn't a bad person. He was practically the only family she had left.

"It's okay, Dad. I'm fine. I'm so glad you're okay. They said you were safe, but I wasn't sure." Her eyes welled up, and she brushed away a tear.

"Mr. Hunter, I insist you sit down. You are on strong narcotics, and it's not safe for you to be up and about."

"Fine. But we're not leaving until I say so." He relented and sat, sighing as they carefully placed his feet on the foot pads.

"What happened?" Marti asked, looking at the thick bandages wrapped around each leg.

"I couldn't find you. No one could. I didn't know where you were, and I didn't trust anyone else to find you, so I went to look myself. I thought you might be trapped in the music room. It turns out that's where the fire started and I ran into some trouble." He held out the cast on his arm as evidence.

"Are you okay?" She noticed scratches on his face and bruises on his other arm.

"Oh yeah, just some minor burns. You can't keep a Hunter down." He winked. "Plus, they've got me on some awesome drugs." He grabbed the armrests and swayed in the wheelchair for effect. The nurse rolled her eyes.

He noticed Adam for the first time. Adam had stepped back and quietly observed their reunion.

"Who's this? I didn't know you had any friends in LA yet." He cocked his head and gave Adam the once-over.

Marti smiled at Adam. "Dad, this is my boyfriend. . . ."

Adam held out his hand. "Adam Jamieson, sir. Nice to meet you."

The two shook hands. "So, you're dating my daughter?" he asked in a stern, fatherly way, which embarrassed her but also made her feel warm and safe. He didn't indicate if he recognized Adam's famous name or not.

"Yes, sir," Adam said, and Marti wanted to kiss his face all over for how politely he was treating her injured father.

"Hmm." Her father contemplated Adam for a minute. "Correct me if I'm wrong, but it must be difficult to play guitar with a cast on your left arm." His eyes twinkled.

Adam grinned from ear to ear. "Yes, sir, it is. Unless you have your arm recast in a specific position."

Her dad nodded. "You're a very talented kid. I like your stuff."

"Thank you, sir. That means a lot coming from you. You're the best."

Her dad smiled. "I like you. Not sure how I feel about my daughter dating a musician, but you seem like a good kid. Let me warn you. Don't you dare do anything to hurt my girl."

"No, sir, I won't." Adam looked at Marti with love in his eyes.

"And call me Steven. 'Sir' makes me sound old, like I should be wearing a business suit and not a hospital gown that shows off all my assets." He laughed at his joke.

"Thank you. I will. Steven," Adam added, his eyes dancing with excitement. Marti couldn't get over seeing her boyfriend and her dad together, both talented guitarists from different generations. She beamed.

Marti's nurse returned. "My, my, we have quite the party going on. Marti, we have a room for you now."

"Mr. Hunter, it's time we get you back to your room as well," his nurse said, seemingly tired of his antics.

"You ladies just don't know how to have a good time. But I could show you one, if you're interested," her dad joked, and the nurses shook their heads and tried to hide their laughter. "Marti, I'll see you tomorrow," he said.

"Good night, Dad." She waved as his nurse wheeled him away. He wasn't gone two seconds and they heard him singing.

"He's a riot!" Adam laughed.

"He's also stoned out of his mind on painkillers." Even so, her world had become so much better now that she knew he was okay.

Marti's nurse released the wheel locks on her bed. "Are you ready to go?"

"Yes, but can Adam come, too?"

Adam offered the nurse his best "pleading teenager" look.

The nurse waffled. "It's awfully late. Perhaps he should get home," she suggested.

"He doesn't live here, and he doesn't have any place to stay. We could go ask my dad if you want," Marti offered with a devious grin. She figured the hospital staff would rather not deal with her dad any more tonight.

"No. I think we should let your father rest. I guess I don't see it as a problem. Your father has you in the VIP wing. I think you'll find plenty of space there for both of you and lots of supervision with nurses monitoring you all night."

"Thank you," Marti said as the nurse rolled her away. She couldn't imagine not having Adam by her side right now.

The next morning, Marti woke, curled up beside Adam. He started out sleeping on the sofa, but she insisted he crawl in with her. She needed to feel the security of his presence. After one scolding by a shift nurse, who thought two teenagers shouldn't snuggle in a hospital bed, they were left alone. She slept great with him next to her.

"Good morning," he said sleepily.

"Good morning." She smiled into his delicious brown eyes.

He caressed her arm. "How do you feel?"

She felt a lot better. "Good."

"I can't believe how close I came to losing you." He pulled the blanket up a little higher and kissed her.

The nursing shift changed, and the doctor came through on rounds, rousing Adam from her side. Marti's lungs were clearing, and her oxygen levels had returned to a normal range. The doctor gave her a thumbs-up. She was free to leave whenever arrangements were made.

Instead of feeling relief and happiness, Marti creased her brow and frowned.

"What's the matter? You look so sad." Adam sat on the bed after the doctor left.

She studied the pattern on the blanket, contemplating her words, and finally looked up. "I don't have anywhere to go," she whispered as tears watered her eyes.

Adam held her hand, which helped anchor her emotions. "I don't even have clothes to wear when I leave the hospital." She looked around the room. "I can't even say I have the clothes on my back."

He rubbed her hand with his thumb. "We'll get you new stuff. We'll figure out what to do next. It'll take time."

His eyes were so wide and loving and willing to do anything for her.

"I know it will, but that doesn't help the fact that I'm homeless, penniless, and practically an orphan. My camera equipment is gone, and so is my laptop with every picture I ever took, my grandma's wedding brooch, and the picture of me and Grandma."

She swiped away a tear. The more Marti thought about it, the more she realized how much she had lost. They were only things, but when she suddenly didn't have them, it became a big deal.

Adam rubbed her leg. It helped a little, but not enough.

"And I lost Kahlúa!" she cried, and covered her face.

"I know. I'm sorry." He wrapped her in his arms.

She buried her face in his chest. "I didn't think I'd get out, and I didn't want her to die, too, so I threw her toward a tree. I don't know if she lived or died, and if she did live, I'll never find her again." Her tears soaked his T-shirt. "I don't have anybody left."

"You have me. I know I'm not the same as your cat, but if you scratch behind my ears, I'll try to purr." He tipped her face up and kissed her sweetly on the mouth. She loved the familiar feel of his lips on hers. She always felt safe with Adam, and he helped her relax and not feel quite as bad.

She sighed against his dampened shirt. He tucked her head under his chin. "What am I going to do? I mean, really? Where am I going to stay tonight?"

"You'll stay with me. I don't know where yet, but I'm sure there's a hotel I can get us into."

She smiled at the implication of being alone with Adam in a hotel room. "Okay, that's fine, but what about when you leave? I can't go back to Wisconsin. I should be starting school next week, but I no longer have a home. I don't even have a school anymore. Do I not go? Do I drop out?"

He leaned back against her pillow. "No, you don't drop out! Slow down. You don't need to have answers to everything all at once. One thing at a time."

"Easy for you to say." She rested her head on his shoulder. Safe for the moment, but what hell storm would start next?

"I know what will help."

"What?" She didn't have the energy to feign curiosity.

"Let's go see your dad. If nothing else, he's good for a few laughs." Adam squeezed her shoulder and kissed her temple.

She couldn't hold back the reluctant smile. Her dad was a character, never a dull moment with that man.

"Okay."

"Martini! Baby, come on in! Hey, Adam, what's up!" her dad welcomed them.

"Hi, Steven, you're looking good today," Adam said.

"Couldn't be happier. I'm alive, Martini's alive, what else could a person want?"

Adam grinned at Marti with a sideways glance.

"Hi, Dad. How are you feeling?" She approached his bed. His legs were wrapped in fresh gauze. She noticed the TV tuned to a news channel.

"I'm high as a kite!"

Marti laughed and pulled a chair up next to his bed. "I'm glad you're so happy."

A soft knock sounded on the door.

"It's been a revolving door through here all morning. Come in," her dad called.

An attractive, middle-aged woman with stylish shoulder-length brown hair entered. She wore beige slacks, a crisp blazer, and a blouse, along with a friendly smile. A Coach bag hung from her shoulder.

"Mom!" Adam looked surprised as his mother entered. "Wow, I didn't expect to see you until tonight." He went to greet her. "How'd you know we'd be in here?"

"Never underestimate the power of a mother." She hugged him tight.

His mother! He never mentioned she was coming.

"Is anyone else with you?" Adam asked, checking the door.

"Just me. Were you hoping for more?" His mother raised an eyebrow, and a smile curled at the edge of her mouth, reminding Marti of Adam's sly smiles.

"God, no!" He turned to Marti. "Marti, I'd like you to meet my mom. Mom, this is Marti."

Marti stood and smoothed down her robe and hospital-issued pajamas. "Hello, Mrs. Jamieson." Suddenly shy, she hoped his mom didn't hate her because Adam had come to LA to see her.

"Hello, Marti. I heard about the terrible fire. I'm so sorry that happened to you. How are you feeling?"

"I'm much better, thank you. This is my dad, Steven."

Adam grinned, obviously enjoying the sight of their parents meeting.

His mother approached the bed with a hand out.

"Nice to meet you, Steven. I'm Karen Jamieson. I wish we were meeting under better circumstances. My sons are big fans of your music."

Her dad shook Mrs. Jamieson's hand. Marti prayed he wouldn't say something inappropriate.

"My pleasure. I met Adam last night. He seems like a nice kid." He winked at Marti, having clearly read her mind about behaving.

"Adam called last night to tell me about the devastating fire. I'm so thankful everyone got out. I hope you're not seriously injured?"

"No, just some burns and a broken arm. They want me to hang around for a few days, and I've got nowhere else to go. So why not?"

An image of the mansion on fire popped onto the TV

screen. "Dad, I think that's the fire!" Marti pointed to the TV.

"I've been waiting for this." He turned the volume up. Adam and his mom took a seat on the couch and they all watched, riveted, as video of the fire played.

"Holy mother of God! Look at that place burn! It's like the fires of Hell struck from the sky!" her dad said, fascinated, as the flames shot a hundred feet into the air and engulfed his home.

Marti stared in horror as the roof collapsed. She replayed the events of the fire in her head, experiencing the fear all over again. She shook it off and looked away.

The newswoman spoke live before the charred ruins. "While the cause of the fire has not yet been confirmed, the Los Angeles Fire Department suspects arson. Officials are questioning Courtney Colburn, former girlfriend of Steven Hunter."

"Yes!" Steven shouted, waving a fist in the air.

"Courtney started the fire?" Marti asked.

"Sure did, the little bitch." He glanced at Adam's mom. "Oops, sorry about that. A couple people spotted her sneaking around. The investigators came earlier, asking questions. They're gonna nail her a . . . to the wall. She'll do jail time. Couldn't happen to a nicer person."

"I can't believe it." Marti let the reality sink in that Courtney knowingly set fire to a house filled with people. How could anyone be so evil? Courtney left them with nothing. She turned her attention back to her dad. "What happens now? I mean, everything is gone. All your guitars and awards."

He pushed a hand through his hair. "I'm not gonna lie, it pisses me off, but at the end of the day, everyone got out safe." He looked at Marti. "I'd happily trade all my worldly possessions for knowing my kid is okay." He took her hand and squeezed it.

Marti smiled, so thankful to have her dad. "So what do we do?" The overwhelming feeling of loss and no direction returned. She longed for answers and to know she had a place where she fit.

"I don't know. My manager is finally gonna earn his pay. He'll figure out the insurance processing, and he's gonna set me up in a bungalow at the Beverly Hills Hotel. It'll be nice to have a change of venue for a while. The band will be rehearsing for the tour. I don't think this has to set us back too much. That'll take up most of my time. I don't need a house for that."

Marti hadn't heard her name mentioned once. Was she supposed to stay at the hotel? Where would she go while he was on tour? Her heart sank. She didn't need much, but she did need a place to live.

"You know, kids, it's a beautiful day, and I hear there is a lovely patio on the rooftop. Adam, why don't you and Marti go find it? Get some fresh air for a while. I'll meet you up there in a little bit. I just want to talk to Marti's dad for a minute."

"Okay," Adam said.

With no other choice, Marti stood. "I'll see you later, Dad."

"Sounds good." He stared at the TV again.

They left and wandered down the long corridor.

"Mom's up to something," Adam said.

"Why do you say that?"

"Call it a sixth sense." He slid his arm around Marti's waist, hooking his thumb in the loop on her robe.

"Is that good or bad?" she asked.

"Hard to say."

A half hour later, Adam's mom joined them on the landscaped patio. She brought three bottles of water. He could see she was in "Mom" business mode.

"This sure is a pretty spot." She handed them each a water bottle and sat on a floral, cushioned deck chair next to Adam.

"Thank you." Marti smiled, taking the water.

Large potted trees and flowering plants decorated the area. A small pond and waterfall highlighted the corner of the elegant patio.

"So, what's up?" Adam asked.

"Why do you always think something's up?"

"Mom, I know you. I can tell when you're up to something."

His mother ignored him. "First things first. I understand

that the two of you had unprotected sex."

Marti's smile disappeared, and her face went pale. "Yes, ma'am."

"Oh my God, Mom! Stop talking. Now!"

"I'm your mother, and when there are concerns with my son, I will ask whatever questions need asking."

"She's not pregnant!" Adam blurted before his mother could say another embarrassing word.

"Oh thank goodness." She sighed and Adam could see her relax. "That's a blessing. Then, next on the list is birth control."

Adam wanted to make her stop but knew she wouldn't. He sank lower in his seat and covered his eyes.

"You are young adults, and I know that no matter what I or anyone else says, you're going to do what you please. That said, before you leave the hospital, I'd like you to speak with a doctor about birth control options. And Adam, you need to take equal responsibility and provide condoms."

Adam fought the urge to crawl under his chair. "Mom, please. You don't have to worry."

"Oh yes I do. I'm your mother, and this is exactly the type of thing a mother worries about. If Marti's grandmother were here, I'm sure she'd agree. And since your mother is not in the picture, and your father is otherwise occupied, I'm happy to make sure the two of you protect yourselves from future scares. Of course, I prefer that you abstain, but I'm not foolish enough to assume that will happen." She eyed them both.

Marti turned scarlet. Adam shook his head and covered his eyes. *Unbelievable.*

"Adam, stop behaving like that. If you're old enough to have intercourse, you're old enough to have this discussion."

He was pretty sure that Marti wanted to evaporate on the spot. He sure did.

"Are we agreed?" She looked at each of them. They both nodded. "Good." She turned to Marti. "I just finished speaking to your father."

Twisting the cap of her water bottle back and forth, Marti nodded. Adam figured she was waiting to see what horrible thing his mom brought up next.

"He is a lovely man, but he clearly has his hands full. He's going to be in the hospital for a while longer and with the loss of the house and many of his legal records, as well as preparing for a tour, he's going to be very distracted for an extended time. In fact, he admitted that he doesn't have a plan for you right now."

Marti spoke up, her face brave yet resigned. "It's okay. I understand. You're trying to say that he doesn't want me anymore."

His mom's eyes filled with concern. "No, Marti, I'm not. Your father and I talked about this at length. He loves you very much. He ran into a burning building to save you, but as a caregiver, he has a less-than-stellar record. What

I'm trying to say is that he doesn't always focus well, and caring for you isn't always his top priority. The next ten months are going to be very chaotic for him. He agreed you'd be better off in a more stable environment."

Adam saw the heartbreak on Marti's face. Her shoulders drooped. Adam wanted to yell at his mother for hurting Marti when she'd already taken so many hits.

"Oh dear, I'm not handling this very well. What I've been trying to say is that your father agreed you should come stay with our family until better arrangements can be made."

Adam sat up. He couldn't believe his ears. "Mom. Are you serious?" Not in a million years did he imagine his mom would suggest Marti live with them. Marti seemed surprised and guarded, unsure of what to think. He had to ask.

"Absolutely. Marti, from what I've learned, you've been facing some very hard times with the death of your grandmother, the challenges with your mother, and now the fire. I'm sorry you've had to go through all of this at such a young age. But you aren't all alone, and I want to help."

She looked at Marti with such kindness and affection that Adam wanted to hug her. "Your father has signed your hospital discharge papers and agreed this would be a good idea, but it's up to you. I certainly would never force you."

Marti looked at his mother, to him, and back. "Are you sure? It's such an imposition. I don't want to intrude."

"Not at all. It would be lovely to have a girl around for a change." His mother reached out and patted her hand.

"That's the nicest thing I could ever imagine." A spark of hope shone in Marti's eyes.

Marti would be with him! They'd be together. "Mom, you are so awesome! I can't believe it!" He hugged her.

"This is only temporary while we work out a more permanent solution for Marti, where she'll be able to live in a stable, secure home. We're going to fly out tonight to Boston. The rest of the family is already there. Adam, I know you don't like the idea of living in Boston, but it's the way it's going to be."

Right now he couldn't care less where they lived. He'd get to be with Marti!

"Marti, why don't you go say good-bye to your father. I'll go pick up some clothes for you and be back in an hour or so. Does that sound okay?"

"I don't know what to say," Marti said. "Would it be okay if I hugged you?"

His mother stood and held her arms open. "That would be lovely."

Adam watched as his mother embraced Marti. His heart burst with pride and hope for the future.

"I'll go talk to my dad now. Adam, if you don't mind, I'll meet you back in my room a little later."

They would be together! This was better than his

wildest dreams. Marti left, and Adam and his mom walked across the patio.

"Mom, why are you doing this? Don't get me wrong. I'm totally happy you are, but you were against me coming to see her and now you're bringing her with us? I don't get it."

His mother adjusted her purse strap. "I've made mistakes in my life. When Peter's girlfriend, Libby, went through hard times, I could have stepped forward and helped. I could have saved that poor girl a lot of heartache, but I didn't take the time to find out what was really going on. I did nothing. I've felt terrible that I let that happen."

She paused and then continued, "If something terrible happened to you or one of your brothers, I would hope someone would step up and lend a hand. I think we've become too callous and self-centered in our world. An occasional random act of kindness is good for all of us."

"I love you, Mom."

"I love you, too." She put an arm around his shoulder and gave him a squeeze. "But don't think you're off the hook for your behavior in New York. You have a lot of explaining to do, and your father is very upset. Your actions reflected badly on all of us."

"I know." And he did. He never should have left like that, but he didn't regret it for a second and never would. Even so, he knew there would be hell to pay.

24

Marti woke up disoriented. She glanced around the room at the smooth, beige walls and slate-blue bedspread. It took her a minute to realize it was early afternoon, and she'd been napping in a hotel bedroom after a red-eye flight to Boston.

After quickly washing up, she ventured into the main hotel suite to face Adam's family. While Marti was ecstatic to be with Adam, and she was grateful to his mom for her help, it still felt weird relying on them for everything.

Adam hunched over on the sitting room couch looking as if he recently woke up, too. His face lit up the moment he spotted her. Her shoulders relaxed and she felt so much better, as if she'd never be alone.

"Hi, Marti," Peter said.

She turned. Peter and Libby sat on the leather love seat, facing Adam. "Hi! I didn't see you two," she said. Marti liked Libby a lot and was glad to see her again.

Libby came over. "I'm so happy you're okay. I couldn't believe it when I heard about the fire." Libby hugged her.

"Thanks, it was pretty horrible."

The door to their suite opened and Adam's mom and two guys entered. Marti assumed by the way they frowned at Adam they were Adam's dad and his other brother.

"Oh good, everyone's here," his mom chimed.

"You must be Marti. I'm Jett, Adam's father." The older man smiled kindly, a look very different from the angry frown he gave his son.

"Nice to meet you. And thank you for letting me stay with you, Mr. Jamieson."

"It's our pleasure. We all feel terrible for you and your father. It's a real shame, but I'm told he's going to fully recover."

"Yes. He has some minor burns and a broken arm, but that's about all."

"Hi, I'm Garrett." Adam's oldest brother gave her the once-over and walked away.

She studied him as he crossed the room. Garrett stood a little shorter than Adam and lacked the genuine warmth of his brothers. His straight, dark hair framed his serious expression. His eyes matched Adam's in color, except they were a little too close together. He was definitely her least favorite of the three brothers.

Garrett came up behind the couch and squeezed

Adam's shoulders. "Adam, you finally bothered to come back." Garrett acted casual, but Marti noticed his knuckles turn white as he gripped Adam's shoulders. Adam stood up to break the viselike hold.

"Yeah, 'cause I missed your obsessive, controlling ways." Adam joined Marti on the other side of the sitting area.

"Hey! You ever pull an asshole move like ditching a performance again, and I'll break your neck." Garrett pierced Adam with a threatening glare.

The mood in the room plummeted to glacial silence.

Marti wanted to slink away out of Garrett's sight. Adam's body tensed.

"Just because I'm here doesn't mean I'm coming back to the band," Adam said, his jaw set.

What?! Marti hadn't heard anything about that!

"Of course you're in the band," Peter interrupted in a calm voice. "No one's quit anything."

"Adam, I've had enough of your behavior. You'd be wise to hold your tongue," his father warned.

Marti didn't know what to do with all the hostility flying around. She and Grandma never fought. At her dad's, she just disappeared when things got ugly.

Mrs. Jamieson interrupted, "Marti, can I have a moment with you? There are a couple of things we need to go over."

Marti checked with Adam. He shrugged. She nervously

joined his mom at the polished mahogany table, hoping she hadn't done anything wrong.

"I thought you'd like to go buy a few things for yourself. Libby offered to take you, and I think that would be a lot more fun than having me around." She dug in her purse.

Libby joined them with a friendly smile on her face. "There's a mall not far from here."

Adam's mom held out a shiny card. "Here's a debit card in your name."

"How did you get that?" Marti asked. She wondered how Mrs. Jamieson had gotten it so fast. She couldn't let them keep paying for her.

"Your father had his business manager set up an account for you at a bank here in Boston," Mrs. Jamieson said. "There is a significant balance on it, so be sure not to lose it. Your birth year is the PIN number. Your father wants you to replace the belongings you lost in the fire. Insurance will cover everything, so don't feel bad about spending the money." She laughed at Marti's stunned silence. "Don't try to buy everything all at once. Just pick up whatever you feel like today."

"Wow! That's really nice." Overwhelmed didn't begin to express her emotions. But thank God she wouldn't have to keep asking for favors.

"There'll be lots of time to shop during the next few days," Libby added with a smile.

"One more thing," Mrs. Jamieson said. "Your father's

business manager will be calling you tomorrow at ten a.m. to go over a few things, including getting you a new phone."

Marti suspected Mrs. Jamieson was behind all of this happening so quickly. Heck, her dad was probably still flying high on painkillers. He likely gave Adam's mom the go-ahead, and she took over from there.

"While you girls are shopping, we have some family business to handle, so take all afternoon if you like." Mrs. Jamieson snapped her handbag shut.

Marti turned to Libby, feeling like she won the lottery. "You want to go shopping?"

"Oh yeah! We can have some fun with that thing." Libby pointed at the shiny plastic card in Marti's hand.

She turned to go get her purse, but remembered she didn't have one. One more thing to buy.

Adam walked her to the door. "Looks like your day has been planned. Sorry about that." He wore a sheepish smile, probably embarrassed by his family.

"I guess so, but I really do need stuff, so this is okay."

"Have fun." Adam hesitated. She knew he wanted to kiss her. She wanted a kiss, too, but as long as his family was around, it didn't seem like a good idea. She offered him a tiny wave and a playful smile as she turned and left with Libby.

Adam closed the door to the hotel suite, glad to see Marti out of his family's line of fire. When he turned around,

Garrett's eyes lingered on the spot where Marti had stood.

"You didn't tell me she was such a hot piece of—"

"Garrett!" their mother warned.

"I'm just saying."

Adam glared. He wanted to knock the smirk off Garrett's arrogant face.

"Can you boys control your tempers while I step away for a minute?" His mother disappeared into the master bedroom.

Adam sank into a cushioned chair. He knew this was going to suck. The time had come for him to pay for escaping New York.

His father sat on the couch and removed his glasses. He pinched the bridge of his nose. Garrett plopped down on the other end.

"So, you want to explain yourself?" his father asked.

Adam crossed his arms. "Not really."

His father's expression switched from mild annoyance to severe irritation.

"However, if I have to, I'll just say that everyone in this family has a voice in the band, except me. You all decide every last detail."

"That's bullshit, and you know it," Garrett said.

"No, what's bullshit is the way I'm shoved around without an ounce of respect. Garrett wants to do an international tour, so bam! We're in Europe! Peter wants to move to Boston to be near his girlfriend, and the next thing

I know, here we are, and Mom is shopping for new curtains!"

Adam turned to his brother. "Sorry, Pete. I'm glad you got what you wanted, but it sucks for me."

"For the record," Peter said. "I never asked them to follow me. I just wanted more space to do my own thing. I didn't expect Mom and Dad to move the whole machine here."

If Peter could have what he wanted, why couldn't he? It was only fair. Addressing no one in particular, Adam asked. "So, what about what I want?"

"We aren't discussing what you want. We're discussing your irresponsible behavior," his dad barked, his face red with frustration.

Garrett piped in, "You left Peter and me high and dry for a live, televised performance! It was *SNL*, nimrod! You know how stupid we looked missing our lead guitarist?"

"It wouldn't be the first time you looked stupid, dimwit!" Adam said to Garrett, then turned to Peter who was always more reasonable. "So what *did* you do?" He wondered how that went, but had been too busy with Marti to ask.

Peter answered, as if there wasn't a family war raging. "They had a guy from the house band fill in. He was actually pretty good, but he couldn't play any of the riffs you do."

"Adam!" his father interrupted. "Walking out on a gig is not how this band or this family operates. I need your word that you will never abandon a commitment like that again." His stern voice boomed across the room.

Adam thought about what he wanted to do. After his time at camp and the last two days with Marti, freedom looked pretty damn good. "You know what? I'm not even sure I want to be in the band the way it's run right now."

His father furrowed his brow.

Garrett clenched and unclenched his fists. "You don't get to quit. Jamieson is not like playing Go Fish, where you get to throw your cards on the table and walk away when you don't win."

"Unless a whole lot changes, I sure as hell do!" Adam spat back. "Bands break up all the time." He leaned back and crossed his arms.

Peter watched closely but stayed silent.

Their mom returned and sat in the chair near Adam. She crossed her legs and looked expectantly at each of them. "So where are we?"

"Adam's pouting about the move to Boston. He's having a temper tantrum and threatening to quit the band," Garrett said.

"Is this true?" his mom asked.

He shrugged, not trusting himself to speak.

"Peter, do you have anything to add?" she asked.

Adam couldn't wait to hear what Peter thought.

Peter sighed. "Adam's got a good point."

Garrett rolled his eyes.

"Go on," his mother urged.

"When we started Jamieson four years ago, it was Garrett and me that wanted the band. Adam was a natural on the guitar. Hell, he's a natural at whatever he tries. But we never gave him a choice. I don't think he wanted to be in the band back then."

His mother contemplated Peter's words and looked at Adam. "Is that true?"

"More or less," he said, recalling those early days when his life changed from running with the neighborhood kids every night to being thrown into a van with his family and promoting the early music of Jamieson.

"Why didn't you ever say something?" she asked.

"Peter asked me not to," Adam confessed, feeling like he just threw his brother under the bus.

All eyes shifted to Peter. "It's true. Adam told me that he liked playing guitar, but that he really wanted to be at home hanging out with friends. I begged him to stick it out because it was my dream and I wanted it so badly." Peter grimaced. "And so he did."

His mom went silent and looked at his dad. Adam didn't know what to think. He liked finally being heard but wasn't sure where this conversation was headed.

"What exactly is it you're asking for, Adam?" his dad asked.

"I'd like to be an equal member of this band and this family. I don't need to be on every little decision, but I deserve to be in on the big ones, like deciding when we're going on tour, what special appearances we do, and song selections for our next album."

"You think you're ready to be treated as an adult?"

"Dad, I've been acting like an adult for the past three years. I handle media, I put in eighteen-hour days. I help Peter with orchestration, and I work with the backup musicians. What more do you want?"

"I want your word that you won't take off the next time you get mad. I want your word that you really want to be a part of this band. If you don't, well, we'll cross that bridge when we get to it. I don't want you coming to me in a month complaining."

"Until now, I've never complained," he said matter-of-factly. "I can't promise I'll want this for the rest of my life, or even two years from now, but for the immediate future, as long as I get time off for myself once in a while, I'm in." Adam meant it. He loved the music and performing, but he needed more downtime, too, for things like camp and Marti. If Marti ended up back in Wisconsin or with some distant relative, he needed time to go visit her.

"How about we make a one-year commitment?" his

mom suggested. "You boys are getting older and may have other things in mind, like college. Perhaps we need to revisit this once a year."

Garrett started to speak, but Peter interrupted. "I think that's a great idea."

"So do I," Adam added.

"I think that's fair. What do you think, dear?" his mom asked his dad.

"Logistically, that will cause a nightmare of problems, but considering Adam and Peter are still teenagers, I think they should have options, too. If I still had to work behind a desk at my state job, I would not be a happy person. The boys deserve to have options and to make changes in their lives if they want, as long as it's done responsibly."

"That settles it," Mom said.

Garrett huffed and shook his head.

His dad held up his hand. "Except for one thing."

"What's that, dear?"

"Adam's punishment." He pinned Adam with a menacing stare that only a father could deliver.

"What?" Wasn't the drama of dealing with his family punishment enough? Changes needed to be made, and thanks to him, now they were.

"You don't steal money from your parents and fly across the country without a word. While I accept you as an equal member of this family, you are still only sixteen. I've always taught you that for every action, there is a reaction," his father lectured.

"And what's my punishment?" Adam frowned, forcing himself not to roll his eyes.

"Before every performance, you will be responsible for taping down all the stage cords. It should take you about an hour each time. The stage manager will supervise and report back to me."

"What?" That was a crew job!

"Until the end of the year," his dad added.

"That's four months!" His dad was out of his frickin' mind!

"And," his mother added, "as long as Marti stays with us, you will be sleeping at Peter's new place."

Peter laughed, then quickly looked away and covered his mouth.

"That's not fair! Leave Marti out of this! She needs me!"

"You'll see her plenty. Do you really want to discuss the reasons for that rule?" His mother arched a telling eyebrow in his direction.

"No."

"Good. Then I think we're finished. Meeting adjourned." She stood, ending all discussion.

Garrett gloated.

Adam muttered as they all dispersed. *Here they go, screwing with my life again.*

"Hey, Mom, do you mind if I run? I've got a lot to do over at my place," Peter said.

"No, that's fine. I've got some calls I need to make. I'll talk to you tomorrow." She pecked him on the cheek.

Peter headed out the door. Adam followed.

"And where are you going?" Garrett asked.

"To my new room!" Adam slammed the door behind him.

25

"*What* do you mean she's leaving? We only got here yesterday," Adam yelled into the phone. He wasn't sure he heard his mom right. The street traffic made it hard to hear. He and Marti were following the Freedom Trail in downtown Boston. It was a walking tour of historical buildings from the time of the Revolution. Today was a Monday; Adam wore a cap and sunglasses and went unnoticed.

His mom responded. "Marti needs a permanent home. You didn't think she'd stay with us indefinitely, did you?"

Yes, he secretly hoped she would. "No, but I didn't think you'd have her shipped off the day after we got here, either." He shared a panicked look with Marti.

"Adam, it's not like that." His mom sounded annoyed, but he didn't care. He hated how Marti kept getting bounced from one place to another. It wasn't fair.

"So where's she going? Are you sending her back to her

mother's? Because that would be the worst thing possible." One glance at Marti's pale face and he knew that she feared the same thing.

"Would you please just come back to the hotel? I think you'll find it works out well for everyone."

"Right. I've heard that one before." He ended the call and looked at the despair on Marti's face.

"I'm leaving, aren't I?" she asked, already resigned to her future.

Adam nodded, a knot of frustration growing in his gut.

They entered the hotel suite in a somber mood. Marti felt like she was about to be sentenced to a long, torturous death. Adam's mom and a pretty young woman chatted on the couch while sipping iced tea. The two women stood as she and Adam walked in.

"Oh good! You're back," Mrs. Jamieson said.

Marti offered a weak smile. She wondered if the stranger was a social worker. Whoever she was, she couldn't be much more than twenty-five.

"Hi, Marti," the young woman said.

The voice sounded familiar, but she couldn't place it. Marti studied the woman's friendly face, her blond hair, and the open familiarity in her expression. She couldn't believe her eyes. "Brandy?"

"It's me." Her half sister smiled.

"Oh my God! I didn't even recognize you." Marti noticed

the similarities of their eyes and noses. She paused, not sure how Brandy felt. They'd never been close growing up. Brandy had been locked in her goth underworld.

"I've changed a bit since you last saw me." Brandy stepped forward and hugged Marti like the long-lost sister she was. "I'm sorry I haven't been in touch with you all these years," she said in her ear before she released her. "I was pretty messed up for a long time and then I spent all my time in school playing catch-up."

Marti soaked up the embrace. She'd never been so happy to see someone. Brandy looked nothing like her former self. She'd lost the dyed-black hair, the nose ring, and the other piercings. "I can't believe it's you!"

Brandy gave Marti the once-over. "And I can't believe how grown up and beautiful you are. Last time I saw you, I think you were still in grade school."

Marti's heart sang. She'd written Brandy off, but now that her sister stood before her, Marti didn't ever want to let her go. She grinned like an idiot, and then she remembered Adam, who had been so worried. "Oh, I'm sorry. I forgot to introduce you. This is my boyfriend, Adam."

"Hi. Nice to meet you," Adam said. He seemed relaxed now to know the mystery guest was her sister and not her mother or a foster care worker.

"Why don't you two do some catching up?" Mrs. Jamieson offered Marti her spot on the couch. "Marti, would you like some iced tea?"

"Yes. Thank you."

Marti joined Brandy. "How did you know I was here?"

"Mrs. Jamieson called. She talked to Dad. He had his manager give her my number. Of course, everything at Dad's place is gone." She touched Marti's arm. "I can't believe you were in that fire. It sounds like it was terrible."

Marti kept staring at her sister. She never thought she'd see Brandy again. They had always lived such different lives. And here her sister was, in the Jamieson's Boston hotel suite.

Adam's mom set down Marti's glass of iced tea.

"Thank you."

"I've been talking too much. I'm just so happy to see you. Tell me about yourself." Brandy picked up her glass and sipped.

Marti paused a moment. Her emotions rolled to the surface. "My grandma died," she said, her eyes tearing up. *Now where did that come from?* She had been so good at forcing back her sadness.

"Mrs. Jamieson told me. I'm so sorry. That's why you ended up back at Dad's place?" She put her glass down and squeezed Marti's hand.

"There was no place else for me to go. My mom is worse than Dad." Marti blinked her tears away.

"Really? That's hard to imagine. Dad is like some middle-aged kid who's never had to grow up. He's terrible as a parent and you can't rely on him for anything. And that's why I'm here."

More than anything, Marti wanted the next words out of Brandy's mouth to be an invitation to live with her. But almost before she got her hopes up, she forced herself back to reality. It was too much to ask for.

"You can't go back to living with Dad."

Thank you! "I know—he's got the tour." Marti rubbed her palms on her new jeans.

"I'm not just talking about the tour. I'm talking about after that, too. Dad means well, and he loves his kids, but he's a train wreck. He almost got you killed living in that house. What I'm trying to say is that I'd like you to live with me." Brandy watched expectantly for her reaction.

Marti's eyes widened. She turned to Adam; his face mirrored her emotions. Happy and scared. If she lived with her sister, when would she ever get to see him? Where did her dad mention Brandy lived? She recalled it was far from LA. Was it someplace out east? That would be closer, but still, she and Adam would be back to square one and never get to see each other. But she wanted to live with Brandy. She liked Brandy, especially the new, grown-up version.

"Are you sure? That's a lot to ask." Marti wanted to make sure her sister really meant it. Too much had been ripped away from her. She couldn't bear it if it happened again.

"Of course, I'm sure." Brandy grinned. "I barely got out of that nuthouse in one piece, and there's no way I'm letting you suffer any more than you already have. My place is no mansion, but you'll get your own room, and we have a great view of the bay. I should mention that you'll have to share the place with me, my husband, Paul, two cats, and a dog."

Marti felt a momentary stab at the mention of cats. Kahlúa was lost forever, her last attachment to Grandma. She changed the subject. "Dad mentioned you got married. Are you sure Paul won't mind?" She didn't want it to be like living with her dad where Courtney hated her guts.

"Are you kidding? Paul has five brothers and sisters. He says our place is too quiet. He's already mentioned remodeling the basement so you can have a hangout place with your friends."

Part of her loved the idea of living with them, and part of this reminded Marti that she would have to make new friends all over again. She gazed at Adam and saw him try to hide his sad resignation. They both knew he wouldn't be able to visit very often. But the reality was that she needed to go with Brandy. She didn't know how she could say good-bye to Adam again. He'd saved her so many times.

Brandy kept talking. "And I checked out the high school, and they have an awesome school newspaper. You could be on the newspaper staff and take pictures if you want. Of course, school started last week, but we can get you registered tomorrow and start the day after."

So soon? Marti needed more time.

"I know it's a lot all at once." Brandy chuckled, unaware of Marti's dilemma.

"Yeah, I was just getting used to the idea that I'm in Boston and now I'll be going to a new city." Her gut lurched at leaving. She wanted so badly to put down roots, but in someplace where Adam could still be in her life.

"Oh, didn't you know? I live in Boston."

Her jaw dropped. "You do?" Marti was stunned. How was this possible? It was too perfect for words. She looked at Adam; he wore the same shocked expression. Marti wanted to jump up and down and scream at how awesome this was.

"Yes, for the past four years. I finished my nursing degree here and work at a clinic in Back Bay."

"So I don't have to move away?" She glanced at Mrs. Jamieson to see her shared excitement.

"Nope," Brandy said. "In fact, I'd love to show you my place. It's about twenty minutes from here. Adam can come, too. We'll order Thai food, sit on the screen porch, and catch up. What do you think?"

Marti looked at Adam, then his mom, who nodded, and then back to her sister. "I'd love to!" She hugged her. "Thank you so much! I can't believe this is really happening!"

Brandy looked just as happy as Marti. "Well, go get your stuff."

"Oh, yeah." Marti popped up. "There isn't much." She wiggled her finger at Adam and he followed her into the bright bedroom. The instant they were alone, she spun around. "Can you believe it? My sister! And she lives in Boston!"

"I know!" He linked his fingers with hers, pulled her forward, and kissed her. "I told you, I wasn't going to let you get away."

A zing of excitement shot through her, like it did every time he kissed her. She thought back to their first kiss. That moment was a snapshot in her mind, one that would last forever. No fire could ever take her memories away. And now she and Adam would get to make more memories together.

She could hardly wait.

26

Four weeks later

"*Where* are you?" Adam asked.

"Just got off the bus. I'm almost home." Marti held her phone and strolled down the sidewalk. Shade trees with bright yellow and deep red leaves dotted her way. Her new camera hung from her neck and her messenger bag was slung over her shoulder. A light breeze swept a few colorful leaves through the air. Marti loved fall, and she loved her new life with Brandy and Paul, but she loved Adam even more and missed him like crazy while he was gone the past week to, of all places, LA.

"I found out today the school paper is using two of my pictures of the homecoming court."

"That's great! So you still want to go?"

"Of course! That way all the kids who haven't bothered

to say hi to me will find out my boyfriend is the world-famous Adam Jamieson."

Adam laughed. "You are so cruel. So you're sure you don't mind having a rocker for a boyfriend?" She heard the teasing in his voice and pictured his gorgeous face.

"Nah, not too much." She grinned. "Hey, when do I get to see you?"

"Soon. Oh, bad news, I'm not going to be able to get a car to drive you to dinner and the dance tomorrow night."

"Oh no. What are we gonna do?" She didn't want to ask her sister to drive. Brandy had already done so much.

"Let's take your car," he said.

"Very funny. My car was ruined in the fire." Marti walked around the side of the hedges that edged her front yard and stopped in shock. In the middle of the drive-way, she discovered Adam leaning against her cute, yellow Mustang.

Adam grinned and lowered his phone.

"Oh my God!" She wanted to run to his arms, but couldn't get over the surprise of seeing her car parked in her driveway. "How did you . . . ?" She walked up and touched the gleaming hood.

"I didn't. Your dad did. It's not your car from LA, it's a new one."

She couldn't believe her dad bought her another car. She turned to Adam and slipped her arm around his waist, still staring at the car. "This is so amazing."

"And there's more!" He smiled with that playful twinkle in his eyes.

"What?" She couldn't imagine what else he could possibly surprise her with. She'd been flying high on happiness ever since reuniting with Adam and then moving in with Brandy and her husband. Both of whom she adored.

Adam reached into the backseat and pulled out a pet carrier.

"You got me a cat!"

He turned the carrier in her direction and a loud meow sounded. "Kahlúa!" She glanced at Adam in disbelief and reached for the carrier's door, her hands shaking. Kahlúa looked at her and mewed another angry cry.

"Come here, girl," she said. Adam held the carrier still as Marti opened the door and pulled out her noisy cat. Marti hugged her and buried her face into Kahlúa's long fur. "How'd you find her?" She tried to hold back her tears.

He returned the carrier to the car. "I didn't. One of your dad's neighbors did. Kahlúa had been sleeping in their windowsill for a couple weeks before they bothered to check her tags and see the last name Hunter." He reached over and rubbed the fur around the cat's ears. "They figured she belonged to your dad. It took a while before they got a message to him. Then your dad heard that Jamieson was in LA and called to see if I wanted to bring her to you."

Kahlúa squirmed in Marti's arms. "I can't believe it. I

thought for sure I'd never see her again. Thank you." She stepped closer and kissed him. "I love you so much. I can't tell you enough."

He wrapped his arms around her, pulling her as close as possible without irritating the cat further. He pressed his forehead to hers. "Sure you can."

"I love you, I love you, I love you." She punctuated each word with a kiss.

He held her face in his hands. "I love you, too."

Now she truly had it all.

Acknowledgments

$\mathcal{A}$ special thank-you goes out to all the teen idols and boy bands who have entertained young girls. From Donny Osmond and the Backstreet Boys, to Justin Bieber and One Direction, every generation has enjoyed at least one charismatic young rocker who keeps the girls swooning.

Thank you to my husband, for understanding that when I tape up photos of rock stars around the house, it's only for writing inspiration; and to my kids, for understanding that Mom just really likes to look at pictures of hot rock stars.

Much gratitude to Jane Dystel at the Dystel & Goderich Literary Agency and her fantastic team for taking such good care of me.

Thanks to my brilliant critique partner, author Linda Schmalz; author Liz Reinhardt, for her undying encouragement and creative swearing; and author Tina Reber, for her generosity. You are gems!

Heartfelt thanks to Sue Balthazar, for sharing her terrifying story of surviving a house fire. Also, to these wonderful people who contributed to this book: Deb Barkelar, Rachel Berens-VanHeest, Kris Hebel, Christine Merrill, Glenn Svetnicka, Tess Thruman, Kristi Tyler, and Chandra Years.

A very special thanks to Meagan Hatfield for inspiring this story.

Hugs to James Dylan of Jason Bonham's Led Zeppelin Experience, for your generous spirit. Keep the dream alive!

Thank you, Rosemary Brosnan, Editorial Director of HarperCollins Children's Books. You make dreams come true! And many thanks to Karen Chaplin and the rest of the HC staff, whom I haven't yet met as this ball is rolling so fast.

And finally to my special group of author friends, both indie and traditional. You inspire me, you get me through the day, and most of all, you make me spew soda at my computer screen! *Viva la Pagina!*